SATAN'S RING

A NOVEL

SATAN'S RING

JOHN F. BAYER

BROADMAN
& HOLMAN
PUBLISHERS

NASHVILLE, TENNESSEE

0-8054-2431-8

Published by Broadman & Holman Publishers
Nashville, Tennessee

Dewey Decimal Classification: 813
Subject Heading: FICTION

1 2 3 4 5 6 7 8 9 10   06 05 04 03 02

DEDICATION

FOR MOM

PROLOGUE

For the third time in less than thirty minutes, the red warning light on the dashboard of Carlos Reza's antiquated and battered Ford van flashed a warning. Carlos swore to himself, sighed with frustration, then pulled the van to the edge of the road. The old van rattled and bucked as Carlos negotiated the graveled shoulder of the country road. It kicked up a small cloud of brown dust as the balding tires skittered across loose stones. Another rattle deep within the engine compartment announced the impending doom of the overheated engine. Steam poured from around the front wheel wells, and at the same time escaped from the frayed insulation surrounding the engine cover within the van itself.

"What's happening, man?" Javier Lopez asked lazily from the single bench seat just behind the driver's seat. The bumping created when Carlos pulled the van onto the shoulder of the road had awakened Lopez, forcing him to adjust his posture, which resulted in an exposed seat spring ripping his frayed and dirty jeans. Javier was not in a good mood.

"Go back to sleep," Guillermo Reza, Carlos's brother growled over his shoulder.

"Stuff it, Billy," Javier shot back, using the anglicized diminutive form of Guillermo's name. "How long this time?" Javier moaned and

1

pulled himself loose from the exposed spring. His jeans ripped further as the spring tore loose from the denim. He started to say something, but his anger was tempered by the thought that both Reza brothers were just as angry as he was. What was it the gringos said in these situations? Discretion was the better part of valor? That was it. He wasn't exactly sure what it meant, but he suspected it applied to this situation. He decided to keep his mouth shut.

"How am I supposed to know?" Carlos replied curtly to Javier's question. He was angry. Nevertheless, he could understand Javier's frustration. It was the same frustration he was feeling, only Carlos was certain his own far outstripped that of his friend in the backseat. After all, it was *his* van belching steam and smoke, *not* Javier's, and that meant having to spend more money—money he didn't have. Money that he and his brother had yet to earn in the local chicken processing plant where they had found employment only weeks earlier. Payday was less than a week off, but it might as well have been a year. Without the van, their efforts to earn enough money to support their families back home in the poverty-stricken village in Nicaragua would be nearly impossible.

Thoughts of home surfaced. Their village had been inundated by a hurricane, forcing most of the men out into the countryside to seek work. Carlos considered himself, along with his brother and Javier, lucky. They had actually made it to the United States, obtained green cards from the INS, and found employment, such as it was. Still, he missed his family: his wife, Tara, his thirteen-year-old son, Daniel, and especially the young twin girls, Marta and Maria. How long had it been now? Months? Years? Or did it only feel that way? How long had it really been since he, his brother, and Javier had come to this forbidding country where the faces were different, the language strange, and the customs odd? Loneliness had a way of rendering time unimportant. One week or one year, it didn't matter. The pain of separation was always there.

As it was, the available jobs paid little more than minimum wage, and the money the men earned barely kept them alive. The work was difficult and dirty, and it would be several months before they could save enough money to send to their waiting families, if then. The three, along with two other men, shared a small apartment miles from the poultry processing plant. The van was essential. And now here it was, regurgitating steam and smoke like a dysfunctional medieval dragon.

Carlos pulled on the emergency brake as the van rolled to a halting stop. He would have one more look at the worn-out engine. Maybe he could do something to get the vehicle back on the road. At least he should be able to get back to their small, hot, miserable apartment. Then they could begin looking for more reliable transportation. Not that they had the money to buy a new car, but one problem at a time was all he could face at the present.

"Pop the cover, Billy," Carlos ordered. "I'm going around back and get the tools."

"Told you guys not to take this shortcut," Javier argued sullenly from the backseat, his posture already slumping into a position that would make it easier to sleep; he had no intention of helping with the repairs. It wasn't *his* van, after all.

"Shut up, Lopez," Carlos said as he opened the door at the back of the van. "We didn't have any choice. The signs said this was the detour route," Carlos continued angrily. He could only take so much of Javier's lip. Carlos retrieved the makeshift toolbox, slammed the door shut, and headed for the engine compartment.

"It don't sound good, *hermano*," Billy Reza said as he manhandled the cover from the interior of the van and onto the ground outside the passenger side door.

Carlos mumbled an unintelligible reply while searching through the toolbox for a pair of pliers to remove the breather cover from the whimpering engine.

"Be careful. That thing is hotter than summer on *la costa de mosquito*," Billy warned, referring to their native land just north of Puerto Cabezas on Nicaragua's Mosquito Coast.

"Nothing is that hot," Carlos chuckled, surprised that he still had a sense of humor despite the problems he faced with the cursed van. He would like to get his hands on the used car dealer who'd sold him this piece of junk, but he knew that would be futile.

Javier Lopez began to snore on the rear seat, and the attention of the Reza brothers was temporarily drawn away from the engine compartment. They glanced at each other, their eyes meeting in mutual understanding. When this was over, they would have to chastise Javier in some form or fashion. The brothers grinned at each other as the possibilities raced through their minds.

Neither heard the sound of the pickup truck pulling to the shoulder of the road a hundred yards behind the van.

■ ■ ■

The white Dodge Ram sat parked on the side of the road, its engine producing the powerful, low-frequency tones through twin tailpipes that told anyone within earshot that this was one bad pickup.

Three men, their faces obscured by the glare of the setting summer sun reflecting off the windshield, sat watching as Carlos Reza made his way around the far side of the van and into the smoking vehicle. They could not hear the conversation within the van, and if they could have, they would not have understood all of it, for the men in the van were "foreigners" and did not speak much English. If the men sitting in the pickup knew nothing else, they knew that much.

The driver, his huge hands working over the steering wheel as if massaging it, never blinked as he stared at the scene before him. The tension within the pickup was broken by the coughing of the man seated in the middle.

The three men waited.

That Carlos Hernandez Reza Salazar, as well as the two men with him, would die within the next thirty minutes was not in question, for it had been ordained. A lesson was required; a lesson would be taught. It would be a harsh lesson.

The time had come for the three men in the smoking van to die. The decision was irrevocable. Orders had been issued; the killing ground had been selected.

■   ■   ■

"We're going to have to hitch a ride," Carlos said finally, his head still buried in the engine compartment of the rickety van, his voice echoing from the depths of the machinery. "I can't get this thing running."

Javier moaned from the rear seat but said nothing.

"Who you think's gonna pick us up out here?" Billy asked.

"No idea, *hermano,* but it's either that or walk to the apartment. This engine's not going to run again in our lifetime."

Billy struck out with his right foot, kicking the door of the van in an act of frustration. The sharp sound reverberated off the van's inner walls. Javier jumped at the sudden racket. The futile gesture only slightly alleviated Billy's frustration, but he was glad he'd roused Javier. "I'd like to get my hands on that used car dealer," he said.

Carlos grinned despite the problems caused by the balky van. Those had been his thoughts no more than two minutes earlier, but he would not let his younger brother know that.

■   ■   ■

The Dodge Ram inched forward, moving like a predator stalking late afternoon prey. Small stones skittered from beneath the knobby, over-sized tires as the pickup moved inexorably toward the smoking van and its three occupants. The sun, now beginning to set in the western sky, reflected off the windshield, making the windshield appear as a single golden eye. An eye whose gaze was firmly fixed on the disabled van.

■   ■   ■

Javier was the first to hear it. At first he thought he had drifted off to sleep after Billy's abrupt display of impatience and that the sound was reaching him in a dream. As the low rumbling sound increased, however, he realized he was not asleep, despite his best efforts and intentions. He opened his eyes and twisted around in the seat where he had been waiting for the Reza brothers to repair their cursed van. Through the dusty rear windows he could make out the slow movement of something large and white moving toward the back of the van. When he realized the shape was a pickup truck, he felt a sudden surge of relief. Here was the help they sorely needed. They would probably have to ride in the bed of the truck, but that would be better than walking.

"*Ya viene, alguien,*" Javier said, twisting back to face the Reza brothers.

Carlos looked up. "What're you talking about?" he asked.

"Behind us, man. Looks like a pickup. We can get a ride," Javier answered.

Both Billy and Carlos came out of the engine compartment and looked back. The movement of the white truck was barely visible through the filthy windows of the van.

Billy craned his neck further, trying to distinguish the make and model of the truck. "Can't see much. Maybe we better go talk to them before they change their minds and take off."

"Go ahead," Carlos told his brother. "I'll stay here and close this thing up."

"Forget it," Javier said as he scrambled for the handle of the van's side door. "Ain't nothin' gonna get this thing back on the road except *una grua,*" he finished as he stepped from the van.

Carlos glared at the retreating figure of Javier Lopez for suggesting that only a wrecker would get the van moving again, but deep down he knew his friend was right. The van had had it. The best thing to do was leave it and catch a ride into town with the driver of the white truck that had just braked to a stop only scant feet short of the rear of the van. Carlos heard his brother say something to the occupants of the truck, but he could not make out what he said. Then he heard a heavy thud and the sound of something hitting the ground just to the rear of the van. *What was that?* he wondered.

Suddenly Carlos felt the hair on the back of his neck stand up and a feeling of uneasiness he could not explain. A chill shot through him.

Carlos craned his neck to see what was happening just outside the van. He could still see the white pickup parked behind them, but with the sun glaring off the windshield, he could not tell who was driving.

Another sound, deep and ominous similar to the previous thud, filled him with a growing sense of terror. Carlos exited the driver's side door. The van was between him and where his brother and Javier had gone to talk to whomever had just driven up. He didn't hear a conversation. All was quiet. Too quiet.

Carlos rounded the front of the van expecting to see his brother and friend talking to the strangers. Instead he glimpsed a wash of color traveling at a high rate of speed and aimed at his head. A split second later the world went black.

■　■　■

"Finish it," the driver of the white Dodge Ram ordered.

The other two men set upon the two Reza brothers and Lopez with the black baseball bats they'd pulled from behind the pickup's bench seat. In less than sixty seconds the three Nicaraguans were dead, their skulls smashed by repeated blows from the bats.

"That'll teach 'em to come up here and try to take over," the smaller of the three men said.

"You got that right," the driver said, standing over the three bodies. "And this will be a lesson to the rest of those 'foreigners' comin' up here. Bannerman County ain't no place for anybody but white men."

"We better get out of here," the third man said, his voice breaking just slightly. He was not sure what he'd expected, but he now knew this was not it.

"What's the matter? You ain't goin' soft on me, are you?"

"Naw. Not me. It ain't that. But we don't want to get pegged bein' out here when the sheriff finds these bodies. Besides, we need to report in on this one. Gonna be a lot of smiles all around when we unload this story," the third man added.

"You're right," the big man responded. "There's gonna be a party tonight."

"Let's get out of here."

"On the way," the driver said. "Get in the truck. Be sure we got everything. Who's got the paint?"

"I got the bats," the third man answered.

"I got the paint. You want me to do it?"

"Be sure to get it right," the driver said.

The man with the paint went to the van and began writing on the wide side panels. When he was finished, he asked, "How 'bout that?" The man stepped back to admire his work.

The driver examined the man's handiwork and nodded. "Now, let's get out of here." He stepped up into the Dodge Ram, waited a few seconds for his two companions to join him, and then spun gravel even as the passenger door was closing.

"Who's getting the detour sign?" the man in the middle asked, his eyes glued to the road in front of him.

"That's not our worry. That's someone else's job. It'll get done," the driver answered impatiently, beginning to wonder about his friend sitting next to him. The man in the middle—nicknamed "Bull" because of his passion for bull riding—was one of the toughest customers he'd ever run across. Surely someone crazy enough to get on the back of a two-thousand-pound bull was crazy enough to do what they'd just done. But something was wrong with Bull. The driver would have to report his doubts about Bull when he reported their successful attack on the brown-skinned immigrants who never belonged in Bannerman County in the first place, and who would never again create another problem within the county's borders.

The driver began thinking of tomorrow's headlines. He could hardly wait to read what that ultra-left-wing newspaper in Spring Valley would write about the murders. It would be something along the lines of how tragic the murders were, how things such as this should not happen in Spring Valley or Bannerman County, how the sheriff's department would have to pursue the killers "with all diligence," how the victims were innocents, and other such junk. It would be enough to make him puke. And it would probably be enough to put the *Spring Valley Courier* back on the hit list. At least he hoped so.

Innocents? *Not hardly,* the driver thought to himself, as he steered the Dodge around an upcoming curve. Innocents wouldn't have left their own country to come up here and take away jobs that should rightly go to the locals. Innocents didn't speak a different language, or practice different customs, or go to different churches. Innocents stayed where they belonged, and didn't bother anyone. Innocents? Not these three. They had broken every rule, and they had paid the price. Now the only thing left to do was read about it in the next edition of the *Spring Valley Courier* and discuss over coffee just how wrong other folks could be about the motives of such killings.

■ ■ ■

Governor Patrick Francis O'Brien slumped into the rear seat of the Lincoln Town Car and rubbed a cold soda can over his forehead, wishing he'd remembered to bring his travel bottle of aspirin. He had decided at the last minute to make this trip at the request of his campaign manager, and now he wished he hadn't. Next to him, the man in charge of his reelection campaign funds, Martin Akers, was talking on his ever-present cell phone. O'Brien sipped at the soda and let his gaze settle on the passing terrain outside the car window. Gently rolling hills, forested with a combination of evergreens and hardwoods, passed by on the right. In sharp contrast, the view from the other side of the automobile was vast fields of corn that would be just right for harvest in the next few weeks. The contrast within the state always surprised him. Diversity was a key element in the lifestyle of the state's inhabitants. Diversity and flexibility. One needed both to make a decent living here, but it was a good state with good people—for the most part. There was an element,

Patrick O'Brien knew, that remained outside the mainstream. The radicals, the misfits, the instigators. But every state had them, and you had to learn to live with them as best you could. At least until an alternative could be found.

"Not tonight," Martin Akers almost shouted into the cell phone plugged into his ear. "Tomorrow. Tonight is impossible. I told you that last week. Get *that* through your head for once."

O'Brien chuckled as Akers punched the button to disconnect the phone. "Take it easy, Marty. You're going to have a heart attack, and where would that leave me?"

"That would leave you with almost four million dollars in a reelection campaign fund and absolutely no idea as to how to spend it all," Akers replied only half jokingly. "And before I forget it, thanks for changing your schedule tonight to be here. You are always more effective than surrogates. I know the members of CAM, and it wouldn't have looked good having someone other than the governor himself at their rally. And ditching the state police escort was a good decision too."

"Thanks, Marty. The Caucus of American Minorities is essential for what I'm planning, and their upcoming convention is going to provide the perfect springboard." O'Brien rotated the soda, watching small drops of condensation trickle down the chilled surface. "CAM is more powerful and influential than the NAACP right now. They definitely are a factor in this election." O'Brien paused, then added, "But another word of advice too. *You* go easy. I can't afford to lose you now."

As Akers's eyes followed the rolling topography outside the car's smoked windows, he answered, "I'm not going anywhere. It's just that I get so frustrated with some of *your* people."

O'Brien chuckled again. That was Marty Akers's way of telling him that the personnel making all the mistakes were not the people brought on board by Akers, but people who'd already been in place long before Akers arrived at the state capital. O'Brien had to admit that his financial manager had a point. "What do you want me to do?"

Akers sighed. "Straighten them out. Explain how this reelection campaign is supposed to work. I can't have everyone and his brother going behind my back making agreements, verbal or otherwise, that I'm expected to honor after the fact. That's not how things are done."

"You're talking about McGrath."

"Him, along with others. But McGrath is enough to chew on right now."

"We need that old man."

"Why? You've got all the money you need to get reelected."

Patrick O'Brien smiled and rubbed the cold can across his forehead once again. "I brought you on board to manage the funds, not the personnel, Marty. McGrath has a large percentage of the electorate in his hip pocket. People we need. Votes we need. He can deliver votes that no one else has a prayer of securing. And that can mean the difference in us returning to the governor's mansion or not."

"He's not a man to cross."

"No one's talking about crossing him," O'Brien said, taking a swig of the soda. "We're just discussing the natural order of things as applied to the democratic process."

Akers cleared his throat to speak, but O'Brien interrupted. "What is it, Marty? You have something to tell me, and I get the feeling you don't want to do it."

"You're as astute as ever, Patrick," Akers replied. "It *is* about McGrath. There are rumors floating around—"

"That he's part of some right-wing, survivalist-type Neo-Nazi group."

Akers looked askance.

"Don't worry about it, Marty. It's all lies. I know McGrath. Trust me on this one." O'Brien smiled. He could tell by the look on Akers's face that the man had not expected him to know about the rumors. *That* was his surprise, the governor thought to himself. He knew more than even Martin Akers suspected.

Akers paused.

"Go ahead, Marty," O'Brien urged. He wanted to know exactly what else Akers knew.

"It's about some money I spent. Fifty thousand dollars."

O'Brien glanced at his friend. "All aboveboard? Totally accounted for?"

"Of course. It's just that—"

"Just nothing. That's your job."

"But the money has to do with McGrath."

■ ■ ■

A powerful Cummins diesel rumbled beneath the hood of the Mack truck, its power subdued, contained, controlled—awaiting only release. The driver watched dispassionately as the Lincoln Town Car made its way down the road, heading for the interstate.

The man's orders were simple and direct, and he would follow them to the letter. So far, every piece of information he'd been supplied had proven accurate. The final evidence that the people he worked for did indeed know what they were doing was now moving in front of him only a few hundred feet ahead.

Supposedly no one had known the car's exact schedule, but here it was, rolling toward the highway at *exactly* the time listed on the small scrap of paper the driver held in his hand. Someone *had* known.

They had known; *they* always knew. Termination had been ordered.

The dump truck was loaded with twelve cubic yards of wet, compacted, construction grade sand, which added deadly ballast to the weight of the already ponderous vehicle. With that much weight moving at better than seventy miles an hour, accidents were bound to happen.

The driver watched as the Town Car wove in and out of the thinning traffic. Soon the driver of the Lincoln would take the on-ramp to the expressway, and he would follow. On the expressway the speed limit was seventy miles per hour. At that speed, the potential energy of the truck with its load of sand was a force not to be encountered by a smaller, more vulnerable vehicle. But that was exactly what *they* had planned to happen in the next few minutes.

They knew.

The driver shifted through the gears; the truck gained speed as it followed the Town Car onto the on-ramp. The lighter Town Car picked up speed rapidly. The truck lagged behind. It didn't matter. The driver knew where the car was going, and the intercept point was more than twenty miles east on the expressway. Twenty miles would provide plenty of time for the driver to overtake the Lincoln.

■   ■   ■

"You're quiet, Marty."

"Not much to say, Governor."

O'Brien smiled. "Tell me about McGrath."

Akers averted his gaze out the window of the Town Car. Low, rolling hills sped by, broken here and there by small cultivated fields of corn, soybeans, and seasonal wheat. He needed to tell O'Brien exactly what he'd learned, but the question was *how*. It was possible he had delved into areas better left alone, but he would never know until he shared the information he'd garnered with O'Brien.

"Come on, Marty. Talk to me. You're not just my financial advisor, you're a good friend. If I can't listen to you, who can I listen to?"

Akers turned back to O'Brien. "OK. You asked for it."

Just as he was about to reveal what he'd learned, the Town Car began slowing. Both O'Brien and Akers glanced through the windshield to see what was happening.

Ahead, in the center of the expressway, barrier signs had been erected. Large arrows pointed toward the shoulder and a nearby off-ramp.

"Looks like a detour," the driver of the Lincoln said over his shoulder to his two passengers. "It wasn't here when we came through the first time, but it shouldn't be much of a problem."

"This is something you can rectify," Akers joked halfheartedly. "The construction delays and overruns on the expressway repairs are causing all sorts of problems. Fix that, and you'll be reelected for the next hundred years."

O'Brien laughed. "If I could fix this, I wouldn't just be a governor; I'd be a saint. Now, back to what you want to tell me."

Akers sighed again and twisted in the rear seat of the Town Car. He was just about to speak when the massive grill of a large truck filled the rear window. Akers had only enough time to scream a chopped-off warning before the truck slammed into the rear of the Lincoln.

■   ■   ■

The driver of the dump truck watched with detached interest as he guided his truck directly into the rear of the Lincoln Town Car in front of him. The huge bumper clipped the very top of the Town Car's trunk. With little or no deceleration, the truck continued up and over the top of the smaller vehicle. Despite the fact that the Lincoln was a formidable automobile, the Mack truck continued its forward progress unimpeded, its speed only slightly reduced. The sound of twisting metal and muted screams reached the driver.

The top of the Lincoln was crushed as the combined weight of the truck and sand rode over the top of the car. The truck's momentum carried it another 150 feet past the Town Car before coming to a stop crossways in the middle of the expressway, miraculously managing to remain upright. The Lincoln, by some miracle, did not burst into flames, but what was left of the expensive automobile more closely resembled the loser in a demolition derby than an executive limousine. An eerie silence engulfed the immediate area.

The truck driver sat, his mouth moving slowly, as if in prayer, but the two words he repeated were not directed toward a heavenly being. The mantra continued until the door of the truck flew open.

"You all right, fellow?" the person opening the door asked.

The driver repeated the last line of his mantra, then looked down at the man. "Yeah. I'm all right. What about the people in the car?"

"Gotta be dead. Know what I mean? You squished that car flatter than a pancake. Another guy is calling 911 on his cell phone. Just sit tight until the cops and medics get here." The man disappeared, heading back to where a crowd was gathering around the destroyed Town Car.

The driver turned his attention to the overpass next to the off-ramp. A single car waited, its engine idling.

They knew.

The truck driver climbed down from the cab of the dump truck and walked toward the waiting car. In less than sixty seconds he was in the backseat, headed north. Understandably, everyone's attention was riveted on the crushed and mangled Town Car and its occupants. No one noticed the truck driver walk away from the accident site. Only when the state police began questioning the witnesses did they discover that the truck driver had disappeared. The only man to have seen the driver could not supply a description to investigators.

Newspapers around the state would have a double headline to display the next morning. It had been a bloody day for the state, but it had been a good news day for the media.

CHAPTER ONE

The small spinner landed lightly on the water's surface, simulating, Drew Chapman hoped, an insect falling from the overhead branches. The small fishing lure sent out small concentric circles as it slowly sank in the river. For Drew, it made little difference if he actually caught a fish this afternoon. He had retreated to the small stream to forget about work for a few hours. Thinking came easily here, wading and fishing the stream located in the northern part of the state. He was not sure if it was the solitude of the river or just being away from the state capital that brought him relief. Probably a combination of the two, but it didn't really matter. That relief found within the tree-canopied river was sufficient. He had decisions to make—major decisions. Fishing was the answer, a repose he'd sought since he had been a boy.

Already Drew looked forward to the coming night. He'd pitched his small tent alongside his old truck, and he could almost hear the diminutive roar of the twenty-year-old brass backpacking stove he'd brought with him. It sounded like a small jet engine and signaled the end of the day and the beginning of an even greater solitude—the solitude of the night.

The gentle babble of the stream brought him back to the present. It was a relaxing sound. He often wondered why people took drugs or drank alcohol, particularly when the sound of clear water splashing over moss-covered rocks produced a more desirable and beneficial effect than all the chemicals one could possibly ingest or inject. Andrew Chapman considered himself a modern outdoorsman. Not by any means like the men he'd known when growing up, of course. Those had been real men, men like his father. His father, now a retired university professor, was an intellectual who had cherished nature. That love for nature had been passed on to Drew, and he enjoyed being alone in the forest, especially near running water. This small river was his favorite.

The afternoon sun was beginning to cast long shadows over the river. As the light rays filtered through the dense tree limbs, the surface of the river began to dance and sparkle like a million diamonds. Drew began to pay closer attention to his surroundings. Summer was always hot in the state, but it didn't seem to matter here at this private place. Trees spread over the stream from both sides, providing a cooling effect in kinship with the gently flowing water. The water was clear, sparkling slightly as the dwindling sun sought flowing ripples in the stream. Multicolored stones littered the stream's bottom, their colors attenuated in the deepening shadows, muted and drab but beautiful nonetheless.

Drew was dressed in worn blue jeans, a navy blue T-shirt with the state police logo emblazoned on the front, worn tennis shoes, and no socks. It was what he called his "wading uniform," and the clothes functioned perfectly in that context. At slightly more than six feet tall, his one-hundred-ninety-pound physique was still nail-hard, honed by daily running and trips to the state police gym. But at forty-two, Drew Chapman was beginning to feel the effects of age. Despite his conditioning regimen, he could feel the flexibility of his once supple body ooze from him. He knew he would be stiff after wading in the cold river water for more than three hours, but it was a sacrifice he was willing to make.

Standing waist-deep in the stream, he slowly retrieved the lure he'd just cast, flipped the bale on the ultralight spinning rod, and cast again, this time near a log slick with black moss. The water near the log swirled and exploded as the lure hit the surface. Drew set the hook quickly, and the tiny rod bent to the weight of a three-pound rainbow trout fighting to free itself from the tiny hook.

Drew felt a surge of excitement. The rod straightened as the fish drove toward him. He cranked the reel furiously, taking in slack line, trying to keep the fish from suddenly snapping the thin line by reversing course.

"Slick," Drew said, the word of admiration subdued but sincere as he watched the machinations of the fish.

The trout reversed course again, this time surging downstream, using the slight current to his advantage, seeking freedom, moving with the current. The small rod bent.

Drew knew he'd lost this battle. He'd not been able to reel in enough slack before the fish reversed its course, and now all he could do was watch the four-pound test monofilament snap as the trout gained momentum on his headlong plunge downstream.

The line parted in front of Drew's eyes. It was not the first time it had happened, and it would not be the last. Sometimes he won this battle; other times, Saul won. Drew had named this particular rainbow trout more than two years ago when he'd first found the secluded stream. The same log had been in the same position, defying the spring runoffs and periodic floods, providing a resting place for the recalcitrant trout. Drew had hooked Saul on his first cast toward the log. The trout had only been a little more than a pound and a half at that time, and Drew had easily landed the battling fish. Once landed, he had released the trout, expecting the fish to flee to the depths of some deep pool in the stream, but that had not happened. Instead, the fish had turned to glare at him in what Drew considered an almost insolent manner. Then, as if he had all the time in the world, Saul had returned to the log. Drew had stopped fishing that day, but he had returned to the stream many times since then; each time his last cast of the day had been toward the shadowed protection of the moss-covered log. Most times, Saul took the bait on the first cast, as if he knew who was making the cast and was eager to engage a familiar enemy. Lately, the advantage had gone to Saul, with his increased weight and savvy.

"Next time, Saul," Drew said as he retrieved the broken line and turned to head for the shore. As he made his way back upstream to a place where it would be easier to exit the stream, the pager attached to his belt vibrated. Enclosed in a plastic sandwich bag and carefully attached at the small of his back, the tiny device was the one concession he made to his work—not because of any sense of responsibility but because it was required.

Drew climbed from the stream and reached around his back to retrieve the small device. He removed it from the plastic sandwich bag and pushed the button. A single phone number popped up on the display; he recognized the number and silently lamented its appearance. It was not the number of the shift commander; it was the number of the state police commander, Colonel Samuel Reardon.

"Not good," Drew said to himself.

He made his way in the deepening twilight. The day was cooling off as the sun set. The sound of the stream murmured in the background, gurgling over rocks as it made its way downstream in an unending parade of crystal clear water. Unfortunately, the tranquility of the stream did not counteract Drew's growing apprehension. Why would the colonel be calling him? He was just a Criminal Investigation Division investigator and not the senior investigator at that. He'd been CID for what? Five years? No. Five years in November. Four years and some months, then. Certainly not senior enough to be of any special interest to someone like Samuel Reardon, although he knew Reardon on a casual basis. But apparently he was of some interest, and that realization was disquieting.

Drew disassembled his ultralight rod, carefully stowed it in its carrying case, placed the small aluminum tackle box next to him on the seat, and balanced the rod in a gun rack in the window of his 1954 Chevy pickup. Unlike some citizens of the state, fishing rods were all he carried in the gun rack.

He pulled his cell phone from the truck glove box and dialed the number displayed on the pager. It was answered on the first ring. He listened, saying nothing, then disconnected. Drew Chapman sat in the truck, his hands on the steering wheel, his head on his hands. What was going on? There had been no explanation from Reardon's secretary, who'd answered the phone. Only a summons to join the state police commander in his office as soon as possible.

■   ■   ■

The city lights came into view as Drew approached the metropolitan area from the north. The old Chevy did not have a dashboard clock, and Drew could not see his wristwatch in the darkness. He knew it normally took two hours to drive Buck to the capital, but that was if he was driving a state police vehicle or his own Ford Taurus. The old Chevy—ol' Blue, he had dubbed the truck—was his fishing vehicle, so he'd driven it upstate. He could only push the '54 Chevy so hard. Fifty miles an hour, tops. Given that, he figured it was close to nine o'clock.

He would go directly to state police headquarters. His jeans had dried out on the drive, even though he'd had to endure an hour or so of shivering in the wet denim. He'd not taken the time to change into the dry clothes lying in the seat beside him. Something had happened, and he wanted to know what.

State police headquarters was a newly constructed labyrinth of buildings west of the state capitol complex itself. Originally in the downtown area, the state police headquarters had been housed in an old military-style set of wooden buildings until the buildings had literally rotted from beneath the occupants. The new complex—all chrome, glass, and aluminum—was still in its first stage and included the central administrative offices. The office of Colonel Samuel Reardon was in the new building. Later stages would include additional administrative offices, laboratories for the Criminal Investigation Division, and advanced training facilities.

Drew Chapman pulled the Chevy into a vacant parking space at the rear of the complex. Several marked state police cruisers along with unmarked CID vehicles were parked in designated spaces. Drew pulled into one whose sign indicated it was "for official use only." Everyone at headquarters knew the blue '54 Chevy. No one would question its presence.

The mood within the headquarters building was somber, heightening Drew's curiosity as his steps echoed down the hallway.

Besides not having a dashboard clock in the old Chevy, there was no radio either. Although the drone of the Chevy's six cylinder was all the companionship he usually wanted when he was driving, he had to admit at certain times that having a radio would prove convenient, if for nothing other than to tune to the hourly news programs. But now, even without the news updates he might have received via a radio, he knew he had been right—something *had* happened.

"Reardon is waiting for you in his office," a uniformed state trooper sergeant told Drew as he entered the foyer.

"I thought as much. I got a call a few hours ago." Drew responded. "What's going on?"

"You haven't heard?" the sergeant asked.

"I'm in ol' Blue. No radio."

"Go talk to Reardon," the sergeant said, checking his watch. "It'll all be clear at ten."

Drew made his way down the long corridor leading to the colonel's office. He paused briefly, knocked, then entered without waiting for a response.

"Who is it?" a voice called from the inner office. Drew had entered the office of Reardon's secretary.

"Chapman, sir."

"Drew. Come in here. The news is just about to come on. It will be the perfect beginning spot."

Drew entered the large office that was furnished in what could be described as ancient eclectic. A huge oak desk, as scarred and weather-beaten as its owner, dominated the room. Photographs depicting Colonel Reardon's sojourn through the ranks of the state police adorned the walls. Earlier photos were all in black and white, depicting scenes from the early sixties. The more recent photos were in color and showed a progressively aging Reardon posing with a variety of civic and political leaders. The photographs were a chronological depiction of Reardon's public service, a concise history lesson of the state police. Next to the photograph display, a glass case displayed an assortment of weapons, from ancient to modern. In stark contrast to the weapon case were the colorful Southwestern draperies hanging at the corner window behind the oak desk. The bright yellow and rust colors would have been out of place in any other office, but for Samuel Reardon, every element seemed to fit—just as Reardon himself fit the old leather chair positioned behind the desk. This man, who was a study in contrasts, worked in an office that revealed more about his character than he would ever reveal about himself.

The colonel was in his early sixties. It was rumored that only the clerks who issued the payroll checks really knew how old Reardon was, and they had been sworn to secrecy on penalty of his infrequent but volatile temper. It was a joke, of course, but nevertheless, no one seemed to know exactly how old he was. His close-cropped gray hair and suntanned face stood in sharp juxtaposition; it didn't seem possible that a man with almost white hair could tan so deeply. The tan also accentuated his chiseled features and deep-set blue eyes—eyes that reflected the inner depths of Samuel Reardon's character. Those eyes told anyone who cared to notice that here was an honest man.

Drew chose the first chair he came to and sat down. Reardon was known for his informality, and the practice kept everyone who worked with or for him at ease. "A perfect beginning spot for what, Colonel?" Drew asked.

"This," Reardon said, indicating the television set he'd just flicked on. "Watch closely."

The set winked on. Drew checked his watch. It was 10:00 P.M. He thought about asking Reardon what he was doing in the office at this time of night but knew better. Samuel Reardon did not punch a clock, nor did he watch it.

"Now for tonight's breaking news," the commentator began. "Earlier this evening, an accident involving Governor Patrick O'Brien; his campaign finance director, Martin Akers; and the driver of the governor's limousine, whose identity is being withheld, sent the three men to the hospital in critical condition. That story coming up. But as if that were not enough, the Bannerman County sheriff's department reports that three men were found beaten to death in rural Bannerman County earlier today. The men were transported to Bannerman County Hospital and pronounced dead on arrival by attending physicians. Doctors say it appears that the three men were attacked with some form of blunt object around five o'clock this afternoon. The only clues are a series of markings police think might have been painted on the victims' van by their assailants. Lieutenant Governor William Benson issued a statement from the capitol steps only minutes ago. For that we go to Alex Barrow who is standing by at the capitol. Alex."

The picture switched from the studio shot to the capitol steps. Alex Barrow stood in the spotlight, a darkened capitol in the background. "Thank you, Warren. This is Alex Barrow on the steps of a capitol that is as dark as this day has turned out to be. As you said earlier, Governor Patrick O'Brien, Martin Akers, and the governor's chauffeur were all injured when a dump truck loaded with sand collided with the rear of the limousine in which the governor was riding. All have been transported to Doctor's Hospital, where the condition of all three men is listed as critical. In addition, the murders in Bannerman County have added to the somber atmosphere of this night. Only minutes ago Lieutenant Governor William Benson announced that in the wake of the accident involving the governor, he is now the acting state executive. In that capacity, he has issued a statement about what is already being dubbed the 'Bannerman County Hate Murders.' Acting Governor Benson is assigning a special task force, funded from the governor's office and staffed out of the state police Criminal Investigation

Division, to investigate and bring to justice the murderers of three Hispanic men in rural Bannerman County. The man chosen by William Benson to head the investigation is CID investigator Andrew Chapman. We will have further details when they become available."

"Turn it off," Samuel Reardon ordered from his chair.

Drew rose and flipped the television off, then returned to his chair without saying a word. He knew Reardon well enough to know when not to speak.

"Benson called me on this one," Reardon began, taking his seat behind the scarred desk. "Excuse me, *Governor* Benson called me." The false emphasis was evident in Reardon's voice. It was no secret that the head of the state police did not like playing politics with his men.

"And you recommended me for the job?" Drew replied incredulously.

"No. I recommended Casey for the job, but Benson was insistent. He wanted you. He made that clear in no uncertain terms. Is there anything you want to tell me about that?" Reardon asked.

Drew moved to the edge of his chair. "Nothing, Colonel. I'm as much in the dark as you are. The only thing that could possibly make any difference is the fact that I was raised not too far from Spring Valley. I grew up in Bannerman County, but I wouldn't expect Benson to know that."

"Nor would I expect him to have any interest in that fact even if he were aware of it. I checked your file and saw that particular bit of information. I suppose if I can get the information, Benson can too; but for the life of me I can't imagine why he would want it." Reardon rose from behind his desk and walked to the corner window. "And Benson didn't bother to enlighten me as to why he wanted you on this case, but he left no doubt that it was you he wanted. I was hoping you would be able to shed some light on it."

"I don't have a clue, sir. Unless, as you say, he knows I grew up around there and thought local knowledge might come in handy."

"OK. You're going to Spring Valley. And you're going tonight. A crime scene van and forensic team are already on the way. The

Bannerman County sheriff's department is working on this too. I want
you to be there first thing in the morning to go over the scene and review
what the forensic guys come up with. I don't want you working from
secondhand knowledge." Reardon turned to face Drew. "But watch
yourself up there. We don't know a thing about these killings, and I have
a bad feeling about them. There are a lot of questions to answer up in
Bannerman County, and they're not the only questions coming out of
what has happened tonight either."

"You're referring to the governor's accident?"

"Exactly. You catch anything strange about the news report?"

"There was no mention of the driver of the dump truck that ran into
the governor's car."

Reardon smiled. "Exactly. We stopped the media from reporting on
the driver."

"Any particular reason?"

"A very good reason. We don't know who he is," Reardon said,
stone-faced.

"You mean he's dead and we haven't been able to identify him?"

"I *mean*," Reardon emphasized, "that we don't know who he is,
where he is, or anything else about him."

Drew stared at his boss for a full thirty seconds before his mouth
was able to form a response. When he did, the sound was only an unintelligible grunt.

"Save the questions," Reardon said, holding up his hand. "I'll tell
you what we know. We know that one man talked to the truck driver.
One of the first people on the scene ran to the truck to check on the
driver. He was fine, according to the witness, so the man left him in the
truck. When our guys arrived on the scene, they began looking for the
driver, but he'd disappeared. Poof—disappeared into thin air. No sign of
him whatsoever."

"And this man who talked to him immediately after the accident?"

"Can't remember a thing about him. It all happened too fast."

"But if the driver disappeared . . . ," Drew said, thinking aloud.

"Then it was probably planned," Reardon said, completing the thought.

"But . . ."

"By whom?" Reardon finished Drew's thought once again. "That's what we're asking ourselves at this very moment. Why? Who? All the questions we're supposed to ask, all to which we have no answers. We're treating this as a deliberate attack on the governor. For all we know it could be some form of local terrorist group or something."

"The same type of cretins who kill three innocent Hispanics along a rural highway?"

Samuel Reardon leaned his elbows on his desk, peaked his fingers beneath his chin, and looked directly at Drew. "*That* has crossed our minds. It's too early to tell, and we certainly have no evidence on which to base such an hypothesis."

"We've got the truck," Drew reminded Reardon.

"We've got it, and it's being transported to the state CID lab at this very moment. We'll go over it with a fine-tooth comb, but I have my suspicions on that too."

"It'll be clean."

"As a pin."

"Then that leaves us with a disturbing question."

"Many, in fact," Reardon nodded.

"Who wanted the governor out of the way?" Chapman asked rhetorically.

"And why?" Colonel Reardon said. "And who wanted to kill three Hispanics in Bannerman County?"

And are the two incidents connected? Drew Chapman thought, realizing the question was as disturbing as the answers would probably be. But the most disturbing realization of all was the one he had not voiced: Did he know the murderers in Bannerman County?

CHAPTER TWO

"When did he get here?" Jordyn Phillips asked, annoyed that she was just now being informed, even though it was only a little past six o'clock in the morning. A pink sky was just beginning to wink the existence of a new day into being.

"Settle down, Jordyn. You heard what Benson said last night as well as I did," Bannerman County sheriff Dewayne Lawrence answered. "He drove in late last night. But it's not that bad. At least we know him. He's one of us."

Jordyn whirled toward Lawrence. "That doesn't help," she argued. "This is a county problem, not a state one."

"The way national news crews are pouring into Bannerman County, it doesn't make any difference what we think up here. It's now a national event, and that makes it a state problem and possibly a federal one too. There are already photos of the markings painted on the van. Those markings provided just what the mainstream media is after: enough ambiguity to be able to put their own spin on the murders. And that's just what they're doing." Lawrence continued, "This is going to be hard enough to handle. Let's not exacerbate the situation by fighting among ourselves."

Word about the killings had gone out even quicker than Lawrence had imagined it would. After the three bodies had been found, it had taken less than an hour for the first media phone call to reach his office. That phone call had come from a daily in the capital, but after that, phone calls had seemingly come from every corner of the United States— all interested in the three victims and strange markings on the side of the van. Combined with the events surrounding the governor and the subsequent appointment of the lieutenant governor to the state's highest post, it was turning into a newsworthy day. Within the next four hours, news crews had begun arriving in Bannerman County in record numbers. The scant few motels in the area had quickly filled, and some of the late arrivals were having to stay as far away as Evanstown and Fort Collins. Television crews were setting up in the court square at this very minute, Lawrence knew. He could see the white lights of the cameras blazing next to Ferguson's Pharmacy. Lacking an official statement, the news personalities were having to make do with interviews with whomever happened by at this time of the morning. Lawrence returned his attention to Jordyn Phillips.

"We're not fighting among ourselves," Jordyn replied easily. "I'm protesting the interference of the state in a county investigation."

Lawrence threw his hands in the air and retraced his earlier steps back to the office window he'd been staring out when Jordyn Phillips, Bannerman County's prosecuting attorney, had barged into his office. He'd known what was coming from the first moment one of his deputies had discovered the three bodies alongside the deserted county road yesterday around 7:00 P.M. Yet it was turning out to be even worse than he'd imagined. He'd spent the entire night supervising the investigation out on Hallis Road, and he was tired. Tired, confused, and angry. Most of all, he was angry.

At fifty-six years old, Sheriff Lawrence had looked forward to serving his remaining years in office with as little fuss and bother as was humanly possible. That meant no undue stress, which meant no more criminal cases with the potential to pique anything more than the interest of the *Spring Valley Courier*. And at times *that*, thought Lawrence, was more than enough. Of course, he could deal with Robert Chancellor, the owner, editor, and publisher of the *Courier*. And he could deal with any other problem that might arise within Bannerman County, as long as the problem remained a county problem. What he was not prepared to deal with, and did not want to deal with, was anything outside the county. Last night's three murders had already short-circuited those hopes. Now, to top it off, he was having to placate Jordyn Phillips before he'd even had his morning cup of coffee. Life was not fair. Not fair at all.

"How long have you been a prosecutor?" Lawrence asked, turning to face Jordyn.

"You already know the answer to that. I was appointed last year," she answered.

"Appointed? Appointed by whom, Jordyn?"

"Cal Webster."

"And Cal Webster is?"

Jordyn strode to the window the sheriff had been peering out of moments earlier. There seemed to be even more white lights burning the early morning peace away as additional news crews arrived in Spring Valley. "You know Cal is the state prosecuting attorney."

"So you work for him, right?"

"I know what you're getting at, Dewayne," she said, her voice calming. "But that's not what I'm talking about."

"No. What you're talking about is your misplaced idea that someone from outside this county is treading on your turf," Lawrence said. Then he quietly added, "Don't you think I feel the same way every time the state sends one of its investigators up here? I had to deal with an entire forensic team last night. But I've gotten used to it. It's the way things are when something like this happens. You haven't been around long enough to appreciate the politics involved, but you'll get used to that too."

Jordyn was quiet for a moment, then said, "It's just . . . ," she paused.

Lawrence replied before Jordyn could continue. "Is it because it's Drew?"

Drew? Jordyn repeated in her mind. No, not Drew, *Andrew*. That's what she'd always called him, all the way through high school and well into the summer just before college. Never "Drew," because that was what everyone else called him, and she'd never wanted to be like everyone else, at least not where Andrew Chapman was concerned.

Jordyn looked out at the brightening dawn. The intensity of the camera lights were surrendering to the birth of a new day. The pink color of the coming day had been swallowed up by the rising sun, and the downtown area of Spring Valley looked as serene and tranquil as she had ever seen it.

She had grown up in this village and she loved it. From the window she could see most of the town square. For Jordyn, the town had not changed substantially over the years. Of course, there had been the continued upkeep of the quaint town square area with its false storefronts and turn-of-the-century ambiance. The streets were still paved with brick and stone, and the small park in the middle of the square retained the look of a turn-of-the-century park, with cast-iron benches and lampposts dotting the brick pathways. When the idea to cover the streets with a layer of asphalt had been introduced in the city council chambers, it had been voted down by a wide majority. Trees lined every street in Spring Valley. Not just a tree here and there, but so many trees that at times it was difficult to see the century-old homes serenely nestled within their branches.

The village was deceiving though. What at first appeared to be nothing but a small village was actually a bustling town of more than fifty thousand souls. From where Jordyn stood in Sheriff Lawrence's office, she knew the perfectly laid-out grid of interlocking streets stretched for more than a mile in every direction. There was no heavy industry in Spring Valley. Light manufacturing companies specializing in everything from custom golf clubs to plastic parts for automobiles made up the bulk of the jobs within the town limits—that and the small private stores that, unlike in many smaller towns these days, still occupied the downtown square that encircled the small park. There had been one attempt at a strip mall on the outskirts of Spring Valley. A bitter, if short-lived, skirmish over the unsightly structure had been waged, and in the end not a single aluminum-framed, glassed-in storefront had been occupied. The developer had slunk out of town, licking his wounds and promising himself in the future to investigate more thoroughly the demographics of his next capital venture. Money procured from private donations was used to purchase the strip mall building, and it was promptly bulldozed into nonexistence.

The Village, as it was known to those living in Spring Valley, intended to remain as it was, and it broached no interloper.

Jordyn Phillips could not have agreed more. Now, as she stood gazing out the window at her village, she wondered what had happened. It was a conscious question rolling through her mind, and she realized it was the first time in her life she had actually asked herself such a thing.

The Village had been a good place to grow up, to go to school, to court, to love, and for most lifelong residents, to die. Spring Valley was not just a disjointed collection of bodies drawing breath and going about their business. The Village was a family. And the family was quickly becoming dysfunctional.

And now Andrew was returning. Was she ready for that? She was not sure she even wanted to answer *that* question. Andrew Chapman had been the one love in her life. They had been high school sweethearts, had had plans to attend the same state university, and eventually marry. But those plans had been derailed by an official letter from the office of the Republican senator announcing Andrew's appointment to the United States Military Academy at West Point. It had been a day Jordyn would never forget, although part of her wanted desperately to erase it from her memory. But another part of her wanted to cling to the memories, and such reflections were all she had of Andrew and of the times they had been together. So she remembered.

Recently, the memories had been infrequent, and she was grateful for that. She had dated, once seriously considering a proposal of marriage, but nothing had come of that. He had been another attorney whose practice had consisted mainly of wealthy commercial clients, and it had taken Jordyn months to realize that as an attorney the man was exceptional, but as a person his ethics were suspect. In her mind, there had always been a standard, fictitious or not. The standard had been inexorably linked to Drew Chapman. The memories had been faint, but they had been there. And now he was coming back.

The dawn was gone; a new day had begun. Jordyn turned from the window where she stood. There was a strange look on Dewayne Lawrence's face as she turned. How long had she been lost in thought, staring out at the wakening village? She felt a slight blush of embarrassment rush into her cheeks. She'd forgotten about Lawrence in that short time. Her thoughts had been on Drew.

"Sorry, Dewayne," Jordyn continued, "but, no. It's not that it's Andrew," Jordyn hedged, hoping the slight break in her voice would not give her away. "It's just that we should be able to handle this locally."

"Not a chance. Benson wants an investigator up here, and it's going to be Drew. Not that it makes any difference, but he is one of the best, you know."

"So I've been told," Jordyn replied, taking her seat. "Any news on the governor?" she asked, wanting to change the subject. Already she could feel the raw nerve endings of her emotions beginning to chafe.

"Nothing definitive. Too early, I suspect. The truck driver still hasn't turned up, though, and that makes it look pretty strange."

"That, I think, might be the understatement of the year. Sounds like someone was out to get him."

Lawrence laughed. "That's one of your problems, Jordyn. You can find a conspiracy in anything."

"And *you* think not being able to find the driver of a dump truck loaded with sand that ran over and almost killed three people—one of whom happens to be the governor of this state—is not strange? People don't just disappear like that. Not without a plan."

"Don't start," Lawrence said, holding his hands up in mock surrender. "I'm just saying, don't read anything into an incomplete investigation. That's all."

"What do we know? Your boys come up with anything out on Hallis Road?"

Lawrence was silent for a moment, as if weighing the question. "Nothing more than the old van and the bodies. Danny Boggs remembered one of the men. Says he thinks he worked over at the processing plant out on Highway 21. But there won't be anyone in the company's personnel office for another hour yet, and we've got plenty to do until then anyway. The state forensic team cleaned up most of it."

"Boggs was out there?" Jordyn asked warily, dismissing the reference to the state's intrusion. Right now she wouldn't go there.

"Sure he was. He was on duty last night along with Reece. They were the ones who found the bodies. And they were the ones out there with the state forensic team when they arrived late last night. Why?"

"Nothing," Jordyn replied, not wanting to discuss her concerns about Deputy Danny Boggs with his boss. The truth was, she *was* concerned. Since taking over the prosecutor's office in Bannerman County, she had had a couple of confrontations with Boggs, and she didn't like the man. More important, she didn't trust him. More than once she suspected pertinent evidence had disappeared, and she suspected Boggs. Mike Reece, on the other hand, was a good cop, and she hoped his presence last night mitigated any effect Boggs might have had on the evidence gathering. She stopped for a moment and smiled. Maybe Dewayne Lawrence was right. Maybe she did see conspiracies at every turn.

"Gotta run, Dewayne," Jordyn said, reaching for the doorknob. "I'll be in touch, and if you turn up something interesting, let me know."

"Does that mean, if I see Drew, to give him your best?" Lawrence joked.

Jordyn turned to the Bannerman County sheriff. "You do what you think best, but I'll tell you up front. I'm about to go find Andrew right this minute."

"He's staying at the Carter House," Lawrence said, smiling. "You'll probably wake him up this time of morning. He got in late."

"Good. We have three murders up here, and he needs to be up if he's going to be the lead investigator. He needs to know that I'm in on it too."

"Good luck," Lawrence said to Phillip's retreating figure. When she was gone, the grin that had been on his face disappeared. He wondered if he should make a specific phone call now or wait. After only a moment's reflection, Lawrence decided to wait for the time being. But he was fully aware that if events continued along the same line as they had in the last twelve hours, he would have to make the call, and that he did not relish. As much as he hoped he was wrong, he was afraid he knew exactly what was about to take place.

CHAPTER THREE

Jordyn left the Bannerman County sheriff's office through the basement exit, avoiding the television crews that had almost surrounded the building. She could identify the crews by the logos on their cameras and other equipment, and she had no intention of being interviewed before she really knew what was going on. And certainly not before talking to Andrew Chapman.

At forty-one years old, Jordyn looked ten years younger. At times that was a asset, and at other times it was a real handicap. In court, she constantly had to be aware of how she presented herself. She preferred to wear her honey blonde hair down, just touching her shoulders. But she had learned that by wearing it on top of her head, she exuded an aura of professionalism and authority that otherwise was elusive. In court, she wore severely cut neutral or earth-tone business suits. This morning, despite the early hour, she had chosen the younger look, hoping to avoid the media teams surrounding the sheriff's office. She was wearing jeans, a plain white blouse, and running shoes. She hoped she looked more like one of the janitorial staff just getting off work than the county prosecuting attorney.

No one paid any attention to her as she exited the building, and she smiled ruefully. It was just another indication that appearance was everything. This time she did not care.

She had parked around the block, next to the public library. It had been a wise choice, she now realized. The town square was beginning to fill with people curious about the tons of electronic equipment, cameras, and people in coats, ties, or designer dresses grasping at any and every person walking the streets who might even look like they knew something about the multiple murders or the strange symbols reportedly painted on the victim's van.

Jordyn had one goal in mind, and it had nothing to do with what was happening in the now overcrowded town square. She wanted to get to the Carter House before someone from a television station discovered the chief investigator assigned to this case was staying at the popular bed and breakfast.

As she unlocked her car and crawled inside, she felt the beating of her heart increase. A narrow line of perspiration popped out on her forehead, and her breathing became short and rapid. If she didn't know better, she would have thought she was having a heart attack. But she knew the reason for the physical symptoms—Andrew Chapman. It had been a long time since she'd felt this way, and she was not sure she liked it.

The Carter House was located in a quiet neighborhood, at the corner of Pulaski and Mesa streets. She had never stayed in the popular B & B but had been inside many times. The large Carter House living room was a popular meeting place for the village's various women's clubs. She liked the old world charm that radiated from the golden oak wainscoting and the white-on-pink flocked wallpaper. The intricate details of the woodwork brought back thoughts of earlier times and proud artisans. The house was furnished with turn-of-the-century English antiques, mostly brought over by the current owner from remote antique shops southeast of London in Sussex, Surrey, and "The Garden of England," Kent. The hardwood floors shown through a variety of woven woolen and cotton rugs from Scotland and Guatemala respectively. The house was comfortable and considering the quality of the breakfast, reasonably priced. She was not surprised Andrew had chosen the out-of-the-way place as an alternative to the higher profile, higher priced motels that lined the highway outside the village city limits.

Jordyn parked on Pulaski Street. The street ran beside the Carter House, and she knew her approach to the B & B would go unnoticed until she was practically on the wraparound porch, which protected three sides of the house. She wondered why she cared, but she secretly knew that she did not want Andrew to see her until she had seen him first. It would be a small triumph, but it would make her feel better.

■　■　■

Drew smiled to himself as he watched Jordyn Phillips approach the Carter House. He was standing in the dining room where he'd just finished the breakfast provided by the B & B's hostess, Maura Kelley, and now he was enjoying a last cup of coffee before beginning what he knew would be a disturbing day. The presence of Jordyn would be the one pleasant event of the morning, he hoped.

Drew sipped the coffee slowly, his eyes glued to the girl he had once loved. Once? Was that how he thought of the relationship now? In the past tense? He looked down at the dark circle formed by the coffee. He could tell himself anything he liked, but in his heart he knew that the memories of Jordyn Phillips had never been completely eradicated from his mind.

Drew went to the English sideboard and placed his coffee cup on the gleaming wooden surface. He would meet Jordyn at the door, but he would not let on that he had been watching her as she had parked and made her way toward the house. He could feel his pulse begin to flutter at the thought of actually talking to her again, but he would not tell her that either. The idea of contacting her had come to him many times, but something always seemed to stop him. The longer he'd waited, the more reluctant he'd been to initiate the contact. Now the meeting was being forced on him, and that made him nervous too. Nervous and excited.

Drew arrived at the front door just as the outer door opened. There was no need for Jordyn to ring the doorbell; everyone knew the Carter House was open to the public.

Drew's first face-to-face glimpse of Jordyn made him wonder why he had not called her. As she came through the door, her blonde hair caught the reflection of the early morning sun. In her jeans and starched blouse, Drew thought he was looking at an angel who'd just come from a picnic. His pulse accelerated even more. He hoped his face was not flushed, knowing all the time that it was and that he was already embarrassed.

Jordyn hurried through the front door and almost ran into Drew. She pulled up short, staring into the CID investigator's eyes for what seemed to be an eternity.

"Hi, Jordie," Drew said, breaking the silence with a nervous smile and using the pet name he'd given her what seemed like eons ago.

Jordyn stepped into the foyer. "How are you, Andrew? It's been a long time," she replied more formally.

Drew looked for a derogatory meaning in Jordyn's greeting but could find none. It was as if she were greeting an acquaintance or business associate she'd not seen in several years. There was no hint of the intimacy they'd shared so many years ago, and Drew discovered he was disappointed.

"Yes. A long time," Drew said, letting the words hang in the air, hoping the absence of explanation would suffice. "How have you been? You're the prosecutor, I hear."

Jordyn stepped into the room. "About a year, now," she answered as she scanned the room, trying not to make additional eye contact with Drew. She could feel his gaze follow her into the room.

"You look wonderful, Jordie," Drew said, closing the door. "Is this going to be a problem? I didn't ask for this, you know."

Jordyn turned to meet his gaze. "A problem?" she repeated demurely. "Not for me, as long as you do what you're supposed to do, and I guess that's to find out who killed three men out on Hallis Road, which won't be easy. Television crews are already inundating the town square. It won't be long before they find you."

Drew sighed and followed Jordyn into the living room. "That's why I'm here, and the sooner I can get to it, the better." Drew's tone of voice changed to match the coolness of Jordyn's own tone. This was going to be more difficult than he'd thought. He was discovering he would have to battle not only the killers but the Bannerman County prosecuting attorney as well.

"I'll be honest with you, Andrew," Jordyn began, meeting his gaze. "I don't want you up here. I don't want any state investigators up here, but that's not my call. You do what you have to do, and I'll cooperate. That's my job. The sooner we can get this out of the way, the better."

"Get what out of the way? This investigation or the memories of our previous relationship?"

Jordyn flushed at the statement, and Drew was pleased to discover that she was not as cold and uncaring as she pretended to be. There was still hope. He could live with that small encouragement for the time being.

"Sorry," Drew rushed on. "That was uncalled for. I didn't mean that. I've already contacted my forensic guys, and I'm about to head out to Hallis Road. The bodies are at the funeral home, and most of the evidence, what there was of it, has been recovered."

Jordyn stared for a moment, then said, "Very efficient."

"I shouldn't be out there very long. You want me to come by your office when I get back and tell you what we know so far?"

"I do," Jordyn said quickly.

Drew smiled. The words had come too hastily, thoughtlessly. She'd had her mind made up before coming to see him, and he found he relished the idea of seeing her again so soon. Maybe the day would be better than he'd anticipated.

"I'm on my way out. I'm finished here—unless you want a cup of coffee or something."

"I'll be waiting," Jordyn replied succinctly.

Drew grabbed a light jacket from the antique hall tree in the foyer and put it on. Jordyn wondered why he'd done that. It was already warm outside, and then she realized she'd not even noticed that he was wearing a small shoulder harness that held an automatic pistol snugly beneath his left armpit. It was just one more reminder of why they had been thrown together again.

Drew held the door, then followed Jordyn out. The sun was up, casting long, cool shadows beneath the porch, promising a warm day in a few hours. Street traffic was nonexistent.

Almost.

From the corner of his eye, Drew caught the flash of sunlight on the windshield of an approaching car. The car was moving slowly, deliberately.

Too slowly.

Too deliberately.

Menacingly.

Drew followed the movement. Suddenly the automobile accelerated, closing the distance between the Carter House and itself. Drew saw long objects protruding from the windows of the car. The sight galvanized him into action!

Shotguns!

"Down!" Drew shouted, throwing himself at Jordyn. He knocked her to the ground, covering her with his body as he drew his own pistol. The only protection was a small picket fence lined with box hedges that surrounded the B & B. No real protection at all. He had to move! Find cover!

He could hear the car now. The deep-rumbling growl of a powerful engine vibrated in the tranquil morning air. Muted voices reached him from within the car despite the sound generated by the powerful engine. Voices of urgency, of command. Voices with purpose.

Death rode in the car.

Drew couldn't make out the words, but the tones were unmistakable. There were men in the car who meant to kill him. Or Jordyn. Or both!

"The porch!" Drew ordered, pulling Jordyn with him. "It's our only chance." Drew sprinted for the porch, seeking the cover of the oak boards and heavy support beams and posts. Jordyn slipped once, going down hard. Drew picked her up, forcing her in front of him, placing his body between her and the approaching killers.

The sound of the accelerating car was now somewhere in the back of his mind. Drew saw only Jordyn; recognized only the necessity to protect her, to save her life. The growl of the killer engine receded in his mind as he raced for the protection of the porch. His footsteps pounded in his brain. *Too slow!* he thought. *Too far to go!* There were only scant yards left. The porch was elevated; the space beneath, dark and beckoning; isolated, sheltering.

Shots erupted in the morning stillness, splitting the tranquil mood of a beginning day.

"Dive!" Drew ordered, shoving Jordyn beneath the Carter House porch. He pushed her, forcing her into the space before him as he turned with his weapon raised and crouched to stabilize his aim.

The heavy beam next to him shattered from the impact of buckshot. The sounds of exploding shotguns, frantic voices, and the powerful engine melded into one, a cacophony of disorder and destruction.

Another beam exploded above his head. He checked on Jordyn's position, satisfied that he'd forced her far enough beneath the porch to protect her. The post to his left splintered as more buckshot rained in toward him. It was impossible to count the number of shots. All around him Carter House was being destroyed. Grass and dirt were disgorged from the yard in front of him. Huge chunks of sod were thrown into the air as shards of deadly wood flew before his face.

Drew's Glock model 32C was in his hand, the automatic bucking, sending shock waves up his arm. It was an unconscious reaction, a fight for self-preservation where flight had not been an option. The automatic stopped, its ammunition expended, the last of the brass shells hitting the ground just as the firing from the powerful car ceased. The automobile accelerated away from the Carter House.

Drew heard a subdued sob escape from the depths of darkness beneath the porch. He watched as the car disappeared from sight before turning to check on Jordyn. There had been no license plates, no overt descriptive markings, nothing but an ordinary car that was far from ordinary.

Drew crawled beneath the porch. Jordyn was tucked into a semifetal position, her head covered by her arms, her jeans soiled from the ground, her blouse filthy. Drew put his hand on her shoulder and felt her trembling. "Are you all right?" he asked gently.

Slowly her arms came down; she turned to Drew. "Wha . . . what . . . was that?" she asked, her voice tremulous, large tears pooling in the corners of her eyes.

Drew gently squeezed her shoulder to reassure her. "I think someone wants one of us, or both of us, off this case. Let me help you out," Drew encouraged, carefully assisting Jordyn as she left the dark protection of the porch.

"Are they gone?" she asked, not sure she wanted to abandon her hiding place.

"I think so. I don't think they wanted to kill us. I think they were delivering a message."

Jordyn's eyes flashed instantly. "A message? What kind of message?" she demanded, her fear evaporating in the morning light, replaced by growing anger.

"To steer clear of these murders, would be my guess."

"That's crazy," Jordyn exclaimed. "They just risked exposing themselves."

"I don't think so," Drew said as he helped Jordyn to her feet. "My guess is, we will never find that car in this lifetime," he commented decidedly as he looked down the street to where the car had disappeared.

Jordyn's fear subsided as anger flared in its place. "What do you mean?"

"Simple. I watched that car until it disappeared, and I'm not sure I can tell you what I saw. It was innocuous, nondescript. I've been trained to observe, and still I would have a difficult time describing it. This was a message that no interference will be tolerated."

"A message? They tried to kill us," Jordyn protested.

"I don't think so," Drew said, stooping to examine the shattered wood beams and posts where they'd taken cover. "Look at this," he said, pulling out a small pocketknife and going to work on the wood. In seconds, he had what he was searching for.

Jordyn moved closer. "What is it?"

"Buckshot," Drew answered, showing her the small lead pellets.

"And you say they were only sending a message?" Jordyn asked incredulously.

"This is number eight or nine shot. Bird shot. Look at the penetration too. Must have been low brass shells. Those kind of shells are used for bird hunting. Not enough penetrating power and too small for larger game. Even if they'd hit us, it wouldn't have killed us. Not at the distance they were shooting from. No, this was a message."

"If that was a message, I don't want any parcel post packages from those freaks," Jordyn replied.

A crowd was growing around the Carter House. Drew wanted to get away, maintain as low a profile as possible. He would have his forensic team check out the damage and the shot to be certain his theory was correct. At the same time, he knew it would be impossible to trace the shot. Shotguns were smoothbore weapons and left no telltale marks on the shot pellets like rifles or pistols left on bullets. The attack had been well thought-out and planned. The obvious question remained: How did the attackers know who he was and where he was staying? Samuel Reardon was right. He'd have to be careful. It looked like whoever had killed the three men on Hallis Road had well-placed informants. Someone had known of his presence, and Drew found that disturbing.

They knew.

"Let's call the police," Drew said, heading back inside the Carter House. As he climbed the stairs, Drew wondered who the men in the car were. There was a chance the men with the guns had at one time been his friends. That thought was more frightening than any other he could come up with.

CHAPTER FOUR

Deputy Mike Reece felt a pang of guilt as he fingered the small ring in his pocket. He glanced at Deputy Danny Boggs as the larger deputy guided the police cruiser down the main street of Spring Valley. They had an appointment to meet state investigators out on Hallis Road in twenty minutes, a meeting Reece was secretly looking forward to. He had discovered the ring last night out on the road near the murder scene of the three Hispanic men just before the state forensic team had arrived, and had picked it up and put it in his pocket. He didn't know if it would prove to be important, and if it did, he would probably have to justify his tampering with possible evidence. But he knew he didn't trust Boggs to deliver the tiny object to the investigators. He'd made up his mind to give it to the lead investigator, a CID agent named Andrew Chapman.

Reece recalled the scene last night as he and Boggs had been patrolling the rural limits of Bannerman County. He had seen some terrible things in his life but none worse than what he'd seen out on Hallis Road. As a New York City cop for almost fifteen years, working split shifts in Brooklyn from East 31st to East 37th south of Linden Boulevard, Reece thought he'd been exposed to the most malignant sector of humanity possible. He'd moved to Spring Valley and joined the Bannerman County sheriff's department to escape the nightly carnage, but nothing he'd seen in those fifteen years had prepared him for what he and Boggs had encountered on the side of the road in rural Bannerman County.

The three men had been beaten almost beyond recognition. Their aging van had been untouched except for the two strange symbols spray-painted on its wide side panels. Nothing in the three men's pockets had been disturbed, which meant this was murder for murder's sake, not robbery. Not that anyone in their right mind would have thought they could get anything of value from the three men.

Reece knew he'd never forget the gruesome scene he and Boggs had found last night. But as ghastly as that scene had been, the reaction of Deputy Boggs had been even more shocking.

The two deputies had discovered the van sitting on the side of the road at about 7:00 P.M. At first Reece thought it was an abandoned vehicle, but that assumption had changed quickly. Upon discovering the three bodies, Reece had been horrified, but Boggs had been almost gleeful, commenting that it seemed as if three more "wetbacks" had gotten exactly what they'd deserved. Reece had been disgusted at the statement but had said nothing. No words could express his own disgust of Boggs.

Reece's grandfather had escaped from Warsaw, Poland, on September 30, 1939, two days after the city had fallen to Hitler's blitzkrieg but before starvation had forced total capitulation. He'd eventually made his way to the United States. Reece still remembered the stories his grandfather had related about the fall of Poland in general and Warsaw in particular. It had taken his grandfather many years to be able to recount the horrors of those days in Poland, and Reece suspected that his grandfather never told them the entire story. Even now the thoughts of those emotional narratives made his hair stand on end. But Reece had understood the point of his grandfather's chronicles and had taken them to heart. For Mike Reece, discrimination was a way of life, and he had identified with the three slain Hispanics lying alone and abandoned beside the road. He had despised Boggs's vile comments. He'd wanted to smash the deputy in the face but knew that would have done no good.

He thought about reporting Boggs to his superiors, but he would have to be careful. Discrimination within the Bannerman County sheriff's department was not unheard of.

Reece's family name had been changed by his father early on after arriving in the United States. It had been Reisman, a recognizably Jewish name. The name had been changed, but that was all. Despite the anglicized name, Reece still faced discrimination within Bannerman County that reminded him of his grandfather's stories about the ghettos in Warsaw. When all was said and done, Reece knew you could change many things in life, but you could not change a person's heart. For Reece, that was the tragedy.

Reece's mode of operation was to work on the system from within. He'd been hired to meet some perceived quota but had planned to use his intelligence and hatred for intolerance to change things for the better. At least that had been the strategy. It hadn't worked out the way he'd hoped, and he had been on the verge of submitting his resignation when the murders had occurred. Now he knew he had to stay long enough to at least have an impact on this investigation. Three souls sought restitution, and Mike Reece would be the avenging angel.

That's why Reece said nothing of what he'd found last night at the murder scene. He'd wait for the right person and the right time, and he hoped the right person would be Andrew Chapman, the man appointed by Acting Governor Benson to head the investigation.

As Boggs was about to turn north and head for Hallis Road, the police radio sprang to life.

"All cars, shots fired at the corner of Pulaski and Mesa Streets. All available cars respond at once. Car twenty-one, your call is code three."

"Miller and Coats are in car twenty-one," Reece said.

"They have all the fun," Boggs replied, the disappointment evident in his remark. A code three call meant using both flashing lights and siren. Per department policy, only one car could be designated code three. Boggs liked the adrenaline rush that came with fast pursuits or code three calls. Today he was being denied.

"Pulaski and Mesa. That's the Carter House," Reece continued. "What the heck is going on?"

"Who knows," Boggs said, accelerating toward the area, his lights flashing but his siren silent. "We'll be there in less than two minutes."

When Boggs braked the police car to a stop on Mesa Street, the area was already jammed with other patrol cars, uniformed officers, and civilians. Some wore the uniform of the Bannerman County sheriff's department, some the uniform of the Spring Valley police department, and some the housecoats and robes of curious neighbors who'd been drawn to the commotion from the breakfast table.

In all, Mike Reece thought it was rather comical. He could see deputies Jeff Miller and Sean Coats talking to the county's prosecuting attorney, Jordyn Phillips, and a man he did not know. The four were standing at the base of the front steps of the Carter House. From where Reece stood, it looked as if World War III had broken out and the Carter House porch had been the target. Just then Coats looked up and spied both Reece and Boggs. Coats motioned them over.

"You both know Jordyn," Coats began. "And this is Andrew Chapman. You never knew him, I know, Mike," Coats said, addressing Reece, "but Drew was the star running back for Spring Valley a few years ago. Drew's the CID investigator from the capital."

"Good to meet you, Mr. Chapman," Reece said, holding out his hand. The handshake was firm without being painful, and Chapman looked him straight in the eyes. Already Reece was impressed with this man he wanted to talk with privately. But now there was a warning flag. Drew Chapman had at one time been one of Spring Valley's chosen. Just how close, Mike Reece wondered, had Chapman been to the rest of the "good old boys" from the village? Too close, maybe. He'd have to take his time on this one.

"Good to meet you, Mike. Call me Drew. And as for a few years ago, it was more than just a few. This is my first time back since my parents retired from here. And I must say, this is more of a homecoming than I'd planned on."

"Looks like someone doesn't want you around," Reece continued.

"Yeah. My thinking exactly."

"Mine," Jordyn interrupted, "is that someone was trying to kill us."

"Maybe, maybe not," Danny Boggs interjected. "But I have to admit that someone was at least out to get your attention," he smiled smugly.

Reece again felt contempt building toward Boggs.

Miller and Coats returned to the report they had been completing. It took a few minutes, and with that finished and the remainder of the police department and sheriff's department collecting photos and evidence, Boggs began again. "We were on our way out to Hallis Road when we heard the call. I think we were supposed to meet you out there," Boggs said to Drew.

"The forensic guys are probably wondering what happened to us. We might as well get out there," Drew said. "Then I'm coming back into town to talk to Jordyn."

Boggs glanced at Jordyn; his eyes narrowed for a moment, then a smile creased his face. "Sounds good to me. We could use a pretty face on this case. Let's go," he said, turning and heading for the police cruiser.

"Don't pay any attention to him," Reece said as he turned to follow. "He never grew up."

■ ■ ■

Jordyn watched as Boggs and Reece got in the cruiser and headed for Hallis Road.

"You'll be in your office?" Drew asked Jordyn.

She sighed and said, "I'll be there as soon as I get these clothes changed. Maybe we can talk about this later this evening."

"Possibly," Drew said as he headed for the car. "I've got a date tonight," he said over his shoulder. "I'll call you."

Jordyn's gaze followed Drew as he walked away, wondering why she was experiencing a sudden pang of jealousy. A date? *Just who does Andrew Chapman have a date with tonight?* she wondered, and then just as quickly, wondered why she cared.

CHAPTER FIVE

Lewis Thomas cursed as he rummaged through the drawer in his night-stand. The drawer was the only place he'd not searched. The rest of his shabby apartment already resembled the aftermath of a medium-size hurricane. Every drawer had been turned out, the contents spread across the floor of the three odd rooms he called home. He had turned out kitchen cabinets, a chest of drawers, clothes closets, the three pairs of jeans he'd left on the floor a week earlier, and every nook and cranny of the tiny bathroom. There was no denying it. The ring was gone. It was just that simple, and Thomas knew that at the next assembly, if he showed up without the ring, there would be repercussions. Serious repercussions.

Thomas thought about phoning Bull and asking him if he'd seen the ring, but if he did that, he'd have to admit to having lost the ring out on Hallis Road, and he was not prepared to do that just yet. The logical course of action would have been to phone Willie Henderson, but Thomas knew better than to reveal the missing ring to Henderson, even if he had probably lost the ring in Henderson's pickup truck. The man was not a very nice person, and besides, Henderson was also the senior centurion for the Spring Valley Assembly. No one messed with Willie Henderson. You could talk to Bull Burton, but not Willie Henderson.

Then it struck him. What if he'd dropped the ring out on Hallis Road? Oh man! He didn't *even* want to think about that possibility. Of course *that* was a one in a million chance. And even if he had, the odds of someone finding it were pretty remote. Still, he would feel better if he could lay his hands on the ring. He would start his search over, and this time he would be more methodical in his approach.

"It has to be here," Thomas said to himself, but the words brought no measure of comfort.

■   ■   ■

"Carla," Sheriff Lawrence called to the outer office. "I'm going to be on the phone for a few minutes. Hold any calls."

"Sure thing, Dewayne," Carla Moore called back.

Lawrence picked up the phone and dialed. The number was a private one, and it was answered on the first ring. "Lawrence here," the Bannerman County sheriff said. "You were right. This situation could get out of hand quickly. It's starting here. Exactly what I didn't want."

Lawrence listened as the voice on the other end of the phone explained exactly what was going to take place in the next few days. Lawrence nodded silent agreement at what he heard.

"Yeah, we were right. The markings on the van support your suspicion, at least." Lawrence replied when a break came. "So I do nothing right now. Just sit tight and observe." Lawrence listened, nodding at the phone, then hung it up. The instructions were understandable, but that did not mean he liked them. He would wait and watch Andrew Chapman for the next few days to see what the CID investigator uncovered. But contrary to what the voice on the other end of the phone had said, he would not sit back and do nothing should intervention be required.

He *had* been right. He could only hope they did not know who he was. But even the words over the phone had failed to provide the assurance he'd been seeking. More and more it seemed they knew. The realization sent chills up his spine.

Heaven above, he prayed silently, *what if they know?*

■   ■   ■

Corey Simmons felt as if his left shoulder was on fire. A single bullet had punched a hole as big as a quarter in his shoulder, and he could feel the blood oozing down his arm and onto his hand resting immobile in his lap. Already he'd lost enough blood to soak his shirt and the car seat beneath him. The bullet had hit something important; that much was obvious. And to make matters worse, none of the men in the car seemed to care whether or not they got him to a hospital or a doctor. The pain was getting worse by the second. At first he thought he had just jammed his shoulder against the inside of the car as he had lunged back and forth dodging bullets. There had been pressure, then numbness. Maybe he'd hit his funny bone, he'd thought. But that had passed. He'd discovered the hole, and now the pain was streaking up his arm, into his chest, and seemed to be making a beeline for all points south. What was that all about, anyway? Whatever it was, he wanted a doctor.

And then he'd discovered the blood. Lots of it, soaking his clothes and pooling beneath him on the ruined seat.

"Move it, man!" Corey screamed through the pain. "This thing's killin' me." He pressed his injured shoulder against the back of the rear seat hoping to apply enough pressure to stem the bleeding and maybe alleviate some of the pain. All he succeeded in doing was spewing more blood over the beige upholstery and intensifying the agony.

"I told you he'd mess this up," Kendall Morris shouted from the driver's seat. "Man never could keep his head down."

"Nobody said nothin' 'bout him havin' a gun," Simmons shot back through gritted teeth. "Whoever missed that little item of information is the man to blame. Not me."

"Shut up, both of you," Willie Henderson ordered. Henderson was in the front seat on the passenger side, and he still held onto the shotgun he'd just used in the attack against Andrew Chapman and Jordyn Phillips. The only difference between the way he'd used his shotgun and the other two men in the car had been that he'd actually intended to kill Chapman. They had all been ordered merely to scare the CID agent and that good-looking prosecuting attorney. Corey Simmons and Hal Jackson had followed the orders to the letter, but Willie Henderson had had no intention of missing. Had he succeeded, there would have been questions about the failure, but that would have been all right with him. Easier to ask for forgiveness than permission.

As far as Henderson was concerned, if Andrew Chapman had been killed, it would have only made things a little easier in Bannerman County. Besides, he remembered Chapman from years ago, and he'd never liked him that much anyway. Chapman had been the star running back, the best student, and the teacher's pet. The pretty boy who went to West Point. Willie Henderson had been the town bully, the resident delinquent, and the object of every teacher's wrath. When Henderson really thought about it, he hated Andrew Chapman and always had.

"Get me to a doctor," Simmons moaned again. He was getting weaker, his demands less strident, less insistent. Blood continued to ooze from the wound, and with every drop, Corey Simmons grew weaker, his face growing paler with every drop of blood that flowed from the wound.

"What do we do?" Morris demanded. "We got to do something."

"Yeah," Jackson agreed unconvincingly from his position next to Simmons in the rear seat.

Henderson turned to Morris and Jackson, his face a mask of anger. "Why? Just tell me why we have to do anything," Henderson demanded, his tone ugly. "Let the jerk die; then we can dispose of him, and he'll be out of the way." Had the words come from anyone other than Willie Henderson, they might have been construed as a vain attempt at a bad joke. But coming from Henderson, no one in the car doubted their sincerity.

Corey Simmons let out a howl from the backseat.

"Shut him up," Henderson ordered, his anger growing with every moan that Simmons let out.

Jackson put a hand out to comfort his wounded comrade.

"What'll we do?" Morris asked, confusion beginning to overtake him as he drove. He was heading out of town, away from the help Simmons was pleading for.

Henderson looked at both Jackson and Morris, then back at the ashen-faced Simmons. "Keep going. Head for the cove like we planned and let me think."

Simmons had quieted down. Blood had stopped flowing from Simmons's wound, the odor of gunpowder replaced by the pungent coppery odor of human blood.

Morris turned the car onto a side road that led further into the forest. Neither Simmons nor Jackson said a word from the backseat. Henderson stared straight ahead, knowing now what had to be done.

"Pull into the cove. My truck's there," Henderson ordered.

Morris guided the car into a clearing that opened up into a small, secluded cove formed by the Spring Valley and Bannerman County water supply reservoir. The road leading to the reservoir was on private property. The high water mark of the reservoir itself was owned by the county, but no one ever ranged as far as the cove. There was no need.

Henderson's white Dodge Ram came into view as Morris pulled to a stop at the edge of the cove.

"Everyone out," Henderson ordered.

Morris shut off the motor. Hal Jackson climbed out of the car from the rear seat. Corey Simmons slumped over onto the seat when Jackson got out. The only sound that came from him was another low moan.

"Get the guns," Henderson said. "And be sure we've got everything else. I don't want anything left in that car. Except Simmons, that is," he added with a cruel smile.

"Wait a minute . . ." Jackson began.

"Wait nothing," Henderson shot back, leveling the shotgun he carried at Jackson. "Leave him. He's almost dead anyway. This way, he's out of our hair. We don't need the headache. Anyway, no one's going to even know he's gone. Why do you guys think we were chosen for this job? None of us is married. You think that was just coincidence?"

Henderson chuckled. "And Simmons don't have any family in these parts. What he does have is two states over, and they're not going to come looking for him for a long time. Simmons has got to go, and this is as good a way as any. We already decided to dump the car in the cove. Simmons is just an added attraction, is all. Now clean out the car, and let's get it in the water."

For the next ten minutes the three men worked around the wounded Corey Simmons who lay in a semicomatose state in the backseat. They removed any evidence that might lead to them. There had been none to begin with, but Willie Henderson was taking no chances. With that done, all three pushed the car to the edge of the cove and over the edge. The reservoir had been constructed for the sole purpose of providing a water source for the surrounding countryside. Because of that, the shoreline drop-off was steeper than would have normally been found in a naturally formed lake. The car bubbled into the water, filled quickly, and sank in the cove to a depth of more than forty feet.

"Now, let's get out of here," Henderson said, heading for his truck. "And don't forget the assembly tonight. Everyone's expected to be there," he said with a touch of warning in his voice. "Don't even think about not showing."

Henderson pulled the truck back onto the road and headed for Spring Valley. His thoughts went at once to Andrew Chapman. The fact that Chapman had had a weapon caused him to seethe beneath an already angry exterior. He had tried to kill Chapman, and the plan had backfired. He would see the CID agent dead before the week was out, he promised himself. And maybe that bothersome prosecuting attorney as well. But first, Henderson thought, he might have to have a little fun with the attorney. The thought produced a smile. After all, he had a score to settle with Andrew Chapman. This would be the perfect way to do just that.

CHAPTER SIX

Drew rolled down the window as he drove along the tree-lined state highway leading to Hallis Road. Despite the heat of the summer morning, he shivered. The shooting back at Carter House was unusual for this part of the state and certainly unusual for him. Being a CID agent, he was more accustomed to the pure investigative portion of a case, not the shoot-'em-up false impressions of many laymen. What's more, it didn't seem possible that such a thing could happen here among the rolling hills and wooded forest. He'd grown up not far from here, and the memories were good ones. It had been a normal, healthy passage from childhood through adolescence to adulthood. Shortly after Drew had been admitted to West Point, however, his father had been appointed the head of the English department at a private college and his parents had moved away from the area. Eventually his parents retired to Florida and Drew had not had the opportunity to return to Bannerman County until now.

As idyllic as the setting was here, Drew knew things such as the murders did occur. It was a world gone mad, which was one of the reasons he'd made the date for tonight. He smiled at the recollection of that. He'd intended to surprise Jordyn with the revelation, but her reaction, as far as he could tell, had not been one of surprise or concern. He planned to call her later on in the afternoon, after his inspection of the murder scene, to invite her to accompany him on the date. That, he grinned to himself, would certainly elicit a reaction of some kind.

Hallis Road came up on the left, and Drew took the turn. The state road on which he'd been traveling had been well maintained, but Hallis Road was the responsibility of Bannerman County road crews, and reduced budgets from a diminishing tax base had left the road in a dismal state of repair. Drew bounced along the road for two miles before seeing the white crime van and the cruiser from the Bannerman County sheriff's department in the distance. Drew braked to a halt at the rear of the police cruiser.

As he had suspected, there was little to learn at the crime scene. The forensic team along with Bannerman County deputies Boggs and Reece had combed the area. They had probed every possible nook and cranny on the side of the road. The van had been transported to the capital only after the forensic crew had snapped literally hundreds of photographs of the vehicle. Drew had discussed the van with his forensic investigators and was pretty sure nothing of any importance was going to turn up in the van. There had been mention of the graffiti-type markings, but that was all. All the evidence pointed to the fact that nothing had actually taken place in the van itself. The three bodies had been lying beside the road, left there by the killers.

The killers. That's what was sticking in Drew's throat. They were butchers, whose apparent motive for such a crime was that they did not like the three men in the van. Drew had no hard evidence to support that conclusion, but he'd seen it before. The media was dubbing this a hate murder, and Drew could not refute the conclusion.

Drew struggled up the gentle embankment. The grass was still moist with dew, and he was being careful not to slip.

"How's it going, Barry?" Drew asked the lead investigator of the forensic team.

"Almost finished, Drew," Barry Michener answered as he packed up some of the equipment he and his team had transported to Bannerman County. "Another few minutes, and we'll be out of here."

"Thanks, guys," Drew said to the other members of the team. "You men too," he added, turning to the two deputies who stood close by.

"No problem," Boggs said, a smirk creasing his face.

"Anything else we can do?" Reece asked, the sincerity in his offer in sharp contrast to Boggs's sarcastic smile.

Drew looked around the area. It had been a good job, rapidly done. Sometimes speed was detrimental to the outcome, but this time he felt certain speed would turn out to be an ally. The state police needed to produce an informed statement, and that could only be done after sufficient evidence revealed a pattern. As the lead investigator, he would have to handle the press. That part of the job was his least favorite, although it was widely believed that he did a superior job of public relations when compared to other CID agents, including handling the media.

But the media here were going to want answers, and Drew was not sure he was quite ready for even a preliminary statement.

"Oh, by the way, Drew," Michener said from where he was finally snapping shut the last aluminum case. "The photos we took are in the safe in the back of the van. There's a set in there for you. We shot digital photos and printed them from our onboard computer."

"Thanks, Barry," Drew answered, making his way to the rear of the crime scene van. He pulled open the doors and saw a manila folder lying within a small metal mesh enclosure. He opened the "safe" and extracted the bulging package. He'd not yet had a chance to examine the photos. He'd heard the rumors though. The murderers had spray painted some sort of figures or symbols on the van. He pulled the photos from the folder and looked. Suddenly he felt his pulse begin to pound in his temples as the images swam before his unfocused eyes. He felt as if he would faint, as if the surrounding trees were closing in on him. He resisted the effects the photographs were having on him.

Was it possible?

The photos were of the van's exterior and interior, but the symbols painted on the van's broad exterior panels were his main point of focus.

He stared at them with increasing distress. His mind traced the mark-ings, remembering a time long ago, not more than a few miles from where he now stood.

"Not possible," he said under his breath. "Please, God, tell me this is not possible," he whispered. For a moment he wondered why he had mentioned God but then smiled to himself. He knew the answer to that question.

"Something wrong, Chapman?" Danny Boggs asked, approaching from where he'd been watching the CID agent. The smug look on the deputy's face revealed nothing.

Drew looked up, meeting the irritating gaze of the Bannerman County deputy. "Nothing I can't handle. Thanks anyway, Boggs." He then turned and left the man standing alone beside Hallis Road.

Drew had to think. The markings on the side of the van were familiar, very familiar. *More* than familiar, he reminded himself. He had to reason this out. What he was seeing was impossible. It had been years since he'd seen symbols similar to those painted on the side of the battered white van, but he knew them as well now as he had then.

"We're pulling out," Barry Michener called to Drew. "We'll process what we've got and get back to you as quickly as possible, but don't count on that being too soon. We've got a lot of stuff to sift through," the forensic scientist warned.

"Thanks, Barry. Make it as soon as possible. You know what we've got here."

Michener nodded. "Yeah. I know. Good luck. I'll be in touch."

Drew watched as the men climbed into the crime scene van and drove away from the murder scene.

"What's that mean?" Boggs asked as he and Mike Reece stood nearby.

"What?" Drew asked.

"You said you know what you've got here. What's that?"

"You don't know?" Drew countered, his anger beginning to build. He didn't like Boggs, but he really wasn't sure what it was about the man that irritated him.

"You're the CID agent. You tell me," Boggs challenged.

"Somebody didn't like Hispanics. They killed them because they were available. And that turns my stomach."

"Nothin' but wetbacks. Probably got what they deserved . . ."

The words were not completely out of Boggs's mouth before the impact of Drew's right fist knocked the deputy to the ground.

Boggs was up in a flash, cat-fast on his feet, moving in on Drew, closing from the right. The deputy was larger than Drew by fifty pounds, but Drew moved with a grace that belied his forty-plus years. Boggs charged, and Drew easily eluded the mindless attack. His hand grasped Boggs's uniform shirt and propelled the deputy in the same direction he was going. Momentum did the rest.

Boggs stumbled once, going down hard.

"Think about it before you get up," Drew warned.

Boggs was up again. This time he warily approached Drew, his weight on the balls of his feet, balanced and prepared to attack yet again.

"What're you gonna do? Arrest me?" Boggs taunted.

"No," Drew replied easily. "I'm going to leave you in the ditch over there and let your boss come pick you up."

Boggs stood erect, his intended attack temporarily halted by the assurance he heard in Drew's voice. Although he was facing a man smaller and older than he was, somehow he believed this man could do exactly what he was threatening. "You think so?" Boggs continued.

"It's not what I think; it's what I know. But I can tell you don't believe me, so come ahead," Drew said easily.

Boggs now understood he was overmatched. He would have to wait. There would be another time and place. Of that he was certain.

"Come on, Reece. Let's get out of here. This is state business now," Boggs said, turning and heading for the patrol car, wiping the blood from his mouth as he walked.

Boggs was closing the door of the car before Mike Reece moved. Reece smiled at Drew. "We need to talk," he said. "Tonight. I'll call you. This is worth your time; I promise," the deputy said before turning and heading for the patrol car.

Drew stood in the middle of the road and watched the cruiser burn rubber down the ill-maintained county highway. He then picked up the photographs from where he tossed them when he'd hit Boggs. He glanced at them once again before stuffing them back in the envelope.

How is it possible? he asked himself. He needed to talk to Jordyn, to explain. But explain what? And how? Would she understand? He was surprised and pleased that he cared enough about her to wonder what her reaction would be when he told her about the strange markings on the side of the van.

He would call her and go ahead with his original plan. He'd ask her to accompany him on his "date." Surely he could find an appropriate time to tell her.

That would be a beginning, but only a beginning.

■ ■ ■

Jordyn Phillips signed the last of the documents on her desk and called out, "Janice, these are ready to go."

Janice Brown, Jordyn's secretary, came in from the outer office. "You don't look too good. Are you sure you're all right?"

Jordyn forced a smile. "Not really. That shooting shook me up."

"I can imagine. Why don't you take the rest of the day off? I've got most of the motions finished, and I'll walk them over to the courthouse and file them. That's about all that's left to do for right now."

Jordyn rubbed her temples in gentle circles. She'd been fighting a headache since this morning, and now she was losing. The shooting had only worsened the problem. "I think you're right, Janice. Call me at home if you need me. Anything else can wait until tomorrow."

"What about the interview?"

The interview. She'd completely forgotten about that. With Drew Chapman out of reach, the media were circling her office like sharks drawn to blood. There had been numerous requests for interviews with the county prosecuting attorney. She'd talked to Dewayne Lawrence earlier, and he was battling the same thing. There simply were not enough people "in the know" to go around, and the media personnel were frantic.

"Not today. I'll sneak out the back. I did the same thing this morning over at Dewayne's office. No one expects me to be the prosecuting attorney anyway." Jordyn thumbed through her personal calendar lying on her desk. "Oh, shoot. I've got CSA tonight."

"I almost forgot. Joy Hartford called to remind you about that," Janice said, the apology unspoken but apparent in her voice.

"No problem," Jordyn said, rising. "I'll go home, take some aspirin, lie down for a couple of hours, and then go on over to the church."

The phone rang and Janice started for her office to answer it, but Jordyn waved her to the one on her own desk. Janice answered and listened for a moment. She placed her hand over the receiver and mouthed to Jordyn, "Andrew Chapman."

Jordyn thought for a minute before waving off the call.

"I'm sorry, Mr. Chapman, but Ms. Phillips is not in the office this afternoon. Could I take a message?"

The response was short, and Janice replaced the phone. "It was something about a date tonight," she continued after hanging up. "Said to tell you that you missed an interesting evening."

Jordyn's puzzled looked caused Janice to smile. "Didn't know anything about a date?"

"Sure, but the date is with someone else, not me. I wonder what he was talking about?"

"Call him. He left his cell phone number."

"I don't think so. I'm too old-fashioned in that way. I'll let him try and call me if he's serious."

Janice smiled wider. "Don't want to appear too excited?"

"*Interested* is a more appropriate word, and you better keep your mouth shut, or you'll be looking for another job," Jordyn said with mock seriousness.

Janice laughed. "No one else will put up with you the way I do, and you know it. Threats will get you nowhere."

Jordyn hugged her, then said, "I'll let you know what happens. In the meantime, I'll be at home and later at the church if anyone we know should try to contact me," she grinned, despite the pounding headache.

"I'll try to remember that. Go home and take those aspirin, or you'll never make it to CSA tonight."

"You're right. And there will be a lot of folks there this afternoon and tonight. We received a whole shipment of clothing from a manufacturer upstate. The items have small defects, so the company normally would have sold them in their own outlet stores, but the state CSA convinced them it would be worth millions in publicity to send them to the CSA stations around the state."

"Great idea. The Community Services Agency is one of the best ideas those boys at the state capital have ever come up with."

"I know. It even surprised me. Benson's the one who rammed the idea through the legislature, and that was even more of a surprise," Jordyn continued. Lieutenant Governor—now Acting Governor—William Benson is not known as the most benevolent man ever to walk the face of this earth."

"He'll be running for governor one day," Janice replied. "The unofficial word on the street is that the governor will be out of the hospital and back in charge. If Benson wants to be governor, he'll have to earn it."

"You're probably right," Jordyn said. "Still, it's not like Benson. But that's another story. We've got CSA, and it's working. That's what counts. OK, I'm gone. Call me at home if you need me."

"Or if someone we both know calls," Janice added with a smile.

"That too," Jordyn said, walking out the rear door of her office. As she settled into the seat of her car, she wondered why Andrew had called about the date he'd mentioned tonight? *Curious,* she mused. *Very curious indeed.*

CHAPTER SEVEN

Time was slipping away as Samuel Reardon poured over the documents covering his desk. Long rays of golden sunlight shone through the partially opened blinds, creating equally long shadows on the far wall, signaling the end of a long day. The air-conditioning hummed in the background, the forced air making a quiet whooshing sound as it cooled the inner sanctum of the state police commander.

Reardon pushed the documents away and concentrated on the far wall. The alternating bands of shadow and light reminded him of the bars of a jail cell. And it was the jail cell that represented for him the height of justice in a society gone berserk. He'd seen it all during his time on the streets, and now, as the state's top law enforcement officer, he was determined to have some measure of influence on the lawlessness around him.

The documents on his desk were preliminary reports from the forensic team that had returned from Bannerman County. The information included photographs of the scene, the van, and the bodies of the victims. Reardon had studied the photos, always returning to those of the van, examining the cryptic markings spray painted on the van's side panels. He'd seen similar markings before, years ago in another place and time, and seeing them again now chilled him to the bone. But more than that, what he *thought* frightened him even more.

The phone rang in the outer office, and then his line buzzed. He sighed as he picked it up. Another problem, to be sure, because that was all he was getting these days.

"Reardon," he answered.

"It's Lieutenant Governor Benson," his secretary told him.

"*Acting Governor Benson,* Marci," Reardon said with a tinge of disgust in his voice at having to recognize the man's authority. "Thanks." He pushed the lighted button. "Reardon here," he said flatly. His voice, he hoped, conveyed nothing, and in that nothingness his true feelings would search for an avenue of escape. He would have to hold his temper and be discreet. It would not be easy.

"Sam, Bill Benson. How are things going over in the new complex?"

To Reardon, it sounded like old home week. *Bill,* he thought. Never had Benson introduced himself to Reardon as Bill, and Reardon also knew he was not free to address the *acting governor* in that manner. "Just fine, Governor," Reardon answered, knowing the reason for the call. "What can the state police do for you this afternoon?"

"Well, Sam," Benson began, "I need some information on that Bannerman County thing. Any word from Chapman yet?"

"Nothing from Chapman, but I've got a preliminary report from the forensic team on my desk. My men are going over the van as we speak, and I've sent some inquiries to Washington."

"Washington? What's Washington got to do with this? Murder is not in their jurisdiction."

"No, sir, but there are indications that this might be a murder that the FBI could help us with. After all, what we want to do is find the killers, not fight a jurisdictional battle." Reardon noticed the pause on the other end of the line before Benson spoke.

"Of course, you're right. It's just that I had hoped to clear this up in record time. What type of information do you have that the FBI might be interested in?"

"I'd prefer to discuss that face-to-face, if you don't mind."

Benson chuckled over the phone. "Must be something pretty important. Have you seen the news reports coming out of Bannerman County?"

"Yes, sir."

"Then we can talk about that, too, when you get here. An hour, shall we say?"

"An hour, sir," Reardon answered, then replaced the phone. He stepped to his desk, picked up the photographs again, and thumbed through them until he got to the ones he wanted. He perused the photos of the van again, noting the markings on the panels that were no doubt left there by the killers for a reason. Those markings were the impetus for his FBI inquiry: he would have to reveal that to Benson. He didn't really like the idea; nevertheless, it would have to be done. He shoveled the forensic report back into the large manila envelope it had come in, placed the envelope in the bottom drawer of his desk, and locked it.

The markings were vivid in his mind, as if they had been burned into his retina by a laser. Yes, he'd seen the markings before, but what gave him pause was the disquieting suspicion that in all probability, Andrew Chapman had also seen the markings. If that were so, in what context had he seen them? For in this case, context was everything.

He had an hour before his meeting with Benson. More like forty-five minutes. It would take him fifteen or twenty minutes to drive to the state Executive Office Building where Benson maintained an office. He needed to talk with Chapman, but that would have to wait. However, he had an idea.

"Marci, get me the personnel file on Andrew Chapman, please," he said over his intercom. He had reviewed the file when Benson had requested that Andrew Chapman be the lead investigator on the murders and had found nothing of significance. But he could have missed some pertinent nugget of information. Something, *anything,* that would shed light on the reason for Benson's insistence on Chapman's assignment.

He would review the file again. Maybe he could find Benson's reasoning behind the request.

It was dark when Marci delivered the file and tossed it on his desk.

"What time is it?" Reardon asked, noticing that the alternating rows of light and shadow no longer adorned his far wall. The sun had gone down.

"Almost eight-thirty."

Reardon looked up. "Why are you still here?" he asked, smiling at his secretary.

"Because you are. Who would have gotten that file for you if I had not been here?"

"The comptroller's not going to like the overtime," Reardon responded, only half jokingly.

Marci Kean did an about-face and marched out of the office. Just before closing the door, she muttered, loud enough for Reardon to hear, "No one asked for overtime."

Reardon smiled again, knowing that there would not be even a minute of overtime on Marci's time sheet. He turned to the file. Thirty minutes, max, he told himself, then to the governor's office. He opened Andrew Chapman's file and began reading.

■   ■   ■

The phone booth where Mike Reece stood had seen better days. Gang tagging and miscellaneous graffiti covered every inch of the booth's flat surfaces in a dizzying array of colors and patterns. To Reece the booth's surface looked like a kaleidoscope gone berserk, expressions of life out of control. He smiled at the thought of gangs in Spring Valley. What passed for gangs in the small burg were nothing more than expanded social clubs, teens searching for companionship, much like he'd done during his high school days. Tagging, those strange symbols painted by the gangs on every available surface, were about as rowdy as things got around Spring Valley. No car thefts, no gang wars, no form of organized intimidation. Sure there was some minor drug dealing, but nothing approaching what could have been. Not like the larger cities. Certainly not like in New York.

Reece stepped into the booth, inserted a coin, and dialed the cell phone number of Drew Chapman. It was answered on the first ring. "We need to talk. An hour," Reece said, his left hand in his pocket, feeling for the ring he knew was there. "There's a hardware store on the outskirts of town, on the capital highway. It's closed. Called Dowinger's. Meet me at the rear."

A meeting established, Reece hung up. He pulled the ring from his pocket, examined it for the hundredth time, then replaced it, wondering why he had violated police procedure so blatantly, yet knowing instinctively he'd done the right thing. He stepped out of the booth and headed for his car. The hardware store was no more than ten minutes from where he now stood. He'd told Chapman an hour. Reece would get there first. He was always first; he wanted to survey the area. Continued personal safety is due in a large part to personal preparedness, and Reece liked to think he was always prepared. He gunned his car toward the capital highway. For better or worse, he'd decided to trust Andrew Chapman. He smiled at that; it sounded like his marriage vows—*for better or worse*. "And we hardly know each other, Mr. Chapman," he laughed aloud. Then the laughter died, suffocated by the reality of the situation. He had a feeling that the situation would get worse before it got better. What bothered him most was that his feelings were seldom wrong.

■   ■   ■

"Follow him," the burley man with the slightly weak chin ordered. "And don't let him know we're back here."

"I know what I'm doing," the driver growled, throwing the car into gear, spewing loose gravel in the wake of spinning tires.

"Subtle," Weak Chin said. "Very subtle."

The driver said nothing. His gaze was fixed on the car ahead of him, its taillights visible in the growing darkness. *This is going to be fun*, the driver thought.

■ ■ ■

The state's Executive Office Building was situated directly across from the capitol—across Fifth Street, a bustling six-lane city avenue known to everyone simply as Capitol Street.

Built in the early 1900s, the building projected a majesty whose cost would be prohibitive in today's modern architectural market. A great granite facade was inset at strategic locations with white marble, and huge columns rose on the portico, symbolizing the power of government. The windows had been changed within the last few years, the smoked glass in contrast to the rest of the building, yet still managing to retain a grandeur in their floor-to-ceiling height. Just across the street the capitol dome glowed in the night, its outline enhanced by hundreds of low-intensity lights. The executive building's grounds were well maintained but lacked the refinement of the more ebullient state capitol complex.

The thought of *governmental power* brought a smirk to Sam Reardon's face as he climbed the granite steps leading to the entrance of the Executive Office Building. Most governments never really knew the power they wielded until faced with outright rebellion on the part of their citizenry, and then most discovered that their perceived power was quite a bit less than what they had thought.

A uniformed state policeman stood guard just inside the foyer. The man recognized Colonel Reardon immediately, saluting his superior as Reardon pushed through the glass doors.

"Working late, Colonel?" the officer said.

"Sure am," Reardon replied. "Getting to be a habit."

"Governor Benson is waiting. His aide called down and said you were coming."

"Better not keep the great man waiting, then," said Reardon as he moved toward the stairs.

"The elevators are working, Colonel," the policeman said.

"Always take the stairs. Helps keep me in shape," Reardon said as the stairwell door closed behind him.

The Executive Office Building consisted of four floors, laid out in the traditional rectangular arrangement with the governor's office on the top floor. The building's layout offered no surprises, and Reardon found a certain degree of comfort in the familiar, the mundane.

As he climbed the stairs, Reardon wondered if Benson had ever seen the inside of the stairwell. "Probably not," he said aloud, the words echoing off the pale green cinder-block walls.

In less than ninety seconds, Reardon exited the stairwell and headed for the governor's suite.

The suite was nicely done without being ostentatious, a must for a frugal state. The outer door, however, was singularly impressive—native oak framed in natural maple with a finish that was almost blinding. A small brass plaque identified the door as the entrance to the offices of the head of state government. Samuel Reardon had long ago ceased to be impressed by the trappings of power. That was one of the reasons he respected Governor Patrick O'Brien. O'Brien's roots went back to a conservative Ireland, and that conservatism had been applied to the state's fiscal policy, as well as everything else O'Brien touched. Reardon briefly wondered about the governor. He'd also seen the photographs of that wreck and knew that it was a miracle anyone escaped alive. He would have to phone the hospital when he got back to his office.

Samuel Reardon took three deep breaths, then knocked on the door and entered.

■   ■   ■

Drew Chapman folded the small cellular telephone and replaced it on his belt. An hour. Forty-five would be better. He'd have to call his "date" for the night and cancel. Better yet, he'd drive by her house and tell her face to face. A call would have been easier, but this woman was special and deserved an explanation. Besides, her house was on his way to his meeting with Mike Reece, and the stop would only take a few minutes. That decision made, Drew walked to his car and five minutes later pulled to a stop in front of the home of a woman he loved dearly.

No more than a cottage, the house reflected its occupant—simple, comfortable, and inviting. Warm yellow light spilled out onto the narrow porch. A small picket fence surrounded the yard. A sense of tranquility that Drew found captivating encompassed the cottage. As he walked up the narrow dirt path leading to the house, the porch light came on and a woman appeared at the door. Even from a distance Drew recognized Nanny Collins, or Nanny C., as he had called her.

"That you, Andrew?" The voice was mid-range smooth despite the years. "I knew you would come."

Drew was instantly glad he had decided to come in person.

"It's me, Nanny C.," Drew answered, his footsteps hollow on the worn boards of the porch steps.

"Drew! God bless you," Nanny said when she saw him.

She moved slowly now, Drew noticed. How old was she now? Seventy-five? Eighty?

Nanny bear-hugged Drew as he threw his arms around her, returning the affection. Here was the lady who had raised him, scolded him, and pampered him from the time he was old enough to remember her until he'd left for West Point. He still remembered sitting at her feet and listening to the yarns she used to spin. It was not until years later that he realized the stories were more than just yarns; they had been her history, her past, and in some cases, her future.

Most of the stories had been about her grandfather and the days he'd spent in the cotton fields of Mississippi and Louisiana just prior to the Civil War. Cotton Collins, her grandfather, had seen it all, from the Civil War to the turn of the century. Nanny had never known her grandfather other than by the stories she'd been told by her father, but she could not have been prouder of any man. Eventually, after emancipation, the family had moved north and never returned to the land of her birth. She'd had no regrets, although Nanny sometimes expressed a desire for a warmer climate.

After her husband died, Nanny found employment with the Chapman family and had bonded instantly with young Andrew. If asked, she would truthfully say she'd never loved anyone as much as she loved little Drew. And the feelings had been mutual. So much so that when Drew's parents once discussed retiring Nanny, Drew had screamed and cried until they relented. Nanny had stayed on until young Drew left for West Point. She then retired on a handsome pension provided by Drew's father. Never in all her years did she regret a minute of the love she'd shared with the Chapman family. And Drew had stayed in touch, despite the distance.

"God bless you too, Nanny C.," Drew said, holding the old woman tighter.

"Mercy, child. You're going to break my bones," Nanny said reluctantly.

Drew released her, holding her at arm's length and looking into her soft brown eyes. "How have you been, Nanny C.?"

"Well, if you would come around more often, you would know the answer to that," the old lady scolded, grinning from ear to ear.

Drew hung his head in mock repentance. "I know, Nanny C. I'm sorry."

"And there's someone else up here who's sorry, too, but we can talk about that later."

Drew tried to decipher the old woman's meaning but decided to let it go for the time being. "And I've got some bad news for tonight."

"You can't spend the evening with your Nanny like you said you would," Nanny said.

"You always did know what I was going to say before I said it."

"And I always knew what you were thinking too. I know you've got business. These murders are frightening. Can you do anything about them? Do you have any ideas?"

"Some," Drew answered evasively.

Nanny looked at Drew, her head twisted to the side so that she was looking out of only one eye, her head inclined to the right.

Drew remembered the look. He'd called it "the magic eye." Every time she had used it on him, from somewhere deep within his soul he had dredged up the truth and told her what she'd wanted to know. This time, he knew he'd have to keep what he knew to himself. "Sorry, Nanny C. I promise I'll tell you when the right time comes. Besides, all I have are suspicions."

"If I remember correctly, your suspicions were usually on target."

Drew laughed. "Touché. You're probably right about this too, but still, I need to keep this to myself for a while yet."

"I understand," the old lady said softly. "But remember, you can always give your burdens to the Lord, and he'll help you carry them. You haven't forgotten that lesson, have you?"

"No, Nanny C. And I'm living proof that what you say is the truth."

"Not me, Drew. The Lord said it, and he meant it. If you got problems, he can help."

"I'll remember. Right now I've got to meet someone."

"Someone who knows something about the Bannerman County murders?"

Drew snaked his arm around the old lady, hugging her as he said, "You need to be on the state police force. No one would ever put anything over on you during an interrogation."

Nanny wrapped her arm around Drew's waist and looked up at him. "*You* never could," she smiled.

"Gotta run. I'll call you tomorrow. I've got someone I want you to meet."

"If you mean that nice Ms. Phillips, we already know each other. Bring her with you. I'll fix supper soon."

"It's a date," Drew said. "Now, I've got to run." Drew bounded down the steps, making for his car and waving to Nanny as he headed for the meeting with Mike Reece. What, he wondered, did the deputy have for him tonight? Whatever it was, he'd know in a few minutes.

■ ■ ■

"He's on the loading dock," the weak-chinned man whispered to his companion.

"Let's do it," the driver said.

"You sneak around the other side. I'll get his attention from this side. Make it quick. If I know Reece, he's got his pistol with him."

"It'll be quick. Quick and dirty, just like I like it."

The driver moved off to the left, skirting the old hardware building. Weak Chin waited a full five minutes, knowing that was more than enough time for his partner to get behind the Bannerman County deputy. He stepped from the deep shadows of the adjacent building, staggered slightly as if drunk, and continued toward Mike Reece.

When the deputy moved from the loading dock to the ground level to investigate the man who was apparently drunk, the driver moved.

CHAPTER EIGHT

When she'd first begun, the number of downtrodden human beings passing through the Bannerman County branch of the Community Services Agency had been disconcerting for Jordyn Phillips. She empathized with many, feeling the pain and loneliness that she saw in their haunting and hurting faces. It was a pain born from separation and desperation—men, women, and children who had not seen their homeland for long periods of time, who were desperate to scratch out a living in this strange new land called the United States. As a volunteer with CSA, it had taken her more than a year to become accustomed to the human misery that paraded through the doors every Monday, Wednesday, and Friday evenings. Tonight was particularly oppressive, especially when she factored in the shooting at the Carter House this morning and the three murders on Hallis Road. It had never occurred to Jordyn that such events could happen here when she'd accepted the appointment as the Bannerman County prosecutor. Her musings over the shooting brought with it the recollection of Andrew Chapman, and she knew she needed to tune out the earlier events and concentrate on the task at hand.

The Community Services Agency of Bannerman County was temporarily located in the unused basement space of Valley Community

Church. The church's pastor, Kerry Hartford, had offered the space when the state first began the CSA program. Hartford's wife, Joy, was named director, and CSA began its benevolent work. Now, more than a year later, the work had grown beyond the expectations of both the state and the church. Additional space had been made available in the church while the state formulated an overall strategy to provide permanent quarters for all CSA branches, now located in every county of the state.

The Bannerman County branch of CSA, like the rest of the branches, was staffed solely by volunteers, except for Joy Hartford. She and the other directors were paid by the state. Many of the CSA sites were located in space donated by local churches, and most of the volunteers were members of those sponsoring churches. The arrangement negated the necessity of maintaining a paid staff and provided sufficient manpower to handle the influx of migrant workers, refugees, and homeless men and women. The churches were highly supportive of the program.

CSA provided clothing, temporary shelter, and food for anyone who walked through its doors, and there were many. More important, it served as an education and employment coordinator for those seeking to better their lots in life. It was an innovative solution whose basis could be found in the benevolent attitude of the many rescue missions dotting the landscape within the United States. The overriding factor for CSA, however, was that it had the financial backing of the state, thus providing a relatively stable platform from which to serve humanity.

CSA had been the brainchild of Lieutenant Governor William Benson. Some found this fact curious since William Benson had never been perceived as a particularly benevolent politician. Nonetheless, CSA had been formed and to date could claim significant success in its stated goals.

Tonight five volunteers, counting Jordyn, tended to the influx of men, women, and children. Jordyn was working at the registration desk. Every person who entered CSA was registered. Names were required, as well as addresses, if available. Any other pertinent information supplied was recorded but not required.

Jordyn sat at the console of the registration computer, which was networked to the central office and all other CSA branches around the state. Information collected was sorted and collated by the central server in the state capital, and the information was used to keep track within the state of the movements of the people CSA served. The system also served to identify any professional freeloaders. If it was determined that the benevolent cause of CSA was being abused, the career sycophant was handled gently by the CSA staff. Failing that, the local authorities were called. The bottom line was that such human parasites seldom returned to CSA once they experienced the tracking capabilities of the system.

Jordyn looked up as yet another family entered the doors. It was a man and wife, obviously migrant workers, with four children. Jordyn's heart went out to them. The father seemed confused and embarrassed. No one liked having to seek help to support his family, but at times, circumstances overwhelmed even the most sincere and hardworking.

"Hi," Jordyn greeted with a smile. "Welcome to the Community Services Agency. How can I help you?"

The confusion on the father's face quickly magnified, the eyes questioning.

"Papi doesn't speak English," the child nearest Jordyn replied quickly.

"OK. Can you translate?"

"Yes," the child said. She was taller than the other three children and was probably the oldest, Jordyn thought.

"I need some information first. Then we'll see what you need."

"What do you need to know?"

Jordyn began with the family name and worked from there, pecking away at the keyboard as the girl supplied the information. Jordyn was almost finished when she realized the girl spoke perfect English with little or no accent, an indication the girl was equally at ease with both languages. Jordyn admired those with such ability. Such skill would be highly marketable in the future.

"That does it," Jordyn said, looking up at the family. The father had visibly relaxed during the process; the other three children clung to their mother's dress. "What can we do for you tonight?"

The girl spoke to her father in Spanish, then turned to Jordyn. "We would like work," she said. "And something to eat, if that's possible. We have been driving two days, and the children need something to eat."

Jordyn was filled with compassion. She'd seen this before, and her heart always went out to the families. No amount of exposure to situations such as this could ever anesthetize her against the feelings that welled up inside her. She glanced at the children. Each of them seemed more beautiful than the previous. Deep brown eyes stared back at her from deeply tanned faces. The mother stood stoically, her hands on two of the children huddled at her knees. The father's hands were gnarled and twisted from manual labor.

"*Si. Por favor. Tal vez, algo para los ninos*," the father said.

Jordyn turned to the older girl.

"Something for the children," the girl translated.

"Come with me. We'll take care of you," Jordyn said, getting up from the computer, her hand reaching out to the older girl and directing the family to the cafeteria area that was always a part of any CSA program.

There was a line waiting when Jordyn returned to her computer. It was going to be a long night but, she knew, a very satisfying one.

"How many do you think?" Joy Hartford asked over Jordyn's shoulder. Joy was in her mid-thirties with a petite cheerleader figure that had not yet succumbed to the ravages of time and gravity. Her dark red hair was pulled into a tight bun high on the back of her head. The few freckles that were spotted across her nose and cheekbones seemed to have been carefully placed there to produce a most attractive synergy with her light complexion. She and her husband, Kerry, presented the perfect picture of a pastor and his wife. It was universally agreed that Valley Community Church was better for having the two of them.

Jordyn tapped a key. "Sixty-seven so far. About average. But there are more waiting."

"Getting the information on everyone?"

"For the most part. There are some blank spaces, of course, but I'm getting the names."

"Don't forget. If they don't have an address, try to get them to give us information about their plans. Tracking movements is critical," Joy said. "Keep up the good work."

"Will do, Joy. It's going to be an average night, I suspect."

"Well, the more we can help the better. Thanks for staying with us, Jordyn."

"I wouldn't have missed this for anything."

The director turned and disappeared down the hallway.

I wouldn't have missed this for anything," Jordyn repeated. But that was not necessarily true. She would have missed tonight if Andrew Chapman had called, and with that realization, Jordyn felt herself blush at her unilateral self-admission.

She turned back to the computer and began the registration process for another family, this one with three children in tow. She could still feel the warmth coursing through her that the thought of Andrew Chapman had provoked.

■　■　■

It was dark. No lights shone at the rear of Dowinger's Hardware. The business had closed when Old Man Dowinger retired, and no one ever reopened the location. There was a feeling of desolation to the place, but it also provided the necessary condition Mike Reece sought for his meeting with CID agent Andrew Chapman—isolation.

Reece had arrived early, just as he had planned; surveyed the surrounding area; and settled in to wait for Chapman. He was mildly shocked when he saw a figure stagger from the deep shadows and move toward him. "A drunk," Reece said to himself, angry at this unwarranted interruption. "Just what I need."

The man staggered on, bobbing and weaving, struggling to maintain his balance.

Reece moved to intercept the debilitated figure, hoping to redirect whomever it was to another location. He was not in the mood to deal with a drunk tonight, and arresting one would result in hours spent back at the courthouse and jail, hours he did not have to spare tonight.

The drunk staggered closer; Reece could smell the liquor now—strong, rancid, and repulsive.

From the smell of the man, Reece could tell he was pretty well wasted. Reece cursed silently, knowing he would have to deal with the drunk.

The drunk moved closer until less than ten feet separated the two men. Still, Reece fleetingly wondered how one man could drink enough alcohol for him to be able to smell it at such a distance. "Must have spilled half of it on his clothes," Reece muttered. And then he realized his mistake.

The drunk was straightening up, coming out of the crouched posture of a drunk and into the upright stance of a man about to attack.

Reece reacted, his mind now functioning on automatic, his movements swift and certain. The man had moved closer. *You made a mistake,* Reece thought to himself. The drunk had revealed himself too early. The intervening space provided more than enough time for him to counter any movement the man might make. The man's only advantage had just been sacrificed. *Unless that was part of the plan,* Reece calculated, realizing his own error in the split second before he was jolted from behind by a battering ram charge.

The Bannerman County deputy went down hard on the paved surface. There were two attackers, both strong and determined.

Reece kicked out with his right foot, but missed. He kicked again. This time he was rewarded with a grunt from the man he'd struck.

Blows rained in on him, fists pounding his face and head. He perilously clung to consciousness. Suddenly a well-aimed kick found his stomach, expunging the air from his lungs. He couldn't breathe. With all his remaining strength, Reece clawed for the face of the man who'd portrayed the drunk; his fingers sought and found the soft flesh beneath the man's eyes. A scream erupted in the darkness. One attacker had temporarily been neutralized.

Reece could feel himself slipping into unconsciousness. There had been more blows to his head than he'd realized. He could feel the warm trickle of blood oozing from open abrasions on his forehead.

The second man was on him, his weight oppressive, pinning Reece to the concrete. Reece pushed with all his remaining strength and kicked with his knee, seeking the second attacker's midsection. His knee found its target, and the second man rolled to the side, freeing the deputy. Reece struggled to his knees. He could see the second attacker writhing in pain a few feet away, but he'd lost sight of the "drunk."

Just before a thousand lights exploded in Reece's brain from an unseen blow, he heard, "Here, this is from the Shepherd." The blow from behind propelled him face down onto the pavement. In seconds the brilliant lights in Reece's head were replaced by a black void. His last conscious thought was, "Who is the Shepherd?"

■   ■   ■

"Man!" the driver exclaimed. "For a minute there I thought we were going down. That's one tough cop."

"Not as tough as this baseball bat," the man with the weak chin exclaimed. "Look what he did to my face."

"Can't see nothing in this light. We better plant the stuff and get out of here."

"Right." Weak Chin knelt over the still body of Mike Reece and stuffed several small plastic envelopes in the deputy's pockets. "That ought to do it. By the time the cops finish investigating one of their own men, no one's going to believe a word he says. Get on the horn and tell them to do the apartment."

The driver pulled out a cell phone and dialed. When it was answered, he said, "Do it," and disconnected.

"I'd like to kill this guy," the weak-chinned man said. "I've got to get to a doctor and get these cuts taken care of."

"I know just the guy to fix you up," the driver said with a smile. "Let's go."

■   ■   ■

The soft glow of rapidly departing taillights grabbed Drew's attention as he braked to a stop. Off to the side he could see a parked car. It had to be Reece's. Drew got out and began walking around to the loading dock area. The night was eerily quiet. Heat lightening filled the sky in the distance. Drew was perspiring heavily. The summer heat had not yet abated, and the heat absorbed during the day by the old asphalt parking lot was radiating heat back into the night air.

"Reece?" Drew called. There was no answer. "Reece?" he called again, moving more cautiously now. Something was not right. His eyes had not yet adjusted to the deep shadows and dark night. Drew stood for a moment, waiting for his sight to return to normal in the low-light conditions.

When his eyes adjusted, Drew could make out a crumpled body no more than twenty feet away. As he moved closer, he heard low groans coming from the prone figure.

"Reece!" Drew surveyed the surroundings. He saw no one else. He raced to the fallen figure and gently turned him over. It was Mike Reece, and he'd been badly beaten.

Drew had his cell phone out and was dialing 911 before he even realized he was doing it. He gave the operator the location and stayed on the line until the emergency rescue unit arrived.

During all that time, Reece emitted nothing more than an occasional low groan. The man was in serious condition. The question was why? Reece had wanted something. He'd wanted to talk. Had it been about the murders? Something else? Something even more fiendish? Was that even possible? What was more evil than the murder of three innocent human beings? The thought that the possibility might exist sent chills up Drew's spine.

Men were rushing in now; red, blue, and white lights illuminated the scene in an eerie kaleidoscope of colors and patterns. Strange hands pulled Drew away; voices, calm but authoritative, issued orders. Life-saving measures were being instituted, and the men and women whose job it was to save lives would brook no interference.

It seemed like an eternity before emergency personnel began loading Reece onto a stretcher. The stretcher's undercarriage dropped noisily to the ground, and the paramedics pushed it into the huge opening of a Mobile Critical Care Unit.

Drew watched with interest but also with a strange detachment. Events were spinning out of control in Bannerman County, convoluted events shooting off on tangents with no apparent purpose.

"You Chapman?" a voice asked from somewhere outside Drew's own consciousness. "Chapman, I said. Are you Chapman?"

"Yeah," Drew responded. "Yeah, I'm Chapman. Why?"

"The guy in the ambulance just came around. He wants to say something to you, but you better hurry. He's in bad shape."

Drew climbed into the rear of the ambulance. What he saw in the glare of the white light was even worse than he'd imagined. He moved to Reece's side. "I'm here, Mike," Drew said, holding the deputy's hand in his.

Give your problems to the Lord, Nanny Collins's voice echoed in Drew's mind.

Mike Reece tried to speak, but the words were indistinct and difficult to understand. Words forced from damaged flesh. "Pocket . . . pocket . . ."

Drew reached into the deputy's pocket. What he came away with was a total shock. Small glassine envelopes containing a white powder filled the man's pocket.

"No . . . no . . . not th . . . that. Plan . . . planted. The other po . . . poc . . . pocket. Found . . . Hallis Road . . .Ring . . ."

Drew shoved his hand into the opposite pocket. His fingers grasped a single item and he extracted it carefully. It was a silver ring. The scroll-work of the ring leapt at Drew. It contained the same markings that he'd seen painted on the van of the three murdered men on Hallis Road—

markings that were linked both to the Bannerman County murders and to hell itself.

Lights exploded in his brain; time expanded and contracted in an instant. Disorientation took over. Was it possible? Not only possible, but probable. Here was the evidence. The ring, the murders, a badly beaten police officer. What more was there?

Convoluted events spinning out of control.

Give your problems to the Lord.

Then, as if to answer Drew's unspoken question, Mike Reece said one more thing before he slipped into a coma.

"Th . . . the She . . . Sheph . . . The Shepherd," Reece said almost inaudibly. "*The Shepherd!*" Reece repeated, the words strong and guttural, a final declaration forced from a severely injured man. Then his eyes closed, and Reece slipped into the anesthetized darkness of unconsciousness.

"*The Shepherd,*" Drew said under his breath. "So *it is true.*" The words, finally uttered aloud, galvanized Drew Chapman's mind and body. He stepped from the ambulance and watched as the emergency vehicle screamed off into the night.

CHAPTER NINE

Light streamed from soft lights situated behind William Benson, backlighting the acting governor of the state and giving the impression of his being surrounded by a golden corona. To Samuel Reardon it appeared as if Benson had purposely positioned the illumination to cast him in the best possible light. Reardon's dislike of the man increased with every step he took into the governor's office.

"Sam," William Benson said as he held out his hand to the state's senior police officer. "Thanks for coming over on such short notice, but I know you're aware of the possible ramifications of this Bannerman County thing. We need to talk."

Reardon shook hands, then extracted his own as quickly as he could. "That 'thing' is a triple homicide, Governor," Reardon responded.

"Sit," Benson said, waving Reardon to a vacant chair, then sitting opposite him. "I know. That might have sounded insensitive, but we need to get a handle on these murders before the situation escalates." Benson settled himself in the chair and continued. "What can you tell me? And what is this information you didn't want to talk about over the phone?"

Reardon leafed through the file in his lap, trying to ignore his surroundings but finding it impossible. The office rightly belonged to

Governor Patrick O'Brien, not William Benson. O'Brien was a law-and-order governor whose heart was anchored in justice from his days as the state prosecuting attorney and then later as a judge within the appellate court system of the United States. As far as Reardon was concerned, William Benson was an interloper. And an uninvited one at that.

"What I have, and what I sent to the FBI for identification purposes, are the photographs taken of the van the three men were traveling in." Reardon handed the photos to Benson. "What you see on the side of the van was certainly spray painted there by the murderers. It's their mark, their calling card. I've never seen those marks before, at least not exactly in the configuration we see here."

"Do we know what the symbols mean?" Benson asked, scrutinizing the photos.

"Yes, sir, but I want to verify my theory with the FBI before releasing any information. I think we're dealing with one of the survivalist-type groups. Maybe even an outright hate group. It takes someone pretty warped to do what was done to those three men." Reardon passed more photos to Benson. "Those are the photos of the men themselves." If Samuel Reardon had been expecting a reaction of shock or dismay on the part of William Benson, he was disappointed.

Reardon glanced out the windows, out onto Fifth Street, where the traffic was already beginning to thin. It was late. Most citizens were home by now, watching the late edition of their favorite news programs, hoping for some morsel of information about the murders in Bannerman County. Not unlike, Reardon thought, what William Benson was doing at this very moment.

"Gruesome," Benson said, handing the photos back to Reardon.

"Yes, sir. It is. As I was saying. It's just possible the FBI or the ATF has information on this group."

"If it's what you think it is. A survivalist or hate group?"

"Exactly. Both agencies keep pretty close tabs on those types of groups. They don't want any more incidents if they can help it."

"Like Waco, Ruby Ridge, or Whidbey Island."

"By Whidbey Island, are you referring to Bob Matthews?"

"I don't recall his name, but the one who killed that talk show host in Denver."

"Alan Berg."

"Berg?"

"The name of the talk show host. Bob Matthews killed him outside his Denver home, then fled to Whidbey Island."

"That's what I'm talking about. We don't need that kind of publicity in this state. Better to keep the Feds out of this if possible."

"Yes, sir," Reardon answered, not sure what Benson was getting at.

"We'll use the information from whatever source, be it FBI, ATF, CIA, or PTA, but if we find out we're dealing with one of these groups, I want it kept quiet. I don't want Washington up here telling us how to run things and then killing a bunch of people, leaving us with the cleanup and the explanation. That's not what I want. We'll be better off handling this internally."

"Just the locals and the state police?"

"That's right. And no one but Chapman up there for the state. Low profile and all that. It'll probably be easier for Chapman. Won't have to be stumbling over a bunch of other agents."

Reardon wasn't sure what it was, but there was a small inflection in Benson's voice, an unnatural pause, an abeyance of not only the truth but of reality.

"I'm not sure I totally understand, sir. With more men, we have a better chance of catching the ones who did this. This is already a high-profile case. Seems to me it would be better to assign a task force large enough to carry out the investigation in a timely manner, as quickly as possible. At least that way, we would be able to show the media and the public that we are taking this seriously."

Benson paused before speaking, running his hands through his hair and then resting his elbows on his knees. He stared directly into Reardon's eyes. "You're going to have to trust me on this one, Reardon," Benson said, all pretense of civility gone. "Chapman is the man in

Bannerman County, and the FBI and ATF are to be left out of this. Is that clear?"

"Not totally, Governor. I'm the senior police officer in this state. That means I decide how to handle these cases. You can fire me if you want, but if you want me to restrict this investigation in any manner, I'm going to need it in writing."

The color rose quickly in William Benson's face, but just as quickly, the acting governor controlled his emotions. "I think that can be arranged, Colonel Reardon," Benson said. "You will have the letter in the morning. Thank you for coming tonight, Colonel."

Reardon rose and headed for the door. He couldn't wait to get out of the office, but he glanced one last time at William Benson. "By the way, Governor. How is Governor O'Brien doing?"

"I'm due for an update on his condition in just a few minutes. I'll forward anything I learn to you via E-mail before I leave the office tonight," Benson said in a voice that clearly indicated he did not want to talk about Patrick O'Brien at that moment.

"I'll be waiting to hear from you then," Reardon said as he left the office, knowing he would seek his own information about the condition of Governor Patrick O'Brien.

Reardon walked slowly from the Executive Office Building, wondering what it was that bothered him so much about Benson. He was absorbed in those thoughts when he got in his car and switched on the ignition. Reardon had not noticed a car next to him when he'd parked. Now, as he carefully maneuvered out of the parking space, a bright flash filled the night.

To Reardon, the explosion was felt as a massive wave of pressure crushing in on the left side of his car. From somewhere in the back of his mind, he knew he'd been the victim of some type of plate bomb, but that was his last conscious thought as ten pounds of TNT carefully positioned behind a steel plate in the door of the other car slammed into Reardon's car with the force of a freight train.

■   ■   ■

He didn't remember arriving at the hospital. Had he known where Reece was being taken, or had he followed the police? Whatever the answer, it was unimportant. What was important was that he was here. More important, Reece had confirmed what he'd thought when he'd first seen the symbols painted on the van at the murder scene on Hallis Road.

The trip to Bannerman County Hospital had been a blur. Drew's mind had rebelled against what he'd heard uttered from the lips of Mike Reece. But the ring he'd found in Reece's pocket, coupled with the symbols on the van and Reece's agonized declaration—"The Shepherd"—had confirmed it. Drew had not wanted to believe what he'd suspected earlier, for in belief was verification, authentication—authentication that a horror had returned to Bannerman County and the state.

"Drew?" The soft voice jolted Drew back to reality. Jordyn Phillips was standing in the doorway of the emergency room waiting room. "Drew, I just heard about Mike Reece," she said, moving to where Drew sat. "I was just finishing my shift over at the Community Services Agency. Do the doctors know anything yet?"

Drew felt his spirits lift at Jordyn's very presence. Her golden hair spilled loosely over a short-sleeved dark blouse that only accentuated the aura about her. Drew felt himself coming out of the self-induced trance he'd been in since he'd heard those words from Reece in the parking lot of Dowinger's Hardware.

"No. Nothing yet. I got to Mike just after it happened," Drew said by way of partial explanation.

Jordyn drew closer, her smile radiant despite the circumstances. "So that was the date you had tonight."

Drew hesitated, confused for a moment, then remembered the "date" with Nanny Collins. "No," he grinned crookedly. "No, that was another date, and I had to stand her up. Mike called me and wanted to meet."

"About what?" Jordyn asked, taking the seat beside Drew. The air in the waiting room was stale with the dry, musty smell of disinfectant and powerful cleaning solutions.

Drew extracted the ring he'd retrieved from Mike Reece and handed it to Jordyn. She rolled the ring around in her hand, examining the markings and the inscriptions.

"These are the same markings that the killers spray painted on the Nicaraguans' van," she said in almost a whisper.

Drew nodded.

"What does it mean?" Jordyn returned the ring.

Drew accepted the ring, turning it over and over in his hand. "Here," Drew said, pointing to the markings. "Remember the ones on the van, the ones that looked like arrows?"

"Sure. I've got a set of photographs in my office. I think I've seen those before."

"You probably have. This one, the one that resembles the tip of an arrow, is called a Tyr-rune. The other one, the one that could be the fletching—the feather end of an arrow—is called a Toten-rune."

"What's a rune?"

"It's a letter of the alphabet used by the ancient Germanic people."

"Germanic?"

"As in German or Germany."

"*That's* where I've seen these. A documentary on the History Channel or maybe the Discovery Channel. These were used in World War II by the Germans. The swastika was a rune, wasn't it?"

"It was," Drew said, shifting in the chair to face Jordyn. Outside in the corridor, white-clad nurses and doctors hurried by. Drew ignored the traffic, absorbed now in the explanation. "The swastika was the symbol for Donner, or Thor, the god of thunder."

"Are you saying these runes are tied to Hitler and World War II?"

Drew inhaled deeply, then continued. "I'm saying that these runes are tied to their meanings. The arrow-looking rune is the Tyr-rune. It's the Germanic symbol for Tyr, the god of war. The other, the Toten-rune, is the symbol for death. That stands for the Brotherhood of the Ring," Drew said, indicating the ring he was holding.

"Then the skeleton head on the ring is . . ."

"The Death's Head of the SS from the Nazi regime."

Jordyn slumped down in her chair, pensive for the moment. Then she said, "So we're dealing with a bunch of neo-Nazis here?"

"Possibly. Look inside the ring," Drew said, returning the ring to Jordyn. As she took the ring, their hands touched briefly. Jordyn looked into Drew's eyes at that moment. The touch had been almost electric.

Jordyn examined the ring more carefully. There were numbers inscribed on the inner portion of the ring. "What are the numbers?"

"During World War II, when Heinrich Himmler wanted to reward his best troops within the SS, he gave them a ring like this, except the runes were different. Whoever made this ring substituted the Tyr-rune and the Toten-rune for the Ger-rune. Himmler was a nut on early Germanic legends. Thor, the god of thunder . . ."

"The swastika," Jordyn added.

"Right. German mythology said that Thor wore a ring of pure silver on which people could take oaths."

Jordyn sat upright. "You mean like swearing on the Bible in a court of law?"

"The same. Anyway, if the ring's owner was killed, the ring was to be returned to the SS. The numbers are registration numbers identifying the owner. And, of course, the skull on the ring is the same Death's Head."

Jordyn looked at the ring again. A shiver ran through her. "It's frightening," she whispered.

"It is that."

"Almost like a ring dedicated to Satan himself," she said in an even lower voice, reluctant even to say the words but knowing they were true.

"Satan's ring," Drew affirmed.

Jordyn tore her gaze away from the ring and looked into Drew's eyes. "How do you know so much about this? I mean, I never knew you were a history buff."

Drew averted his gaze, wanting to be any place other than where he was at the moment. He could feel the nearness of Jordyn. A warm feeling had infused him from the moment she'd set foot in the waiting room. The last thing in the world he wanted to do was disappoint this lovely woman next to him. Just as he was about to speak, a white-coated emergency room doctor interrupted.

"You the cop?" the young doctor asked without preamble.

Drew stood up. "That's me."

They stepped further into the room. "Officer Reece is in critical condition. We've got him stabilized for the time being, but it's going to be close. I've got a call in for a neurosurgeon. He took some nasty blows to the head. We'll probably have to go in to relieve pressure on the brain. We'll know more in a few hours." The doctor finished his update and left without giving Drew a chance to ask questions.

"That was short and sweet," Drew muttered.

"You were about to tell me how you know what you just told me about this ring," Jordyn said, her hand on Drew's arm.

Drew took a deep breath, then said, "I was a member of the Brotherhood of the Ring."

CHAPTER TEN

Smoke from the thirteen candles rose in the still air of the sepulcher, seeking escape through strategically placed ventilation holes in the roof. The number of candles was significant, a representation of those now gathered in the semidarkness. Only the light of the candles intruded, a portrayal of the lives of those who were privileged to the secrets of the Brotherhood and its sepulcher, a sacred place known to the thirteen members as the Kingdom of the Anointed. Tonight, one member was missing.

The lives of the thirteen were bound by a warped sense of honor, united by a distorted view of humanity. They were not the first to hold such views, but they were the most recent, the most fanatical, the most depraved. Compromise was not part of their philosophy; mercy, never an option.

These were the members of the Brotherhood of the Ring.

The twelve members present flowed in unison, their movements accentuated by the gentle sway of the flames, their long robes sweeping the floor beneath their feet. The gentle swish of the blood-red robes they wore lent an air of mystery to the ceremony. Low, almost inaudible mantras—words chanted by memory in honor of the one true leader—

filled the sepulcher with an eerie resonance. No one spoke in tones louder than a whisper as they made their way to their assigned positions.

Thirteen chairs arranged around a circular heavy oak table waited for the members to occupy them. The table was constructed of thick wood stained dark from overuse. The chairs were equally heavy, their high backs deeply carved with figures representing all that was sacred to the Brotherhood, their seats as hard and unyielding as the members who occupied them.

The location of the chairs represented points on the compass; the thirteenth—and most important chair—was located at the carefully defined pinnacle of the table, the point represented by true north. For the Brotherhood, it was more than a symbol; the northern chair represented the zenith of ascendancy, the position of power and knowledge. This was the position reserved for the Shepherd.

The sepulcher itself was round. The walls were of thick stone construction, their upper limits reaching three stories into an inky blackness. The oak table—almost fifteen feet in diameter—occupied the central area of the sepulcher. The room itself seemed to move and flow with the members, the light not quite reaching the far recesses, as if the illumination were not welcome—for in the light lay exposure.

A narrow ledge rimmed the interior of the circular wall. No more than two feet high and two feet wide, the ledge held small white crosses representing the earlier members who had given their lives in the pursuit of the Brotherhood's ideals. Some of the small statues represented other warriors for the cause who had never been members of the Brotherhood but whose names were nevertheless rallying cries.

The Brotherhood's origin was as benign by comparison as its intent was diabolical in its nature, for these were members whose purpose in life was defined by their membership in the organization, not by another criteria extraneous to the goals of the Brotherhood.

The twelve positioned themselves around the table, hands on the back of the oak chairs, fingers caressing the deep carvings.

"Members of the Brotherhood, please take your seats," the member nearest the northern chair spoke.

The members silently took their places.

"We are here tonight to inaugurate the greatest movement in the history of this state and this country," the senior member said. "All of us recognize the authority that has been passed to this group. The dedication with which we seek to fulfill the destiny of the Brotherhood is truly an honor bestowed on us by the greatest authority to have ever walked this earth. We will fulfill that destiny in a manner befitting the Shepherd's vision and purpose."

A murmur rose within the sepulcher voicing fanatical support of the Brotherhood's objectives.

"We are here tonight without one member," the speaker continued, "a member whose vision and vitality is responsible for the success and acceptance of the ideals represented by you, the leading members—the heart and soul of our Brotherhood. We will have a moment of silent prayer, praying for the continued provision and providence of the Brotherhood, praying for our leader who is not able to be here tonight. Let us enter into a season of prayer for the Shepherd."

All heads bowed. So silent were the prayers that the flickering of the candles could be heard throughout the sepulcher. In unison the twelve members finished the prayer.

"Now, we will address the progress to date, the time schedule, and the contingency plans that have been put in place."

All heads turned toward the speaker. Voices were recognizable, but that was all. Each member wore a blood-red hood that matched his robe. The Death's Head was emblazoned across the forehead of the hood. Along the right sleeve of each robe, the Tyr-rune was embroidered. The left sleeve carried the Toten-rune.

"What is the reaction of our people to the latest strike against our enemy?"

"We have the wire service reports. At this point, there is, of course, an investigation beginning, but there are no solid leads, nor will there be any. The explosion that ripped into Reardon's car cannot be traced to any member of the Brotherhood. Not even the FBI will be able to make a connection, despite their so-called sophisticated laboratory techniques." The speaker was the Brotherhood member who occupied the due east compass point chair.

"There is the question of the advisability of the attack at this time," another member spoke.

"The order came directly from the Shepherd," the first member said, addressing the speaker, his voice resonating within the stone chamber.

"What of the investigation into the three Hallis Road enemies?" another asked. There was a general murmur of interest around the table.

The moderator waited for the murmuring to subside before he spoke. "As we know, our soldiers in Bannerman County successfully completed the first step in our campaign to reclaim our birthright. Carlos Reza, after only a few weeks on the job, was in the process of forming a union in the poultry plant where they all worked. These people are not content to find work; they find it necessary to change the system. A system that works. A system that has provided security and prosperity for decades. Unacceptable. But as planned, a CID agent sympathetic to our cause was assigned to the investigation. The attack on that devil Reardon precludes a change in the agent's status—"

"But we're not certain Chapman *is* sympathetic to our cause," another member interrupted. Again a general murmur filled the room. Heads nodded around the table; a general undercurrent of disquiet accompanied the mutterings.

"Members of the Brotherhood. Please," the moderator said. "We were aware of that possibility. It is not necessary that Andrew Chapman share our beliefs at this point. It is sufficient, if you recall, that we instill a feeling of confusion, of disorientation. Time is what we require, and Chapman's previous involvement with the Brotherhood should provide the disorientation we require, thus providing the time. You will recall it was on advice of the Shepherd that Andrew Chapman was assigned to this investigation."

"It is my understanding that Chapman is not exactly following our planned scenario."

"Oh, but he is," an as yet unspoken member replied in a quiet voice. "The scenario is, as our moderator suggests and as the Shepherd planned, that we utilize the confusion of Chapman to delay the Bannerman County investigation while we initiate the next stage of our campaign."

"Quite true," the moderator agreed. "Which brings us to the next stage. What have we heard in relation to Bannerman County?"

"Agreement all around," a member said.

"Exhilarating," another said.

"Extraordinary."

"Exciting."

"Superb. The seed has been planted."

"Good. There are those who would see us stopped, but the majority of our polls show unequivocal support for our actions," the moderator continued.

"Except for men such as Robert Chancellor," a member interjected.

"Of course," the moderator agreed. "We expect as much from the esteemed publisher of the *Spring Valley Courier*. And there are others. Perhaps not as outspoken as he, but they exist. He is of course a radical liberal, and we may well have to deal with him within that context. Right now, however, any action against him would be detrimental to our cause. Too much publicity is not what we want."

"Too much of the wrong kind of publicity is what we don't want," a member said. "And killing Chancellor would be the wrong kind."

"You are correct, my brother," the moderator agreed. "We can persevere against the publicity we receive over the extermination of the three Nicaraguans, but murdering Chancellor would affect the movement in an unfavorable manner—a manner we cannot afford at this critical stage in our plans. Better to let the man alone for the time being. We will monitor his actions, and should it become necessary, take the appropriate steps. Now, what about stage two of our strategy?"

Multiple voices once again were raised within the sepulcher—excited, animated voices mixing with the darkness and faint odor of candle tallow.

"We are on schedule," a dominant voice rose above the others. All eyes turned to the member who occupied the southernmost position at the table, a position of importance just below that of the Shepherd.

"Continue, brother," the moderator urged.

The man stood. "As I was saying, we are on schedule. We are waiting only to secure a certain report. As you recall, when we have the report in hand, that will be the signal to continue our strategy."

"That investigator's report."

"Yes," the man nodded. "Garrison's report. When it is secured, stage two will be set in motion. Within days we will begin the elimination and expulsion of our enemies from this state."

A muted cheer rose in the confines of the darkened chamber.

The man's hand rose to quiet the outburst.

"Remember, we are all in this. Each of us has a part. Failure is not an option. We must rid this state of all unwanted riffraff and foreigners. These *mud* races. We must return this state to the purity it once enjoyed, to the way of life we deserve, to the true morality and stainless virtue embodied by our leader. We must return to the integrity of our Christian identity."

"To the Shepherd," the moderator intoned.

"*To the Shepherd,*" the twelve voices articulated in unity. All rose in a fusion of mind and spirit, blood-red robes rustling against the harsh wood of the chairs. Twelve voices continued in perfect agreement, the volume building to a crescendo, the words repeated incessantly.

"The Shepherd"

"*The Shepherd*"

"*The Shepherd!*"

■   ■   ■

Erika Molinar sat at a table in King's Pizza Parlor, studying for her final exam in organic chemistry. She did not enjoy summer school, especially when it involved courses such as organic, but she had to do it in order to get accepted into the state's only medical school and begin classes in the fall.

At twenty years old, Erika had progressed through the state university's rigorous premed curriculum in just under three years. Coming from Buenos Aires, Argentina, her heart's desire to study medicine in the United States had been realized when she'd won highest honors at Lincoln Academy in Argentina's capital city. As valedictorian, she'd been awarded a full scholarship to study in the U.S. She had left her homeland for the unknown.

Erika was a dark beauty in the Latin tradition. Dark eyes and olive skin were framed by long, flowing dark brown hair. The hair was a perfect complement to her thin face, and many a male student had been attracted to her—until they discovered she had no interest in any romantic entanglement this side of a medical residency and an active practice as an orthopedic surgeon. Her only other interest was her almost fanatical involvement with student government. She was the first minority member to have been elected president of the student body.

Outside the restaurant, a warm wind was building, and Erika's focus was momentarily distracted by the sound of a plastic garbage container tumbling down the sidewalk outside. She smiled. "I'll never get used to this place," she said quietly. It was more than a simple statement; it was a self-confession that she knew went much deeper, penetrating her very soul. She missed her mother and father—and BA, as natives called Buenos Aires.

A constant stream of letters and E-mails between Argentina and the United States maintained contact, but it was not the same as being home. She missed Sundays when her mother prepared *asado, ensalada mixta, papas fritas,* and *mate,* the green tea of the gauchos. She remembered the smell of meat cooking on the grill while her mother prepared the mixed salad and french fries turned a crispy brown in the deep fryer. She had many good memories, and occasionally she indulged herself in such reminiscences—but not too often. They always induced a sort of melancholy that she could not afford right now.

Erika forced the memories away, compelling her mind to concentrate on the chemical formulas before her. Suddenly something caught her eye. A movement, slight but distinct, caused her to glance back out the window. Across the street a boy was leaning against a utility pole. His face was familiar; she had seen him before. But where? He was staring at her through the broad expanse of glass. An involuntary shiver ran through her.

She forced her attention back to her studies, but the boy's face remained in her mind. When she glanced back out the window, he was gone. She sighed. "Silly goose," she whispered to herself. That was what her mother used to say to her when her imagination would run amok. Surely that was what she was doing now.

■ ■ ■

He moved normally, not wanting to attract attention to himself. For Henry Durrell it was the beginning of what he considered retribution. He was fed up with his low-paying job and the constant demands of an overzealous boss who never knew, nor cared, what it meant to occupy the lower rung of a corporate ladder with no possibility of grabbing the next rung. It was not that Henry considered himself unqualified for advancement; rather, he'd never been given the breaks he deserved. After all, this was *his* country; he should be enjoying the benefits of a natural-born citizen. Benefits he was entitled to. Benefits appropriate to his status as a white male. There were certain advantages that should naturally accrue to him, but every day those advantages seemed to slip further and further out of reach. Most of it was due, he knew, to the influx of outsiders who did not deserve the advantages of a natural-born citizen—outsiders who continued to siphon off resources meant for him and those like him. The girl sitting at the table in the pizza parlor was a perfect example of what he was talking about.

Durrell tapped on the back glass of a van parked at the corner of the street just across from the restaurant. The door opened, and Durrell climbed in.

"What do you think?" Joseph Casey asked, as Durrell settled onto a wooden box in the rear of the van. Casey had accompanied Durrell to the restaurant. He considered himself another of the downtrodden whose entire history of misfortune was tied to foreigners who stole the best jobs, received promotions due him, and generally made life miserable for the more deserving of society.

"She's there, all right. Reading or something. Who knows. It don't matter. We can wait her out. That pizza joint's gonna close in a few hours."

"A few hours! Look, it's hot in this van. We can't wait that long. We'll fry."

"The sun's down, man. Get a grip. We can wait her out right here. We can see the door from here, and as soon as she comes out, we follow."

"Then I gotta get something to drink," Casey said.

"Then do it, and hurry up. She might come out any minute now."

Casey stepped out of the van just as Erika Molinar got up from the table where she'd been sitting.

"Too late," Durrell announced. "She's moving. Probably heading for campus. Get in here. We'll follow."

Casey grumbled but returned to the van. "Let's go get this over with."

"No hurry," Durrell said, starting the van. "We know where she's going, and we want to make sure everyone knows who is responsible for this."

Casey laughed. "Don't worry about that," he said, pointing to a design tattooed on his left arm—a Tyr-rune and Toten-rune combined to form an arrow. "The Brotherhood strikes again."

■   ■   ■

"Drat," Erika muttered to herself as she raced from King's Pizza. She glared at her watch as if the instrument was responsible for her forgetfulness. She was due at the university's library where she worked part-time as an assistant librarian. It would take a miracle for her to reach the library in time.

She glanced up and down the street before she decided to jaywalk. The traffic light was against her, but at this time of day and in this neighborhood, there was little danger. She stepped from the curb, confident that if all went well, she would be no more than five or ten minutes late. Even at that, she would have to endure a minitirade from the library's director, Dr. Phil Yeager. She could live with that, provided of course, that the final exam in organic went well. It would be disconcerting to do badly on the exam *and* endure Yeager's wrath.

The yellow light flashed as Erika crossed the street. "See," she said to herself, "even the light is helping me."

Erika heard the screeching of tires and the distant acceleration of a vehicle but paid little attention as she continued to cross the street.

■   ■   ■

"Check the cross traffic," Casey said, as he steered the van toward Erika.

"Nothing in sight. Gun it!" Durrell ordered.

The van responded to Casey's heavy foot, accelerating down the deserted street. He watched his intended victim as he jammed the accelerator to the floor. She apparently paid no attention to the sound.

"She's not even hurrying," Casey said, his gaze fixed on the figure of the girl now beginning to fill his windshield.

"Yeah, man. Yeah!" Durrell exclaimed from the passenger seat.

The van gained speed rapidly, closing the distance between itself and Erika. The transmission shifted into its highest gear, the speedometer twisting toward fifty miles per hour.

"Square her," Durrell said over the roar of the engine.

"I got her," Casey responded, concentrating on the task at hand.

■ ■ ■

It was an apparition straight from hell, Erika thought as she looked up. *What are these guys doing?* she wondered. She could see two men behind the expanse of the van's windshield. The van was now almost upon her, accelerating toward her unerringly. It was not as if she were in the wrong traffic lane. She knew she had already crossed into the opposite lane, meaning that the van had altered course. There was no other explanation, other than the possibility that the men in the van were drunk. But the van was closing quickly, and she could see the men's faces now. There was a strange, demonic countenance on both of them. Gringo faces. White faces. *Angry faces,* she could tell, although she had no clue as to why.

The van kept coming. Erika searched for a way of escape. The sidewalk was close but not close enough. Her mind automatically calculated the remaining time before the van would strike her, and she realized she could not escape the inevitable impact of the two-ton vehicle. She briefly wondered if her body would be shipped back to Argentina for burial. A split second later the impact of the van threw her fifty feet and onto the sidewalk.

Erika Molinar was dead before her lifeless body came to rest on the hot concrete. Flashes of lightning produced by a swiftly building thunderstorm flashed in the distance.

■ ■ ■

The shock of impact was greater than either Casey or Durrell expected. The windshield shattered on contact. One large area of destroyed glass indicated the impact point of the girl's head. The sound, too, was unbelievable. It was as if a large bag of rocks had been hurled into the front of the van. The combination of the impact and the resultant sound temporarily disoriented Joseph Casey.

The van bucked out of control, its radiator and windshield destroyed. With little deceleration, the van continued down the street, the carrier of death on a summer evening.

The thunderstorm broke now in all its ferocity. Rain pelted earthward in huge drops as the wind swept down the street. The hot asphalt surface threw the rain back into the air in the form of steam. The whole scene was surreal, otherworldly.

Casey struggled with the van; the tires lost traction on the rain-slick pavement. The van careened to the left, its top-heavy design causing the vehicle to tilt crazily.

"Stop it!" Durrell shouted.

"What do you think I'm trying to do?!" Casey screamed.

Before either man could respond again, the left front tire caught on the raised curb. The van flipped into the air, rolling and tumbling in an instant, sending the men inside flying. Neither had a seat belt buckled. The van rolled seven times in rapid succession before coming to rest against a utility pole. Steam erupted from the radiator as gasoline leaked from the breached fuel tank.

The top of the van was flattened; every window, broken. Gasoline inched its way along the gutter formed by the raised curb, seeking the lowest point, propelled by gravity and the laws of physics. The gasoline fumes, invisible but deadly, found the superheated exhaust manifold and exploded in a muffled *whump*. Screams burst from the interior of the van—shrieks of agony from a battered, metal coffin.

Joseph Casey had managed to drag himself half out of the destroyed van when the gasoline ignited. Both he and Henry Durrell died in an agony that neither had known existed—but both would endure for eternity.

CHAPTER ELEVEN

"Rain," Drew said offhandedly as the bright flashes of lightning lit the distant sky.

"Still a long way off," Jordyn replied softly, relieved that Andrew had finally broken his self-imposed silence. He hadn't said a word since they left the hospital. Not since he'd confessed to his involvement in the Brotherhood of the Ring.

Drew had been deep in thought as Jordyn drove them toward the outskirts of town. He had expected things to be different between himself and Jordyn after all these years, but he hadn't expected to have such conflicting emotions. On the one hand, he sensed a barrier between them, a wall of isolation. At the same time, he felt something straining against it, a resurgence of emotion that was both exciting and alarming. How long had it been since he'd felt the gentle touch of someone he cared for? He couldn't remember, and that realization troubled him. Emotions were surfacing that he'd thought dormant—feelings long forgotten, suppressed to the point of nonexistence. He'd forgotten the feeling of being alive, he realized, and that was what he was feeling now. Emotions bubbled to the surface like a wellspring seeking release from eternal confinement.

Jordyn parked the car; lightning flashed again, this time closer. They were still in the city, but on the outskirts, where trees predominated.

Isolation. Solitude.

Drew couldn't remember getting into the car. The trip had been a blur, and as he looked around, he wondered where they were. And then the words flowed.

■   ■   ■

The *Spring Valley Courier* was housed in twin storefronts on the village square looking out on the brick pavement and the deep green of the central park's oaks and maples. For as long as most residents could remember, the newspaper had been located in the exact same place. Only those who had lived longer than ninety years could claim remembrance of when the original editor and publisher had first set up shop in Spring Valley. In those early days the paper had been located in a small log cabin on the outskirts of town. Throughout the years, the *Spring Valley Courier* had been a symbol of stability. Beneath the masthead of the paper appeared the motto: "All the truth, always." For most of the residents of Bannerman County, the motto had never been in question, nor had the integrity of the paper's various publishers.

Robert Chancellor had been editor and publisher of the *Courier* for twelve years. Twelve years was not long enough for him to be considered a native, for only natural-born citizens of Bannerman County could claim that title, but it had been long enough for readers to accept his premises based on their own conservative history. Most agreed with his editorials and his method of presenting *all the truth, always*. But acceptance of Chancellor's views had never been universal, and the publisher knew it.

Chancellor gazed out on the town square. He held a cup of coffee in his hand, as yet untouched. He could just make out the cold front that was sweeping through the upper Midwest, preceded by a line of thundershowers and lightning. The lightning was still a long way off, but he watched as the flashes highlighted the approaching clouds. For

Chancellor, the approaching storm was a metaphor of his life in Bannerman County. Since he'd purchased the *Courier*, his life had been a series of crises interspersed with periods of relative calm. But the calms never seemed to last long enough or offer sufficient respite, and lately, the periods of calm were becoming fewer and fewer.

Chancellor was a tall man with a full head of white hair. The residents of Bannerman County and Spring Valley referred to him as "our own Perry White," the white-haired publisher who was Clark Kent's—aka Superman—boss in the DC comic strip. At sixty-three, Chancellor was anything but the typical grandfather type. There was still a passion burning deep within him to reveal the truth, in whatever form it came, and to expose injustice in all its forms. He did not consider himself a crusader, at least not in the classic tradition. When he was in his most reflective moods, he admitted to himself that the *Courier* was not the best forum to carry out his campaign, but it was the one available to him.

He had to admit to a certain amount of success. There was a Pulitzer Prize hanging on the wall in his disheveled office at this very minute, attesting to his tenacity. But that had been awarded for a story far less malignant than the one he was currently working on.

Chancellor looked out at the large pile of papers occupying every inch of space on his desk. The stacks contained stories and research data. Data he did not trust to the mechanical workings and capricious whims of electronic memory. Data he had painstakingly collated by hand, with beginning dates that reached back years. Data that revealed a disturbing sequence—the continuous and systematic elimination of people of certain ethnic origins.

All the truth, always.

Robert Chancellor turned and headed back to his office. The only lights burning in the *Courier*'s building were the ones in his office. A dim glow from his computer screen reminded him he was still connected to the Internet. He'd begun some research, and what he'd read had been so disturbing that he'd needed the cup of coffee. Now he would return, fearing what he would read there, but knowing it was the truth.

All the truth, always.

The computer was still connected to the Knight-Rider wire service. Chancellor could just make out the logo indicating that a breaking news story was about to be downloaded. "Maybe something interesting," he said to himself as he moved around to view the computer screen from a better angle.

He was almost at his desk when the sound of shattering glass filled the office. The publisher turned, rushing toward the source of the sound. His steps crunched on the fragmented shards of glass from the destroyed window. Framed in the broken window stood two figures, each holding shotguns.

Strange, he thought. He'd only heard the shattering of the glass, not the discharge of shotguns. Chancellor dove for the protective cover of the high counter in the small reception area. He knew the shotguns could easily blast through the thin veneer of paneling covering the counter, but there was an old-fashioned Victoria Safe and Lock Company safe positioned beneath the counter, and it was that small area he sought. The safe had been manufactured in Victoria, Texas, just after the turn of the century. Chancellor had acquired it in the early fifties and had used it since for the storage of noncritical papers. He liked the style and ruggedness of the safe. Now he was depending on it to save his life.

The shotguns exploded in the night, adding the erupting fire from their barrels to the lightning from the approaching storm outside. Intermittent muzzle flashes illuminated the walls of the darkened reception area.

Lightning flashed; thunder followed in slow succession, indicating the storm was some distance away. The shotguns spoke with unerring accuracy, their buckshot ripping and tearing at the walls and counter of the *Spring Valley Courier*. Photographs and memorabilia exploded from the walls where they hung. Huge slugs of lead tore into the old plaster walls, sending white dust into the dark night. There was not a square inch within the reception area that was not destroyed by the guns. Wood splintered, glass exploded, walls buckled under the onslaught. The sound was horrific, the sound of the fury of hell unleashed on earth.

As quickly as it began, it was over. Robert Chancellor had found the protection he'd sought. The old safe had performed very well indeed, as he had known it would. He heard the squealing of tires and the acceleration of a powerful engine as the shooters made their escape. He waited several minutes more, long enough to hear the sound of running feet heading in the direction of the paper's office.

"Chancellor," a voice yelled through the destruction.

The publisher recognized the voice. "Here," he yelled from behind the destroyed counter.

The sound of more breaking glass meant that someone was coming through the shattered window, walking over the shards of glass that lay on the floor.

"What happened?" Sheriff Dewayne Lawrence asked, reaching down to assist the aging publisher from where he'd been crouching.

Chancellor ran his hand through his hair, trying to compose himself. As he looked around the room, he suddenly laughed at what he saw on top of the counter. The cup of coffee he'd never touched rested on the corner of the counter—intact. The men and shotguns had not so much as chipped the ceramic of the cup.

"What's going on?" Lawrence repeated.

The phone rang in Chancellor's office. He went to his desk and picked up the receiver.

"A warning, Chancellor. You were lucky tonight," a horrible voice hissed over the phone line. "Next time, we will kill you if that is what it takes. You have been warned. The Brotherhood will prevail."

The phone connection was severed, and Chancellor was left holding the dead line.

"Who was that?" Sheriff Lawrence asked, surveying the damage as he gingerly stepped over broken glass and destroyed memories. The reception area of the *Spring Valley Courier* was a scene of total destruction.

"The Brotherhood visited me tonight," Chancellor said without reservation, his voice shaking.

The Bannerman County sheriff felt the blood drain from his head; a slight case of vertigo ensued. "You . . . you know about the Brotherhood?"

Chancellor met the gaze of Lawrence. "Of course. They have been threatening me because they know I'm trying to expose them. And with these three murders out on Hallis Road, I've got a good chance of doing just that. And I won't be surprised to find out they're the ones responsible for the explosion that put Samuel Reardon in the hospital."

"How did you hear about that?" Lawrence asked, his astonishment evident.

"I'm a newspaper man," Chancellor answered, regaining his composure, "and I've got a computer. Even if I don't like the cursed machine, it has its advantages. The story about Reardon came over the wire service just before the two goons showed up. What's happening, Dewayne? Is the whole world going crazy?"

"How do you know it was the Brotherhood?" Lawrence asked, ignoring for the time being Chancellor's question about the world.

Chancellor reached for the cup of coffee. He held it up and asked, "Want a cup?"

Lawrence shook his head. "The Brotherhood. How do you know it was them?"

"Easy," Chancellor said as he stepped over broken glass and chunks of wood and plaster. "When the window exploded inward, there were two men, both with shotguns. I would have had to be blind to miss the blood-red robes and hoods they were wearing. They wanted me to know who they were. And if that were not enough, the phone call was from one of their more educated spokesmen—from an unlisted number, of course. There was nothing displayed on my caller ID box."

"They wanted you to know they were out to kill you?" Lawrence asked with bewilderment.

"Not this time. I don't think they are brave enough to take on the press—yet. They are basically cowards. These types of people always are. Still, it's beginning to appear as if they have the whole state in their grasp."

"That's a pretty bold statement. You're talking about the attack this morning on Chapman and Jordyn?" Lawrence queried.

"I am," he said. "This morning was a warning, and I think this attack on me was the same thing. I repeat my question, Dewayne. What's going on?"

Lawrence took a deep breath, wondering if he had a logical explanation for Chancellor, and even if he did, could he share it with the publisher?

■   ■   ■

"It was in April 1975," Drew began slowly, his reticence obvious.

"Vietnam. The fall of our embassy."

"Right. I still remember the sight of the helicopters taking off from the roof of our embassy in Saigon. There were five of us watching that day."

"You were only sixteen years old," Jordyn said soothingly, not wanting to affect the strange mood that seemed to have enveloped Drew.

"I remember the shame and sense of defeat I felt that day when I watched that scene. It was not a popular sentiment in those days, but all five of us felt the same way. We all thought that being a soldier was the grandest occupation in the world. We were idealistic fools, but we didn't know that then."

Lightning flashed again, and a spattering of rain began to spot the windshield. Jordyn waited, knowing anything she might say could put an end to Drew's introspection. The storm was building from the west. The darkness was more profound than Jordyn would have thought possible. More rain pelted down.

"We wanted to win," Drew continued. "The sight of our troops being humiliated was more than we could stand. We—all of us—

decided to join a society that stood for the preservation of honor. It was stupid, I know now, but it seemed like the right thing to do." The words were flowing now—soft, hushed words of confession and confusion. Words and emotions bound to the past. The pain was there, exposed like raw nerve endings.

"We joined a group, five adolescents thinking we were men, doing something constructive, something patriotic. Idealism run amok."

"The Brotherhood of the Ring," Jordyn interjected, urging Drew to continue. The van photographs of the murdered men on Hallis Road flashed through her mind, the spray-painted graffiti falling into context with what Drew was saying. Jordyn waited, her heart going out to this man she thought she'd known so well. She was listening to a confession from Drew's heart, from his soul.

"That was the beginning. And when I think about it, I suppose that was also the end." His voice was stronger now, the recollections coming more quickly, with more certainty. The emotions were restrained. Strength had returned to his voice. "We never really did anything. We attended a couple of meetings. We never even met the head of the Brotherhood—the Shepherd—but it was obvious, even in those days, that everything the Brotherhood did was dictated by him."

Jordyn glanced at Drew, her eyes widening, her breath coming in shortened gasps. "The Shepherd?" she whispered.

"Rather arrogant, wasn't—isn't—it? The title, I mean."

Again Jordyn waited.

Lightning flashed again; thunder quickly followed. The storm had struck. Rain beat down on the car, the sound almost drowning out the words.

"I think we thought, all of us, that the Shepherd would somehow be the savior of our national pride."

"Savior?"

"Arrogance exemplified. *Foolishness*. We were all churchgoers. We knew who Jesus Christ was. He was the Savior, the true Shepherd. But the Brotherhood promised no less to this country at a time when this country despised everything we believed in. At least, that was the way we looked at it."

For Jordyn, the explanation was simplistic, but it revealed a side of Andrew Chapman she had never envisioned. She could feel the coldness she'd exhibited earlier, her own indifference when she'd first met Andrew at the Carter House, melting within the context of the tortured words.

"It was utter insanity, but we couldn't see that then. Time has a way of adding perspective to one's character," Drew whispered, his voice barely audible above the sound of the storm that beat at the car.

"And you think you still have a responsibility in all this?" Jordyn asked, not sure she wanted an answer, but knowing one was necessary.

Again Drew hesitated, his eyes scanning the darkness outside the rain-spattered window as he searched for a response, no longer able to deny his culpability.

"Not after all this time." Drew stuttered, the words difficult to form. "Still, I have to wonder if some of those who were with me then are now part of this more malignant form of the Brotherhood."

"And you wonder if you are looking for killers who used to be friends?"

Drew turned from the window, his eyes slowly focusing on Jordyn. "That's *exactly* what I've been wondering. I haven't kept in touch with any of the others since I left Spring Valley. The photographs showing those symbols of the Brotherhood were a shock. The murders were not something I ever envisioned the group doing. If some of the people involved are the same ones who were in the group back then, what happened to them? What are they thinking? How did this happen?"

Jordyn took the lead. She knew what Drew was feeling. "I don't think you can tie what you did so many years ago to what has happened here. Certainly not the murders. If something *has* gone wrong—and I'm not convinced *that* has happened—it has nothing to do with you."

Drew looked deep into Jordyn's eyes, his own filling with gentle tears. He reached out, taking Jordyn's hand in his, its warmth in deep contrast to the cold rain beating down outside. He felt the gentle pressure of her hand; his heart and spirit leaped within him.

"I think we need to talk with someone in town," Jordyn said.

"Who do you have in mind?" Drew asked.

"Robert Chancellor. The publisher of the *Spring Valley Courier*. He's been writing about these hate groups for a long time. Quite honestly, I haven't paid that much attention to the editorials, but from what I have read, he seems to know what he's talking about."

The storm continued without any signs of letting up. Lightning streaked across the sky, and thunder rumbled in an almost instantaneous rejoinder. Rain buffeted the car. Inside, however, Drew felt the warmth of Jordyn's hand pulsate through him in waves that matched the intensity of the storm. Jordyn was right; they would talk to Robert Chancellor. There had to be an answer to the madness, to the insanity. But sanity would have to wait for morning.

Just as another lightning bolt burst forth in white hot brilliance, Drew's cell phone rang. He regretted the electronic intrusion, but he answered it. He listened for a long moment, saying nothing. A look of horror and disbelief was etched on his face as he ended the call.

"What is it?" Jordyn asked, her eyes wide at the sudden change in Drew's expression.

"Samuel Reardon is in Doctor's Hospital. Someone tried to kill him outside the Executive Office Building using a bomb. He's in critical condition," Drew said softly.

"The world is out of control," Jordyn said angrily.

"And we're going to find out who's responsible," Drew added. "I want to see Chancellor tonight."

Jordyn started the car. "He'll be at the newspaper office. I don't think he ever goes home." She threw the car into gear, the tires slipping on the wet surface, the car accelerating toward Spring Valley and Robert Chancellor.

CHAPTER TWELVE

The corporate headquarters of McGrath Oil Company, Inc., was not what most people expected when they visualized the corporate offices of one of the world's top twenty oil companies. The office complex was situated on eighty acres in the middle of rolling hills that were populated by century-old oaks and massive pines, most still standing per the orders of Joshua McGrath himself. The site was located more than twenty miles from the nearest metropolitan center, at the southern edge of Bannerman County. Each of the buildings was a custom-built replica of an original log home or business that had once populated the area. The office buildings were by necessity much larger than the originals but retained the character of those earlier buildings right down to the light-colored chinking between the logs. The complex had been an architect's nightmare; faithfulness to the original structures had been mandated, with no compromise possible. The offices had been custom designed and manufactured by a company in northern Montana called Freedom's Homes.

McGrath had wanted it that way. He saw himself as one of the pioneers of the region, even though he'd arrived only twenty years ago. His father and grandfather had established McGrath Oil in the Permian Basin of West Texas in the early 1920s, about the same time the Texon Oil and

Gas Company came into existence. The McGrath clan built their company on the Scottish ideals of austerity, hard work, and perseverance. The fledgling Texas oil fields had fulfilled all of the hopes and aspirations of the McGraths. Seeing a still more profitable avenue, McGrath Oil sold its oil field holdings and moved the distribution and refining portions of the company to the Midwest, positioning itself midway between one of the largest oil deposits in the United States and the largest center for fossil fuel consumption in the world—the bustling Northeast corridor of the United States. McGrath Oil also expanded into the business of oil transportation, assembling a fleet of tanker trucks that were used to supply the vast gasoline and fossil fuel needs of the burgeoning automotive industry in the north as well as the heating oil needs of those who lived there. Later the fleet grew to include more than twenty massive supertankers that plied the seas in an effort to quench the desire of the world's most voracious consumer of crude oil.

Over the years McGrath had learned the hard lessons of the West Texas oil fields, the Midwest union riots, and the eastern corporate web of deceit. He'd put all to good use, and McGrath Oil now stood as an independent beacon in the heart of a multinational industry whose only loyalty was to the cheapest oil producer and whose altar was the hallowed head of an oil barrel.

McGrath was the prototypical wildcatter, although his ancestors were the ones who could truly lay claim to such a title. Joshua was the only McGrath to possess even a hint of formal education. He'd graduated from the Colorado School of Mines in engineering. Knowing that would not be enough, his father had immediately enrolled young Joshua in the Harvard School of Business, where he earned an MBA. Now, as the chief operating officer and principle stockholder of McGrath Oil, Inc., Joshua McGrath was fond of saying that he had a whole lot more education than he showed. And it was true.

McGrath was sixty-two years old. At a time when most men his age were contemplating early retirement, morning golf games, and afternoons free of social significance, McGrath was just beginning to enjoy the fruits of his efforts over the past twenty years. He had no intention of abandoning a goal he had sought for so long.

McGrath stood six feet four, weighed just over two hundred pounds, and possessed the wind- and sunburned features of an outdoorsman. His hair was cut painfully short, yet his tanned features were accentuated by what little gray hair he allowed to grow. He scrutinized everything around him with intensely dark eyes whose color defied definition. At one time McGrath had been married, but the relationship required more time and effort than he was willing to give, so one day his wife simply walked away. He never heard from her again, nor did he attempt to find her. In fact, he had been pleasantly surprised and gratified to realize that he really did not care if he ever saw her again or not. When his attorneys advised him that she had every legal right to claim a portion of the growing McGrath Oil Company, Joshua stated unequivocally that should such a request be made, he would simply dispose of her. His attorneys had been dutifully shocked, advising him that it was against his best interest to think such a thing, much less express such an opinion to others. McGrath agreed. He fired those attorneys, hired new ones, and kept his mouth shut about a wife who may or may not appear one day.

McGrath was a hard man—as hard as the life he'd built for himself—and he loved it. The head of McGrath Oil possessed one trait that, had the general public known about it, would have condemned him, but one which he considered the true driving force in his life: he hated anyone who was not of his own Caucasian/European ethnic origin.

McGrath stalked around his office, a single piece of paper in his hand. The creases and folds in the paper were evidence that on first reading of the message, he'd crumpled it and thrown it against the far wall. Joshua McGrath was angry.

"What's the meaning of this?" McGrath turned to Jeff Caine.

Jefferson Caine did not move from the chair where he sat. He was accustomed to McGrath's explosions. "It came from our contact in the governor's office," Caine replied evenly, knowing no amount of logic would quell his employer's anger at the moment. "I just got it over the computer's high-speed secure line. That's the printout."

The office was large, but not overly so, at least not for a multibillion-dollar corporation. The furnishings fit the expression of austerity McGrath liked to display to the public. There were no carpets covering the gleaming hardwood floors. The only adornments on the real log walls were early photographs of oil wells in the Permian Basin and the original corporate offices of McGrath Oil—two sheet-metal sheds with a single hand-painted sign hung between the two motley structures. McGrath's desk was made of oak. It had been rescued from an early schoolhouse when McGrath had first moved the offices to the Midwest. A matching oak schoolmaster's chair stood behind the scarred desk. Two wooden slat-back chairs occupied space in front of the desk. Jefferson Caine sat in one of these, his legs crossed, his hands in his lap, waiting for McGrath to finish his harangue.

"What about Akers? We knew he was going to be a problem. What had he found out?" McGrath asked, turning back to Caine.

"Not much more than we knew before. He hired a private investigator to look into any connections that might exist between us and the Brotherhood. We know who the investigator is, and we know he finished the report, but we haven't been able to find out what the report says."

McGrath flared at the answer. "What do you mean you haven't been able to find out? You know who the investigator is, don't you?"

"Yes, sir."

"Get to him. Offer him more money than he got from Akers and find out what's in that report. And if that doesn't work, get some of our own men to break into the offices and get the information."

Caine took a deep breath before he replied. "We can do both of those, sir," Caine said, knowing the key to successful negotiations with Joshua McGrath was first to agree with his ideas. Only after that could one express opposition, and then only gradually.

"Then get to it," McGrath ordered.

"Perhaps there's a better way, Mr. McGrath," Caine offered.

McGrath shot a withering gaze at his assistant, then relented. "What's that?"

"We can certainly offer the investigator more money, but wouldn't that have the effect of confirming the very association we seek to conceal? What I mean is, if we go to them and make the offer, wouldn't that be like admitting that there *is* a connection between McGrath Oil and the Brotherhood? We *do* want to conceal that fact, don't we, sir?"

McGrath thought for a moment. "Good point, Jeff. Yes, we want to keep the connection from entering the public domain, as it were. Nothing good could come from revealing even the connection. Not at this time."

Caine relaxed; his tactics were working as usual. "Then there's the idea of breaking into the office of the investigator. We can do that any time you order, Mr. McGrath, but I was thinking that that might have exactly the same effect. It would indicate to the people we least want to alert that there is a connection—a relationship, shall we say, to the Brotherhood. It would be difficult to deny such a connection if our first step was either of these two plans. Perhaps we would be better off to consider another path of action, at least at this early stage, and leave the more definitive approaches for later, should we need them." Caine was using a stratagem he had used before with McGrath: offering options while conceding that McGrath's own scenarios were valid and viable, even if they were asinine.

McGrath paused, walked over to the schoolmaster's chair, and sat down. He slowly read the message he still had in his hand. As his anger abated, his mind began working along more constructive avenues. "Yes, Jeff, I think you may be right. We will maintain our options in this matter. We will employ less drastic measures now and hold in abeyance these two actions should they be needed."

"Very good, sir," Caine agreed, as if the entire idea had been McGrath's.

"Here's what we will do concerning Akers's report. I want you to go to the hospital as a liaison between McGrath Oil and the governor's office. We are, after all, one of the major contributors to O'Brien's campaign. It's ironic that the money Akers spent to investigate a connection between McGrath Oil and the Brotherhood was probably donated by McGrath Oil." The big man chuckled at the thought.

Caine relaxed further; he'd won another battle of wits with his employer.

"Go to the hospital. Talk to Akers and O'Brien. I'll set it up from here; otherwise you probably could not get within a hundred feet of either. See what you can find out from Akers. Offer our condolences, our support, and our prayers. Assure him that McGrath has nothing to do with the Brotherhood, and offer to open our books to him or anyone who might be interested. Be open, cooperative."

"Sounds good, sir."

"What about Reardon?"

Caine shifted his weight in the hardwood chair. His backside was becoming numb from the pressure of sitting in the rigid chair. "Reardon's just come out of the operating room. All signs are that he will recover, but it will take him some time. He won't be a problem for several months."

"Good. *Good*. That's just the way we planned it. Now we only have a couple of other busybodies to deal with."

"We've got Andrew Chapman in Bannerman County. His presence will provide breathing space, if by nothing more than the doubts he may have. He was Brotherhood. His natural tendency will be to hesitate, and any hesitation on his part will give us time."

"Again, my idea," McGrath replied.

Caine smiled. The idea had been his, but he had manipulated McGrath as deftly as he'd just done with the Akers's investigation. "Yes, sir. And a good idea. We've also got the state's prosecuting attorney and the newspaper publisher."

Joshua McGrath sat back in his chair and smiled. "I don't think the publisher of the *Spring Valley Courier* will be giving us much trouble after tonight."

Caine sat forward in his chair, the change of position a relief. But what he'd just heard from Joshua McGrath caused instant concern. "Why is that, Mr. McGrath?"

"Because the Brotherhood visited our Mr. Chancellor tonight. They left a message with him that not even he could ignore."

Caine felt his pulse begin to race. "What kind of message?"

"The only kind a Zionist sympathizer can understand."

"What happened?" Caine asked, concerned.

"Not much, really," McGrath answered. "A couple of our men stopped by the offices of the *Spring Valley Courier* to request that Chancellor stop his investigation into the Brotherhood, as well as his two-bit editorials about what he thinks would be the appropriate disposition of Brotherhood leadership."

Jeff Caine sat back in the hardback chair and let out a deep sigh. McGrath's audacity and stupidity never ceased to amaze him. It would do no good now to explain how such a move would in all probability accomplish just the opposite of what was desired. Caine realized he would have to act quickly to possibly mitigate the results of tonight's attack. However, explaining such actions to Joshua McGrath would do nothing to alleviate the situation.

"How is Governor O'Brien?" McGrath asked.

"Reports are that he's holding his own, the same as Akers. The driver died a few hours ago. Both Akers and O'Brien are going to make it."

"That may be good news after all. We miscalculated on this one, but it was an honest mistake."

Caine wanted to remind McGrath that what had happened was the result of McGrath's own "Lone Ranger" method of operation, but he refrained. It would do no good at this point.

"I'll be at the hospital first thing in the morning. You can call and set it up. It might be best if I see Governor O'Brien first, just to let the press think he's the primary concern of McGrath Oil. Then I can stop in on Akers, just as a courtesy."

McGrath reached for the phone. "I'll set it up right now. You be there when the doors open, and then get back to me as soon as you're finished with Akers."

"Yes, sir," Caine said, rising from the uncomfortable chair. Sharp pains shot down his legs as he rose, reminding him why he hated sitting in the office of his employer. "I should be back before noon," he said as he closed the door behind him.

McGrath watched Caine close the door behind him, his smile widening. He would never let on to Jeff Caine that all the young assistant's sophisticated manipulation and psychological mumbo jumbo could not conceal the fact that Caine thought he was controlling the head of McGrath Oil. The fact was, McGrath presented to those around him the face he needed to present in order to accomplish his own desires. Jeff Caine was just another man who, in thinking he had the upper hand, surrendered to Joshua McGrath his very will and power of reasoning. McGrath knew he was in control, and nothing would ever change that.

McGrath picked up the phone.

■　■　■

Willie Henderson was just finishing the third can of beer from the six pack he'd just bought at the corner convenience store when the phone rang. Willie cursed, crushed the can and tossed it at the overflowing trash can, and cursed again as the empty can rattled off the edge of the container and hit the stained linoleum floor with a hollow ring. He picked up the phone while he ripped another can of beer from its plastic binder.

"Who's this?" Henderson snarled into the phone.

"You know who this is," McGrath replied evenly.

Henderson felt his pulse begin to pump in his temple. Was it the beer or the call? Or both? He wasn't sure. What he did know was that he was not crazy enough to mess with Joshua McGrath. He put the beer can down, unopened.

"Yes, sir. I know who it is," Henderson stuttered.

"What about the girl?"

"We took care of her."

"We? *We?*" McGrath repeated just as evenly as his first statement. "What actually happened just came on the late news. You *are* aware of the circumstances?"

Henderson swallowed hard, wishing he'd not put the beer back, wishing he'd already downed the other three and passed out before the phone rang.

"We had a little problem," he replied.

"You call accomplishing the task you are assigned, then killing yourself when you wreck the van you are driving a little problem! We wanted the world to know who killed the girl, *but not names*! You better hope those two can't be traced back to me."

Willie Henderson glanced longingly at the three cans of beer remaining, then forced them from his mind. He had to answer. "They were the best I could find in that part of the state. They did what they were told to do, didn't they?" he asked, instantly regretting his tone of voice in the question.

There was a pause on the end of the line as McGrath let Henderson think about the possible consequences of his tone of voice, then he said, "I wanted the Brotherhood to take credit for the murder; I *did not* want two bodies piled in the middle of the street that might lead to other connections, connections better left alone. Do I make myself clear?"

Willie had to think for a moment. What was McGrath saying? Finally, through the alcohol haze, he understood. "No. No! Don't worry. There's no connection between those two idiots and me or any of my men. Guaranteed. Certified."

"I'm glad to hear that. Because if a connection could ever be made to you, it would be a very unhealthy situation," McGrath said, slamming the telephone down so hard it rang through Henderson's brain like a church bell.

Henderson replaced the receiver, McGrath's last words echoing through his mind. *It would be very unhealthy. Very unhealthy.* He shuddered at the chill he'd heard in those words. He shuddered even more when the meaning eked its way into his numbed brain.

Henderson plucked a beer from the plastic holder, popped the top, and guzzled half the contents before allowing himself to think of the consequences of his latest actions. Even with all the data available to him, his mind kept returning to its starting point, a point he'd recognized earlier: all his problems seemed to have arrived along with Andrew Chapman, and *that,* he knew, was something he could rectify.

CHAPTER THIRTEEN

It was a glaring anomaly, proof that a madness had infected Spring Valley. White-hot lights blazed in the falling rain, casting garish shadows around the town square. The intense light produced miniature rainbows that glowed like multicolored coronas set in space. People milled about the scene, most soaked to the skin by the drizzle. The more fortunate wore raincoats or slickers. Television cameras were covered in makeshift tents of plastic, their operators left to the mercy of the elements. News crews jockeyed for position, forcing what casual onlookers there were away from the scene of destruction.

The news crews that had earlier focused on the murders of the three men on Hallis Road now converged on the destroyed twin storefront of the *Spring Valley Courier*. The more innovative on-camera personalities linked the two incidents as they broadcast this latest happening to the rest of the world.

The steady drizzle lent an air of despondency to the scene as Jordyn parked her car across from the courthouse, away from the glare of the lights and away from the primary focus of the news teams.

Drew and Jordyn got out of the car. The sounds from across the square filtered through the falling rain. Voices, strident and demanding, mixed with others, subdued and reflective, forming a panorama of sound that was softened by the increasing downpour. The media was doing its thing, and *that* depended on the audience being influenced.

Drew and Jordyn inched toward the scene, each careful not to draw attention. They wanted to talk to Robert Chancellor, but from their current vantage point, it appeared impossible. The focal point for the moment was the desolation of the *Spring Valley Courier*.

"Crazy, isn't it?" a network electrician remarked as he became aware of Drew and Jordyn.

Drew answered without turning toward the speaker. "Crazy isn't the word for it. We just got here. What happened?"

"Two nuts in red robes and hoods tried to blow away the editor of the newspaper. Guy named Chancellor, I think. This is the craziest place I've ever been, and I've been in some crazy places."

Drew felt Jordyn's hand on his forearm.

"How long ago?" Drew asked, his attention focused on the shattered windows and the hoard of people caught in the glare of the lights.

"Not more than half an hour at the most," the man answered. One of the lights illuminating the scene flickered, and the electrician cursed. "It's the rain. Gonna play havoc with the wiring. Got to check it out." The man was gone.

Drew stood in the rain, watching the insanity escalate in Spring Valley. The twin plate-glass windows of the *Spring Valley Courier* had been blown out. Beneath the glare of the lights, he could just make out the interior of the office. Destruction was everywhere. The walls were pockmarked with what could only have been shotgun pellet holes. Shotguns?

Shotguns!

It seemed like an eternity now, but it had only been a few hours since the same weapons had been trained on both himself and Jordyn. The attack at Carter House had been accomplished using shotguns! The madness was spreading like a virus, a disease incubated in a laboratory of insidious hate.

Jordyn pressed Drew's arm. "We need to talk to Chancellor," she said in a hushed voice. "I think you will want to hear what he's got to say about this madness."

Drew nodded. "I want to hear what anyone has to say about what's going on. This is not just a murder case about three men. This is insanity on a grand scale."

"Hate does strange things to people."

"Hate gone unchecked, unexplained, unrestrained, perhaps. None of which are acceptable in a structured society."

"Maybe that's the key."

Drew turned to Jordyn. "The key?"

"You said it. *None of which are acceptable in a structured society.* Maybe someone is trying to restructure society."

"You mean, someone like the Brotherhood of the Ring?"

"The Brotherhood is not the only group. Groups such as these have always been with us, or so it seems. That's why I want you to talk to Chancellor."

The news crews were beginning to disperse, their pictures taken, the tape sequestered for use on the next newscast.

"Come on. Let's find Robert," Jordyn said, moving through the quickly dwindling crowd. No one paid attention to her; everyone was more concerned with their own functions. Cameramen and electric techs were breaking down and storing equipment. On-camera personalities were self-absorbed. It suited Jordyn just fine. As long as self-importance outweighed the desire to pursue the truth, she and Drew would be freer to seek the real truth.

Drew followed Jordyn, marveling at her independence and assertiveness. He readily admitted to himself that neither quality had been attractive when he'd known her earlier, but now he found that both had certain appeal, if not a certain charm. Had he changed that much? What had he been thinking when he'd left Spring Valley and Jordyn Phillips?

There was no time for Drew to answer his own reflective question. They had arrived at the shattered entrance of the *Spring Valley Courier*.

The destruction was even worse than Drew had thought. Both large plate-glass windows were blown away, the shards of glass littering the floor inside the office. The pellet holes were large. Double O buckshot, Drew knew without having to extract the pellets from the wall. Not the birdshot used against him and Jordyn earlier. The shot here was larger, meant to maim and terrify. Someone wanted Robert Chancellor to receive a definitive message. There was nothing within the office that had not been affected by the barrage.

Three uniformed deputies were busy inside the office. The only one Drew recognized was Danny Boggs, the deputy he'd hit earlier that morning out on Hallis Road.

Drew noticed Boggs's glance when he and Jordyn entered. The look was one of pure hatred, but the deputy turned and went back to gathering evidence.

Robert Chancellor was talking with Sheriff Lawrence near the entrance.

"I'll get someone down here from the hardware store. All they'll be able to do is secure the place with plywood and come back in the morning and take the measurements for the replacement glass," Lawrence was saying.

"Thanks, Dewayne," Chancellor replied.

Drew and Jordyn moved closer, the crunching of the shattered glass beneath their feet alerting the two men.

Sheriff Lawrence turned. "Ah, Jordyn. Good to see you." He turned back to the newspaper publisher. "Bob, this is Andrew Chapman, the CID agent assigned to the murders on Hallis Road."

The gray-haired editor held out his hand. "I've heard of you, Mr. Chapman. It's a pleasure to finally meet you."

Drew took the hand. The grip was surprisingly firm coming from a man he knew to be at least twenty years his senior. Drew had the idea that Robert Chancellor might be full of surprises.

"The pleasure is mine, Mr. Chancellor," Drew said honestly, "although I must say the circumstances are less than ideal."

Chancellor glanced at the sheriff and Jordyn before he spoke. When he did, his words carried a tone of sincerity. "I'm not so sure about the last part. I think this just may be fortuitous—for both of us."

Drew met the publisher's gaze; their eyes locked. "How so?"

"Is there somewhere we can talk?" Chancellor asked.

"My office," Jordyn volunteered. "I think we all need to hear what you have to say to Andrew," she said.

■ ■ ■

It was late, but not too late for Nanny Collins to flip to one of her favorite passages in her worn Bible. She sat in her favorite chair, the lamp next to her the only source of illumination. This was the way she liked it—alone during the quiet night with her Bible and prayer list. On the top of her list were two names—joined as one—for she prayed for both in the same breath and with the same fervor. The names were Drew Chapman and Jordyn Phillips.

Nanny smiled to herself as she thought of Drew and Jordyn. "A match made in heaven, Lord," she said in her low, husky voice. "What are we going to do with them, Lord?" she said, before getting down to a concerted prayer time, knowing in her heart that the Lord had heard her question as surely as if he had been in the same room, which, she reminded herself, he was. *That* thought ended in an even broader smile. "We both know what should happen, Lord, but I think they're going to need some help pretty soon. Lord, protect those two young folks like only you can do."

Nanny put the Bible aside, remembering why Drew had returned to Spring Valley. The three murders out on Hallis Road were only the latest atrocities to afflict Bannerman County. People had disappeared—people she knew, at least in passing. There was an evil in the county, and Nanny Collins was certain Andrew Chapman had been sent to ferret out the baneful entity. She also knew Jordyn Phillips would be involved. She would have to pray very hard for both of them and anyone else whose war was against—as Nanny put it to her closest friends—*Satan come to Bannerman County*.

■   ■   ■

It had taken only a few minutes for the foursome to settle into Jordyn's office. On entering, Jordyn had flipped on the ever-ready coffee-maker, and the aroma was already filling the office. Outside, the lights from the news teams had finally been extinguished, which, along with the continuing rain and storm, lent an eerie feeling to the village square. The night was punctuated with sharp clashes of lightning, which produced elongated shadows reminiscent of the cartoon shadows from *The Legend of Sleepy Hollow*. Drew expected the headless horseman to ride into the office at a moment's notice.

Jordyn flipped on more lights, and the ghostly effect dissipated quickly.

Drew noticed the tastefulness of the office. The building had once housed the Spring Valley post office. The post office had long ago moved to the outskirts of the village, leaving the old building available for general sale. Jordyn had purchased the building for private practice but now operated out of the renovated office space as the Bannerman County prosecuting attorney.

Drew was impressed. There was no part of the renovation that was particularly impressive, but the cumulative effect was stunning.

The general areas were large and airy. Walls had been removed or relocated, giving the office a spacious, inviting feel. Bold splashes of color on carefully selected wall spaces heightened the subdued effect of the generally off-white décor. The furnishings were either refurbished English oak or exacting facsimiles, which Drew noted were simple and effective. But the part of the office Drew found particularly engaging was the ceiling. Overhead, base-relief panels—formed at least a hundred years ago from copper sheets—were painted the same off-white. Drew recognized the designs as English landscapes. His own concentration on the ceiling drew the attention of the other two men.

"Nice, isn't it?" Sheriff Lawrence said knowingly.

"Beautiful," Robert Chancellor parroted. He, like Lawrence, recognized the artistic value over their heads.

"They came from the old train station," Jordyn said, ignoring the effect the office had on Drew. "I redid them all myself."

Drew forced himself to ignore the copper plates and followed after Lawrence and Chancellor as they walked into Jordyn's office.

"Sit down, gentlemen," Jordyn motioned with a sweep of her hand. "It's not as elegant as the waiting area, but it will do."

They all took seats. Jordyn sat in the chair nearest her desk, establishing her own identity and authority within her personal domain.

Jordyn began the conversation. "I'm not really sure where to start. I know what I've read in your paper, Bob, and I know what Dewayne and I have discussed over the past months. Now Andrew is here investigating the three murders on Hallis Road, and I can't help but think that there's a common thread in all of this. Bob," Jordyn addressed the publisher, "your editorials and investigative pieces have been . . . how should I put this? . . . not typical of a normal small-town newspaper. But that's not much of a surprise."

Chancellor smiled ruefully. "I hoped that was the effect I was having around here." Chancellor turned to Lawrence. "Dewayne, how far can I go with this?"

The sheriff took a deep breath, collected himself, and answered. "It's more than a small-town problem now. I thought for a while we would be able to contain certain information, at least until we could get a handle on what's been going on. But it's gone past that."

Drew sat forward in his chair, his eyes wide, his comprehension acute.

Jordyn noted Drew's change of posture but said nothing. Words were about to be uttered, the truth spoken, and nothing in this part of her world would ever be the same again.

"Start at the beginning, Bob," Lawrence suggested. "Tell your story."

"The beginning?" Chancellor muttered reflectively. "Only God knows the true beginning, but let me start with my coming to Spring Valley." The publisher's voice was low, his words exact—the phrases and syntax of a writer.

The gray-haired editor began. "I came to Spring Valley twelve years ago. Not by chance, I might add. What I'm about to tell you began long before then, but it took a specific act for me to become personally involved." Chancellor's voice took on the tone of a man who knew evil, hate, and loss at an intimate level. He was weary, and it showed.

"My wife was killed thirteen years ago. It was a case of mistaken identity, or so it was supposed. She'd been shopping, driving my car, and the speculation is that someone who had a grudge against me thought I was driving and killed her while she was stopped at a traffic light. Investigators said there was no way to trace the killers. They'd used shotguns, just like tonight. Cowards and murderers with no conscience."

"Shotguns," Drew repeated, his voice a low whisper.

"Just like this morning," Lawrence said, reinforcing the thought he knew was running through Drew's mind. "And just like tonight."

"Shotguns. Impersonal, chickenhearted weapons. Men to whom words and ideas—particularly words and ideas that run contrary to their own beliefs—are more frightening than blood and death." Chancellor continued, the strain of recounting the story etched on his face. "They were never identified except by the organization to which they belonged. I received a note a few weeks after the funeral. It said that I would be next if I didn't begin printing the truth about the organization. My wife's death had been a warning. But they were stupid men, men who did not understand that they had removed the only leverage they might have had with me. I would have died for my wife. She was my life, even more important to me than my writing. I wrote the truth, and these people could not tolerate the truth."

"What truth?" Drew asked.

Chancellor was speaking with his head lowered, his chin resting in open palms. He did not raise it to acknowledge the question. "I'm coming to that. But as I was saying, these men had removed the only possible leverage they might have had with me, so I continued printing the truth. Anything I could dig up on the group, I printed. I attempted to discover names, to identify the membership, but it was impossible. The

group was closemouthed. They were stupid, yet they were also disci-
plined. Still, I was just as determined. If I couldn't get to them via a single
avenue, I would do it by combining methods. I began keeping records of
every strange death that occurred in the state, particularly deaths of
minorities. African-Americans and Hispanics were of special interest to
me because they seemed to be either dying or disappearing in numbers
that defied their demographic proportions."

Here Chancellor paused. The telling of the story was a release for the
old man, but it was not without a cost. The price was memory, reminiscences dredged from the past. The memory of lost love.

"There seemed to be no connection, other than the ethnic origins of
the victims, but I seemed to be the only one interested in the facts."

Again Drew interrupted. "Facts? What facts?"

Chancellor ignored the question again and continued. "I contacted
everyone—the state welfare offices, the INS, state and federal employment security divisions, anyone who might provide even a shred of evidence as to what I suspected." Chancellor paused; the silence spoke
volumes. "When I got all the raw data, I analyzed it. The conclusions
were obvious."

"Which were," Jordyn probed gently.

"Someone was systematically eliminating minorities in this state."

Drew felt his breathing catch in his throat. He glanced around the
room; no one else seemed surprised at the conclusions drawn by the
publisher. "How is that possible?"

Chancellor's smile was cold. "Rather easily, actually. Consider where
most of my data came from. Most of the information is unofficial at best.
Even the Immigration and Naturalization Service doesn't try to keep up
with every registered alien. That's changing now, after September 11, but
it's still a government agency, and they don't turn on a dime. They have
their hands full with the influx of illegal aliens. Under the current system,
it's impossible to keep track of every noncitizen entering this country. The
welfare roles and employment security divisions are only interested in those
applying for employment or welfare. The lists don't necessarily coincide."

Drew was aghast. "But you're saying someone is intentionally killing minorities."

"That's what I'm saying. I believe there's a deliberate effort to eliminate every minority from this state, whether by terror, murder, or a combination of both."

"And that organization?"

"The Brotherhood of the Ring."

Drew felt the blood drain from his face. The room swam before his eyes. He gripped the arms of the chair where he sat, waiting for the feeling to pass.

Before he could speak, Chancellor continued. "I should say, the organization you joined a few years ago is not the same organization you thought it was. I know about your membership too. You were kids—teenagers—playing at games." Chancellor glanced at Lawrence. The sheriff nodded almost imperceptibly. "Dewayne and I have discussed it. Your membership, that is. Games, nothing more than games. This is different. It has evolved into a hate group that far exceeds any other group I've ever heard of."

"And they're behind the murders," Drew said, knowing Chancellor would know he was talking about the three men killed on Hallis Road.

"Their sign was all over it. You've got the photos. You know the markings on the van were the Brotherhood's. They're killing people all over the state and maybe the nation. People whom no one misses until it's too late."

"People who don't trust the authorities to protect them," Sheriff Lawrence added.

"Exactly. Their agenda is white dominance. Pure and simple," Chancellor said. "And that's not all."

All eyes were on the publisher now.

"The Brotherhood and the rest of these hate groups appear to be forming alliances. Something is in the wind. I don't know exactly what the full intentions are, but I do know what they're calling it."

"There's a name for it, whatever *it* is?" Jordyn asked.

"They call it Operation Resurrection."

"Resurrection? Resurrection of what?" Drew asked.

"*That* is the question I'm afraid to ask," Chancellor said as his gaze met that of the CID agent.

Drew reached into his pocket and extracted the ring he'd received from Mike Reece. He held it out for all to see, the light glinting off the silver surface. "Here's just another link to the killers," Drew said. "Reece found it on Hallis Road. I got it from him before he was transported to the hospital." Drew looked at Jordyn. "I know what you're thinking."

"Do you?" Jordyn asked, her face revealing nothing.

"That the ring is evidence and the integrity of the chain of evidence has been violated."

Jordyn nodded.

"It was too late to worry about that when Reece gave me the ring," Drew continued. "We will have to work with what we have."

Jordyn nodded unhappily. "What about Reece? How's he doing?"

"It was a severe beating, but he'll survive," Lawrence supplied. "I spoke with the emergency room doctor. Reece is a tough kid."

"The ring," Chancellor said, retuning to the item in Drew's hand. "Someone will be scrambling to find that. I've heard about the rings, but this is the first time I've seen one."

"What we have is the Brotherhood and an operation called Resurrection. What we need to know is how are the two connected?" Drew asked.

"Well, I can't go into that tonight," Chancellor said. "I've got to get back to the paper and see to the temporary repairs."

"And I've got to check out the evidence that's been collected. You coming, Drew?" Lawrence asked.

"Right behind you," Drew said, rising.

"Let's meet tomorrow," Jordyn suggested. "We're on to something. By collating our joint information, we may be able to uncover exactly what's going on."

"Agreed," the Bannerman County sheriff said. Everyone nodded.

Drew gazed at the ring in his hand. He could feel the evil it represented, the feeling heightened by the stormy night.

■   ■   ■

"They were together. I saw them coming out of the broad's office."

"By 'the broad,' I assume you're referring to Jordyn Phillips, the prosecuting attorney for Bannerman County?" McGrath's voice was silky smooth, yet the hint of threat was not disguised by the tone.

"Yeah," Danny Boggs replied. "Phillips's office. They were in there for almost an hour after the attack on Chancellor's office."

"So it's happening," McGrath mumbled, as if talking to himself.

"They're going to meet again in the morning. I heard Lawrence telling the dispatcher."

There was silence on the other end of the phone; Boggs waited.

"All right. Let them meet. Find out what's said in that meeting. We need to know exactly what they know."

Boggs stuttered, "How am I supposed to find out what's said? It's not like I'm invited."

"You know how. We have our sources inside Phillips's office. Contact them and let them know about the meeting in the morning. There are ways to monitor such a meeting. But you be sure it's done, Boggs."

Boggs felt sweat on his forehead and in the palms of his hands. McGrath had not said, *"Be sure it's done, or else,"* but he'd not had to.

"I'll get it done and call tomorrow." Deputy Boggs quickly replaced the phone. Too many things were beginning to get too complicated for his liking. And he was beginning to greatly dislike Joshua McGrath. He didn't care how much money McGrath had or how much he was contributing to the Brotherhood, something was going to have to be done

With that thought, Boggs picked up the phone again and dialed. He would see that the meeting was monitored. What he would do with the information after that was his decision, and *that* thought gave him some comfort.

CHAPTER FOURTEEN

The night had produced little sleep and no rest for Drew Chapman. His dreams had been a jumble of various themes, the most important, by his standard, being those involving Jordyn Phillips. Drew now stood on the porch of the Carter House sipping a steaming cup of coffee. Had it only been yesterday that he'd started the day in the same manner? It seemed more like a month. It all seemed like a dream, a malicious nightmare sprung from the wellspring of hate. He had shed no light on the murders of the three Hispanics out on Hallis Road, but he was beginning to think that might not be his primary goal in this investigation. Too much had happened, too much had been said, too much revealed. More was yet to be revealed, and Drew found himself looking forward to the coming meeting in Jordyn's office.

The morning sun was just beginning to warm the earth. The long shadows were shortening, and a slight hint of a breeze tickled the lush vegetation surrounding the Carter House. Flowers swayed in the breeze, and the long fingers of hanging ferns waved a salute to the new day.

To Drew, it seemed to be a facade. A horror was living in Spring Valley and Bannerman County, at least according to Robert Chancellor, and all the beauty of God's earth could not conceal it. He and Jordyn had been attacked and almost killed; Deputy Mike Reece was in the hospital in critical condition, as was Samuel Reardon. Robert Chancellor had said there appeared to be a movement afoot to rid the state of minorities, and as if to prove the point, the *Spring Valley Courier* had been virtually destroyed by red-hooded hoodlums with shotguns.

Drew had to admit that had he heard of such a conspiracy under different circumstances, he would have found the idea laughable. A secret organization dedicated to the expulsion of minorities was ludicrous, absurd. But circumstances were not different. An attitude of hate and discrimination infected Bannerman County, and if he needed additional proof, there was the ring he still carried in his pocket, the ring he'd taken from the pocket of a terribly injured man who'd looked into the face of hatred.

Drew felt for the ring and held it out in his palm. A single shaft of sunlight seemed to focus on the ring, causing it to gleam a brilliant white-hot silver in the morning sun. As he turned the ring over in his hand, he noticed once again the inscriptions carved into the ring. The runes and the Death's Head represented everything that was wrong with a society gone mad.

Drew checked the time; he had only thirty minutes before the meeting in Jordyn's office. He would call Nanny Collins later in the day. Right now, he knew, she would be having her morning devotional. Morning and night, it was always the same. He pictured her in his mind with her worn Bible and a dog-eared prayer list that always seemed to be battered and soiled, no matter how current the latest names were.

Drew smiled to himself at the thought, realizing he loved Nanny Collins as much as his own mother and father. And the thought that he knew she'd be praying for him caused his smile to broaden as he entered the Carter House to return his coffee cup to the sink, grab his holster and jacket, and head for downtown Spring Valley.

■　■　■

The man sat behind the wheel of the car, partially concealed, but not conspicuously so. His orders were specific, detailed. Constraints had been put in place; action forbidden.

He was to observe and report, nothing more. The man he watched was named Andrew Chapman, and he knew Chapman was assigned to the state Criminal Investigation Division. He knew this Chapman had come to investigate the murder of three Hispanics out in the county. He knew little else and cared less. His assignment had come from the one man he revered, idolized, as had the other men he knew were carrying out similar assignments at this very minute. There were at least three others, perhaps more. It made no difference; he knew his duty, his loyalties.

The man pulled the hat he wore down over his eyes, appearing to be stealing a few winks while waiting to be joined by other workers. His clothes matched those of the town's residents. The car was plain but not too plain. There were times when too little was as dangerous as too much. Yet today if anyone in the neighborhood were asked to provide a description of the man and his car, the only adjective that would come to mind would be "ordinary."

The man's gaze sharpened, his attention drawn to the front of the bed and breakfast where Andrew Chapman rented room C, the one with the full bath and antique bed and matching dresser. His subject was coming out, getting into the state licensed car, and heading toward downtown. The man waited until the car turned the first corner, then threw his own into gear and followed.

At the end of the day, he would provide a detailed report to the man who'd ordered the surveillance—the man he knew only as the Shepherd.

■   ■   ■

Robert Chancellor surveyed what remained of the *Spring Valley Courier*. In the harsh glare of daylight, the damage was even greater than he'd remembered from last night.

The shattered windows had been boarded up with great slabs of plywood, bolted into place with huge bolts inserted into hastily drilled holes. The combination of shadow and light only served to highlight the destruction. It didn't seem possible that any human being could have survived the onslaught of buckshot, but he had.

"A miracle," Chancellor said to himself as he took one last look at the destruction before heading for Jordyn Phillips's office.

"You don't believe in miracles," Dewayne Lawrence said, coming up behind Chancellor.

The newspaper editor turned, a wry grin on his face, his eyes red from lack of sleep. "Not the kind of miracles you're talking about, perhaps, but consequences of time and space, yes."

The sheriff laughed. "*Consequences of time and space?* Now that's something I've never even considered before."

Chancellor started walking, heading in the general direction of Jordyn's office. He spoke, knowing Lawrence was pacing him. "Maybe you should consider it, then. It makes more sense than a bunch of mumbo jumbo based on some religious creed or whatever."

"Come on, Bob. You still think that anyone who proclaims belief in a supreme deity is crazy?"

"As a road lizard."

"Don't tell Nanny Collins. You know you're at the top of her prayer list, don't you?"

Chancellor stopped in the middle of the street he and Lawrence had been crossing. He turned, his face twisted in disbelief. "You've got to be joking. The woman doesn't even know me."

The blare of horns honking jarred the two men into action. Both skittered across the street to safety.

Lawrence laughed heartily. "No joke, Bob. Nanny Collins is famous for her prayer lists."

Chancellor resumed walking. "So I've heard, but I thought the woman was just senile. Surely you can't put any stock in such nonsense?"

The sheriff hesitated before answering, as if trying to frame his answer in such a way as to explain the inexplicable. "I guess it was fifteen years ago, come this September," Lawrence began quietly. "Gracie was ill. That was a few years before you came to town. Doctors here sent her to the capital, down to Doctor's Hospital. Same hospital the governor's in at this very minute. Best doctors in this part of the country. But they couldn't figure out what was wrong with her. Talk was of sending her to the Mayo Clinic or down to M. D. Anderson in Houston. Everyone thought it was some form of virulent cancer, or some strange disease. Whatever it was, she was losing weight by the bushels. Wasting away before our eyes. Nanny Collins heard about it and made a trip down to Doctor's to see her, just to let Gracie know she was praying for her. Said a prayer right there beside the bed and then left. Everyone knew Gracie was on the top of Nanny Collins's prayer lists in those days."

Lawrence paused, his throat constricted, his eyes beginning to water. He pulled a handkerchief from his pocket and dabbed at the moisture, then continued. "The next few days were critical. The doctors found the problem. Some form of lymphatic cancer, sure enough. They talked about it for about two days, coming up with treatment protocols, they called them. When they'd finally decided on the right drugs, they put together a concoction and ordered it administered to Gracie. They'd already told me what to expect. It would take a miracle for the drugs to work, and the process would be painful to watch. The drugs would either cure or kill."

"I didn't know any of this, Dewayne. I'm sorry," Chancellor interjected.

"No matter. Like I said, it was before you arrived in Spring Valley. Anyway, the morning they were scheduled to begin the treatments I arrived early at the hospital, just to be with Gracie. We'd been married for twenty years then, and I couldn't think about going on without her. When I got to her floor, there was a big hubbub going on. Something had happened. It still didn't register with me, not until I realized all the commotion was going on around Gracie's room. My heart was in my throat. I thought she'd died."

"Don't tell me—"

"Wait. Let me finish," Lawrence said as the two men continued to walk. "I thought the worst, but it was just the opposite. The doctors were all gathered around her bed, and Gracie was sitting up, eating breakfast.

She'd been hungry when they woke her for the treatment. Completely out of character. She hadn't eaten anything for weeks. That was one of the symptoms, loss of appetite. Anyway, there she was, sitting up, smiling like she'd just been awakened from a good night's sleep. She felt so good, the doctors held off on the treatment until they could run a test. The test came back negative. No cancer. No sign of it. No sign of anything else, either. Gracie was cured."

Chancellor chuckled. "And you want me to believe that Nanny Collins's prayers cured her when the doctors couldn't. Don't think so, Dewayne."

"Nope. That's not what I had in mind. I didn't believe it either, not even when the doctors told me that what had occurred was a true miracle. I wasn't a believer then. My reaction was pretty much the same reaction you just had."

Chancellor stopped on the sidewalk. They were only yards from Jordyn's office. "Then what exactly is the point of your story? If it wasn't a miracle, then what was it?"

"I didn't say it wasn't a miracle. I said I didn't believe the doctors."

"And your point is?"

"I believed Gracie."

Chancellor felt a chill run up his spine at the simple statement. What was going on here?

"Gracie told me what happened in the middle of the night. She described how two angels had appeared beside her bed and how they had just smiled. Somehow, she said, she knew that Nanny Collins was praying at that very moment and that God was answering her prayer, the prayer of the faithful. I didn't believe Gracie at first, but her story never changed—and the cancer never came back."

"She never had cancer then," Chancellor challenged.

"I had that thought too. The doctors ran the test on blood they'd drawn earlier. The cancer was there. Then they ran it on the blood they'd drawn that morning, and the cancer was gone. Never been back, either. You can believe or disbelieve whatever you want, but if you talk to

Gracie, you'll know a miracle happened that night, and that angels exist, and God answers prayer."

Chancellor glared at the sheriff before saying, "Not in a million years. There's an explanation. No one's found it yet."

Lawrence placed his hand on the editor's shoulder and looked him straight in the eye. "You believe what you want, Bob. But bank on it: one day, some day, you'll believe. I just hope it's not too late when you do."

"No more hocus-pocus, Dewayne. Let's get in here. I've got some things to show you, Phillips, and Chapman. I think you'll find it interesting. As a matter of fact, here comes Chapman right now."

Drew pulled to the curb and got out of his car. "Morning, gentlemen. Let's get to this. I have a feeling we've fallen into a pit of vipers, and I want to know who the vipers are."

Chancellor said, "You are correct. And what I've got to tell you will confirm it."

■ ■ ■

From three separate vantage points, three men watched as the Bannerman County sheriff, the publisher of the *Spring Valley Courier,* and the CID agent from the state capital entered the office of Jordyn Phillips, the Bannerman County prosecuting attorney. A fourth man shifted his gaze from the three men, picked up a cellular phone, and punched in a number.

"Woman's on the way. The other three have already arrived" was all he reported before turning the small instrument to the off position. Now he and the other three would wait for further instructions. The man hoped the instructions would be to kill some or all of the four subjects now under surveillance.

CHAPTER FIFTEEN

The storm from the previous evening had cleared the air in Spring Valley, and as she walked to her office, Jordyn marveled at the beauty of the village. The air was crisp and clean; the day before it had been hot and humid—sticky. She glanced at the antique clock tower that dominated the village square just across from her office, noting that she had five minutes to get to her office before Chancellor, Lawrence, and Andrew were due to arrive, but knowing them as she did, Jordyn would not be surprised to find the three men waiting on her.

Jordyn was wearing a stylish navy blue pantsuit with matching pumps. The dark blue highlighted her blonde hair hanging loosely over her shoulders. Normally during the summer months she eschewed dark colors, but the weather was too nice to miss the opportunity. She also realized that she was hoping Andrew Chapman would notice the contrast between her freshly washed hair and the dark suit. The combination, she knew, could be devastatingly alluring to the right person.

As she neared her office, she could see the mangled front of the *Spring Valley Courier,* its boarded-up windows glaring in the morning sun like festering scabs. News crews who had the day before been intensely interested in the destruction of the newspaper offices and the earlier murders had yet to make their appearance in the town square. But they would return, seeking increasingly graphic coverage. "Thank goodness for minor miracles," Jordyn said to herself as she crossed the street. The notoriety that gripped the village had not yet infected the morning.

Out of the corner of her eye she noticed movement that did not fit in with the normal hustle and bustle of the village square. What was it? She stopped as she reached the edge of the sidewalk and scanned the surrounding area. It hadn't been her imagination, had it? After yesterday, anything was possible. "Jumpy, Jordyn," she said to herself. "You're getting jumpy," she repeated as she pushed through the outer door into her office.

■ ■ ■

The man whose instructions had been to maintain surveillance on the prosecuting attorney stepped from behind the shrubbery surrounding the clock tower in the center of the village square. He'd gotten careless, he knew. That would not have been a valid defense if Jordyn Phillips had seen him. She was smart, this one, he thought to himself. And a looker too. Too bad his contract was just to observe and report. Too bad.

■ ■ ■

Jordyn's entrance, as she swept into the waiting room, had the same effect on Drew as the night's previous storm had had on the atmosphere. The dark suit she wore, coupled with her glistening blonde hair spilling over her shoulders, was mesmerizing. Drew wondered if either Chancellor or Lawrence were aware of the pure magnetism Jordyn Phillips exuded. He glanced at the men and flushed when he realized they were looking at him with the same questioning gaze.

"I may be older than you are, Mr. Chapman," Chancellor said, "but I'm not blind." Chancellor's smile told Drew that the publisher knew what he was thinking.

Lawrence, on the other hand, seemed impervious to Jordyn's charms. Then as if to answer the unasked question, the sheriff said, "Don't think I don't notice too. I just hide it better."

Drew flushed even more deeply, knowing that both the men knew exactly what he was feeling at this moment.

"Good morning," Jordyn said as she moved closer. "Let's go into my office. Sorry if I'm late."

"Not at all, my dear," Chancellor said with a sly grin. "I think it did the three of us some good to get here just a little early."

Drew glanced at the newspaper man, noting the insinuation and wondering if his own reaction to Jordyn's entrance had been as apparent to her as it had been to the others. The thought brought more embarrassment, and Drew felt himself flushing again. It was going to be a long morning.

"Janice," Jordyn called to her personal assistant and secretary, "would you get coffee all around, please? Gentlemen, let's get started."

Janice Brown went to the coffee service and filled four cups; placed them on a tray with cream, sugar, and artificial sweetener; and carried them into Jordyn's office.

"Thanks, Janice. I'll call you if I need you. Close the door on the way out, please," Jordyn ordered, establishing immediate superiority in her office again, just as she'd done the previous evening.

■   ■   ■

Janice quietly closed the door behind her, pressing a small, concealed button behind an antique set of lawyer bookcases just outside of Jordyn's office as she passed. Her hands were sweating now, and her head was pounding, but she did as she'd been ordered. She wondered as she did so what Jordyn Phillips would say if she knew of the betrayal.

■   ■   ■

"Let's begin where we left off last night," Jordyn suggested, sipping at the coffee.

Chancellor picked up the suggestion, speaking first. "As I was telling you last night, there's something in the wind. Something big."

"Operation Resurrection," Drew supplied.

"Right," Chancellor reaffirmed. "You all know now why I came to Bannerman County and Spring Valley. These are the same people who killed my wife, and I'm going to expose them. But the organization—"

"Or organizations, plural," Sheriff Lawrence interjected.

"Organization or organizations," Chancellor agreed, "because Dewayne is right. I have the feeling there are several different organizations involved in this."

"What organizations?" Jordyn asked, hearing this part of the publisher's suspicions for the first time.

Chancellor extracted a folded piece of paper from the inner pocket of the sport jacket he was wearing, referring to his notes. "Any number of organizations whose basis is in the mutually held idea of Christian Identity."

"Maybe you better explain what you mean by Christian Identity," Drew suggested. He knew exactly what the publisher was suggesting; he'd seen the FBI and ATF reports. "Just so we'll all be on the same page, so to speak," Drew added.

"Right. Christian Identity has its basis in the Old Testament, with the formation of the tribes of Israel. These groups use Deuteronomy 7:6 as a basis for their beliefs."

"Which is?" Drew asked. He was suddenly in new territory.

Chancellor read from his paper. "'For thou art an holy people unto the LORD thy God: the LORD thy God hath chosen thee to be a special people unto himself, above all people that are upon the face of the earth.'"

"And these groups consider themselves the chosen people?" Lawrence asked.

"They do. The idea, in a condensed version, is that the chosen people of God began with Adam, whose name, they say, means 'to show blood in the face.' Or to put it more bluntly, to be able to blush."

"The Caucasian race," Drew explained.

"Skipping a few centuries, there was Eber, whose descendents were known as Hebrews. Abraham was a direct descendent. Abraham was chosen by God for a special covenant with God and to receive special blessings. Abraham passed these on to Issac, who passed them on to Jacob, his son. Jacob's name was changed to Israel, and he had twelve sons, the foundation for the twelve tribes of Israel. About 700 B.C. . . . ."

"The Assyrian captivity," Drew added quietly, remembering his Sunday school lessons.

"Right," Chancellor continued, his gaze resting momentarily on the CID agent. "The Assyrian captivity. These groups hold that the captive tribes escaped, made their way west, and became the Caucasian European nations. Furthermore, they say that the United States and Canada are the only nations on the face of the earth that fulfill the prophesied place of the regathering of all the tribes of Israel."

For almost a minute, the group was quiet, absorbing what they'd just heard.

"You're saying these groups believe they have a mandate from God," Jordyn broke the silence.

"Exactly."

"Now we're back to who *they* are," Lawrence said.

"Under normal circumstances, these groups go their own way, operating according to their own agendas. It's only been in recent years that there has been proof of any connection between them."

"Them?" Drew asked.

"The white supremacist groups."

"Like the Brotherhood of the Ring," Drew whispered.

"There are others. Many others, as I'm sure you're aware. The Southern Poverty Law Center in Montgomery, Alabama, keeps track of most of them. The SPLC monitors the activities of these groups, or attempts to. It's become a massive undertaking in the last few years. Groups are multiplying like viruses," Chancellor said. "Groups like The Covenant, Sword, and Arm of the Lord; The New Patriots; The Order, an offshoot of everyone's favorite, Aryan Nations. Groups like The White

Aryans, The Group, The Branch of the Lord, and the National Alliance. There are more, many more. But there's never been a concerted effort to assimilate all the groups into a single unit. At least, not until recently."

A chill filled the room, as if the air-conditioning had been suddenly turned to a lower setting. Only this chill filled all four from the center of their being. It was a chill that began in the soul and expanded, seeking release and relief.

"And the idea is that these groups are now banding together to accomplish what they could not as individual units?" Jordyn asked.

"That certainly appears to be the goal," Chancellor answered. He extracted another folded paper and peered at it for a moment.

"What's that," Drew asked.

"Another list," the publisher answered. "A list I compiled from my research, mostly in this state, but there are others also. This," Chancellor said, holding up the paper, "lists the people I am almost certain were killed by one of these groups."

"Or by a combination of groups," Sheriff Lawrence interjected.

"Could be," Chancellor said. "But in most of these cases, I don't think so. It's just recently that the groups could actually claim any sort of cohesive alliance. Most of the names on this list go back several years, except, of course, for the most recent."

"The murders out on Hallis Road?" Drew asked, certain he already knew the answer.

"Those three and one other on the other side of the state. A young college student. President of the student body and the first Latina to be elected. It just so happens that the killers lost control of the van they were driving and crashed. One of the men, the driver, had tattoos identifying him as a member of the Brotherhood of the Ring. We may be able to link those men to others."

Jordyn glanced at Drew. Drew nodded in affirmation. "I got the report last night when I called to find out how Samuel Reardon was doing."

"Which brings me to what I believe is an expansion of the activities of these groups. To what end, I'm not sure, but I suspect when we discover what Operation Resurrection is, we will know the answer."

"The answer to what?" Lawrence asked. "This all sounds too fantastic to be true."

"Samuel Reardon was attacked coming out of a meeting at the Executive Office Building, a meeting with William Benson, the acting governor of this state. The car carrying Patrick O'Brien was demolished by a runaway truck that could have been nothing more than a deliberate attack on the governor. Whatever is in the hopper, the timetable is being accelerated."

"You're suggesting that all of these latest events—including the governor's accident—are linked in some morbid way?" Jordyn replied, edging up on her chair.

"I am. There's too much coincidence."

"But you have no idea what?" Drew asked.

"Not in the least."

"What about those names?" Lawrence asked.

"Have a look for yourself. You'll see that I've added the governor's name; Martin Akers, the governor's campaign manager; the governor's driver; Samuel Reardon; and Mike Reece. We can only speculate about them, but the attacks fit the pattern."

Lawrence scanned the list. One fact was readily apparent in the list— if hate groups were involved in the murders or disappearance of the people listed, then they were targeting minorities, especially Hispanics. The majority of names were obviously Hispanic. The others were also minorities, although not identifiable by ethnic origin.

A small gasp from Jordyn caused all three men to turn in her direction.

Jordyn covered her mouth with her left hand, the list of names in her right. The list was shaking uncontrollably, and Jordyn was pale beneath what little makeup she wore. Her gaze alternated between the shaking list and Drew.

Drew rose and went to Jordyn. "What is it?" he asked gently, his hands on the arms of Jordyn's chair as he kneeled.

Anger flooded Jordyn's eyes; she made no attempt to conceal it. She grew even more pale as she continued to scan the names on the list. Tears appeared in the corners of her eyes.

"For heaven's sake, Jordie," Drew said quietly. *"Tell me."*

Jordyn finally became aware that Drew was kneeling before her. When she spoke, her voice was just above a whisper, and the words she said had the same chilling affect within the room as a blast of arctic air.

"I . . . I know some of these . . . people," she answered. "Oh, heaven above," she cried. *"I know them."*

CHAPTER SIXTEEN

Doctor's Hospital occupied a chunk of prime real estate in the bustling southeast section of the capital. Along with the corresponding and obligatory Doctor's building, the medical complex was the premier facility of its kind in the state. It was no surprise that both the injured governor of the state and the chief law enforcement officer had both been admitted to Doctor's.

For Jefferson Caine it made the task assigned to him by Joshua McGrath all the more easy. Rather than traipsing around the entire city in an effort to uncover the information he was seeking, he would only have to gain entrance to a single facility. Of course, given the circumstances of the previous days, such entrance could prove more difficult than normal.

Caine parked his car in the multilevel parking garage and began walking toward the entrance of the Doctor's building. He could see uniformed and nonuniformed police officers standing around the entrances to the medical building and the hospital. There were direct connections between the medical building and the hospital at every level, Caine knew. McGrath had said he would clear the way, but Caine knew full well that when the lives of two of the state's chief operating officers

151

were in question, it was possible that even the name McGrath would not gain entrance or audience.

Two uniformed officers moved to intercept Caine as he approached the entrance.

"Excuse me, sir," the larger of the two officers said. "Are you a patient, or do you have business here?" the man asked.

Caine instantly thought that the question was stupid, but he smiled. "My name is Jefferson Caine. I work for McGrath Oil, and Mr. Joshua McGrath was supposed to have called ahead. I'm here to check on Governor O'Brien and Samuel Reardon, at Mr. McGrath's direction."

The smaller officer quickly produced a handheld computing device, activated the screen, and scanned the information that appeared. "Jefferson Caine, administrative assistant to Joshua McGrath?" the officer asked.

"That's correct, officer," Caine answered.

"Could we please see some identification?" the man said.

Caine produced his driver's license. "The photo's not the best," Caine joked, handing the laminated card to the officer.

The officer activated another series of buttons, waited, then said, "It all matches, Mr. Caine. Thank you." The man returned the license.

Caine took the plastic card, then asked, "How are you so sure about me?"

The officer with the handheld computer smiled, then turned the screen toward Caine. There on the screen was a perfect copy of the license he'd just handed the policeman, complete with photograph and additional biographical data.

"Impressive," Caine commented.

"Yes, sir," was all the man said.

"You may go up, sir," the larger policeman said.

"Old McGrath really came through," Caine said to himself as he stepped through the automatic doors of the building. What no one knew, except for Joshua McGrath, was that Caine was actually here—if possible—

to interrogate Martin Akers, the campaign manager for Patrick O'Brien's reelection efforts.

After checking at the information booth just inside the foyer, Caine took the elevator and stopped at the floor where the state's governor and chief policeman were being treated. It was also the floor on which Martin Akers was being treated. All three rooms—O'Brien's, Reardon's, and Akers's—were close. O'Brien and Reardon were next to each other, and Akers was directly across the hall, effectively reducing the security perimeter. Again, a group of uniformed and plainclothes officers were outside the rooms. Intermediate guards were posted at the ends of the corridors, and the first of these stopped Caine just as he exited the elevator.

Caine automatically produced his identification. The first guard checked it, then waved to the next guard, who came from where he was standing, took the ID, nodded, and waved for Caine to follow him.

Caine did as he was ordered. The guard pointed to a metal detector set up to one side of the corridor, and Caine stepped through it.

"Can't be too careful," the officer announced.

"I understand completely. Keep up the good work."

A white-coated doctor was just exiting the room Caine knew to be that of Governor O'Brien.

Caine stopped the man. "I'm Jefferson Caine, assistant to Joshua McGrath. How is the governor?" Caine asked the man. Under normal circumstance, Caine knew that such information was private. But within this state, the name McGrath carried more weight than even that of the President of the United States. Caine could see the doctor had no intention of withholding information sought by the wealthiest man in the state, not to mention the largest contributor to the medical complex.

The doctor consulted the chart in which he had been writing. "We've just changed his status to satisfactory. Governor O'Brien was lucky. It seems that most of the impact and rollover was absorbed by the car he was riding in. He'll need some rest, a few more tests to confirm what we think, then we'll release him with instructions to take it easy for a couple of weeks. He should be fine."

Caine made notes in a small notebook he'd pulled from his pocket, then asked the same thing about Samuel Reardon. As he wrote, he asked, "And what about Martin Akers? Is the report on him as good?"

The doctor nodded briefly. "More or less. The governor and Mr. Akers were in the backseat. It looks like the truck that struck them rolled up and over that portion of the car. Our only explanation is that the additional structural material of the trunk area must have protected them. The same is not true for the driver. His crush injuries were more serious. He died a few hours ago."

Caine continued to write, concealing the feeling of satisfaction at the news of the driver's death. "I do not want to disturb the governor, but I can assure you that Mr. McGrath will be grateful for the information, Doctor . . . ?"

"Klein."

Caine smiled. "Dr. Klein. Thank you so much for your cooperation. Just one more question. Would it be possible to see Martin Akers? If he's doing as well as you say, I would like to speak to him."

"I don't see why not. Don't stay too long though. Mr. Akers's recovery is on track, but I don't want him tired out. I'm sure you understand."

"Perfectly, Doctor."

"Officer," Doctor Klein motioned for a uniformed officer standing near the door of Martin Akers's room. "I'm going to let Mr. Caine speak to Akers for a few minutes."

"Yes, sir," the officer replied.

Jefferson Caine reached for the doctor's hand and shook it. "Thank you again, Doctor. I'll see that Mr. McGrath takes special notice of your cooperation." Without waiting for a response from the stunned doctor, Caine entered Akers's room. The uniformed guard stepped aside, allowing him to enter.

The room was set up as a semiprivate room, but the second bed had been moved to the side, and a cluttered desk now occupied the space, along with multiple telephones and a small file cabinet. There was no one else in the room, but Caine knew that Akers was feeling well enough to conduct as least a semblance of reelection business from the now-converted suite.

Akers's bed was next to the window, and when Caine entered, the campaign manager turned toward the sound.

What Jefferson Caine first saw in the eyes of Martin Akers was a weariness that seemed to penetrate to the man's marrow. Akers's face was black-and-blue, the bruises giving him an almost comedic appearance. Even the effort required to roll over in bed was apparent as Caine neared the bed. Medication was being dispensed from a digital machine through a single intravenous line in the back of Akers's right hand. The exposed portion of the arm was also bruised, but with just a hint of yellow around the edges of the darker bruises. Martin Akers's body was already in the process of healing itself.

As Caine drew nearer, he saw Akers focus on his face; the man's expression changed dramatically. "Joshua McGrath's bulldog," Akers said in a low, painful tone.

"Mr. Akers. Good to see that you are continuing to work for the reelection of our popular governor," Caine said, indicating the desk and phones.

Akers remained silent.

"But I've heard some disturbing rumors, Mr. Akers. As one who normally dismisses such rumors, I tried not to pay too much attention to them, but they seem to continue popping up." Caine pulled one of the chairs near the desk beside the bed. "Mr. McGrath would really like to know if the rumors are true. I assured him that you would talk to me. The governor is doing well, you are doing well, and you both will be out of here before too much longer." Caine drew nearer, his voice low, his mouth near the left ear of Martin Akers. "Now, here is the question, Mr. Akers," Caine said in a conspiratorial tone. "Where is the report generated by your rather foolish expenditure of fifty thousand dollars?"

Akers said nothing, but Caine watched the campaign manager's eyes closely. What he saw there told him all he needed to know at this point, for what he noted in Akers's eyes was the emotion of unbridled fear—a fear so profound that even the deep facial bruises couldn't conceal it.

"Just what I thought, Mr. Akers. You see, I wasn't certain until now that such a report even existed, but I see in your eyes that it does, and that fact alone greatly simplifies my position. Verifying the report's existence is enough for the time being. I will have that report, Marty. That's what Governor O'Brien calls you, I believe. Marty. Well Marty, I will have the report; it's only a matter of time. You lay here and think about it. Mr. McGrath is the largest contributor to this campaign, as you well know, and he expects . . . how shall I put this? . . . certain accommodations? He looks on his contributions as investments, and Mr. McGrath expects a return on his investment. I'll be back, Marty. Count on it. I want the report."

Martin Akers started to speak, but Caine held his hand up, stopping him.

"This is important. Right now you have possession of that report. It's of value to you only while you control it. You can turn it over to me, or I can find it. The first produces far superior results for you. I hope you understand what I'm saying here, Marty," Caine whispered as he moved closer, "because I wouldn't want there to be any misunderstanding. You can give me the report, or I can find it on my own. The first option is the only one that will allow you to live. We all know that accidents happen, don't we, Marty. After all, you are recovering from one. Let's not have another."

Jefferson Caine rose and walked from the room without another word.

■　■　■

Martin Akers felt his pulse race, the blood pounding in his temple; his mouth was dry, and his head ached. The room swam before his eyes. Had he actually heard what he thought he'd heard? Had the personal assistant to Joshua McGrath actually threatened him, and by extension, the governor of this state?

Akers thought about the report. It was safe for now; Caine could not find it. But how did Caine even know about the report? It was the same report he had been about to reveal to Governor O'Brien when the dump truck had plowed into the governor's car. The report dealt with a movement so diabolical that he had not believed it possible at the outset. But it was becoming clearer now. What had the report said? Garrison had briefed him over the phone, but the details were hazy. He was having trouble remembering. Memories seemed to come and go, details clear one minute, vague the next. What had Garrison *said?* What was the operation mentioned? Operation *what?* It was from the Bible; he remembered that much. Operation Shepherd? No! Not Shepherd! Shepherd was something else. *Someone else.* Operation what? Resurrection? *Operation Resurrection? That* was it! *Resurrection!*

But what exactly was Operation Resurrection?

■   ■   ■

Caine scanned the surrounding area once again. There was only one course of action open to him involving two distinct elements: he needed the report Akers had paid for, and then he needed Akers dead. The report shouldn't prove to be much of a problem, but killing Akers was another matter altogether.

He would never be able to do it while the campaign manager was still in the hospital. Security was too tight. Or would he? Hospitals were notorious for causing, rather than curing, infection. Maybe there was a way to get rid of Akers now.

Caine walked slowly down the corridor, observing as he went. The only people who seemed to be oblivious to the security were the hospital employees. White-clad technicians, nurses, and doctors came and went with dizzying regularity, none seemingly subject to the security measures as he had been. Maybe that was the answer: subterfuge in white. He would think about it after he had the report. He might even share his thoughts with Joshua McGrath, but he would really have to consider that before taking action. Some things McGrath was better off not knowing.

CHAPTER SEVENTEEN

"What do you mean, *you know them?*" Drew asked, still kneeling in front of Jordyn, her hands clasped in his.

The tears were gone as quickly as they had appeared, and a renewed determination had replaced them. The anger that had quickly flashed in Jordyn's eyes returned, her jaw set firmly, her mouth a thin slash across her face.

"I know them," she repeated, then after a short pause, "or I should say I recognize the names."

"How so?" Lawrence asked. The Bannerman County sheriff had seen the same reaction Drew Chapman had seen, but to him it was not a surprise. He'd seen Jordyn Phillips in action in the courtroom; he'd seen the anger she now displayed in a dozen divergent incidences. Jordyn, he knew, was tenacious and tough, two attributes that served her well as a prosecuting attorney. But the other quality that was even more valuable was Jordyn's ability to empathize with the stricken. The combination more often than not produced justice in a courtroom where Jordyn was present.

Chancellor moved closer, now sitting on the edge of his chair. "How do you know these names, Jordyn?" he repeated the question Lawrence had asked.

Drew went back to his chair, moving it closer now. The circle of four had suddenly become quiet, more intense, more focused.

Jordyn ran her hand across her face, pinching the bridge of her nose to relieve a sudden pressure behind her eyes. "I . . . I'm not sure," she replied, suddenly confused. She was thinking, reviewing the names on Chancellor's list, trying to place them. She *had* seen them before. She *did* recognize them, but *why?* Had she seen them in legal briefs? In some other county or state document? She wasn't sure.

Near the end of the list were the names of the men who'd been killed on the deserted stretch of Hallis Road: Carlos Reza, Guillermo Reza, and Javier Lopez. She even recognized those names. When she'd seen them in the paper the day before, something about the names had struck a discordant note. She'd forgotten that until this very minute. The names *were* familiar, but why? she asked herself.

"Tell me, Jordie," Drew pressed, now sitting on the edge of his chair, as were both Lawrence and Chancellor. An air of expectancy filled the room.

Jordyn shook her head. "I don't remember exactly. The list, *this list,*" she said, holding up the piece of paper, "did something. The names are familiar. At least some of them."

"Three of them were the men killed recently. Their names were in the paper and splattered all over the television," Chancellor interjected, the suggestion obvious.

"I know. And I read the paper and watched the news broadcast, but that's not why I recognize the names. There are others here too. Names that were not in the paper, names I've never heard via the media."

Drew sat back in his chair. "Where did you see them, Jordie?" he asked in a low voice. He could feel the emotion streaming from the beautiful woman now seated in front of him. It was difficult for him to maintain his focus. The sheen of her blonde hair highlighted against the dark navy blue of the suit produced a stunning effect. The emotional response to the names only added an attractive quality to Jordyn's already enviable allure.

"You deal with a lot of legal issues," Sheriff Lawrence said. "Maybe you recognize the names from that arena. You could have seen them in legal documents, court cases, court orders."

Jordyn nodded. "It's possible, but I don't think that's it," she said, her mind racing to identify the source of her recognition. "I remember documents and dates from cases. This is something else, something different." And then it came to her. Was it possible? Did her perceived source even make sense? *It couldn't be!*

Drew saw the glint of remembrance in Jordyn's eyes. "What?" he asked.

Jordyn shook her head again, this time with determination. "Nothing," she said. "I thought I might have had it, but I don't." Jordyn felt the internal impact of the lie she'd just told. She *did* know. The source was valid, requiring only confirmation. "The names on this list are not just confirmed deaths, are they?" she said, turning to Chancellor.

"No, they are not. As I said, I began compiling this list a long time ago. The names on the list are names of people who in some form or fashion are no longer in contact with a representative agency of the government or a charitable organization. When I say that, what I mean is that the names came from various sources, such as the INS, the FBI, state and federal assistance programs, private foundations, and more. With the exception of the ones I've marked with asterisks—meaning those are names of confirmed deaths—the others are names of people who are no longer active within that system."

"You're saying they disappeared," Lawrence clarified.

"That's what I mean," Chancellor confirmed.

Drew reached for the list. Jordyn handed it to him. He scrutinized the list, reading the names one by one. What he realized made his blood run cold in his veins. He looked up from the paper, directly at the editor/publisher of the *Spring Valley Courier*. "All the names on this list, from what I can determine, are names of minorities," Drew said in an angry tone, the outburst seemingly directed at Chancellor.

"Don't get yourself in an uproar," Chancellor defended himself. "I only compiled the list, I didn't choose the ones to be included."

Drew quickly retreated. "I'm sorry, Bob," he said instantly. "My anger was not directed at you. It was directed at the obvious."

"The obvious being just what we talked about last night," Chancellor said. "There is an organized effort to rid this state of minorities."

"It's incredible," Drew responded. "We've got three murders . . ."

"And several attempted murders," Lawrence added immediately.

"Right. If we're looking at this as a conspiracy, then we have to assume that the accident involving the governor's car was no accident. Especially since the driver of the truck disappeared. And we know there was an attempt on Samuel Reardon's life. Bombs don't just instantaneously appear."

"And Mike Reece," Jordyn added.

"And Mike," Sheriff Lawrence confirmed.

"Someone is escalating this thing into an all-out war, pushing the envelope, the time frame, whatever that might be." Drew said quietly.

"That's my assessment," Chancellor confirmed.

"It's insane," Drew said.

"That's the nature of insanity," the editor replied.

Drew turned back to Jordyn. Even in the atmosphere of revelation, Jordyn's beauty struck Drew again, and he secretly wondered how he could so easily divide his attention between what he'd just heard and the loveliness of Jordyn Phillips. Then he realized it was not something that needed to be analyzed; he could simply accept it. "What about the names, Jordie?"

Jordyn had determined her course of action. She would confirm the basis of her recognition before revealing it. There was a possibility that she was wrong, but the more she thought about it, the more certain she was that she knew the source of the names. She *did* know the source, and the revelation sent involuntary chills through her body.

Drew felt Jordyn's involuntary shudder. It was as if a chilling wind had swept through the office. There was a look on Jordyn's face, a look of determination and tenacity. "What is it, Jordie?"

Jordyn returned Drew's gaze, looking directly into his eyes. Drew knew she wanted to tell him exactly what she was feeling, exactly what she thought was possible.

Jordyn shrugged. "It's nothing," she said. "I think I may be over-reacting to the situation. Some of the names are familiar to me, but I can't remember why."

Drew pulled away and took his seat again. The look he had noticed earlier in Jordyn's eyes had changed. What had he seen earlier? At first he thought it was fear, but now as he looked at Jordyn he realized what he was seeing was a look of determination. Jordyn had pulled back within herself. "I need a copy of that list, Bob," Drew said.

"What have you got in mind?" Chancellor asked.

"I am going to head over to the capital to run this list through the state's computers and see if I get a correlation between these names and what we have just discussed. It is still difficult for me to believe that there is some type of conspiracy working in this state to eliminate all minority groups. Besides, I need to check on the condition of Samuel Reardon."

"I'll have Janice make a copy of the list," Jordyn said.

"I want the list also," said Lawrence. "I'll have some of the boys at the office go over it. Maybe between us we can come up with something."

"Good," Drew said. "We can work on this list from both ends. Bob's speculation here is frightening. I'll take the list with me to the capital today, and I will be back later tonight." Drew turned to Jordyn, his eyes meeting hers. "While I am gone, Jordie, I don't want you doing anything with this list. Promise me that."

Jordyn's gaze calmly focused on Drew. "I promise not to get in any trouble while you are gone," Jordyn said demurely. "That is the best I can do for now," she smiled.

Drew felt his heart flutter within his chest at the smile. He would only be gone for a few hours, but now a few hours seemed like an eternity away from Jordyn. "I suppose that will have to do," said Drew. "In the meantime, Sheriff Lawrence can run this list by some of his deputies—some very specific deputies, Dewayne." Drew's meaning was clear.

Drew turned and focused on Robert Chancellor. "Robert, you can do the same thing with your resources, and when I return, we can collate all the information each of us gets."

"And what exactly do you want me to do?" asked Jordyn, her eyes scanning the three men before her. "I get the feeling that some of you in this room think I am totally helpless," she said with a tinge of anger in her voice.

Lawrence and Chancellor looked at each other and grinned, knowing they were seeing the beginning of a true relationship between Drew and Jordyn.

Jordyn reached across her desk and thumbed the button on her intercom. "Janice, would you come here for a moment please?"

The assistant appeared almost immediately at the door. "Yes, Ms. Phillips. What can I do for you?"

Jordyn handed her secretary the list of names. "Make half a dozen copies of this list, please," Jordyn said. Janice disappeared through the office door with the list. "She will have the list back in just a moment, gentlemen. Now what?"

"When I return from the state capital tonight, we will get together and go over our results," Drew replied.

The office door opened and Janice came in carrying the copies of the list. Jordyn took them from her secretary. "Thank you, Janice. I will let you know if I need you again. Here are copies, gentlemen," Jordyn said, facing the three men. "Try not to get in trouble with them," Jordyn smiled.

"It should only take me a few hours to get to the capital and back," Drew said. "We can meet back here later tonight." He glanced at Jordyn for confirmation.

"How about ten o'clock?" Jordyn said.

"That sounds perfect," Lawrence said.

"Ten it is," Drew agreed.

Lawrence and Chancellor rose, tucked their respective lists into their pockets, and left the office.

Drew turned to Jordyn and said, "Be careful while I'm gone. While I'm at the capital, I'm going to see Reardon in the hospital. The last report I got was that he was all right, and I need to know what he knows about the situation. You stay put until I get back."

"Is that an order?" Jordyn asked.

"Actually, it's a request," Drew smiled.

"In that case I'll take it under advisement."

Drew looked deep into Jordyn's eyes, a feeling of utter helplessness sweeping over him. "I'll take what I can get for now." He bent over, kissed Jordyn on the forehead, and was gone.

Jordyn watched Drew leave the office, her pulse racing and her heart pounding. She could feel her face flush. Her hand slowly rose to her forehead where Drew had just kissed her. She allowed herself an embarrassed smile.

In seconds the smile was gone. Her eyes riveted on the list she held in her hand. She knew exactly where she'd seen the names on the list, and the recollection caused the blood to chill in her veins. As sure as there was a God in heaven, she remembered.

Now she needed to contact Joy Hartford at Valley Community Church.

■　■　■

Janice Brown waited until Jordyn left the office. For the first time in her life she actually felt as if she had betrayed someone. It wasn't that she had not been aware of what she was doing, for the possibility had existed for a long time, ever since she'd been enlisted by Danny Boggs. It was just that this was the first time she had actually done it.

As she extracted the tape from the concealed recording machine, she felt as if she was being watched. The machine was located in a desk drawer in the office adjacent to Jordyn's. The office was used for storage, and it had been easy to conceal the tape recorder without any of the other office staff knowing about. She had done it because Danny had asked her to.

She slowly opened the drawer, pressed the ejection button on the tape machine, and removed the tape. A simple phone call, and she knew the tape would be picked up within the hour. What would happen after that she did not know, and when she thought about it, she really didn't want to know.

CHAPTER EIGHTEEN

"You're certain?" Joshua McGrath growled over the phone line.

"Absolutely," responded Jeff Caine. Caine had called McGrath to report on the meeting with Martin Akers in the hospital. What he had seen in Akers's eyes had left no doubt about the existence of a report detailing at least partially the actions of the Brotherhood of the Ring. And after seeing the reaction of Martin Akers, there was no doubt as to who possessed the report at this time. That had been the easy part. Mid-America Information and Demographics Service had been employed by Martin Akers in the past. William Garrison was the best at what he did, so it only made sense that the report had been compiled by him this time too. Garrison had the report. Working on that assumption, Caine had already dispatched men to keep Garrison's home under surveillance, with strict orders to do so at a distance. He would check with the team after he finished his report to McGrath.

"How many copies are there?" asked McGrath.

Caine hesitated a moment before answering. "There's no way of knowing at this point," he said. And *that,* he knew, was a dangerous lapse in the information cycle. He needed to know exactly how many reports existed and their locations before moving on Garrison.

"But I assume there's a way to find out," McGrath said.

"It shouldn't be that difficult. I have already dispatched a team to question Garrison. I'm on my way to join them. I sometimes have a very persuasive manner about me," Caine said lightheartedly, hoping his lack of confidence did not transmit over the phone line. Garrison was ex-military and tough. Information from the detective would not be easy to extract.

There was silence at the end of the line. McGrath did not have a highly developed sense of humor, and Caine's levity grated on him. "Find out and get back to me," McGrath ordered bluntly.

"I'll have that information by tonight," Caine answered, replacing the phone. "Sometimes I hate that man," Caine muttered.

■   ■   ■

William Everett Garrison threw the empty coffee cup across the room with all his strength. The heavy ceramic cup bounced off the wall and clattered to the floor, doing more damage to the wall than the cup. Bill Garrison had been angry before, but nothing like this. Normally in his line of work, the anger was generated by his failure to accomplish a specified task. In this case, however, the anger was generated by cold fear. He didn't like being afraid—it was not in his nature—and this fear was the deepest kind, a fear jointly generated by self-doubt and the unknown.

The quandary had started days ago when he'd first read about the accident involving the governor's limousine and had quickly degenerated into an all-consuming terror.

Garrison gazed at the report that lay on his desk and silently cursed Martin Akers. Not because Akers had requested the report—he could have refused the assignment—but because the governor's campaign manager had failed to fully inform him of the nature of the investigation. Now Garrison was wondering if the fifty-thousand-dollar fee he'd been paid was worth it.

The report on the desk was one of three copies. The other two were safely locked away in a savings and loan safe deposit box in another city.

The one on the desk was to have been delivered to Akers the same day as the accident that put both Akers and Governor O'Brien in Doctor's Hospital. Garrison had shared the salient facts of the report with Akers twenty-four hours before the accident. Accident? Perhaps he should classify the "accident" as attempted murder, because in his estimation there was no other explanation. And this realization terrified Garrison.

Bill Garrison was the sole owner and operator of Mid-America Information and Demographics Services, a euphemism that concealed the real aspect of Garrison's work: Garrison was a private investigator. As he had done during his years in the military, he operated alone because trust was an elusive commodity and having no associates provided one less problem to worry about. A secret known by more than one person was no secret at all, Bill Garrison was fond of saying. He kept his own council.

The investigator operated from his residence in a quiet, middle-class neighborhood. Quiet neighborhoods were safer, easier to defend. Not to mention the fact that strange vehicles or people were more easily identified. There was a certain paranoia felt by strangers when they saw the "neighborhood watch" signs posted on every utility pole. Garrison also knew that his seven-house cul-de-sac offered greater stranger-recognition than most locations. He knew each family in the other six homes, and he even had what he called an "uncle-nephew" relationship with the teenage boys in two of the houses. They were interested in military careers, and Garrison was an endless fount of information and exotic stories that held the boys mesmerized for hours on end.

Garrison had come out of Naval Intelligence in the post-Vietnam environment—an environment of national distrust and global subversion—and as far as he was concerned, little had changed in the last twenty-five or so years. The World Trade Center and Pentagon attacks had affected attitudes, but very little of substance had changed. Distrust and subversion still existed, although in highly different forms. National distrust had easily been exchanged for political distrust; global subversion was now the staple of current politicians. There was certainly nothing in his latest dealings with Martin Akers that had changed his mind. He'd taken the job because the money had been good, and it had been Marty. He'd known Martin Akers for years, had had previous dealings with him, and up to now, had trusted him implicitly.

"The last time I take a job from a friend," Garrison said to himself. "No matter how much it pays." He looked across the room to where he'd heaved the heavy cup, got up and retrieved it, and went to the coffeemaker next to the microwave. He filled the cup, spooned in sugar and creamer, and returned to the table.

It didn't take a genius to know that the information contained in the report was at least partially responsible for the latest series of murders within the state. Three men in Bannerman County and a young med student. It was the classic case of the chicken and the egg. Which had come first? The hate groups or the murders? Not that it mattered a whole lot, for the results were the same—chaos.

Garrison was not sure what he had expected when he'd begun his work, but the information contained in the report had been totally *unexpected*. He'd known he was investigating certain groups, groups whose primary focus was survival of their own race—specifically, survival and subsequent dominance by the white race. The contacts he'd made had been his first foray into the strange world of the white supremacist, and not one he cared to repeat. It was the first time in his life he could remember spending nights in a cold sweat, fearing for his own life.

He'd uncovered the information Akers sought and much more. It was that *much more* that concerned him. The one thing in particular that bothered him was what he'd learned about a group calling themselves the Brotherhood of the Ring.

Originally, his information indicated that the Brotherhood was nothing more than a fringe group, much like Aryan Nations or the Covenant Sword and Arm of the Lord. Groups whose ideals were cemented in the theory of Christian Identity, a concept in and of itself abhorrent to Garrison and not at all connected to true Christianity. And he had made the classic mistake all investigators try to avoid. He'd accepted the information supplied by his client as truth and started from there. But the Brotherhood was more than just another off-the-wall white-supremacist hate group, with lopsided biblical principles. After discarding his original assumptions, Garrison learned the Brotherhood acted as a rally point for most of the more radical hate groups. The Brotherhood was actually composed of the most militant and active members of other groups, every member subscribing to the warped doctrine of Christian Identity. The groups were listed in alphabetical order in the report, but Garrison still could not believe what he was reading when he read the facts he, himself, had compiled. It made no sense, at least not in any logical sequence he was accustomed to. But beyond the information, deep within the fabric of a disoriented and disillusioned citizenry, lay a cancer about to metastasize. An outpouring of hate and loathing was about to boil over in the cauldron that was the United States. That was what was so frightening about what he had learned.

Accommodations had been sought; arrangements made. Men—leaders—had been reached, compromised, threatened.

The Brotherhood of the Ring was about to seek retribution. Or to be more specific, in the vernacular of the Brotherhood itself, resurrection lay on the horizon. The Brotherhood was activating what they called the Christian Initiative. The Christian Initiative was Christian Identity with feet on it. That was the way Garrison thought of it. A full-scale operation of hate and destruction.

Operation Resurrection.

But as ominous as the idea of Operation Resurrection was, there was another piece of information—a name—Garrison had gleaned from the massive files he'd combed through. The name was not a name at all, but a title. A title that, within the context of the Brotherhood of the Ring, sent chills down Garrison's spine. The name that produced the terror he now felt.

It was the person known as the Shepherd.

A mixture of fear and loathing was still creeping up Garrison's spine when he heard the sound, a sound out of context for the location. His worst fears were realized, and Garrison had no doubt as to what the sound was: the Brotherhood had found him.

■   ■   ■

Janice Brown slid the tape into its plastic case. Even as she did so, her hands were shaking. *What was going on?* she wondered. She certainly had never had this reaction before. Her hands shook, and a low-grade headache was developing behind her eyes.

She'd already made the phone call telling her contact that the tape was ready, but the idea of betrayal was distasteful to her. She'd always realized the possibility existed, but that had been in the abstract. This was reality. Was this how Judas felt when he betrayed Jesus? If it was, how had he lived with himself? And then she remembered that Judas had hanged himself. Well, that may have been well and good for Judas, but she had no intention of beating herself up over this issue. She knew the truth when she heard it. And what she had heard recently made all the sense in the world.

With that thought in the back of her mind, reinforcing her conviction, she noticed that her hand had quit shaking. The headache was still nestled just behind her eyes, but even that was going away. It was amazing, she thought, what the truth would do for an individual. *You shall know the truth, and the truth shall set you free.* Wasn't that what the Bible said? And wasn't the entire doctrine proposed by the Brotherhood of the Ring taken directly from the Bible?

Knowing she had the truth firmly fixed in her mind, Janice Brown put the cassette tape in her purse and waited.

■   ■   ■

Deputy Danny Boggs braked to a halt in his normal parking place just east of the county courthouse. He'd received a radio message to call Janice Brown only twenty minutes earlier, and he'd found the nearest phone immediately. What Janice told him had excited him. She had not listened to the tape, but she told him whose voices were on it. Just the idea of the four people present during the taping was enough to shift Boggs's imagination into high gear. He would deliver the tape to its final destination within the hour, but first he would review its content. Not because that was his job, but because he was curious. What's more, information is power, and Boggs had no doubt that the information contained on the tape would certainly enhance his current position within the Brotherhood of the Ring.

It was going to be another hot and humid day, Boggs noted as he exited the air-conditioned comfort of the county cruiser. The sun was already beating down relentlessly on the city streets of Spring Valley as the deputy walked across the street to the office of Jordyn Phillips. Just inside the glass door, he saw a lone figure standing. The glare of the sun on the glass made it all but impossible to determine who it was, but he had a good idea.

Sure enough, Janice Brown was standing at the door waiting. As he neared the door, he saw a worried look on her face. He smiled to himself. He and Janice had been dating for just over six months. It had proved an expedient relationship, but Janice did not always control her emotions as well as he would like.

Boggs stepped up onto the sidewalk, looking in all directions before entering the office.

The air-conditioning within the office felt good. He removed his hat as he entered. "What you got, Janice?"

His girlfriend displayed the nervousness Boggs had noticed through the door. She glanced back toward the office area, being certain that no one was listening. "They just left," she said in a low voice.

"They?"

"Jordyn, Chapman, Chancellor, and the sheriff," she answered in a low voice.

"You got the tape?"

She produced the cassette. "I haven't listened to it."

Boggs smiled. His orders were to deliver the tape as expediently as possible. To him that meant after he'd had the opportunity to listen to it. Boggs slipped the tape into his shirt pocket. "I'll take it from here," he said.

Boggs ambled back to his squad car, settled himself in, and pushed the tape into the cassette player. He was immediately amazed at the quality of the recording. He was easily able to identify the four separate voices on the tape. As he listened to the conversation, a small smile creased his face. *They're on the right track,* he thought to himself. And there are people who would pay for such information. Boggs briefly entertained the idea of making a copy of the tape, then just as quickly dismissed the thought. He checked his watch; he was already running behind. He needed to deliver the tape ASAP.

Boggs threw the car into gear and accelerated away from the Spring Valley square.

CHAPTER NINETEEN

His thoughts were now regulated, ordered. It had been a struggle to orient himself. Too much was different, strange. But he was now prepared. Operation Resurrection was underway, and it could not be stopped. It *would* not be stopped, for he was the Shepherd, and *he* had ordained it. The truth lay in the words of Deuteronomy: revealed, inalterable, inviolate.

In his mind, he quickly reviewed the current status and smiled to himself. It would not be long now, not long at all. The goals of the Brotherhood would be carried out. The odious minorities, or at least their arrogant leaders, would be expunged from the land, their influence mitigated to a degree never before seen in this country. And it would be *his* influence that had brought about this miracle of God, for he was the Shepherd.

A satisfied smile crept onto his face, a smile that reflected all the hatred that had ever existed in the world. But it was only the beginning, for the revelation that he expounded would be spread from sea to shining sea, and the sea would indeed shine once again. It would shine, he told himself, for those who deserved the riches and rewards of a true democracy. The theology of Christian Identity demanded it; the dynamic of Christian Initiative dictated it.

Operation Resurrection was the quintessential statement of the chosen people. He could never lose sight of that, for such was the driving force—the divine power—that empowered every member of the Brotherhood.

The Brotherhood.

"The Brotherhood of the Ring," the Shepherd intoned with a touch of reverence. The words rolled easily from his tongue, the Brotherhood's philosophy crystal clear in his mind. They, *he,* was the seed of Jacob. "*We* are the chosen people," he whispered to himself.

The Brotherhood.

The very name brought tears to his eyes. The name said it all. He could feel his throat constrict at the mere mention of the words. These were *his* people, the people of God. It was this categorical certainty that had placed him in his current position, and it was his God who would elevate him even higher as he performed the necessary tasks that lay before him. The three men who were sacrificed in Bannerman County and the young med student were only the beginning, the spearhead—actions that would rock the world.

The Shepherd reached for the Bible that lay by his bed and opened it to Deuteronomy. He gently thumbed to the seventh chapter and began reading. "It's true," he said in a reverent whisper. "It's all true." The man known as the Shepherd continued to read; time lost all meaning.

■   ■   ■

Nanny Collins couldn't put her finger on it, but somewhere in the back of her mind the thought that something was about to happen tugged at her. Those poor men who'd been murdered out on Hallis Road were the beginning, she somehow realized. And she'd just read in the paper about the young college student who'd been run over by a van, a van driven by members of what the media was calling the Brotherhood of the Ring. Some of the media had uncovered the organization's name and were calling it the Brotherhood of Hate. She had to agree.

"Now just what are you worrying about? You know the Lord is going to protect you," she said to herself as she headed for the kitchen and a fresh cup of coffee. She could make out the sounds of Spring Valley outside her window. She poured a cup of coffee, returned to her spartan living room, and reached for her Bible.

When the whole world began to twist and contort and seemed to go crazy, she knew she could open the well-worn Bible and find sanity and truth.

Nanny Collins mouthed a silent prayer, asking for protection, not only for herself, but for Drew and Jordyn. "They's in this, Lord," she said as she knelt at the foot of her favorite chair. "You protect them and help them expose this evil that's got everyone going crazy, Lord. Amen." With the prayer said, Nanny crawled into the large easy chair and began reading. It was well into the night before she lay the Bible on the coffee table and went to bed. She didn't notice the two men just outside her house, resting easily in the deep shadows of the night.

CHAPTER TWENTY

"Joy," Jordyn addressed her friend across the table, "I need your help." Jordyn had phoned Joy Hartford from her office after the meeting with Chancellor, Lawrence, and Andrew. Andrew's suggestion about her being careful had been chauvinistic, at least from Jordyn's point of view, and she had no intention of following his advice. Besides, she remembered where she'd seen at least some of the names on the list that Robert Chancellor had compiled. Now she and Joy Hartford were sitting in a small booth in Spring Valley's only deli-type restaurant, Banners—so named for the display of flags from every state in the union, as well as many foreign countries, all of which the current owners claimed to have visited. Banners was popular, particularly with the young professional crowd, but at this time of day it was virtually empty. Two coffee cups, each with a different flag painted on it, sat on the table. The coffee was always good at Banners. The house brand was from a small Panamanian company, Ruiz. The brew was dark and rich, yet it now sat untouched in a cup with a Panamanian flag painted on it.

"Anything I can do, you know I'll do, Jordyn," Joy answered with a smile. "What's it all about? You sounded mysterious over the phone."

Jordyn felt foolish for a moment, then remembered that the three dead men out on Hallis Road were anything but apparitions, and if she needed an additional reason for the phone call, the list Robert Chancellor had provided was neatly folded and snuggled in the pocket of her suit. The attack outside Carter House was also still fresh in her memory. She shuddered at the recollection.

"Technically, it has to do with a case I'm working on," Jordyn began quietly, pushing the memories from her mind. "I need to ask you to keep everything we say here confidential. At least until I know more about what I'm dealing with."

Joy Hartford's smile slowly disappeared. "You *are* mysterious," she said in a voice that matched Jordyn's. "Now you've really got my curiosity working overtime. Does this have anything to do with Drew Chapman being back in town and that shooting incident you and he were involved in?"

Jordyn felt her pulse quicken at the question. She wasn't certain why. Was it the mention of Andrew's name, the shooting, or the case he was working on? Or was it the list of names in her pocket? Probably a combination of all of them, she told herself, but whatever it was, there was no doubt that Andrew was definitely included in the mix.

"Don't start reading anything into this," Jordyn joked. "It's just what I said it was. I'm working on a case, and I think you can help me."

"OK. Shoot. Whatever it is I can do, I'll do."

"I need to access the Community Services Agency computer at the church."

Joy stared at Jordyn for a moment. "You know that information is confidential. When you began helping out over there, you signed the same confidentiality and nondisclosure statements all the rest of us signed. A pledge not to use any of the information for any reason other than the intended one."

Jordyn felt her face flush. "I know I did, Joy, but this is different. I can't tell you any more right now. If you will trust me, I can promise you that the information I'm looking for won't compromise that pledge."

"Besides, you could always get a court order to access the information, right?"

Jordyn had thought about that very thing, knowing that under the circumstances, she could easily find a judge to sign a court order releasing the data in the CSA computer. But Joy was a friend, and Jordyn wanted to keep it that way. Access on a friendly basis also meant that Joy was unlikely to say anything about what Jordyn was doing.

"I'm not talking about court orders, Joy, just the verification of some information. What do you say?"

"I say we need to get over to the church. Let me call Kerry and tell him we're on our way over. If he hears someone rummaging around the lower levels of the church, he just might get suspicious since this isn't one of the days we are normally open."

"Thanks, Joy. I'll get the bill while you call Kerry."

■   ■   ■

Robert Chancellor watched almost dispassionately as workmen swarmed over, in, and around the offices of the *Courier*. The temporary plywood sheets covering the windows had been removed, and new aluminum window frames were being installed. The din the workmen were creating had a disconcerting effect on Chancellor. He found himself wanting to be anywhere else.

"Quite a mess," one of the workmen said as Chancellor stepped over the various tools and other paraphernalia littering the newspaper's floor.

Chancellor nodded. In the light of day, the damage was more revealing on a gut level than he'd thought earlier. The damage, while extensive, was even more frightening in its intent. Chancellor knew he'd put up a good front when he'd revealed his list in Jordyn Phillip's office. He'd displayed the right amount of anger and tenacity, but he knew in his heart it had been a masterful act.

He was scared. There was no other way to describe the emotions that flowed through him at this very moment. It was fear mingled with an overwhelming sense of guilt. This very crusade had resulted in his wife's death. It made no difference that someone else had actually committed the crime. In his soul, down deep where truth resided, he knew it had been his own stubbornness that had caused the men he sought to act, and he'd never forgiven himself for it. He would continue to seek the men who'd destroyed his life, but he knew he would have to face the dread that infused his being to the marrow: his wife had died because of him. On a certain level, he recognized the futility of such irrational thoughts, but logic alone would not dispel the emotions he felt regarding his own culpability.

"We should be finished here by this afternoon," Len Carson, the job foreman, said when he saw Chancellor enter the interior office.

"Thanks, Len," Chancellor said absently. "Not much hurry. The *Courier* is going to miss this week's edition."

"Sorry to hear that. Most of the town feels the same way. Don't make any sense, this kind of thing."

"Makes all the sense in the world from a certain warped perspective."

"Maybe, but that don't mean that all of us in Spring Valley agree with this kind of stuff."

Chancellor looked at Carson. Something in the man's voice caught his attention. "How do you mean that, Len? Sounds like you've got a bone to pick with the *Courier*."

Carson laughed. "That's your problem, Mr. Chancellor. You say, 'the *Courier*,' as if this paper has a life of its own. This is *your* paper; *you're* the paper, not this building or anything else. You can't separate the two."

"I suppose you're right, Len. It's a habit most newspapermen fall into. For us, a paper does have a life of its own. A certain perpetuity. It's like our child. It has to be fed, nurtured, and taught to do certain things."

"That's too deep for me, Mr. Chancellor. All I know is what I read in the paper, and I know who wrote it. Like I said, there's no difference between you and the paper."

"I guess you're right when you put it like that. There's no difference, just a manner of semantics."

"Whatever that is," Carson responded, picking up a power drill and heading toward the window frames the other workmen were finishing up. "Got to get back to it."

"Len. One question."

The foreman turned around but said nothing.

"You believe in miracles?"

Carson smiled easily, a wariness lining his face. "Is this an interview or a simple question?"

It was Chancellor's turn to smile. "Just a question. Do you?"

"If you're asking if I believe in things happening that have no explanation, then, yeah, I guess I do."

"What about miracles performed by God?"

Carson looked around the destroyed offices of the *Spring Valley Courier,* sweeping his hand in a great circular motion indicating the extensive damage that glared in the morning light. "Take a look around, Mr. Chancellor. Do you really think if there was a God, he would let this happen? No sir, I don't believe in miracles like that." That said, Carson went back to work.

Chancellor stood amidst the carnage of the night before, trying to reconcile what he'd just heard, and what Dewayne Lawrence had told him about the supposed miracle involving the sheriff's wife. What was the difference? Was there one? What were the common factors? He wasn't sure, but he decided in an instant to pursue not only the men he sought for the murder of his wife, but to pursue the questions Lawrence had raised. And for some reason, the two apparently divergent positions did not seem so far apart. He knew where the lady known as Nanny Collins lived. He went to his desk, pushed aside the rubble that littered the top, and made a note to go see her later.

■   ■   ■

Sheriff Lawrence watched as Deputy Boggs drove away from the County Courthouse, headed away from the village center, and turned north. Lawrence knew where Boggs was headed, and the reason for the trip was not lost on him.

Lawrence turned toward the high-pitched sound of power tools coming from the storefront offices of the *Spring Valley Courier* and watched as workmen repaired the damage from last night's assault. The assault was the latest in a pattern, a pattern Robert Chancellor had correctly identified. At least up to a point, Lawrence reminded himself, for the pattern was much more inclusive, more diabolical, than even Spring Valley's editor imagined.

Lawrence's attention almost immediately returned to the lists he carried in his pocket. Along with the list he'd gotten from Chancellor, he carried an additional one. Neither Chancellor nor anyone else knew that a second list even existed. The list the editor of the *Courier* had provided was a list of victims; Lawrence carried a comprehensive list of suspects. The suspects were men and women who had committed crimes in the name of God and country. For Lawrence, such crimes were an abomination before God. He knew the rationale used by the groups, and he abhorred not only the names on the list but the warped vision of humanity that such men and women embraced in the name of the Bible.

Among the names were the connections he sought, but for the moment, he could not reveal even a single name.

Lawrence turned and headed for his office. Once inside, he pulled the second list from his pocket and reviewed the names. He experienced the same physical reaction he had every time he looked at the list. Words such as *suspects, alleged,* and the like did nothing to placate him. For Lawrence, the list represented a concrete link, a cause and effect, and the effect was as chilling as the cause.

True, he'd told himself more than once, no one on the list had been proven guilty or even indicted, but that was just a matter of time. The sheriff knew—had argued incessantly—that there was a wide chasm between technically correct judicial guilt and true guilt. The names on the list were guilty, even if it were never proven.

Innocent until proven guilty was a nice platitude but one that did nothing for the victims or their families. That was where Dewayne Lawrence's pragmatism took precedence over his conscience. As a law enforcement officer, he was mandated by statute to uphold the theory of the law, but as a man, he had difficulty accepting that same law.

"I need a cup of coffee," Lawrence told himself as he dropped the list on his desk. He poured a cup from a pot he knew had been cooking too long, but he didn't care. His thoughts were now on Drew Chapman and what the CID agent would learn on his quick trip to the state capital. Already Lawrence knew that both the governor and his campaign manager would recover. Both were due to be released from the hospital. But the same was not true for Samuel Reardon.

Reardon was still in the hospital, put there by the explosion that would no doubt be traced to the Brotherhood of the Ring, Lawrence suspected. That was their method. He also knew that Drew Chapman planned to see the state police colonel, and if he did, he would learn certain things that would accelerate not only the investigation but the pending incident known as Operation Resurrection. When that happened, people were likely to die, and one of them just might be Drew Chapman.

CHAPTER TWENTY-ONE

Drew Chapman watched the cloud formation in the distance. A broad cold front had swept across the Dakotas and into the Midwest. The National Weather Service was calling for rain later in the day; the storm front was rapidly approaching.

For Drew, the drive to the capital had been without incident, if you didn't include the thousands of thoughts that had been running through his head during the drive. He'd not planned on staying more than a few hours. Just enough time to clear his head and order his thoughts. He was confused, not only by the swirling events around him but by his own reactions and emotions. Those emotions were wrapped up in the latest events in Spring Valley, the attacks on the governor and Samuel Reardon, the attack on him and Jordyn outside the Carter House, but mostly in his thoughts of Jordyn Phillips.

Jordyn. He would not have believed the depth of feeling he had for Jordyn Phillips. Had the feelings always been there—ignored, depressed, subjugated to reality? And if not, why the sudden rush of emotion where Jordyn was concerned? But his thoughts about Jordyn had to be suppressed for the time being. There were other things with far-reaching ramifications that needed to be dealt with.

What was going on, really? The whole world was falling apart around his ears. What did he know for sure? He had three men murdered just outside Spring Valley. Murdered, he was certain, because they were a different race, had been born in a foreign country, and spoke a different language. He had the editor of the local newspaper propagating conspiracy within a group of which he'd once been a member. He had a name for the conspiracy: Operation Resurrection. He had a name or at least a title responsible for the nightmarish leader: the Shepherd.

Drew was thrust back to reality by a honking horn. His brooding thoughts were replaced by the sounds of the city.

Drew needed to talk to Samuel Reardon, his boss, but the last report had not been good. Reardon was still in intensive care. The only visitors allowed were the immediate family and the governor, Patrick O'Brien. That meant the governor was up and active, and that was good news. The latest news release had pegged O'Brien's release from Doctor's Hospital for day after tomorrow. The same was true for Marty Akers, the governor's campaign manager.

That's an idea, Drew thought. Marty. He and Marty played racquetball together about twice a month when their schedules permitted. Marty might have access to some elusive detail that had escaped him. Marty. That was it. Drew needed to talk to Marty Akers, and Marty Akers was still in Doctor's Hospital.

One thought had haunted Chapman from the beginning. It was something Samuel Reardon had said, but the state police commander had not had the opportunity to expound on it. William Benson, the lieutenant governor and now acting governor had wanted Drew on the case, and only Drew. It had been a ploy to mitigate the damage done to the Brotherhood by the investigation, Drew was certain. Which meant Benson was somehow involved in what was happening. Drew was convinced that Benson knew about his past membership in the Brotherhood of the Ring. But to what end? The question haunted him, and so far there were no good answers. Maybe Marty Akers could shed some light on the odd circumstances, Drew thought to himself.

He had also talked with the forensic investigators at state police headquarters and reviewed the forensic evidence. There was a lot of it, but nothing that was conclusive without the murderers themselves. Drew had formulated the basics of a plan. He would talk to Marty Akers first. What bothered him was that there really was no rational reason behind the decision, just a gut feeling that said this was the right thing to do. What he thought he would get from Akers, he was not certain, but the gut feeling was there. The feeling that told him that Marty Akers might know something about the insanity that was occurring all around. Drew's musings were once again interrupted. The traffic was becoming heavier as he neared the hospital. His was the next exit.

As Drew neared the hospital, his thoughts went to his parents. If he were being manipulated by William Benson for some unknown reason, that meant any leverage point could be useful, should it come to that. At least, he thought, his parents were out of harm's way in their gated retirement community in Florida. They were relatively safe. They could not, and probably would not, be used as leverage against him should he turn up something concerning Operation Resurrection and the Brotherhood of the Ring. But there were other leverage points should the Brotherhood decide to exploit them. That was standard operating procedure for such groups. Strike at the vulnerable, divide and conquer. Use whatever necessary to advance a warped doctrine. Nothing mattered but the agenda, even if the doctrine supporting the agenda was fatally flawed.

"Chaos," Drew said to no one. He needed to say the word aloud to define, if only marginally, what was going on in the state at this moment. *Chaos* was the word, the concept. Nothing else made any sense, but the Brotherhood had never made any sense.

Chaos made sense. Leverage made sense. Terror made sense.

Murder?

"Yes, murder," Drew said aloud. Even that made sense. It was the tool of wholesale acquisition. One the Brotherhood would not hesitate— had not hesitated—to use when necessary. Murder was leverage. Death eliminated problems.

Leverage? What was he thinking? There had been the attack on him and Jordyn outside Carter House in Spring Valley. It had been a message, an unmistakable directive to abandon the case of the three murdered men. Forget about them. Forget about Bannerman County deputy Mike Reece. Forget about the attack on Governor O'Brien and Marty Akers. Forget about Robert Chancellor's conspiracy theory and Operation Resurrection. Forget the list of names. Forget what he was doing, what he thought. Forget it all; leave Spring Valley.

That had been the intention all along, Drew knew. *That* was why William Benson had appointed *him* to the case. Benson knew Drew had once been a member of the Brotherhood and probably thought that once the connection was made, Drew would at least mitigate any possible damage to the Brotherhood by delaying the investigation until Operation Resurrection was well underway. Whatever the operation was. Leverage. Pressure points. Intimidation, should it come to that. The guilty protecting the culpable. An ex-member of the Brotherhood preserving the ideals of the current Brotherhood out of a sense of loyalty and identity. A sense of Christian Identity.

It made sense. Heaven above! The logic was as distorted as ever, but in the minds of the warped and distorted, *it made sense.*

Drew headed for the hospital parking garage. The feeling deep inside told him this was the right choice. He *would* talk to Marty Akers.

■ ■ ■

The white Dodge Ram pickup eased into the parking lot of Doctor's Hospital only seconds behind Drew. Willie Henderson had followed him from Spring Valley. His orders had been specific and limited. Parameters had been set, instructions issued, but Henderson had paid little attention. He was to follow and observe. No more. There was one exception: Should Andrew Chapman discover the true purpose of Operation Resurrection, the CID agent was to be killed immediately. The extermination order was based on contact with certain people, a list of whom Henderson carried in his shirt pocket. The list of names was short.

Henderson had them memorized; he'd read and reread them. At the moment, Chapman appeared to be headed directly for one of the names Henderson had locked in his memory. Henderson smiled to himself. Any day he got to kill for the good of the Brotherhood was a good day, and it was going to be a good day.

Henderson had considered the kill order the sweetest words he had heard since Andrew Chapman appeared in Spring Valley. Henderson had made a unilateral decision, a decision that was personal. Regardless of the reality, he had already decided to kill Chapman. He would worry about validating the kill later, should it become necessary. Anyway, once Operation Resurrection was activated, there would be little time to question the motives and actions of one of the Brotherhood's premier soldiers. No. There would be no questions, no recriminations—only relief. And Henderson would be elevated to the status of a near god, for he would be the one to save the Brotherhood's operation from premature exposure by one Andrew Chapman.

For Henderson, Chapman's death would be a single moment of ecstasy to be enjoyed over and over. He would delight in the execution of the simple plan he had already outlined in his mind.

As Henderson watched Chapman pull into the multilevel parking garage, his gaze rested on the ring on his left hand. It was the ring of the Brotherhood, the mark of a loyal soldier. The silver finish reflected the sun, the barren skull of the ring coming alive in a single shaft of white light that peeked through a growing cloud cover.

For Henderson, the nickname that had been given to the ring was not a derogatory surname but one of honor. Sure, he knew the alleged reason for the existence of the Brotherhood—all that garbage about some Old Testament book containing some obscure verse, and the will of the Lord. But to Willie Henderson, it was all nonsense. He knew whose directions he followed, and it had nothing to do with the Bible. Henderson wore Satan's ring with pride.

■   ■   ■

Drew already knew he would not be allowed to see the state police colonel. Samuel Reardon had been moved down two floors to ICU. He would remain there for at least another week, and no visitors other than family were permitted in the room. Drew had been informed of this once he got to headquarters to examine the evidence.

The evidence: it was almost laughable. Not that there was none. The forensic team had gathered every blade of grass and grain of sand that might be of some value. No, the problem was, even with the multitude of physical evidence, there was absolutely nothing to tie it to any particular individual.

Now inside the hospital, with all the security checks completed, Drew took the elevator to the floor where Marty Akers and the governor of the state were being treated and guarded.

Drew showed his ID to the guard outside Akers's room and entered. Marty Akers was sitting in a chair next to the window overlooking the peaceful landscape several stories down. Akers turned as Drew entered, and Drew was shocked by what he saw. Marty Akers's face was pasty white, almost as if some insane makeup artist had used too much pancake makeup in an effort to duplicate the face of the dead.

Akers turned back to the window without a word.

Drew walked over to where Akers sat. "Marty," Drew said. "What is it?"

Akers turned back to face Drew, and this time Drew recognized what it was he was seeing in Marty Akers's face—fear.

Drew repeated his question, this time almost in a whisper.

The answer came from Akers in a voice Drew Chapman did not recognize, a voice that reflected the true depth of terror the governor's aide was feeling. The answer escaped in a muted sob.

"They know," Marty Akers whispered. *"They know."*

Drew Chapman crouched next to the chair Akers sat in. "Who is *they,* and what do they know?" Drew asked.

"They know," Akers repeated in yet another tortured whisper.

Drew moved around in front of Marty Akers. He had known this man for years. He did not appear to be a man who could be easily intimidated. But now there was no mistaking the fear conveyed in Akers's demeanor and tortured words. Something or someone had terrified the man.

"Marty. Listen to me. Who is *they,* and what do they know?" Drew repeated. "Talk to me Marty."

The look on Akers's face suddenly changed, as if for the first time since Drew entered the room, he was recognizing him.

"Drew," Akers said at last. "How long have you been here?"

"Take it easy, Marty. Do you remember what you just said?"

Akers smiled. "I'm not that far gone, Drew. I said, 'They know.' "

"Know what? And who is *they?*"

Again Akers smiled. "The Brotherhood knows," Akers said.

"Knows what?" Drew asked, the hair on the back of his neck standing up at the mention of the Brotherhood.

"About the report."

Drew felt the short hairs on the back of his neck bristle even more. "What report, Marty?" Drew asked, his pulse now racing as his mind collated the possibilities of what Akers was saying.

"The report on the Brotherhood and something they call Operation Resurrection," Akers said in an urgent voice. "You have to stop them, Drew. They know about the report, but they don't know where all the copies are. They probably know who compiled it since they know about the money I paid to have it done," he rushed on. "You have to get the report. You have to get to Garrison before they do. Get a copy of the report. Read it. Stop them." The words were once again the words of a desperate man.

"Tell me about the report, Marty. What does it say? And who is Garrison?"

"Garrison. Bill Garrison. He's a private investigator. You should know him. Garrison came out of Naval Intelligence. He's tough. Look him up. He's got the report. That will tell you all you need to know, but you've got to get to him before the Brotherhood. Get the report."

Drew saw Marty Akers's face as it once again changed, reverting to the pasty white look of a man who was attempting to deal with a terror in his life that was overwhelming. Drew pressed the aide. "I need more. Where does Garrison live? Where's his office?"

But already Akers had retreated into himself. Drew pressed some more, but the man said nothing. Drew left him staring out the hospital room window. *Bill Garrison,* Drew thought. The name was familiar. He *did* know the name. And if Garrison was now working as a private investigator, there would be a license on file at state police headquarters. It would only take a phone call to get the address of the man's home and office.

As Drew exited the hospital, he was so absorbed in what Akers had said that he failed to notice the white Dodge Ram pickup that fell in behind his car as he paid the parking toll and headed away from Doctor's Hospital.

If he'd had any doubts as to the validity of something called Operation Resurrection, he no longer harbored those doubts. The repeated mention of the operation from divergent, unrelated sources was too much to ignore. He needed to know what the operation was, and he needed to talk to Bill Garrison.

Drew dialed the number of state police headquarters on his cell phone and in a few short minutes learned that Bill Garrison had no formal office. The man worked out of his house, and Drew had that address. He headed for the west section of the city and the address he'd just received.

CHAPTER TWENTY-TWO

William Benson looked around the office of the highest official within the state. The recent events that had led to his occupation of the governor's office had not gone exactly as planned, but they had had the effect he had sought. Now it looked as if all his planning was about to pay off. He walked over to his desk—the governor's desk—and picked up the reports that had just arrived. They told part of the story but not all.

He knew Drew Chapman was at Doctor's Hospital talking with the governor's campaign manager, Marty Akers. He knew Chapman was being followed and by whom. He also knew what Drew Chapman sought—the report paid for by Marty Akers out of monies from the Campaign to Reelect O'Brien Fund. But when it came to what exactly the report was and what it said—William Benson was in the dark. It was one of the things he dearly wanted to learn.

Benson picked up the cup of coffee he'd poured a few minutes earlier; it was already cold. He replaced it after an ill-advised sip and thought of Drew Chapman. Had his selection—his insistence—on Chapman heading the murder investigation of the three men in Spring Valley been a tactical error?

There had been reasons for his insistence. Valid reasons. Chapman knew Spring Valley, it was true. His early life had been spent in the area. He'd gone to school there. But that had not been the overriding factor in choosing the CID agent. Andrew Chapman had been a documented member of the Brotherhood of the Ring, and that made him, in Benson's eyes, the perfect man for the job at hand.

Tied to the investigation of the Brotherhood was the inherent danger of exposing Operation Resurrection. William Benson sighed once, looked at the abandoned coffee cup, and walked to the window that looked out on the beautifully landscaped area just outside the capitol building.

For all practical purposes, it was a gorgeous day outside. But a storm was brewing. The sun cast deep shadows across the bluish-green grass of the carefully manicured lawn. Benson could make out the shadow of the capitol dome above him, cast in the shadows across the lawn like an abstract sculpture.

Operation Resurrection.

Operation Resurrection was tied to the Christian Initiative.

The Christian Initiative was tied to the theology of Christian Identity.

The theology of Christian Identity was the basic worldview of the Brotherhood of the Ring.

The conclusion: Operation Resurrection was intricately woven into the very fabric and belief system of the Brotherhood of the Ring.

William Benson walked back to the desk and glanced one last time at the coffee. The creamer he'd spooned into it almost twenty minutes ago was beginning to form a scum on the surface. The desire for a fresh cup he'd felt a few minutes earlier was gone.

Benson fell into his chair and picked up a neatly bound report that lay there. He began thumbing through it. He knew the contents by heart, but that did not stop him from rereading certain sections again.

The Brotherhood of the Ring, the report from the Southern Law Poverty Center stated, had been born early during the Vietnam era, had disappeared for a time, and had reappeared during what was called the Higher Conference held in the Midwest early in 1997. For a short time it appeared as if the patriot movement had lost steam. Most of the militias—the armed, semimilitary groups of fanatics who had in many instances overlapped the membership within the patriot groups—according to a Southern Law Poverty Center intelligence report had suddenly declined from 858 groups to 523. Patriot groups now numbered slightly less than 200, of which more than 70 were counted as militias.

The Higher Conference had been the resurgence of the patriot groups. It had been this conference, the report continued, that had tied many of the existing hate groups to the patriot groups.

Benson read on, his mind now working, absorbing details he realized he'd missed in earlier readings.

The Southern Poverty Law Center classified hate groups into seven categories: Ku Klux Klan type groups, Neo-Nazi, Racist Skinhead, Christian Identity, Black Separatist, Neo-Confederate, and other. There were currently 602 such hate groups operating in the United States.

William Benson put the report down and gazed out the window. Already the sun had worked its artistry on the shadow sculptures on the capitol lawn, rearranging them, juxtaposing some on others, overlapping lights and darks. *Much like this world,* he reflected.

Benson went back to the report. The number of hate groups, including the patriot groups, had declined. The weak, the faithless, the visionless, had been weeded out of the mix. Like all patriot movements, the current version of the Brotherhood of the Ring had emerged stronger, more virulent, more radical than its predecessor.

And now the Brotherhood had set in motion its Christian Initiative—Operation Resurrection.

The morning newspaper lay on the corner of the desk where Benson's secretary had placed it earlier in the day. The headlines glared at him in their vivid black-on-white letters: Governor O'Brien to Be Released Early.

Too soon, Benson knew. Too soon to hope that Drew Chapman would accomplish what Benson most wanted. Too soon to give back the office he now occupied. Too soon to hope for nonintervention from O'Brien.

Too soon. He would have to arrange for a longer hiatus from the governor's office for O'Brien. That was a must.

Benson laid the report on his desk and wondered again if he'd made a mistake by appointing Drew Chapman to the investigation of the three murdered men on Hallis Road in Bannerman County.

Was it possible that Chapman could actually stop Operation Resurrection?

Whatever the possibilities, William Benson needed to generate extra time, and time, by any measure, was the most elusive commodity on the face of the earth.

■   ■   ■

Joshua McGrath looked out on his world, a world that in a few short days would be made better for all the people he cared about and loved. Most could not understand his emotions, his caring. To most of the world, he was a hard, inflexible, tyrannical man. The assessment, in McGrath's view, was harsh. An indictment undeserved. But he could live with that. His course was set, his path ordained. The Brotherhood of the Ring had ordained the direction. The Brotherhood's interpretation of Deuteronomy 7:6 was the authority. It was predestined.

McGrath recognized the feeling of impatience as it welled up in him, but he understood the need for the careful execution of a plan that had been so intricately developed.

Waiting was difficult, but McGrath told himself, as he watched the landscape change with the sun's movement, it would all be worth it.

At the moment, the oil mogul knew that Willie Henderson was trailing Drew Chapman, following him to Doctor's Hospital in the capital city. A phone call from Jefferson Caine a few minutes ago had confirmed that Chapman was actually at the hospital. McGrath grinned. It was amazing to him how single-minded the enemies of the Brotherhood seemed to be. Chapman, he knew from both Caine and Henderson, had talked to Martin Akers, the governor's campaign manager. There was no doubt Chapman would learn of the report Akers had authorized and with that, the report's location. And if Chapman knew the location of the report, it would not be too long before the Brotherhood also discovered the location. With the report in hand, yet another obstacle to the commencement of Operation Resurrection would be removed. As difficult as it was, patience was the key, at least for now.

McGrath felt a surge of pride as he thought about the coming operation. The Brotherhood would certainly take full credit for its successful implementation. There was no reason not to. After the completion of Operation Resurrection, the chosen people of the United States would understand what the Brotherhood was seeking to accomplish. Everyone would understand, and the vast majority would support the Brotherhood. At least those who counted most would support the implementation of the Christian Initiative. For McGrath, it was not possible to think otherwise.

Operation Resurrection would take place under the enlightened leadership of the Shepherd.

■　■　■

William Garrison pulled the Browning Hi-Power from his waist holster. Most law enforcement agencies and the military had long ago adopted either Beretta or Glock automatics, but Garrison preferred the smaller classic Browning automatic. It had never failed him, and he hoped it would not this time either.

Garrison eased through his house, moving like a cat, trying to identify the origins of the sounds. There were at least two sources, and probably more if the Brotherhood of the Ring had found him.

It was still daylight, and the idea that the Brotherhood would come after him in the light was disquieting. Then he realized the daytime was the perfect time. The cul-de-sac consisted of single-family dwellings. These days, most parents worked during the day, leaving the dead-end virtually deserted. Children were away doing whatever it was that children do these days. There might be an odd housekeeper in some of the houses, but that was the extent of it.

Garrison moved through the hallway, coming to the control panel of the alarm system that was centrally connected to one of the nation's premier alarm companies. He verified that the alarm was set and then moved toward the kitchen. The kitchen had only a single window and door. It was a restricted-access location. If the men from the Brotherhood—he assumed they were men—tried to force their way into the house, the alarm would signal the intrusion, and the police would be on their way in short order. At least that was the theory. Garrison realized he'd never had to test the theory, and now it was too late. At least any intrusion would be announced by the loud blaring of the alarm horn.

And then William Garrison heard a sound that paralyzed him: the high-pitched sound of an electric tool. As with any modern home, weatherproof electrical plug-ins were located on the outside of the house. That meant power for whatever tool the intruders had brought with them. The added advantage of the electrical tool was the limited range the high-pitched sound would carry. There was a very real chance that whatever the Brotherhood had in mind, it might not be discovered until it was too late.

There it was again! The sound! What was it? Where had he heard that sound before?

Garrison could hear voices now. Quiet words spoken with calculated accuracy. Specific orders.

A new sound reached Garrison. Someone was on the roof!

The roof!

That was it! The sound he'd heard was an electric chainsaw! The invaders were coming through the roof! There would be no activation of the alarm system. No one ever wired the roof into the security system!

Garrison heard the terrible sound of wood and shingle being cut apart. It was the one structure so often overlooked. The roof was nothing more than a layer of asphalt shingles nailed over, at most, a five-eighths-inch-thick sheet of plywood. Not much protection when it came down to it. Certainly easily breached with the chainsaw.

The sound now reverberated through the house. He would have to set the alarm off manually. He needed to be back in the hallway to do so. That meant leaving the relative safety of the kitchen, but there was no choice.

Garrison moved easily, the Browning held lightly, the safety clicked to the off position. The front door was wired into the alarm system, but the door was a multilight door, with several panes of opaque glass in it. Even through the cloudy glass it was possible for the men outside to detect movement within the house. Given the relative merits of shooting through the glass to kill him and thus setting off the alarm or waiting until he set the alarm off manually, Garrison had no illusions as to which the killers from the Brotherhood would choose. He would have to be careful.

The chainsaw was eating though the roof effortlessly. Could he get into the attic before the killers cut the hole? That was another option.

Garrison moved through the house, checking every possible firing point as he approached. He could be shot at any moment through any of a half dozen windows.

He entered the hallway. The long passage ended in a small bedroom whose window was exactly aligned with the corridor. There was movement in the window! Shadows spread across the glass. Two shadows! Two men! Two killers!

The men of the Brotherhood!

Garrison turned, the Browning pointed in the direction of the two shadows. He fired. The bullet shattered the glass; the alarm bellowed its warning. One of the shadows fell.

Why hadn't he thought of that earlier? All he'd had to do was shoot out his own window, and the alarm was activated. He'd given the killers an extra ten minutes at least. Garrison cursed to himself for his oversight.

The whining sound of the chainsaw had ceased. The roof was breached! The killers had penetrated all defenses! Garrison prepared to fire again at the second shadow. It was gone. The alarm blared, the sound strident and penetrating, hindering rational thought. A face appeared at the window. The second man. Garrison could make out the shortened riot gun the man carried. The gun would be loaded with buckshot—a favorite killing device of the Brotherhood. The buckshot would splinter the interior of the house like shrapnel from a hand grenade.

The man raised the weapon. Garrison could see the smile on the man's face, but nothing happened! The man did not fire.

Garrison knew now. These men, these killers from the Brotherhood of the Ring, wanted him alive. They needed him alive. He knew where the reports were hidden, and they needed that information.

Garrison fired at the smiling face, but it was gone. Windows exploded inward now. Shotguns were ripping the house apart. All semblance of subterfuge had been abandoned. The alarm had already alerted the authorities, and these men had to get to him before the police arrived.

Heavy footsteps bounded down the stairs from the upstairs area. The men who'd come through the roof were close.

Garrison pivoted, the Browning barking as he turned. Bullets slammed into the wall, boring neat, round holes in the sheetrock walls.

"Give it up, Garrison," a man's voice ordered from the stairwell.

Glass shattered behind him. The investigator turned. Two men . . . no three, rushed him from three different directions. Their weapons were holstered.

Garrison fired at the first and was rewarded with a scream. He moved to the second man. Just before he pulled the trigger, he was hit from behind. A man on the stairs had hurled himself from the banister, slamming into him with all his weight. A sharp pain shot through his back; his legs went numb. Garrison landed on his back. His head rang. Colors swirled before his failing vision. There were more shadows. This time they were above him, standing around in a small circle.

"The report, Garrison. Where is it?" one of the shadows asked.

"Stuff it," Garrison answered.

"In here," a distant voice called. "I've got it."

"Well, Mr. Garrison, it appears we don't need you after all." The man leveled a shotgun at the investigator. Garrison had miraculously held onto his Browning through the struggle. He fired, the bullet slamming his would-be assassin against the far wall. The man slumped against the wall, then began to rise.

William Garrison wondered if he was hearing correctly. Then he knew. Each man wore a tight-fitting bodysuit of bulletproof Kevlar, with gloves and boots to match and strangely deformed masks. The screams he heard when he'd shot would have been screams of pain, for the Kevlar suits would have prevented penetration of the bullets he'd fired, but the impact would have been bruising and painful.

■ ■ ■

What time was it? How long had he been out? What was the incessant sound that seemed to penetrate his body? The alarm, of course. It was still blaring. But there was another sound. Sirens. Police? Emergency medical technicians? Whoever they were, they were responsible for saving William Garrison's life.

Bill Garrison closed his eyes. His back burned with pain. Suddenly words spoken in quiet tones penetrated his consciousness. Who were these people?

Uniforms. They were wearing uniforms. The police had responded to the alarm, but the men of the Brotherhood were gone.

William Garrison smiled to himself. The Brotherhood now knew what was in the report, but they only had a single copy. Two more still existed, and he would see to it that those reports stopped the nightmare he'd uncovered.

CHAPTER TWENTY-THREE

If Jordyn Phillips had had to dream up the perfect church building, she would have conjured up a building precisely like Valley Community Church. Jordyn attended a smaller denominational church on the west side of Spring Valley, but Valley Community was still the most beautiful church building within a hundred miles.

The church sat on a small knoll overlooking much of Spring Valley. Nestled in a copse of pine trees, the church's white clapboard exterior walls were accented by the sun's rays reflecting off the four stained-glass windows set in each side. The windows were not identical, and Jordyn relished the idea of the story that was told by the eight colorful windows. The original building had been built sometime in the early nineteenth century, and it reflected a classical church architecture.

"Beautiful, isn't it?" Joy Hartford said as she and Jordyn pulled into the church parking lot.

"My dream church," Jordyn said in a quiet voice, as if even in the parking lot, reverence was the order of the day.

"I particularly love the view at night with the lights of Spring Valley shining in the darkness. They remind me of thousands of small diamonds sparkling in the sunlight," Joy continued.

"I know. I like to come up here at night myself." Jordyn parked the car and got out. Hers was the only car in the parking lot, and she remembered Joy saying she was going to call Kerry to let him know that they would be working in the basement at the Community Services Agency computer. So where was Kerry's car? Jordyn wondered to herself. *Probably out on an emergency call of some kind,* she thought. After all, he was a pastor, and pastors were like policemen and firemen, always on call.

Before she had time to ask the question, her gaze settled once again on the church. The sun was washing the white boards in a yellow splash that enhanced the beauty of the building. The helm roof steeple rose above the church, a beacon for the community to rally round. Just below the steeple at the cornice, an intricate filigree design had been woven in curved carpentry. Jordyn had never really noticed the design before now, but found it intriguing. The design added to the character of the old church, providing a sort of mystery while serving as an anchor for the surrounding community. And that was how Kerry Hartford saw the church, too, Jordyn knew.

Kerry and Joy Hartford had come to Spring Valley less than two years ago. Kerry had been a pastor of another congregation somewhere in Illinois or Indiana. Jordyn couldn't remember which. The Spring Valley community had immediately accepted the affable pastor and his wife. There were other churches in the community, but Valley Community was the quintessential church, and it was the attitude that Kerry Hartford displayed that made it what it was, at least to the nonchurchgoers of Spring Valley. Kerry Hartford took an interest in everyone, religious or not. To put it succinctly, Kerry Hartford cared. Valley Community was the church that all the others wished they were, and it was mostly because of Kerry and Joy.

When the state-sponsored Community Services Agency had needed space, Kerry had been the first to volunteer, offering the church's basement area. Kerry had even financed some of the changes to the basement area out of his own pocket, Jordyn had heard, to make it more functional for CSA.

Joy Hartford was the perfect pastor's wife. Always involved in some community affair, always volunteering, always seeking a way to serve. The overwhelming consensus was that the Hartfords and Valley Community Church were made for each other.

"Let's get to the computer," Joy suggested, heading for the church building.

"Right," Jordyn answered, walking with Joy. "I want to get started and get this over with as soon as possible."

As they moved toward the glowing church, Jordyn felt a strange sensation. Even though Valley Community Church was not the church she attended, for a brief moment, she wondered what it would be like to walk down the aisle of the church to meet Andrew Chapman as her husband-to-be.

That thought was quickly banished as Joy opened the door, and both women proceeded down the stairs to the church's basement area where the CSA computers were housed.

■ ■ ■

The dark-tempered man didn't particularly like the turn of events, but he knew if he were to voice his concern to his immediate superior, he would be told to go along with what was happening. There was a rigid hierarchy within the Brotherhood of the Ring, and he would have to have a very good reason to violate the structured chain of command. The man was not yet prepared to do that.

He would wait, observe the two women he had been assigned to follow, and report as he'd been ordered.

The man pulled his truck beneath a pine tree, cursing the events that had brought him to Valley Community Church and made it necessary for him to park beneath the cursed trees. Pine tree sap would no doubt drip onto his pickup, making it necessary to wash and wax the truck later, but he had no choice. The pine trees were the best hiding place for the vehicle. He would leave the truck among the trees and make his way to the lower level of the church. It wouldn't be difficult. The man knew the church layout by heart. After all, he was an elder at Valley Community Church. Maybe he would bring up the possibility of removing the pine trees at the next elder's meeting.

After Operation Resurrection was completed, that was.

The man pulled a blued Smith and Wesson Model K38 from the glove box and pushed the weapon into his waistband at the small of his back. Next he retrieved a small metallic box that had been next to the pistol and stuffed it in his pocket. He pulled the keys from the truck, checking the key ring to verify that the church key he'd been given was still there. It was. He would go around to the rear of the church, enter through one of the basement doors, and find out exactly what that nosey prosecuting attorney was up to.

He'd never approved of the access Jordyn Phillips had to the church as a volunteer with CSA. She was not a church member, and that made all the difference. Most people did not understand the theology of Valley Community Church. Few cared to delve into the complex theology. That ignorance made them dangerous, and the Phillips woman was no exception.

Before he moved toward the church, however, he reached for the small cell phone attached to his belt and thumbed the off switch. He didn't need the instrument at the moment, and he didn't want it going off at an inopportune moment.

■　■　■

"Hit the light switch," Joy said to Jordyn.

"I've never been down here this time of day," Jordyn responded, flicking the light switch on and flooding the basement room with white light. "I don't know why, but it seems a little spooky."

Joy laughed. "I keep telling Kerry that, but he says I'm crazy. But I agree with you. There's nothing spookier than an empty church."

Jordyn picked up on the reference to Joy's husband. "That reminds me, where is Kerry? I thought you called him to let him know we'd be here? I didn't see his car in the parking lot."

Joy hesitated before laughing again; the mirth was strained. "He probably had some kind of emergency and had to go out before we got here. Happens all the time."

"I suppose it does," Jordyn said, moving toward the computer system that housed the information for the CSA.

"Sometimes I think I'm married to a policeman or a country doctor. Kerry's out at all hours of the day and night. I've told him he needs to stop making house calls. Even doctors stopped that a long time ago."

"He might burn out if he's not careful," Jordyn said. She sat down at the computer and powered up the system. As she waited for the operating system to boot up, she pulled the list she'd received from Robert Chancellor from her pocket.

"What's that?" Joy asked, moving closer to Jordyn and the computer system.

"A list of names I want to check against some of the names in the CSA database."

A worried look crossed Joy's face. "This isn't going to get us in trouble is it? We do have a responsibility to the people we serve, you know. Confidentiality and all that. I'm the administrator for Bannerman County, you know. I'd hate for you to have to prosecute me for something you did," Joy joked.

Jordyn looked up from the list and smiled conspiratorially. "Not as long as we don't say anything about it. Besides, if what I think is true, the state will probably be subpoenaing every CSA computer in the entire state, along with the databases and programs."

"I don't understand," Joy said, moving closer.

The computer system was online, programmed to automatically display the CSA menu. Jordyn clicked on an icon, then said to Joy, "This is a list of names. When I first got it, some of the names looked familiar, but I couldn't place them. Then I remembered where I'd seen them before. The names I recognized on the list were all names that I'd seen before, and the only database that made any sense was the CSA database. That's why I want to run the names on this list against it."

"What exactly is the list?"

"Names of people who have died, been murdered, or have just been reported missing. Something is going on in this state, and if what I think is happening actually is happening, it's probably going on in surrounding states too."

"And that is?" Joy said, a worried edge in her voice.

Jordyn missed the change of tone in her friend's voice as she began typing names into the formatted screen. "I think people are being systematically eliminated. Killed. Kidnapped. Whatever you want to call it. I don't know why, but I think the CSA computer system may provide a lead."

"Is this something you should be doing?" Joy asked again.

Again Jordyn missed the increasingly agitated tone expressed in Joy's question. "Someone has to find out what's going on. I guess I can tell you. I got the list from Robert Chancellor."

"Mr. *Spring Valley Courier*."

Jordyn laughed at the description. "One and the same. He also shared with us—"

"Us?" Joy interrupted.

"Yes, Andrew Chapman and the sheriff were there too. Robert gave each of us a copy of the list. Robert thinks there's some kind of conspiracy going on to eliminate minorities in this state. It sounds fantastic to me, but I did recognize some of the names on the list. Robert's been at this longer than the rest of us. He's got more information on the missing and murdered, but I haven't gone so far as to examine what he's got."

Joy's eyes narrowed at the last bit of information. Then she asked, "And some names from the CSA computer tie into whatever it is that Robert Chancellor is investigating?"

Jordyn continued to type as she spoke. "Right. At least I think so. It took a while for me to realize where I'd seen the names before, but when I finally remembered this computer, it all began to come together."

"Who else did you tell about the CSA computer system and your idea about the names being in the system? I mean, who else knows you recognized the names from working for CSA?"

Jordyn pecked away at the keyboard as she answered. "No one. I wasn't really certain. That's why I wanted to access this information and verify my theory before I sounded like some zealot or alarmist." Jordyn finished typing, pressed enter, and waited. Neither she nor Joy said a word as information scrolled across the screen, stopping as a name was highlighted by the moving cursor.

"Is that one of the names on the list?" Joy asked, moving behind Jordyn to view the screen.

"That's one," Jordyn said, her mind now preoccupied with the computer. She pressed enter again and the computer immediately scrolled to another name and stopped. "That's the second name," Jordyn said, her mind now fully occupied by the magically scrolling screen, the excitement impossible to eliminate from her voice.

■ ■ ■

The caller had been right, the man realized. The call had come less than an hour ago, and now Joy Hartford and Jordyn Phillips were accessing information via the Community Services Agency computer in the basement of Valley Community Church.

The man had quietly entered the church basement using the key provided him as an elder of the church. Now he was standing no more than ten feet away from the two women as they examined the displayed information. It looked as if he would have to use the apparatus in the metallic box he'd jammed into his pants pocket.

The man gently opened the box and extracted the hardware he needed. He would wait a few more minutes to be certain what he was about to do was necessary, then he would act. No one in Bannerman County would ever see Jordyn Phillips again in this life.

■ ■ ■

"You could do a global search for all the names rather than type each one in one at a time," Joy said to Jordyn as she watched the screen in front of Jordyn Phillips fill with information.

"I could, but I want to know more about each of these names. Where they came from, family members, previous locations, last known locations, that sort of stuff. Might help me put all this together."

"But so far every name on that list is in the CSA computer?" Joy asked.

Jordyn didn't look up from the screen when she answered. "Every one of them. And there's more. There seems to be some sort of designation within the system that I've found on each of these names. A small icon appears to the right of each of these names, as if they are being identified in some way." Jordyn turned to Joy. "Do you have any idea?"

Joy moved closer. "What sort of designation?"

Jordyn typed briefly, then pointed at the screen. "Right here, for example," she said, indicating an unusual icon. "That symbol appears by each of these names when I first call up the information."

The icon was small, resembling the fletching of an arrow standing on end.

"Looks like the feathers on an arrow," Joy said, moving even closer to the screen.

Jordyn felt the hair on the back of her neck prickle at the description. Joy was right. The icon was the Toten-rune, one of the Germanic runes associated with the Brotherhood of the Ring.

The Brotherhood again!

■   ■   ■

The man moved quickly, the small syringe in his hand. His target was preoccupied at the moment, and there was no doubt that she now knew too much and was about to discover more. He could not allow that.

It was time.

■   ■   ■

Jordyn felt Joy's arms encircle her, and she wondered what her friend was doing. As a burning sensation erupted in her arm and a red-hot heat spread through her body, she realized what had just happened.

The room began to blur; her tongue was thick, her mouth dry; she couldn't speak. Her breath came only at the expenditure of a tremendous amount of energy. The last thing Jordyn remembered before her eyes closed on a deep blackness were the words in the design along the frieze on the interior of the wall. She wondered why, in all the times she'd been down in the Community Services Agency room, she'd never noticed these things before.

As Jordyn Phillips's head fell on her chest and her eyes closed, she wondered why she'd never recognized the combined Tyr- and Toten-runes incorporated into the design above the biblical verse encircling the basement at ceiling level—the words of Deuteronomy 7:6.

CHAPTER TWENTY-FOUR

It was a nightmare played out in three dimensions and living color.

Drew Chapman had seen the flashing lights, heard the wailing sirens, and had wondered what was going on. Now he had that sickening feeling he always associated with bad news.

Drew turned into the cul-de-sac where William Garrison's home was located. Instinctively he knew that the house where the city's yellow mobile intensive care unit and the blue-and-white patrol cars were crowding around belonged to William Garrison. Something on this small dead-end street had gone dreadfully wrong.

Yellow police barrier tape was strung from trees and shrubs, effectively isolating Garrison's house. Drew could see the house number displayed beside the front door on the fascia board. His instincts had been right; this was Garrison's house.

"Hold it," a uniformed police officer said as Drew stopped his car and got out.

Drew reached for his identification and showed it to the officer.

"What happened?" Drew asked the uniformed man as he replaced his wallet, his eyes riveted on the macabre scene before him.

"Not sure. This is as close as I've gone. Detectives are in there right now, along with the guy who lives here. The corpsmen are working on him in the house."

"Corpsmen?" Drew asked with a hint of amusement. He'd never heard emergency medical technicians called that before.

"They're all corpsmen to me. I spent ten years in the Marine Corps. Navy corpsman saved my life once."

"Understood," Drew said. "Mind if I check with the detectives?"

"Go ahead. Guy's name is Garrison, by the way. The police were called by the security company. Someone set off the alarm. Uniformed men were here first, then detectives and medical folks."

"OK. Thanks," Drew said as he walked away from the policeman. Despite the activity, there was an eerie silence about the place, heightened by the bizarre effect of the flashing red, yellow, and blue lights. *A Salvador Dali painting in motion,* Drew thought as he approached the house. Surrealism in action. He did not like the effect.

The area was obviously residential, and Drew wondered about the neighbors and what some of them might have seen. The thoughts were banished from his mind as medical personnel rolled a stretcher from the house with a body on it. The man was strapped to a backboard, and his head was stabilized.

Drew showed the men his identification as he'd done with the uniformed policeman and asked them to stop.

"How is he?" Drew asked the lead medical technician.

"He's in a lot of pain. Someone or something hit him in the back. We won't know until we get the X-rays."

Drew turned to Garrison. He could see the pain reflected in the man's eyes. "My name is Andrew Chapman, Mr. Garrison. I'm working for the governor. Can you answer some quick questions?"

The medical technician started to intervene but stopped when Garrison somehow pulled his hand loose from the straps and handed an object to Drew. "Two more," Garrison said with obvious effort.

Drew looked at the object. It was a key. A safe deposit box key. There was a coded sequence of numbers on the key, but nothing that immediately identified the bank where the box was located.

"Twelve-seventy-five. Get the reports," Garrison finished before he dropped his hand to his side and closed his eyes.

"He's sedated. For the pain. We got to get him to the hospital," the EMT insisted.

"Take him," Drew replied, staring at the key in his hand. How had Garrison known why he was there? Intuition? A good guess? Divine intervention? Drew smiled at the last option. Divine intervention would be Nanny C.'s answer to the dilemma, but Drew wasn't too sure he was ready to go that far. Nevertheless, the fact that he had even considered it as an option in the normal deductive process made him wonder how much of Nanny's faith had rubbed off on him.

He had told Garrison he was working for the governor just before the man had handed him the key. That statement seemed to have precipitated the action on Garrison's part. *Now,* Drew thought, *the question is: Which governor does William Garrison think I'm working for? Patrick O'Brien or William Benson?*

Drew stared at the key once more. Garrison had provided the safety deposit box number, but there was nothing on the key to indicate which bank the key belonged to. But Drew reminded himself that he was a cop, and he knew someone who could find out.

■   ■   ■

"You were right," Willie Henderson said into the cellular phone. "There must be more than one report. Garrison gave Chapman something. It must have something to do with the extra reports. I'll follow him until we know for certain, and then I'll take him out."

"Be sure to get the reports first," Joshua McGrath replied over the wireless connection. "We have to be sure that there are no more. Until then, we let Akers and Chapman live. When we have all the reports, you can kill Chapman, and Caine will take care of Akers. Until then we have to hold off. Stay with Chapman," McGrath ordered.

"Done," Henderson replied. He pressed the off button on the cell phone and smiled to himself again. He could wait. Anticipation usually heightened the experience, he told himself. First, he would find out exactly what Chapman was after, then he would kill him. It was all coming together, just like McGrath and the Shepherd had said it would.

Chapman would die.

Akers would die.

That meddlesome broad of a prosecuting attorney, Jordyn Phillips, would die. That was the only thing that bothered him. He would get to kill Chapman, but he really wanted to be there when the broad died. But, Henderson told himself, even *he* had to sacrifice some things for the Brotherhood.

CHAPTER TWENTY-FIVE

For Pierre Cardenas, the offspring of a Mexican father and a French mother, the structure was the most impressive thing he had ever seen. What was even more impressive for the foreign-born, naturalized citizen was the fact that the state's top public official, Governor Patrick O'Brien, was to be the keynote speaker for the scheduled event that had brought Pete (as only his closest friends called him) to the structure.

To every person in the United States, the structure was known simply as "the Bubble." The software company whose corporate name was appended to the structure and who had paid fifty million dollars for the naming rights was justifiably appalled that their corporate name seemed to have very little meaning when associated with the Bubble.

For Cardenas, the Bubble was the outward sign that universal acceptance and economic prosperity were within his grasp.

Cardenas had come to the United States from Quito, Ecuador, in 1998 when that country's economic situation had been devastated by the weather phenomenon known as El Niño. He had been associated with a multinational corporation whose corporate headquarters were nominally located in Delaware. The corporation had secured a provisional work visa for the petroleum engineer, and Cardenas had moved his entire family to the vast central sector of the United States known as the Midwest.

While in Chicago on business, the Ecuadorian, already enamored by the industrial and business savoir-faire of the United States, encountered for the first time the basis for such economic might: diversity. Diversity not only in the manufacturing and industrial sectors, but in the people whose control was essential in those sectors—the financial management environs.

But even diversity had its own inherent limits, and those limits stopped just short of full social acceptance for someone who spoke English with a trace of Spanish accent.

Social acceptance for Pete Cardenas had at long last come when he discovered the Caucus of American Minorities. CAM, as it was known, was composed of minorities who, like himself, experienced the boundaries of diversity in this country, and Cardenas had embraced the organization with the fervor of a drowning man clinging to a life raft.

Given the political and ecomonic turmoil in his Native Ecuador, he would never have considered exercising his assumed political and social rights there. The United States was different. The people were different. The word *diversified* popped into his mind, and he smiled.

Diversity. That was where strength lay. Diversity and organization.

The Caucus of American Minorities provided the organization.

A large banner was being strung between huge support beams in the upper reaches of the Bubble. It read: "CAM Welcomes Governor Patrick O'Brien." Cardenas watched with pride as the banner was secured and the workmen climbed down.

As the current president of CAM, Cardenas had experienced a sinking feeling when he'd first heard of Governor O'Brien's accident and his subsequent hospitalization. Cardenas had been working on this conference for the better part of two years, and the appearance of O'Brien was to be the crowning event of the entire conference. Of course, Cardenas told himself, it didn't hurt that the minority vote in the state bordered on 13 percent and that CAM was responsible for the formation of voting blocks within the minority factions that could assure political viability for the astute politician who recognized that fact.

Now the announcement had been made that Patrick O'Brien had been released from the hospital. What's more, O'Brien still planned to address the National Convention of the Caucus of American Minorities, offering, Cardenas was certain, more than what the governor wished to but less than what CAM had asked for. Compromise, after all, was the heart of the political system in the United States. Still, whichever way one looked at it, the conference would be a huge success, and CAM would emerge as a major player in regional and national politics.

For Pierre Cardenas, the CAM convention was a dream come true.

CHAPTER TWENTY-SIX

The flight status board behind the Delta Airline ticket agent showed no delays, but Andrew Chapman wondered how long that would last. It was the time of year when thunderstorms appeared unexpectedly throughout the Midwest, always carrying the threat of heavy rain, lightning, or tornadoes. With these weather systems came airline delays, and a delay for any reason would be unacceptable today. Drew needed to get to Cincinnati as soon as possible.

"Your plane will board in fifteen minutes, Mr. Chapman," the young lady behind the ticket counter said.

Drew checked the status board once again, then nodded. He rechecked the electronic ticket he'd purchased online, verified the gate, and headed for the boarding area. As he walked, his hand went unconsciously to the two items he carried in his left pant pocket. He pulled them out, which he realized was just as well. He would need to place them and his pocket change in the plastic tray near the airport's metal detector when he went through. The ring that resembled the Nazi Death's Head ring and the safe-deposit-box key he'd been handed by William Garrison seemed to be in stark contrast to each other as he placed them in the plastic tray. The ring represented everything that was wrong with the world. The key, on the other hand, represented the potential for good that existed. The question now was: Could the potential that existed in the form of the key overcome the evil represented by the ring?

The key? The representation of potential good. What had William Garrison seen in him that had precipitated the trust—trust sufficient to hand over the key. And what did the key lead to?

It had only taken Drew one call to the CID agent in charge of fiscal and monetary investigations to find out the name of the bank housing the safe-deposit box. The coded numbers on the key had proved sufficient. The key belonged to a box at a federal savings and loan in Cincinnati, Ohio. Once Drew learned that, he immediately went online, accessed the Delta Airline Web site, and purchased a ticket to Cincinnati/Northern Kentucky International Airport.

After passing through the metal detector, Drew retrieved his belongings and proceeded down the concourse to his boarding gate. State National Guardsmen still maintained a heightened sense of security within the airport.

The more he thought about it, the more bizarre the current situation became. The key and the ring that he now held in his hand accentuated the situation.

The headlines blaring back from the racks in the airport's news kiosks announced the quick recovery of Governor Patrick O'Brien and his subsequent return to the governor's office in the state capital. O'Brien was scheduled to speak at the National Convention of the Caucus of American Minorities. There had been some doubt about his appearance, but now the speech was confirmed.

So, Drew thought, *if I'm working for the governor, am I now working for O'Brien or Benson?* That was the same question he'd asked himself when Garrison had handed him the safe-deposit-box key. The answer lay with Colonel Samuel Reardon, his boss. Reardon had made it clear that it had been Lieutenant Governor—then Acting Governor—Benson who had requested Drew be in charge of the investigation in

Bannerman County. Had there been an ulterior motive in that request? Had Benson been sincere in wanting the murders of the three men on Hallis Road cleared up, or had there been an underlying reason? Now that O'Brien was back, would that affect the investigation? Hallis Road? How had he gotten from Bannerman County to here? Had the progression been logical? Sane?

There were too many questions without answers, Drew realized, and as far as sanity was concerned, it seemed elusive at the moment. Nothing made sense.

"Delta flight 5656 for Cincinnati now boarding at gate B-59," the public-address system announced.

Drew could see the gate marker just ahead. Another news kiosk was just to his left as he headed for the gate. Small groups were standing around reading the different renditions of the news from the various newspapers on sale.

Drew handed his boarding pass to the gate agent and walked down the stairs. The aircraft turned out to be a Canadair Regional Jet. The enclosed jetway was not available to this type of aircraft, so boarding was done in the open. Drew was grateful that it was not raining.

As the CID agent boarded the aircraft, a single set of malevolent eyes were riveted on him.

■   ■   ■

Willie Henderson watched as Drew Chapman climbed aboard the small regional jet and cursed his luck. He possessed an e-ticket for the same flight, but he'd not realized until now that the plane was a small commuter-type aircraft. Had it been an MD-80 or Boeing 737, he would have risked boarding, even with Chapman on board. He didn't want to lose contact with the CID agent, but that was impossible now. There were what? Twenty-five, thirty seats on the aircraft? It was one long, thin tube with no place to hide and not enough faces to blend in with. No, he could not board this aircraft, and that left him with only one option.

Henderson walked back up the concourse to the public phones he'd passed on the way to the boarding gate. The battery charge on his cell phone was getting low. He needed to preserve what charge he could for emergencies. He pulled a credit card from his wallet, along with a small book. He dialed a number and waited impatiently while the connection was made.

"He's on his way to Cincinnati. I couldn't get on the same plane. Too small."

"I'll make the necessary arrangements," Joshua McGrath answered back. "You stay at the airport. He has to return. I'll make contact there. Someone will pick him up when he gets there. If he gets the reports, be sure you get them. Do whatever it takes."

Henderson started to say something, but the line went dead in his hand. He cursed again, this time his anger directed at McGrath. Henderson slammed the phone back into its cradle and headed for the ticket counter.

He would have to tell the ticket agent he'd missed his flight and battle for a refund. It was an unexpected setback but one he could live with. Especially if Chapman took the turn-around flight back from Cincinnati, which Willie suspected would be the case. Chapman had carried nothing with him for an overnight stay. He would wait. The idea of killing Chapman in a public facility had a certain allure.

■ ■ ■

The Canadair Regional Jet bumped and bucked its way into the Cincinnati/Northern Kentucky International Airport.

The flight had lasted only thirty minutes, but for Drew, as well as the other ten or so passengers, the turbulence aloft had made the flight uncomfortable. As soon as he was out of the arrival gate area, Drew pulled out his cell phone and called Jordyn Phillips's office. There was no answer, not even the secretary or the answering machine. He tried her house. No answer there either. *What next?* he wondered. *Where could she be?*

Drew powered down the phone, then pulled the list Robert Chancellor had given him from his wallet. He examined the names. Most were names he could only haltingly pronounce. The majority were of Hispanic origin, but not all. He remembered Jordyn's reaction when she'd first seen the list, and that worried him. Did the fact that he couldn't reach her now have anything to do with the list? The very thought made him uneasy. Drew replaced the list in his wallet.

Delta flight 5656 was actually a Comair flight, Delta's regional carrier, and as such utilized Cincinnati's C concourse, which was separated from the main terminal. Drew headed out of the building to catch the shuttle bus that ran between the separated terminals. Downtown Cincinnati, where the federal savings and loan was located, was about thirteen miles away. That meant a bus, a taxi ride, or a rental car. He checked his watch: 1:45 P.M. His return flight was scheduled to leave from the same gate at 5:40 P.M. and arrive back at the capital at 5:26 P.M. It seemed odd to have an arrival time before the takeoff, but the change in time zone accounted for that.

Drew had less than four hours to get to the savings and loan, open the safe-deposit box, retrieve whatever was there, and return to the airport for the flight back. He needed a taxi. A bus would make too many stops, and he didn't want to take the time to rent a car. A taxi it was.

The shuttle bus arrived and Drew stepped aboard. A two-minute ride deposited the passengers just outside the main terminal. Drew hailed a taxi and gave the driver the name of the savings and loan and the address. As the taxi pulled away from the terminal, Drew glanced back, his attention drawn to movement that seemed out of context with the surroundings. A maroon pickup truck, its driver seemingly oblivious to the surrounding crowds, had barreled past the terminal building and taxi stand, almost running over an elderly couple in the crosswalk. Angry words were exchanged, words Drew could only guess at from a distance. Drew shook his head. Courtesy was a thing of the past in this modern era.

Drew turned back and settled in the rear seat of the taxi, the incident with the pickup forced from his mind. The ten or fifteen minutes it would take to reach downtown would be a small respite. He needed to think. He needed to think about Jordyn Phillips. That was his primary concern, and he was surprised at that. And just what was his concern with Jordyn, he wondered. Was it a connection, perhaps with what Robert Chancellor called Operation Resurrection, the Brotherhood of the Ring, and someone known only as the Shepherd? Somehow they were all connected.

■   ■   ■

Gordon Larkin had barely made the intercept. When Willie Henderson had called and told him to get to the Cincinnati/Northern Kentucky International Airport ASAP, he had been at least thirty minutes away. He knew that the Comair flight he was supposed to meet would only be in the air that long. Considering all Comair flight gates were located in terminal C, it only took ten minutes after the aircraft was on the ground to get out of the terminal. Certainly no more. Therefore, Larkin had had forty minutes at the most to get to the airport, identify the man he was to follow, and get in position.

He'd almost blown it. What's more, two old folks who'd just stepped into his path at the crosswalk had not done anything to settle his nerves. He'd almost hit the idiots, slamming on his brakes at the last moment and slewing almost sideways in the process. People had scattered at the sound of screeching tires and the smell of burning rubber. He'd cursed the couple but had accelerated through the crosswalk. Now the taxi he'd seen his quarry enter was just ahead, obviously headed for downtown. From here on in, the assignment should be uncomplicated. He had no idea why he was following the man in the taxi, but he had orders to call the moment the man reached his destination.

Larkin glanced beside him on the truck seat where his cell phone lay. His orders were to call a certain number as soon as he was sure his man was headed back to the airport. He'd been assured the man would do just that. After that, he would be free to go about his business.

Gordon Larkin wondered, not for the first time, if he'd made a mistake by joining the Brotherhood of the Ring. He forced the thought from his mind. The Brotherhood was the only sane entity in a crazy world.

CHAPTER TWENTY-SEVEN

Robert Chancellor concentrated on the keyboard in front of him. The screen of his computer terminal was beginning to blur before his eyes, but he continued his quest. Somewhere, he was certain, in the world of cyberspace and electronic information was a clue to the nature of Operation Resurrection. He'd already been to the Web site operated and maintained by the Brotherhood of the Ring, along with a score of other hate Web sites that espoused the same poisonous dogma. What he found on such sites didn't surprise him anymore. And while, as a journalist, he advocated free speech and freedom of the press, it continued to amaze him that sentiments such as those espoused by the Brotherhood of the Ring had any type of following at all. But they did, he knew, and right now such freedom of expression might well serve two masters.

He had tapped into hate Web sites ranging from militia groups to what the Southern Poverty Law Center called neo-Confederate groups. They all had their own particular agendas, but there were also connecting threads: the twin threads of intolerance and violence.

Chancellor typed some more. He'd returned to the Brotherhood Web site. The other sites had been interesting in a malevolent way, but he'd been unable to establish a concrete connection between them and the Brotherhood site.

The Brotherhood site was well done. Whoever constituted the membership, it was obvious they were well-backed. The site was multi-leveled. Hyperlinks were prevalent throughout, directing the browser to various locations within and without the site. There were links to doctrinal statements, operational statements, vision and mission statements, and even links to other Web sites whose information could be advantageous to the average Brotherhood member.

But there was nothing he could find that provided even a hint as to what Operation Resurrection was, when and where it would be instituted, or who was the mastermind behind it.

Chancellor rubbed his eyes and sat back in his chair. He was tired. He looked around the office. It was still a shambles from the earlier attack. The windows had been replaced, but the interior was riddled with bullet holes. It still seemed miraculous that he wasn't killed.

Miracles? Chancellor leaned forward, closed the current computer screen, and brought up a search engine. He typed in the word *miracles* and waited for a response. It was not long in coming. He marveled at the number of sites the search engine had located.

For the next hour Chancellor was absorbed in the information he found on his screen. Miracles seemed to be as commonplace as air. Everyone had a story to tell, and every story, just like all the hate Web sites he'd located, had a common thread running through them. Only this time that common thread was not a black thread of hate but a golden thread of love, respect, and honor. God was that common thread. Chancellor sat mesmerized, reading with a new intensity.

His mind went to Nanny Collins. Everyone in Spring Valley knew the old lady was a religious fanatic. At least, that was the description most often appended to the old woman. But he was seeing Nanny Collins in a new light now. Just the last hour had opened his eyes to the possibility that miracles—true, supernatural exponents of an omnipotent God—actually existed.

Chancellor sat back again. His shoulders were tight and knotted, almost painful. He looked at his watch. Had he really been reading about miracles for the last hour? Where had the time gone?

But his investigation of miracles was not why he'd begun his research. There still loomed the specter of Operation Resurrection and its true intent. There was still the Brotherhood of the Ring polluting cyberspace with their wayward and warped doctrine. There was still the list of names of the dead and missing. And there were still no answers.

Maybe he did need a miracle. Maybe the whole state needed a miracle at this moment.

Chancellor got up and walked out into the town square. Clouds were building in from the west, and the sky was darkening. It seemed almost a precursor to whatever Operation Resurrection was. The clouds were dark and malevolent, almost angry in their texture. He could see lightning streaking from cloud to cloud, but the storm was too far away for the thunder to erupt in Spring Valley. It would not be long, however, before the storm broke with all its fury, and Chancellor wondered if the storm and the Brotherhood of the Ring would erupt at the same time.

The newspaper publisher turned left at the corner, and before he knew it, he unknowingly headed for Nanny Collins's house. *When you need a miracle,* he told himself, *go directly to the expert.* Nanny Collins was the expert on miracles, at least miracles in Spring Valley.

■   ■   ■

Where the feeling came from, Nanny Collins was not certain. But she never questioned the sensations that told her something was about to happen.

The television was switched on; she never missed the evening news programs. There was always someone needing prayer, and Nanny faithfully watched the news to discover prayer needs. She kept a pencil and paper by her chair so she could jot down the needs as they came across the screen.

The teasers tonight had mentioned flooding in India, a train crash in England, and, of all things, some sort of ruckus in the state's capital city. It was unusual for her own state capital to make the international news scene, but it was there tonight. She would have to pay particular attention to that story.

The news commentator came on, all slick and relaxed, standing in front of a set that attempted to convey a professional casual ambiance. For Nanny, the attempt fell short, but she was not interested in the setting, only the information.

". . . local police have said only that an apparent break-in went awry today. William Garrison, a local private investigator and ex–Naval Intelligence officer, was injured when alleged intruders cut their way into Garrison's house with an electric chainsaw. Garrison was taken to Doctor's Hospital and is reported in guarded condition. We will keep you updated on his progress." The cameraman pulled back to reveal a mass of emergency vehicles and police cars surrounding the scene.

Nanny scribbled the name, William Garrison, on her pad, then glanced back at the screen. Just as the camera was about to fade to black, she recognized a face in the crowd. Andrew Chapman—her Drew—was making his way into the house. *That was it!* she knew. Her prayers would be for William Garrison and Drew Chapman. The feeling was there, and now the television was confirming the object of tonight's prayers.

Nanny picked up the television remote control and switched off the device. Tonight she really needed to concentrate on her prayers. Just as the screen flicked off, there was a knock at her door. When she opened it, Robert Chancellor, the publisher of the *Spring Valley Courier,* was standing there.

Chancellor looked rather sheepish, Nanny thought, but she also had an inkling as to what brought the man to her house. She stepped aside, and the publisher entered without a word.

This, Nanny Collins thought, *will be a night to remember.*

CHAPTER TWENTY-EIGHT

Information flowed in from various sources. The Shepherd read and reread the scraps of reports he'd received in just the last hour.

He was sitting in an ornate room in his favorite chair. The wall was lined with books, mostly concerning theology, religion, and manifest destiny. A small glass of apple juice sat on a small end table along with the reports and a newspaper. It was his favorite room in the house, a place where he could be alone. A place to think. No one dared interrupt him when he was in this room.

The Shepherd glanced at the latest report. Brotherhood members were following Andrew Chapman, Robert Chancellor, and Sheriff Dewayne Lawrence. Jordyn Phillips was in Brotherhood custody at the moment, taken from the basement of Valley Community Church. State police colonel Samuel Reardon was still in ICU at Doctor's Hospital, well guarded. Now the worrisome William Garrison had just joined Reardon and Marty Akers at Doctor's Hospital. Garrison, Akers, and Reardon: three problems all wrapped up at one location, just waiting for the launch of Operation Resurrection. Once begun, the consolidated location would prove to be a tremendous advantage; Akers, Reardon, and Garrison could all be killed in one fell swoop.

Chapman was in Cincinnati, under constant surveillance by a Brotherhood member. As soon as Chapman had the Garrison reports, there would be no need to keep Chapman alive. Obstacles would be eliminated in rapid succession.

It was all coming together. The timing was precise. The cause was just. Operation Resurrection would be a new beginning—a definitive statement about the supremacy of his people over the other races of the world.

The early morning edition of the state's leading newspaper lay on the stand next to the Shepherd. The headlines were subdued and prophetic. "In Surprise Turn of Events, Governor O'Brien to Address CAM Tonight," the headline read. That would be the beginning, he knew. What was planned for the National Convention of the Caucus of American Minorities would show the world that the Brotherhood of the Ring was serious.

Operation Resurrection would begin in the Bubble. It would then sweep across the country like a massive scalpel, excising cancer from a diseased land. It was a grand vision, one with purpose and design. The theology of Christian Identity had defined the Operation, and the implementation of the Christian Initiative would see that Operation Resurrection functioned according to plan.

But there was one point of contention, one unknown factor. How much had Jordyn Phillips learned by accessing the CSA computer? The report was that she had acted alone and had told no one of her theory that a connection existed between Operation Resurrection, the Brotherhood, and the CSA computer system.

The Shepherd reached for the apple juice and sipped it delicately. It was still good and cold, with just a hint of bite. He replaced the glass and let his mind wander back to the creation of the huge database system the state had installed ostensibly to provide increased services to track groups and such. He smiled at the irony of it.

The CSA system did all it was designed to do—and much more. Still, he was a little dismayed that the worrisome Bannerman County prosecuting attorney had so easily seen through the subterfuge.

The Community Service Agency had been his brainchild. He had understood the necessity to identify the various minority groups that invaded the state periodically, groups whose only purpose seemed to be to drain the good, tax-paying citizens of resources. The Brotherhood had long ago prophesized the need to control or eliminate the troublesome "third-world races" from the state. The CSA computer had been one of the tools needed to accomplish just that. The system had, of course, been used for other purposes, some of them good. At least, that was the perception he—the Shepherd—had fostered. Perception was reality, reality was perception, and reality was about to take a twist.

The Shepherd chuckled to himself. Operation Resurrection was close; sanity was within reach, for that was what it actually meant. Sanity had been the victim of the latest influx of outsiders, people who did not belong, people who sucked the life from the very land to which they owed their existence.

But a new day was coming.

The phone next to the chair chimed. The Shepherd picked it up and listened for a moment. He said nothing; nothing was necessary. The Shepherd's acquiescence was in his silence, his compliance understood by the party who had called. He replaced the phone and smiled. Andrew Chapman had reached the federal savings and loan in downtown Cincinnati. It would not be long now.

CHAPTER TWENTY-NINE

The room was spinning, the walls, ceiling, and floor interchanging in a revolving series of colorful lights—an entire spectrum displayed against strange surroundings. Jordyn tried desperately to focus her vision, but she couldn't. She was cold, yet heat seemed to be rising from her body in a marked inconsistency. What was happening?

What had happened?

Jordyn sat up; her head hurt. There was a light source she couldn't identify. There was a burning sensation in her neck. Where had that come from?

Where had she been? Her memory was playing tricks on her. Hadn't she been in the basement of Valley Community Church with Joy Hartford?

Joy! *That was it.* She *had* been there at Valley Community. She'd been accessing the CSA computer program. The names!

The list!

Jordyn rubbed her neck as she tried to stand. Her rubbery legs would not cooperate, but her eyes were beginning to adjust to the gloom of the room. She remembered now. She'd been drugged. But by whom? To what end? Why? The questions flooded her brain; the answers did not come—at least not in this room.

The room. Where was she? She would begin with that question, find the answer, and move on from there.

Jordyn examined her surroundings. The room was circular, with stone walls and a high ceiling. The space had an oppressive feel about it. It was dark, with yellow light from a dozen candles providing the only illumination. If a room could be evil, this was just such a room. It was not just the feeling that an evil presence, a malevolent spirit, occupied the room; it was as if the walls, the floor, the ceiling—the very nature of the room itself—was evil.

Jordyn rubbed her eyes again, forcing herself to concentrate, forcing her brain to function and examine the room more closely. Her head still hurt. She rubbed her temples gently as she tried to force the pain from her head and neck.

Her eyes were becoming accustomed to the dim lighting, to the smoke rising from the candles. There was a large table in the center of the room—a round table constructed of oppressive wood. Equally heavy chairs surrounded the table. She counted thirteen chairs. It reminded her of the stories she had read as a child about King Arthur's Knights of the Round Table. The thought seemed silly and out of place, but she didn't smile at the image.

Jordyn slowly raised her head and peered into the darkness above her head. She could not clearly distinguish the ceiling. Her view went to the walls. They were stone, massive and heavy, like the room's furnishings. But there was something else too.

Around the circumference of the room, low and squat, was some sort of structure. A ledge set low into the wall, no more than two feet high, extending from the wall equidistantly. Jordyn moved toward the ledge, the headache and burning in her neck now forgotten.

There were objects situated on the ledge—small, white crosses that seemed to grow from the living rock. She moved closer.

"Interesting, don't you think?" a voice echoed against the hard walls.

Jordyn jumped, her heart racing, her pulse pounding in her veins.

She'd thought she was alone in the room, but now she knew better. She turned.

It had been a man's voice, but in the dimness she could not see anyone. From across the room she detected a swishing sound and saw the gentle movement of cloth. A figure materialized from the gloom.

The figure was of medium height and wore a blood-red robe with a matching hood. On the hood the Death's Head seemed to be laughing at her. As the figure approached, she could make out embroidered designs on the sleeves of the robe. They were the arrowhead and the feather images she had seen back at Valley Community Church, the ones Drew had explained to her, the emblems representing the Brotherhood. One was the Tyr-rune and the other the Toten-rune. The figures were chilling in their effect, frightening in their reality.

The man moved closer, making no attempt to remove the hood and reveal his identity.

"It's morbid," Jordyn answered, forcing herself to speak through mounting fear. Her words were weak; she recognized the effects of the drugs that had been administered. Joy had been there when that had happened. *Joy had held her!*

"Not so, my dear," the man said, his voice familiar.

"Morbid and probably illegal," Jordyn said, her strength beginning to return, fueled by the anger growing inside her.

The man laughed, the sound harsh and invasive in the enclosed, hard-walled space.

"Yes, illegal. If not, why hide down here in a dungeon, concealed from the rest of the world?" Jordyn was moving now, the movement forcing the effects of the drugs from her body. With each step, she felt stronger, more in control. The control she felt translated to her voice, revealing her determination. "You hide down here like rats in a cellar. Why? Who are you? What is it you want?"

The man moved slowly, closing the distance between Jordyn and himself. Jordyn was aware now, watching closely as the man moved, gauging the distance, estimating the man's strength by his movements, by his stature. The robe hindered further evaluation. If he was alone, she might have a chance. One-on-one. Even though he was a man, she was determined and just frightened enough to possibly overpower this apparition in the red robe.

"Rats in a cellar, you say?" the man answered.

Jordyn knew that voice! Where had she heard it before? Her mind was operating, but the drug's effects were still inhibiting her thought processes. The answer would not come.

"Rats in a cellar," the man repeated. "Not so, my dear. Saviors risen from the sepulcher would be a more accurate description," the man said, moving closer.

Jordyn's anger exploded to the surface. "Saviors? *Saviors?* I'm afraid you have an overinflated estimation of your value. I don't know what it is you think you are doing down here," she said, waving to take in the full extent of the oppressive room, "but I can certainly tell you that you are anything but a savior."

The man continued to move slowly, the hem of his robe brushing the stone floor. "You don't know what is about to occur? Do you expect us to believe that?"

Us? The man had said "Us." Plural. What did that mean? Was there someone else in the room, someone she could not see? Someone concealed deeper in the gloom? Or was he speaking of a group? A group like the Brotherhood of the Ring? Jordyn stood her ground as the man approached, straining to hear some other noise, something that might indicate that someone else was in the room. She heard nothing.

"I don't know what you are talking about." Jordyn replied. "What do you think is about to happen?"

The man laughed again, deep and bilious. "Think? I do not *think,* as you put it. I *know* what is about to take place. The machinery is already in motion, the wheels turning. It cannot be stopped. It *must* not be stopped."

Jordyn's fear returned. The last words had been spoken with a vehemence she recognized as pure hatred. There was something about hatred that renders even the most intelligent person immune to common sense and decency. Hatred was the most insidious infection in the world, and there was no antibiotic that could cure it. She sensed that kind of hate now. That was what this room and this man represented: hatred. Pure, unadulterated hatred.

Jordyn had never felt such revulsion before. She'd been exposed to murderers, rapists, and thieves, but none made her feel the way she felt at this moment. The detestation seemed to flow from beneath the red robe like a tidal wave of loathing that no amount of reason could staunch.

Her mind was functioning now, her body responding to her commands. Reason had returned; the effect of the drugs was gone.

Jordyn decided to take a chance. "You must be referring to that pathetic effort you people call Operation Resurrection. Surely you don't think you can get away with that. Not now. Now that your plot has been discovered."

Jordyn was not prepared for the reaction her words elicited. It was as if she had struck the red-robed figure with a baseball bat. It was not, she realized, the fact that she knew about Operation Resurrection, but the way in which she had described it that affected the man.

She could hear the breath catch in his throat. He stopped in his tracks, the red robe moving in and out as the man seemed to try and comprehend what he'd just heard. Then a scream erupted from him, the anguish of pent-up hatred and loathing.

The man attacked, moving swiftly, his robes shuffling along the stone floor.

The reaction caught her by surprise, but she quickly recovered. Jordyn waited. The man might be stronger, but the robes that he so proudly wore were turning out to be the one advantage Jordyn needed.

The man charged, an unearthly shriek coming from behind the red hood. Jordyn waited until the last moment, then easily stepped aside, like a bullfighter baiting an unsuspecting bull. She moved lightly, the effects of the drugs completely gone.

The man's momentum carried him past Jordyn. She watched him stumble into the far wall, crashing against the low-slung ledge of stone, scattering some of the small white crosses.

Her eyes had adjusted to the dim light. Details that had escaped her earlier were now in plain view. The darker recesses of the chamber were now in focus, revealing a larger area than she'd previously thought. There were two doors set in the stone walls. The small white crosses that adorned the small ledge came into focus. The height of the ceiling still seemed to reach into the heavens, but she could at least discern its limits. She quickly calculated that the ceiling was at least thirty feet high. Too high to offer a means of escape. The only chance was through one of the two doors. But even as she focused on the two doors, she realized escape was impossible.

She could hear the man in the red robe regaining his posture. But it was not the man's recovery that eliminated all hope from her mind. It was the three men standing along the perimeter of the circular room, their presence previously unnoticed due to their stillness.

The men all wore the same blood-red robes with the arrow and feather designs on their sleeves. These were the men of the Brotherhood of the Ring, she knew. And she knew that these men—for she knew they were men by their sheer size—were there for only one reason: to see that she remained in this place of hate and death.

"Forgive me in my haste," the man who'd charged said from behind her.

Jordyn turned now, resigned to her temporary fate. "I must have hit a nerve," she said smiling, hoping the smile was evident in the gloom.

"What you have done, my dear," the man said as he pulled at his hood, "is confirm what we suspected." The hood came off.

At first Jordyn stared in disbelief. Then suddenly it all began to make sense. *"You!"* Jordyn managed to say before she felt the sting of a second needle as it entered her flesh. The face she'd so easily recognized burned into her memory as darkness once again engulfed her.

The nightmare continued.

CHAPTER THIRTY

The ride from the airport had taken longer than anticipated. The taxi had departed the airport and headed for Cincinnati, crossing over the Ohio River on the Interstate 71 bridge. Drew had seen Paul Brown Stadium on his right as the taxi crossed the bridge, but he'd ignored it. He'd had time for introspection; his thoughts going to Jordyn, Spring Valley, and to what he had learned about the Brotherhood of the Ring. Drew realized he did not have as much evidence as he would like. Still, he had the ring Mike Reece had discovered out on Hallis Road. Hard evidence was scarce, but at the same time, the Brotherhood seemed to want credit for the atrocities in Bannerman County. He'd not turned the ring in as evidence, retaining it as a reminder of what had happened and what was driving him. He was a cop, but that was not enough. Not now.

It had been too many years, Drew thought. Too many years doing what he was now doing and too many trying to disguise what he really wanted from life. Nanny Collins knew. Drew smiled at the thought, the nostalgia of the past intruding. Nanny C. always seemed to know, right down to his innermost thoughts. He had no doubt that Nanny had prayed last night. Prayer was her ministry, she'd always said, and Drew was just beginning to understand what the old woman meant by that statement. He felt like praying right now. He craved the inner peace that seemed to come naturally to Nanny C. But praying for what?

Jordyn? She was one of the reasons this sudden feeling of melancholy had so unexpectedly expressed itself during the taxi ride. He'd not been prepared for his reaction at seeing Jordyn again after so many years. He thought he'd successfully pushed the earlier memories of her from his mind. But the vision of her that first morning at the Carter House had been one he'd been unable to purge from his memory, despite repeated attempts. And he foolishly had to admit that he'd not been trying that hard lately. She'd been a vision of loveliness. The loveliness had been only the beginning. She had exuded quiet confidence and not-so-common practicality as well. Drew had no doubt that she would be a formidable opponent in a courtroom.

And the sight of Jordyn had stirred him even more deeply in the same way the short visit to Nanny Collins had reawakened a longing he'd thought long dead. Between the two, Nanny C. and Jordyn, Drew knew everything he wanted in life seemed to be located in Spring Valley, and for the first time since the Hallis Road investigation had begun, Drew knew what he would do as soon as he finished the investigation of the Brotherhood.

"We're here, mister," the taxi driver said over his shoulder.

Drew peered out the window of the taxi. Second Ohio Valley Savings and Loan occupied a redbrick building whose door lintel proudly displayed the construction date of 1908. The mud for the brick had been dug from the Ohio River a year before the construction date. Eighty years later the building's exterior had been renovated and returned to its original state. The cab driver informed Drew that the area was known as the German area. Drew acknowledged the information, but it meant nothing to him. His only interest lay in what he would find in the safe-deposit box in the savings and loan.

"Wait for me," Drew said to the driver. "I shouldn't be more than a few minutes, and then I'm headed back to the airport."

"Will do," the driver answered. "I'll be in the parking lot."

Drew got out and went in. The inside of Second Ohio Valley S & L was a masterpiece of turn-of-the-century architecture, obviously as lovingly restored as the outside of the building had been. Drew went directly to the window marked as the safe-deposit-box window. He'd known the S & L would refuse access to anyone but the original signer of the application form, so he'd hurriedly arranged for a federal court warrant authorizing access. In minutes he was through the process and had handed the key he'd gotten from William Garrison to the young woman in charge. She inserted two keys, opened the box, and then left discreetly.

Drew waited until the woman was out of sight, then opened the hinged top of the box. Two separate but identical bundles lay in the box. Drew pulled them out and opened the first. It was a formal report produced by Garrison. It resembled a legal brief, the pages enclosed in a blue cover carefully stapled at the top. He quickly scanned the report, picking out key phrases and words as he perused the document. The Brotherhood of the Ring was there, as well as Operation Resurrection. In the first few pages there were no proper names, nothing to indicate who was behind the operation. The report detailed the process through which Garrison had obtained the information, but little else. Drew scanned the remaining material quickly, searching for names, for specifics, for *proof.*

On the fifth page names began to appear. Drew recognized powerful men within the state's political and business environs. He felt the hair on the back of his neck stand up. What he was reading was an obscenity.

Impossible! Insanity!

Operation Resurrection was an abomination against not only the citizens of this state, but against all mankind.

Still, one crucial name was missing, Drew realized. Nothing pointed to the titular head of this nightmare. The identity of the Shepherd did not appear in the pages.

■　■　■

Gordon Larkin parked his red pickup across the street from Second Ohio Valley Savings and Loan and wondered what the heck he was doing in the German section of Cincinnati. Not that it mattered much. His assignment was to stay with the man who had just gotten out of the taxi and entered the building. There was no need for Larkin to expose himself by following. The man would come out, and since the taxi had pulled into the parking lot of the S & L, it was obvious the man would be coming out shortly.

Larkin leaned back against the seat and peered at the front door of Second Ohio through narrow slits of eyelids. He couldn't chance falling asleep, but a short rest while he waited for the man to exit was not out of the question. Larkin involuntarily closed his eyes. The sun streaming through the windshield worked on him like a mild sedative. In less than a minute he was asleep.

■   ■   ■

Drew found it on the seventeenth page. It was not exactly what he was searching for, but it was more than he had before. He read the text with growing interest and dismay. His dismay quickly turned to horror as he comprehended what Garrison had written.

It was pure speculation on Garrison's part, Drew realized as he read. But the man's conclusions were based on logic and good detective work. The conclusions were supported by the details.

Operation Resurrection was a nightmare in the making, and if what he was reading was even close to the truth, it had already begun.

Drew bundled the two copies of the report together, closed the safe-deposit box, and headed for the waiting taxi.

"Where's the nearest bank?" Drew asked the driver as he got in the taxi.

"You just left it, mister," the man answered, a slight tinge of amusement in his voice.

Drew ignored the man's tone. "Not this one. Another one. Another federally chartered bank."

"Ohio National has a branch just down the street."

"Take me there," Drew ordered.

The driver shook his head, and again Drew ignored the implications. The taxi exited the parking lot and headed for Ohio National Bank.

■　■　■

Gordon Larkin jerked awake when he heard the taxi come out of the parking lot. He'd gone to sleep! He knew if he lost his prey, he would be in big trouble. He frantically looked around, catching a glimpse of the yellow taxi in his driver's side mirror. The taxi was headed in the opposite direction from which he was facing.

Larkin gunned the idling pickup, the tires squealing on the pavement as he jockeyed the truck around and behind the retreating taxi. He cursed as he accelerated down the roadway. He'd almost blown it.

■　■　■

Drew heard the squealing tires and turned in his seat. The same red pickup he'd noticed at the airport was behind him now. There were no coincidences anymore. The man in the truck was following him, which made the man a member of the Brotherhood.

The taxi wheeled into the parking lot of Ohio National Bank. "This is it, mister."

Drew was out of the taxi in seconds. "Wait," was all he said.

Twenty minutes later he was back. "To the airport," Drew ordered.

"Whatever, mister," the taxi driver said. "This is going to cost you, you know."

Drew tossed a hundred dollar bill over the seat. "Take it out of that and keep the change. When we get to the airport, find a place where you can let me off without someone following us and seeing what is happening."

The taxi driver perked up. "You mean someone is following us?"

"Just do what I said," Drew shot back.

The driver concentrated on his driving, and the ride back to the airport took less time than the ride to the S & L.

"I can let you off around this corner," the driver announced. "You want me to stop or just slow down?"

"Slow down. Be sure the red pickup behind us can see us as we round the corner, but be certain he's out of sight when I get out."

"The red pickup," the driver repeated. "Got it. I thought that might be the one. He's been staying with us the whole time. Never had anything like this happen before. My wife's not going to believe it. Corner coming up."

The taxi rounded a corner formed by the convergence of two airport buildings. Drew waited, his attention focused on the red pickup. True to his word, the driver slowed just as the red pickup disappeared from sight. Drew hurried out of the vehicle and walked briskly toward the access door.

The taxi sped away, lengthening the distance between it and the truck as the truck came around the corner.

Drew watched from inside the building. The ploy had worked, but the realization that the Brotherhood was solidly on his trail was bothersome. He would have to be more careful.

Then a thought that was even more worrisome struck him: if the Brotherhood of the Ring was watching him this closely, how closely were they watching Jordyn, Chancellor, and others?

Jordyn. He hadn't heard from her. If the Brotherhood was worried about what he would find out, how far would they go? What he'd read in the Garrison report told him the group would stop at nothing to fulfill Operation Resurrection. And that meant eliminating him and others. Among the others was Jordyn Phillips, and that he could not allow. Not now.

The return flight was announced just as Drew entered terminal C, and he went directly to the boarding and check-in area. He would have a flight of thirty minutes or less. His concern for Jordyn's safety would make those thirty minutes seem like an eternity.

CHAPTER THIRTY-ONE

Henderson stormed as he listened to McGrath curse Gordon Larkin.

"What do you mean, 'He lost him'?" Henderson asked over the phone.

"Just that. That fool Larkin lost Chapman at the airport. It's a good thing you didn't make it to Cincinnati. You can pick up Chapman when he gets back there."

"Did Larkin say Chapman found the reports Garrison wrote?"

McGrath's voice came back instantly. "Larkin says Chapman went to Second Ohio Valley Savings & Loan and came out about half an hour later with something. He couldn't be sure what it was."

"The reports. It has to be," Henderson interjected.

"Maybe. *Probably*. The problem is that Chapman went directly to a branch of Ohio National Bank, stayed another half hour, then came back and headed for the airport."

"Why would he do that?" Henderson asked.

This time McGrath's voice conveyed the frustration he was feeling with Henderson. "He probably put a copy of the report in another safe-deposit box, making certain it was in a federal installation."

"Guy's smarter than we thought."

"Maybe smarter than you thought, but I was afraid of something like this. It won't matter. When Chapman gets back, you kill him."

Henderson hesitated, his pulse quickening at the direct command, then asked, "What about the copy in that Ohio bank?"

"Chapman will have the registration papers for the second safe-deposit box on him. You get to him first, kill him, retrieve the papers and the copy of the report he's carrying, and we'll be home free. Even if we don't get the copy in the bank, it will just sit there. If we can't get it, no one can."

Henderson felt a flush of anticipation as he listened to McGrath disconnect on the other end. The time had come, and he planned to relish the experience. The question was when, where, and how to do the job. He checked his watch. He could assume that Chapman would be returning immediately, which didn't leave him much time. He needed to formulate a plan, a plan that would do away with Andrew Chapman.

It's a good day after all, Henderson thought as he headed for the Delta ticket counter to check the incoming flights from Cincinnati.

■ ■ ■

Bannerman County sheriff Dewayne Lawrence wondered what was happening. He had just returned from Robert Chancellor's office, but the newspaper publisher had not been there. He had called the office of Jordyn Phillips and was told Jordyn would not be in the office for the next few days. A similar attempt to locate Andrew Chapman had been equally unsuccessful.

What was going on? There was one more call he could make. The person with whom he would speak might have an idea of Chapman's location. It was unlikely he would know about Chancellor or Phillips.

Lawrence pulled the evening edition newspaper toward him and scanned the headlines again. The headlines for the later edition were substantially different from the early morning edition. The lead story that garnered his interest concerned the substitution of William Benson, lieutenant governor of the state, for Governor Patrick O'Brien as principal speaker at the National Convention of the Caucus of American Minorities scheduled to begin tonight at the Bubble. It had been a last-minute substitution.

Something was not right. Although he had no facts or concrete evidence to support his conclusion, Lawrence felt deep in his gut that whatever Operation Resurrection was, it would begin tonight at the Bubble.

Sheriff Lawrence picked up the phone and dialed an unlisted number. It was answered immediately.

"What's going on?" Lawrence asked the man on the other end. He listened intently before disconnecting. His gut feeling had been correct.

Tonight was the night.

■   ■   ■

McGrath felt the blood rushing through his veins at breakneck speed. He knew if he looked into a mirror, an act which he seldom did, he would recognize the flush of unrestrained anticipation.

He'd just ordered the death of Andrew Chapman, and that alone was enough to boost his spirits. The mere thought of having the power of life and death was an exciting one. But his flush of excitement was due to more than just the order he'd issued to Henderson a few moments ago. Mostly his exhilaration was directly tied to what he read in the newspaper.

William Benson would be the speaker at the Caucus of American Minorities tonight. It had first been reported that Governor Patrick O'Brien was well enough to be the speaker, and that would have put a serious kink in the plans for the inauguration of Operation Resurrection. Now, however, O'Brien was claiming a slight relapse. A spokesman for the governor's office said that the governor did not have the strength to attend, so Benson would fill in for him.

McGrath smiled. After all, that had been the original plan. It was imperative that William Benson address the CAM convention this night.

A soft knock on the door drew McGrath's attention away from the newspaper and his musings.

"Come in," McGrath ordered.

The man who entered was dressed in what has become known as "business casual." The man's slacks were neatly pressed, his knit shirt was buttoned at the neck, and his black loafers gleamed.

McGrath was not certain he liked the new protocol. He was a suit-and-tie man at the office and a blue-jeans-and-work-shirt person outside. The idea of "business casual" seemed to be a major drawing card to the younger generation, but McGrath didn't like the look or the underlying attitude that came with it. Even though the young man was one of the up-and-coming members of the Brotherhood and an expert in the development of overseas resources, McGrath worried about the man's depth of commitment.

"What is it, Eddie?" McGrath asked.

Eddie Trevor stopped in his tracks. "The girl. What do you want us to do with her?"

McGrath turned his back and looked out on the compound that was the headquarters of McGrath Oil. He'd just ordered the death of Andrew Chapman, but there was something about ordering the same thing for Jordyn Phillips that ran contrary to his nature.

"Let's hold off on that decision for a while. We'll have a clearer picture after tonight. She won't be a problem where she is. Just keep an eye on her."

"Joshua—"

"*Mister* McGrath," McGrath corrected Trevor. That was another thing he didn't like about this generation. They thought they had the right to call anyone by their first name, as if they were casual acquaintances. Informality, as far as Joshua McGrath was concerned, was just another sign that Operation Resurrection must go forward as quickly as possible. The operation would be an eye-opener for more than just the minorities in the state and around the country. It would usher in a more civil society, one based on respect and influence. The change was long overdue, McGrath thought.

"*Mister* McGrath," Trevor said, an edge in his voice. "We can watch her, but we will need to make a decision shortly."

"And we will. *I* will make the decision, and *I* will decide when to let you know what that decision is. In the meantime, keep her locked up and out of sight. You got that?"

"Yes, sir," Trevor answered. He turned and left the office.

Tonight, McGrath thought. Tonight would be a new beginning.

His next move would be to contact Jefferson Caine in the capital and give him the go-ahead to eliminate Martin Akers.

Operation Resurrection was on track.

CHAPTER THIRTY-TWO

Hate is an interesting emotion, the Shepherd thought to himself. It was an emotion said to be born in anticipation and nurtured in darkness and shadows, making it an emotion to avoid. But that was wrong, he knew. Hate was not always bad; there was a creative pulse to hate, an overriding imperative that demanded the objects of hate be worthy of such a strong emotion. And certainly the objects of hate as expressed by Operation Resurrection were worthy of the hatred he now felt seething within him.

Too long the hate had been quelled—subdued and suppressed according to the "politically correct" agendas of a culturally restricted society. But a society that ignored the basic tenets of what the Brotherhood believed was no society at all. A society that shunned the clear interpretations of the Bible, particularly the teaching found in Deuteronomy, was nothing more than a chaotic accumulation of polar ethnic backgrounds—a grab bag of individuals seeking only what was best for themselves, caring not for their fellowman. *That,* he knew, was the basic flaw in society today. All the talk about a multiethnic, multilingual, multifaceted society was nothing more than a semantic smokescreen. Such a society was not possible. Regardless of what most people in the United States thought, all men were not created equal, and no one understood that underlying rationalization better than he. After all, had not God himself chosen his people?

But the world would know when this night was over. Everything was set in motion. Operation Resurrection would initiate the beginning of national change. Of course, some would call it national regression, but again, those were the ones who did not understand the Brotherhood teachings.

Unfortunately, there was a fly in the ointment, and that fly was Andrew Chapman and his cohorts. Chapman, according to all accounts, had obtained copies of the report Marty Akers had funded and William Garrison had penned. Those reports must not see the light of day. Apparently Chapman had placed one copy in a branch of Ohio National Bank in Cincinnati. He had the other copy with him. As soon as Willie Henderson killed the troublesome investigator, that copy would be secure. The other copy would simply remain indefinitely in the bowels of the bank.

Jordyn Phillips would disappear as well. Robert Chancellor and Dewayne Lawrence were the other two people who had the list of names that could create havoc for the Brotherhood. Even though the names were not all-inclusive, they were important. The two men would have to be dealt with.

The Shepherd's mind relaxed. Contingencies were covered. Operation Resurrection would go forward tonight. Those who thought they were in a position to stop it would be dealt with.

Order would be restored.

■　■　■

Cecil Barlow had worked for the maintenance division of the Midwest Convention Center and Sports Complex—the official name of the Bubble before advertising rights had been sold to that cursed software company—since the structure had opened almost twelve years ago. In all those years he had never dared dream it might be possible that he would have the opportunity to make a significant contribution to the plans of the Brotherhood of the Ring. But now, not only was he about to contribute greatly to the cause—in this case, Operation Resurrection—he was an all-important factor in the initial act that would begin this night.

Barlow skirted the central power control room and headed to check his work. He, along with eleven other Brotherhood members, had waited seven years for this night. It had taken that long to put in place all the necessary material and personnel. Getting the men in the necessary positions had been the most difficult. Since the administration of the Bubble fell under the state's civil service codes, the Bubble maintenance workers were all state employees. It had taken seven long years to get enough Brotherhood members in strategic positions to prepare everything that would make tonight successful.

Barlow pulled a master key from his pocket and opened the door in front of him. He needed to make the last-minute checks to be sure all was ready. He checked the time. Already the members of that despicable organization—the Caucus of American Minorities—were filing into the huge building. Barlow grinned to himself. This would be the last night of their miserable lives, he told himself. With that thought in mind, Cecil Barlow closed the door behind him, thumbed the button on his cell phone, and began the final countdown to death.

CHAPTER THIRTY-THREE

Jordyn slowly regained consciousness. She opened her eyes. What had she been injected with? Her head hurt and she could tell by her reactions that some of the drug was still in her system. Lights and colors still swirled before her eyes. Not so drastically that she could not think, but enough to be annoying. Still, her mind was working, and that was a good sign. The effects of the drug would soon be gone.

Jordyn sat up and looked around. This was not the room she had been in before. Not the dungeonlike room where she had seen . . .

Had she really seen what she thought? Had any of it been real? If so, how was such a thing possible?

Jordyn rubbed her temples between her thumb and forefinger. The pain was fading slowly, and the lights and colors were swirling less and less. She could think.

The last truly coherent recollection she had was of being in the basement of Valley Community Church. Joy Hartford! That had been the beginning.

She had been working at the CSA computer when she had been attacked.

But attacked by whom? And why? Joy had been holding her arms when she'd felt the sting in her neck. She'd been drugged, and Joy Hartford had been in on it!

Jordyn's mind raced now. What exactly was Joy involved in? The conversation at Banners had led to the Community Services computer. Jordyn remembered the list of names. Where was the list? She looked around, but the list was nowhere to be found. Where had it gone?

Joy! Again the name rang as clearly as a bell in her mind. Joy had the list. There was no other explanation. But why would she want it? What was the connection? Thoughts were beginning to tumble and fall over themselves. She was becoming confused. *Back up, Jordyn,* she told herself. Take your time. Think. *Reason!*

Start from the beginning.

The beginning. Banners. The conversation with Joy. The CSA computer. The list of names. The burning sting of the injection and Joy Hartford holding her arms while the drug took effect. It was too bizarre to believe. Joy had something to do with the missing and murdered people whose names appeared on the list and in the Community Services Agency computer system.

The CSA computer system was a state system whose central server was located in the Housing and Urban Development Division building of state government. She remembered that someone had pushed the CSA program through the state legislature, but who was it?

Her mind was working but not as rapidly as she'd first thought. Who had taken the lead in the development of the CSA system?

Benson. That was it! Lieutenant Governor William Benson had pushed for the system. The lieutenant governor had strong-armed and manipulated the state legislatuare to put the CSA system in place—a system whose main function was to track documented and undocumented aliens and provide community support and living services for them.

Except. Except what? What was it? Jordyn shook her head. Thoughts tumbled over thoughts, intertwining themselves in a confusing montage of information. The colors were fading, waning as the drugs in her system were metabolized. Surely she could figure this out.

The Community Services Agency was a good thing, a provider for the less fortunate, a bulwark against the unknown. But that was not all it was, Jordyn now realized.

Every name on the list Robert Chancellor had shared with her had been in the computer. Names had had notations beside them. The Toten-rune. Every name had had a direct connection in the state system.

The Brotherhood had somehow tapped into the CSA system!

The truth hit her like a hammer. The Community Services computer was not just keeping track of aliens; it was providing pertinent information for the elimination of those same people.

The state system was helping to kill people!

"You know," a voice said. It was not the voice of the person she'd seen in the dungeonlike room last night. It was *last night,* wasn't it? Jordyn realized she had no way of knowing. There were no windows in the room where she was being held. No clocks. She checked her wrist; her watch was gone. How long had she been here?

The voice spoke again. "Confusing, isn't it? Not knowing the hour, day, or even the week?"

The week! Jordyn felt panic rise in her throat. *Week.* Had she been sequestered for weeks instead of just hours? Had she been trapped in this place that long? No, she decided instantly. All her physical signs pointed to having been held for no more than a few hours. She would have to be more careful, more attentive to herself, to what her body was trying to tell her. The first thing was that while she was thirsty, there were no signs of feeding tubes or IVs that would certainly be necessary to maintain a noneating human being in such conditions. The other clue was simpler yet: her clothes still fit her. Not even massive, continuous IVs could maintain body weight over the course of weeks.

No, she had been in this awful place only hours, a day at the most.

"You're thinking. I can see it in your eyes. That's what got you here in the first place," the voice said.

Joy Hartford! It was her voice, but not exactly. The voice was coming over a speaker system. The distortion was minor, but it was there.

"Why, Joy?" Jordyn asked, hoping the inclusion of her name would jolt the woman.

"I think you've already figured that out, Jordyn," Joy answered over the speaker system. "And even if you haven't, far be it from me to tell you."

"In the church. The Scripture verse out of Deuteronomy. It's the basis for the philosophy of Christian Identity. You and Kerry are Brotherhood members."

"I told everyone you were too smart," Joy said.

"But you can't be part of that. It's insane."

The voice from the speaker rose to an agonizing timber that reverberated within the chamber where Jordyn remained trapped.

"Insane? *Insane?* I'll tell you what's insane," the pastor's wife continued, her voice rising and falling as if in agony. "Insanity is letting every foreigner who arrives at our borders uninvited into this country to take advantage of what we've worked for. They are the dregs of the earth, the mud races who were discarded by God. *We* built this country, and now there are those who would flush it down the toilet all in the name of liberalism and good conscience. Garbage!"

Jordyn felt the headache returning, but not because of the drugs. What she was hearing spew forth from the mouth of her friend was more than she could comprehend. It wasn't possible! She'd never thought such hate existed in a rational world. But perhaps that was the problem. Certainly Joy Hartford was anything but rational at the moment. Her voice was not that of a clear-thinking person. It was the voice of someone whose entire being was consumed by hate and loathing.

"You've got to let me go, Joy," Jordyn said in a level voice, hoping the soothing tone would have an effect on her friend.

"After tonight, we will set everyone free," Joy said, her voice harsh and dry.

"What do you mean?"

"You already know."

"Operation Resurrection," said Jordyn in a low, almost reverent voice.

"Yes. Operation Resurrection. It begins tonight, but tonight is only the beginning. After tonight's success, we will stand united in our quest to save this nation."

A sharp click signaled that the speaker connection had been terminated.

"Joy?" Jordyn called. There was no answer. "Joy!" The speaker remained silent.

Tonight was the night, but what exactly was about to take place? And who would stand united? Jordyn thought about the other groups, the hate groups Robert Chancellor had named. Were all these groups about to come together to wage open war against all of humanity? Jordyn felt a chill sweep over her, almost as if someone or something had entered the room with her. Had that been the case, Jordyn realized the only thing that could have such an effect on her was the presence of pure evil.

And pure evil was what she'd heard over the speaker system only moments earlier. Whatever Operation Resurrection was, it was totally evil.

CHAPTER THIRTY-FOUR

The Canadair Regional Jet touched down only twenty-one minutes after takeoff.

"We had a little tailwind," the pilot said over the cabin intercom. "We've arrived nine minutes early. Use the time wisely," the young pilot joked as he taxied to his assigned gate. He did not know, nor would he ever know, that those nine minutes would save Andrew Chapman's life.

▪ ▪ ▪

Drew retrieved the Garrison report from the empty seat next to him and followed three men and one woman off the jet. He'd studied the report during the twenty-odd minutes they'd been airborne, reading it through twice while making small notations in the margins, some with question marks. What he had gleaned from the readings was even more troubling than what he initially thought.

Several points were clarified. Operation Resurrection definitely existed; Robert Chancellor had been right about that. The operation was a plot of the Brotherhood of the Ring, and from what Drew could tell, it would commence at a place and time not disclosed in the report. What the report *did* say was that the operation would involve Brotherhood members and a large group of minorities, apparently a *single* large group of minorities. The idea, as far as Drew could tell, was to kill as many members of designated minority groups at one time as was feasible. The groundwork for the operation had already been laid. The whole idea was so abhorrent to Drew that he had had to stop reading at that point. It was beyond belief that so much hate could be based on nothing more than ethnic origin. Still, Drew knew that such hate existed. In fact, it always had. Yet there was one factor even more disturbing which was part of the Brotherhood's rationale: they used the Bible—out of context—to justify the mass murder.

Drew thought back to his Brotherhood days. All in all it was an innocent and carefree time. Protesting had been about the only form of rebellion he'd participated in—certainly nothing like this. Over the years, the Brotherhood had somehow taken an execrable twist and had undergone a change in philosophy that not only supported the hate process but demanded it. Yet even the word *hate* did not seem an adequate expression of what Drew had read in the Garrison report. *Revulsion* was more descriptive. And the fact that such revulsion existed on this earth was, for Drew, beyond belief.

But exist it did, and Drew had pondered that thought as he'd perused the report. To do what was outlined in the Garrison report would require a large number of minorities to be present in one place at one time.

Drew walked up the ramp and into the terminal building. The news kiosk in the center of the concourse caught his eye. The headlines announced the beginning of the National Convention of the Caucus of American Minorities. CAM was meeting tonight in the Bubble.

CAM! The Caucus of American Minorities!

Tonight! The Bubble! Close to thirty thousand men and women of varying minority groups all meeting at one place at the same time!

That was it! It didn't take a genius to know that such an environment was too target-rich to be passed over by the warped mind-set of the Brotherhood.

Drew picked up the paper.

"If you're going to read it, buddy, pay for it," the man behind the kiosk counter said.

"Sorry," Drew said, handing the man a five-dollar bill and turning away.

"Hey. Your change, mister," the kiosk operator yelled to Drew.

Drew kept walking, his thoughts absorbed in the story he was reading.

■   ■   ■

Henderson checked the arrival monitor on his right as he headed for the arrival gate of the Delta flight on which Andrew Chapman would arrive. His eyes caught the flashing icon next to Chapman's flight. He stopped dead in his tracks. The flashing icon indicated that the flight had already arrived.

The flight was early!

Henderson broke into a jog. Normally, "arrival" meant the plane had touched down on the runway. It was not necessarily an indication the plane had made it to the gate. The problem, Henderson realized, was he did not know how long the arrival icon had been flashing.

He cursed as his jog changed to an all-out sprint. He had his orders. They had come from Joshua McGrath, and that meant they had to be carried out.

Henderson skidded to a stop at the arrival gate of Chapman's flight and looked in horror at the parked plane. A service crew was already scurrying around the tiny aircraft, preparing it for a return flight. That meant all passengers had disembarked.

He felt his stomach muscles constrict painfully. He quickly scanned the crowd, hoping to catch a glimpse of Chapman. The CID agent was nowhere to be seen.

Henderson headed back up the concourse the way he'd just come. It was the only exit route Chapman could have taken, and despite the fact that he did not know the exact time of the plane's arrival, it couldn't have been that long ago. Chapman had to be in the terminal, and if he was, Henderson knew he could find him.

What really irked him was the dawning fact that he had passed Chapman on the concourse! In his haste to reach the arrival gate, he had run past Chapman.

As he jogged back up the concourse, Henderson carefully examined each face he passed. Chapman was not among them.

Henderson couldn't believe it. He'd formulated the rudiments of a plan after he'd received the phone call from McGrath, but the plan he'd envisioned included picking up Chapman as he disembarked the plane. Now those plans were changing as he hurried up the concourse. What if he couldn't find Chapman? Larkin in Cincinnati had lost him at that airport, and Henderson remembered McGrath's reaction. Now it looked as if Henderson had compounded the error. McGrath would not be happy. And if McGrath was not happy, how would the Shepherd feel? Chills ran up Henderson's spine at the thought.

Just as he rounded the last corner of the concourse, where all the concourses joined, he caught sight of a bobbing head that resembled Chapman. Henderson pushed through the crowd, following the bobbing and weaving head. It had to be Chapman.

If it was, he would have to follow him. It would have been easier to kill the CID agent within the confines of the building. Henderson would have simply shot the meddlesome agent and walked away. It worked every time, just like when Michael Corleone had killed that stupid police chief and his Sicilian boss in *The Godfather*. Panic would have reigned. The resulting chaos would have provided sufficient cover. The police would have received a different story from every interview conducted. Yes, it would have been easier, but if the man now exiting the terminal was Chapman, the alternative plan Henderson was hatching would work just as well.

■   ■   ■

Drew walked rapidly to his car which was parked in the short-term parking area. Considering all he had learned about Operation

Resurrection from the Garrison report, now learning that the CAM convention was tonight was too much of a coincidence for him to be comfortable. He had to get to the Bubble.

The news story also said that Lieutenant Governor William Benson would be the keynote speaker. The governor's health had prevented his appearance. That meant Benson would be present when Operation Resurrection began, if it began in the Bubble. Benson again. The evidence was almost irrefutable.

Drew searched his memory for a connection between the Brotherhood and Lieutenant Governor Benson but could not immediately connect the two. Nevertheless, Drew was certain that whatever Operation Resurrection was, Benson knew about it, perhaps had a hand in it, and it was important for Benson to be the keynote speaker at tonight's meeting of the Caucus of American Minorities.

Maybe, Drew thought, the speech contained some triggering phrase, some coded message, that would set Operation Resurrection in motion. That had to be it. And whatever that phrase or code was, he had to stop it.

■   ■   ■

It was Chapman!

Willie Henderson watched as Chapman got into his car and headed for the parking lot exit. Henderson ran to jump behind the wheel of his nearby pickup and pulled out, keeping Chapman's car in sight, knowing with almost 100 percent certainty where the CID agent was heading.

Henderson had caught a glimpse of the blue bound report and guessed it was the Garrison report. Chapman also had a newspaper, probably the one containing the front-page story about tonight's convention of the Caucus of American Minorities. The Garrison report most certainly contained a reference to the event, if not in specific phrasing, certainly in terms specific enough for Chapman to link Operation Resurrection and the CAM convention. Henderson had no doubt that Chapman had figured out that something was going to happen tonight.

Henderson paid his parking ticket when his time came, his eyes glued to Chapman's car. He was right. Chapman was headed downtown. Downtown meant the Bubble and the CAM convention.

Henderson smiled. Chapman may have put most of it together, but it would do him no good. Henderson opened the glove compartment and pulled out a Smith and Wesson .357 magnum pistol. The powerful pistol had enough penetrating power to blow right through the thin veneer of Chapman's automobile. Even if he couldn't get a clean shot at the CID agent, the pistol's inherent power would make up for the shortcomings.

Henderson accelerated, his eyes locked on Chapman's vehicle. It would have been easier in the airport. There was no doubt about that, but he was finding that the adrenalin rush he was feeling at the chase more than compensated for missing Chapman in the airport. Willie Henderson was in his element.

CHAPTER THIRTY-FIVE

The official attendance count was slightly more than twenty-nine thousand. The National Convention of the Caucus of American Minorities had exceeded even its own expectations. CAM members had come from every state and territory.

The agenda for the first night was simple: the opening speech of welcome and the passage of a single resolution expressing CAM's support of the current president of the United States in his effort to stem the overwhelming violence and chaos in Third-World nations. It sounded like an innocuous resolution, but passage would carry a message to the rest of the world: this U.S. president had the broad-based support he needed to address injustices, not only in the Third World, but in the U.S. as well. It was a serious statement coming from CAM, and there was speculation that the resolution would cause a ripple effect throughout the entire civilized world. Such was the influence and dedication of CAM members.

Governor Patrick O'Brien had been scheduled to offer the keynote address, but an apparent relapse had shifted the responsibility to Lieutenant Governor William Benson.

The Bubble was ablaze with lights, banners, and displays. The economic prowess of the varied ethnic groups within the United States had long been recognized, but seldom had it been on display as it was this night. The almost thirty thousand people moved en masse, their movements akin to a tidal wave moving inland from an open sea.

The convention's opening address by Pierre Cardenas, CAM's president, was scheduled to begin at 7:00 P.M. sharp. Lieutenant Governor Benson's address was scheduled for 8:30.

Operation Resurrection was scheduled for 8:35.

■ ■ ■

Cecil Barlow made the final checks to the equipment that would shoulder much of the burden for the accomplishment of Operation Resurrection, at least in the initial stage. All the necessary equipment was in place, connected, and functioning. The plan was brilliant in its simplicity, Barlow thought, a testimony to the brilliance of the Brotherhood leadership, particularly the Shepherd.

Barlow was checking the last of the external units that had been connected to the internal systems of the Bubble. The explanation for the additional equipment now ringing the exterior of the huge facility was so simple that he had as yet not been questioned about it. Nor did he anticipate any questions. Of course, should a query arise, the clarification was succinct and easily understandable.

The vibrator on his cell phone notified Barlow of an incoming call. He thumbed the activation button.

"Barlow here." He listened as the voice on the other end spoke. "Understood," Barlow answered when the voice ceased. "All my men are ready. We will activate when Benson gives the word," he continued. "Eight-thirty should be just about right. Maybe as late as nine o'clock, but not much later than that. It makes no difference, though. The Brotherhood is prepared."

As the maintenance supervisor of the Bubble thumbed the button on his cell phone to cut the connection, a thin shaft of light reflected off the Death's Head of the ring he wore. At that moment, Cecil Barlow felt all the power and pride that had drawn him to the Brotherhood of the

Ring. Barlow was unaware that it was the power and pride of hell and death.

■   ■   ■

Robert Chancellor halted momentarily at Nanny Collins's front porch. He noticed a slight movement in the growing shadows just to the right of the house, where overgrown bushes mingled with the shadows. When he looked more closely, however, nothing was there. *Did I imagine it?* he wondered. He looked to the left. There was something in that direction too. There *was* movement—furtive, restrained, as if someone wanted him to know they were there but nevertheless was reluctant to advertise the fact to others. Chancellor swiftly redirected his gaze back to the original location where he thought he had first noticed the surreptitious movement. It was gone; all was deathly still. He swung back to his left. *That* movement was gone too. Whoever had been there—and he had no doubt there had been someone in both directions—they were both gone now.

Who were they?

Chancellor felt his body respond to the external stimuli. His pulse raced now, driven by the intensified beating of his heart. Cold sweat broke out on his forehead. It was entirely possible the Brotherhood had him under surveillance, waiting only for Operation Resurrection to begin, at which time he would be dealt with as only the Brotherhood dealt with people. Chancellor shook off the feeling.

Warm light spilled from the interior of Nanny Collins's house, inviting and tranquil, a pool of serenity in a lake of disorder and turmoil.

Tranquility. *That's* what he needed, Chancellor reflected. Since the murders out on Hallis Road, the destruction of his newspaper office, and his sharing of the list of names with Lawrence, Phillips, and Chapman, life had become a discordant series of events, all seemingly linked to a shadowy presence he knew only as the Shepherd and the Shepherd's diabolical organization, the Brotherhood of the Ring.

Of course, these were only the most recent manifestations with which he'd had to deal. Since his wife's death, life had been driven by the single obsession to find those responsible for her death. He was close now; he could feel it. As he stepped onto Nanny's small porch, he wondered why he had sought out this old woman.

Did it have to do with the faith in God the old woman endlessly professed? He was not a religious man. Theology was a valid study only in that it revealed to man a deepening divide in man's own soul. Was that his problem? Did it have to do with him? Was he searching for something in his life—in this case those responsible for his wife's death—that would never bring him peace, no matter what he accomplished? The thought was frightening. What if all he'd done up to this point really turned out to be fruitless? Did punishment and justice equal peace of mind? Peace within one's soul? What if he found those responsible? Would that bring the peace he sought, or simply closure? They were not the same, he now realized.

Closure would be welcome, but peace—true peace, if there were such a thing—would be a balm to his tortured soul.

Chancellor stepped to the door and knocked softly. It was instantly opened. Nanny Collins stood inside.

"I was expecting you, Mr. Chancellor," the old woman said in a gentle voice.

Robert Chancellor was surprised. The beads of cold sweat that had formed in response to the furtive shadows only moments earlier were gone. Despite a feeling of apprehension, there was something inviting in the old woman's manner, something that was drawing him into the tiny cottage, something that was drawing him into a warmth he had never before known.

■　■　■

As the door shut, two huge men emerged from the shadows where they had sought refuge when Chancellor had appeared. No words were spoken; none were needed. Each knew what his task was.

When Operation Resurrection began, their job would also begin. And that task would be accomplished, for it had been ordained.

CHAPTER THIRTY-SIX

Traffic had slowed to a crawl as Drew Chapman neared the downtown area and the Bubble. He'd taken the first exit coming from the airport, hoping to skirt the congested areas created by the influx of CAM conventioneers into the city.

He was certain he knew exactly what was going to happen. The objective was clear, the method was still in question, but the principal actors in the situation were firmly fixed in his head.

Lieutenant Governor Benson had been the one responsible for his appointment to the investigation of the Brotherhood murders on Hallis Road in Bannerman County. That alone did not make any sense—there were other, more senior investigators—unless you took into account that Benson knew he, Andrew Chapman, had once been a member of the Brotherhood. If Benson were involved with the Brotherhood and Operation Resurrection, then it made perfect sense. Benson needed someone he could count on to stall the investigation—knowingly or unknowingly—without his issuing overt orders to do so, at least until Operation Resurrection was well underway. After that, Newtonian Law took over: an object set in motion will remain in motion unless acted upon by an outside force. Operation Resurrection would provide its own impetus, its own natural momentum. The question now was: Could he provide sufficient outside force to alter the direction of Operation Resurrection?

In the same way, the attack on Governor O'Brien made perfect sense. Benson needed O'Brien out of the way so he, Benson, could initiate the operation. *That* was another point that was still hidden in the shadows. *How* was Benson going to do it? And what about the others who were in the way, people like—

Jordyn! He had forgotten about her. A pang of uncertainty and horror pierced his heart. *How* could he have forgotten Jordyn? Her face, framed by the spill of blonde hair that first day at Carter House, came to him. He could no longer force the debate within himself. He was in love with Jordyn, and it did no good whatsoever to deny it.

He had tried to reach her earlier but had been unsuccessful. Where was she?

Drew picked up his cell phone and dialed her number. Once again the phone rang without being answered. As far as he could tell, Jordyn was out of the picture. But where was she? Was she safe?

Safe? Drew realized it was the first time he had raised that question. The thought produced a twisting pain in his gut.

Drew was filled with anxiety as he contemplated the question. The possibilities he imagined were more in the form of nightmares than rational deductions as he envisioned the worst happening. He did not want to lose Jordyn again. He *would* find her as soon as he addressed the problem of Benson and the Brotherhood's Operation Resurrection.

Traffic was moving slowly but inexorably in the direction of the Bubble. He was only a few city blocks away. Banners announcing the meeting were splayed everywhere, bright splashes of color mixed with surrealistic fonts thought to be hip by a too-young advertising agency caught the eye from every direction.

There was a festive air about the city, particularly in the center business section where Drew was heading.

Suddenly, without warning, the left rear window of Drew's car exploded inward! In quick succession, three heavy thuds shook the car. The windshield exploded, its laminated construction the only thing keeping the broken glass in its frame!

Someone was shooting at him!

■   ■   ■

Willie Henderson grinned from ear to ear, not seeing the horrified look of the passengers in cars closest to his truck, and not caring as he fired the .357 magnum from out his window. This is what he had been waiting for. The time had come.

He had fired four times, the big Smith and Wesson bucking each time he shot. The pistol had a comfortable feel to it, like an old friend. Henderson had used it many times before, but never had he felt the satisfaction of using it as he did at this moment.

Two rounds were left in the big revolver. With luck he could get closer to Chapman and kill him with those two. Not that it made much difference. He had plenty of ammunition preloaded in speed loaders on the seat next to him, but there was an element of pride involved—he wanted to do the job without having to reload.

Henderson had intentionally missed with the first four shots. Sort of an *awakening,* as he called it, for Chapman. A call to arms, of a sort, that he hoped would scare the living daylights out of the CID agent. It had worked to a degree. He had seen the startled face of Chapman as the agent realized what was happening. The next best thing would be when Chapman realized *who* was shooting at him. Henderson wanted the agent to know who was about to kill him, and he wanted him to know, also, that the order had come directly from the Brotherhood.

Traffic was still heavy, and Henderson cursed under his breath. High-rises loomed in the near distance as they approached downtown and the area near the Bubble. The streets were beginning to narrow, and a wall of buildings rose into the night sky, giant reminders of when the city had been a vibrant, beautiful place—before the detestable minorities had moved in. Henderson grinned at that thought. After tonight, that would change too.

He could see Chapman's car moving toward the curb. Was the CID agent about to park? That would make his job even easier. He pulled across the lane of traffic to his right, causing a motorist to blare at the white Dodge Ram pickup with his horn. Willie ignored the tonal assault and continued across the traffic lanes to where Chapman seemed to be heading.

"This is going to be easier than I thought," Henderson said to himself with a hint of disappointment. After all, he considered himself a hunter, a stalker, and for the prey simply to give up took much of the anticipation out of the game. "But," he said as he pulled across the horn-blaring traffic, "I'll take what I can get."

■　■　■

Drew couldn't see out the shattered windshield. When one of the bullets had pierced the glass, it had spiderwebbed before his eyes, limiting his vision. Traffic was heavy. The combination of downtown office workers and executives leaving the area and the CAM conventioneers arriving made for a madhouse. Cars clogged the streets. Pedestrians, mostly CAM members who could not park closer to the Bubble, were jaywalking between the moving vehicles, heading for the convention site. The effect was generalized chaos.

On top of that, Drew's overriding imperative now was to escape the person or persons who had fired at him. He knew the gun being used was a heavy-caliber handgun, a .357 or .44 magnum. His car had been shaken to its foundation when the bullets hit, but the bullets had seemingly stopped on contact, meaning whoever was firing was using bullets designed to expend their power on contact: people-killers. At least, Drew thought, their use would limit the possibility of collateral damage. There were too many people in the area, too many possibilities. Drew had to get out of the car, to distance himself from this area, from the killer, and he needed to identify the shooter. That would not be possible in this tightly congested arena.

Drew slammed the car against the curb, stomping on the brakes. The brake lights blazed in the growing darkness; car horns blared in response to Drew's drastic action. Because there was no parking in this area, the maneuver would cause even greater chaos. Drew hoped the planned pandemonium would provide an opportunity for him to not only escape but to identify the assassin who had been sent for him.

Drew retrieved the Garrison report, slid across the seat, and was out the passenger side door in a matter of seconds. He deliberately headed in the opposite direction from most of the people around him. The move would provide the assassin a chance to identify him as well. It was a general rule in detective work: look for the incongruous, the inconsistent, the out-of-character action. Moving against the general flow of bodies was certainly that, but it was a tactic that worked both ways. The assassin would have to follow. Whoever was after him, whoever the Brotherhood had sent—and Drew had no doubt he was dealing with the Brotherhood—that person would have to park his vehicle and pursue Drew on foot. It would be a matter of who could identify the other first. Who would recognize the contradictory, the incompatible, first? Who would obtain the advantage? *Sort of like a Wild West "walk-down,"* Drew thought as he moved along the sidewalks flanked by the high-rise buildings of the city.

Horns were blaring, a cacophony that seemed, in and of itself, incongruous, out of place. Drew's attention was drawn to an area where an inordinate amount of commotion seemed to be originating.

There it was. The *contradictory!* The *incompatible!* A white pickup truck was forging its way through the burgeoning traffic, causing vehicles behind to alter course in order to avoid collision! A white Dodge Ram. Willie Henderson drove such a truck.

Willie Henderson! It made sense. As much sense as William Benson being the Shepherd and the head of the Brotherhood. As much sense as anything else in this crazy world of hate and revenge.

Drew watched as the Dodge Ram bullied its way to the curb just behind where he had parked his damaged car. The truck lurched to a stop. The driver ignored the oncoming traffic and exited from the driver's side. Horns blared as tires squealed in response to the driver's actions.

Drew pressed against a building—waiting, watching. It was Henderson. Drew recognized the man's face in the glare of oncoming headlights. A sharp glint from the pistol he held reflected back to Drew. Henderson didn't care who knew he was armed. In a situation such as this, with surging bodies and pedestrian congestion, the presence of the weapon gave Henderson an advantage: people instinctively ran from a man with a gun.

Drew felt for his Glock beneath his jacket. The automatic pistol rested easily in its holster. Now was not the time to pull it. The reaction of the people around him would be the same as the people he saw sprinting away from Henderson. The action would serve as a locator, helping to identify him. He didn't need that now.

"However," Drew whispered to himself, "in chaos there is opportunity." Drew recalled the line from the movie *Operation Petticoat,* and the theory certainly applied here.

Drew moved away from the building, now moving at the pace of the crowd in the same direction as the mass where possible, eliminating the inconsistent, the incongruous. He was working his way toward Willie Henderson. People who had yet to see the gun held in Henderson's hand were still moving toward the killer. Others, who had seen the weapon, were running from the armed man. Bodies collided into each other, some escaping, others wondering what was happening. Confusion reigned.

Drew moved in coordination with those around him. Some still moved along the sidewalk, unaware of the danger that lay yards ahead. Others, on discovery of the danger, sought safety; bodies moved in opposition to each other. Henderson, Drew could see, was scanning the crowd, his weapon held high.

"Keep it up," Drew said in a low voice. Henderson's action caused more confusion. The sight of the weapon had caused more congestion in the crowd. Drew moved in concert with the mass, as much as was possible. He didn't want to appear as the single body out of sequence.

Look for the incompatible. The contradictory.

He had to avoid that, so he moved slowly, at the speed of the mass. He could make no movement that might reveal his presence to Henderson.

Henderson had stopped. Drew moved on, drawing closer to the Brotherhood assassin. The crowd nearest Henderson had thinned. There was an open killing ground, an area of relative emptiness around the killer.

Where are the police? Drew wondered. Surely such a commotion would have drawn the attention of the city's finest. The CAM convention would have required additional policemen to maintain order and traffic flow. Where were they?

■   ■   ■

Willie Henderson cursed at the top of his voice. "Move it!" the big man screamed at the people around him. His strategy was not working out as he planned. He thought the exposed .357 magnum pistol would have created a clear pathway to the one person who would know why he was carrying the pistol. Willie had thought Chapman would have become evident among the fleeing bodies of the general public. But that was not happening. The fools around him were careening headlong into one another, obscuring the area, making it more difficult to identify individual faces.

To top it off, the sun had gone behind the high-rise buildings, casting deep shadows across the area. Bodies moved, but not in any coordinated manner. Some moved toward him, others away. This was not the way he wanted it.

Suddenly Henderson no longer felt like the hunter; he was the hunted. He had stepped into the killing field of another and only too late had realized his mistake.

Somewhere in the mass of rushing, running, careening bodies, Andrew Chapman stalked him. Henderson felt a dull fear overtake him. Small rivulets of chilling sweat ran from his shoulders to his waist. Fear was something Willie rarely experienced, but he felt it now.

He was about to head for his Dodge Ram and let McGrath worry about Chapman when he felt the cold metal tip of a pistol jammed against the base of his skull with such force that a small drop of blood appeared at the contact point.

"Don't move, Henderson, or I *will* shoot you," Drew Chapman said in a voice as controlled as it was cold.

CHAPTER THIRTY-SEVEN

The lights in the sepulcher were dimmed; thirteen candles illuminated the chamber, casting long shadows against stone walls. As before, the light from the candles did not reach into the upper reaches of the chamber.

Thirteen figures, clothed in blood-red robes, moved as one into the sepulcher. Candle flames flickered and danced as the gentle breeze created by the movement of the heavy robes reached them. The effect was eerie, surreal.

"Members," one voice spoke. "Please take your seats."

The members of the Brotherhood of the Ring shuffled quietly to the hard oak chairs surrounding the huge slab of oak that was the table.

When all were seated, a single figure—the thirteenth man—took his seat. The delay in this figure taking a seat was in deference to his position, the position of a servant. And yet, as the servant of others, he was viewed as the head of the organization—the Shepherd.

He spoke. "Tonight, my brothers, we will begin the long-anticipated restructuring of a society whose moral decay has become all too evident in these past years. We, the Brotherhood of the Ring, shall show not only this nation, but the entire world, the power of true believers coupled with tenacity and hard work. We shall illuminate the minds of those who, like us, are destined for a heavenly reward, and we shall strike fear into the hearts of those who have come to believe in the power of the diverse, the advantage of multiplicity, the ascendancy of the multicultured. Such beliefs are abhorrent and contradictory to all that we believe. For we know that we, the members of this race, as members of the Brotherhood, have been blessed with superior knowledge and understanding, and having so been blessed, have the obligation and the duty to use these gifts in the cause of true humanity."

A soft murmur filled the room; no one moved.

"Tonight it begins," the Shepherd said to those gathered in the dark chamber. "Operation Resurrection will give this nation back to those who can best administer it. To those who most deserve it. To those whose ancestors founded this great nation. To those to whom it was promised in a time so long ago."

This time the murmur was stronger, the response of the fanatical, the devoted.

One figure stood, a cup in his right hand. "To the Shepherd," the toast was raised.

"The Shepherd," the remaining voices cried in unison, each raising the cup before them.

The Shepherd rose. "The word will go forth as of this night. I shall begin the process, and the process shall continue until all undesirables are purged from this land, as Joshua crossed over into the Promised Land as recorded in the Old Testament, the victory already secured, so shall it be after this night. The victory is ours. There is nothing left to do but claim it."

A shout rose from the group, the words lost in the darkness above them, the menace rising with the chants that now came from the members gathered in the sepulcher.

The voice of the Shepherd concluded, "We shall rise from this sepulcher carried by the winds of a resurrection designed and implemented by this body to occupy our rightful position in this our promised land."

This time the cacophony of cheers and shouts was lost in the soaring expanse three stories above the chamber. Ecstatic roars were swallowed by the encroaching night.

"And you, my dear," the Shepherd said, turning to the single figure present in the chamber who did not wear a blood-red robe, "shall have the privilege of seeing and hearing the beginning of the Brotherhood's ascendancy to power. And then you shall be sacrificed, as one Andrew Chapman is now being sacrificed, on the altar of truth and justice."

■   ■   ■

Jordyn felt her eyes widen at the last words she heard before being whisked from the dark chamber by strong, unseen hands. Her wide eyes filled with tears as she realized what was taking place. Operation Resurrection was as real as the twisted and warped minds of these Brotherhood of the Ring members who thought themselves saviors of the country. What had the madman said? *And then you shall be sacrificed, as one Andrew Chapman is now being sacrificed, on the altar of truth and justice.*

"What have you done to Andrew? *What have you done?*" she called over her shoulder as she was forced from the chamber. She no longer tried to hold back the tears that flowed freely down her cheeks. *"I know who you are!"* she called back, her voice cracking in terror. But even in that moment she knew it was not fear of the Brotherhood that motivated her tears; it was a fear for another. Concern not for herself, the state, or even the nation in which she lived, but concern that was much more specific: fear for Andrew.

Where was he?

And then you shall be sacrificed, as one Andrew Chapman is now being sacrificed, on the altar of truth and justice.

They had Drew! The Brotherhood had not only discovered what she and the others had been doing, but they had successfully nullified their efforts to stop Operation Resurrection. They had discovered the list Robert Chancellor had provided. They knew about her and the names she had found in the CSA computer system. Joy Hartford was one of them. Heaven above! *Joy was one!*

But Joy's relationship with the Brotherhood only explained Jordyn's own capture and incarceration. What about Andrew? And Dewayne Lawrence? And Robert Chancellor? The odds were that at least one, and maybe two, could have exposed the lists by now.

But to whom? Who would believe them? Without the corroborating evidence she'd found in the Community Services Agency computer, the lists of names were nothing more than morsels of paper, crumbs left to the scavengers.

In her heart, Jordyn prayed for Andrew. The prayer was finished even before she realized she had been praying.

■   ■   ■

Jordyn's prayer joined forces with those now coming from the small cottage in Spring Valley where two huge men stood watch and where Nanny Collins was teaching Robert Chancellor about the meaning of prayer and the existence of miracles.

CHAPTER THIRTY-EIGHT

"Don't move," the first uniformed policeman shouted, his service automatic leveled at Drew. A single squad car had responded to a frantic call by a store owner along the street where Henderson had been stalking Drew. The two-man car had pulled to a screeching halt only yards from where Drew stood behind his would-be assassin, his Glock automatic jammed into Henderson's head.

"My pocket," Drew said, not relinquishing his hold on his own automatic. His voice was even, commanding. He held his position, keeping the barrel jammed into Henderson's skull. "I'm a cop. CID," Drew continued quickly, a detectible amount of urgency in his voice.

There were two policemen now, both with guns drawn. The closer officer was being covered by his partner ten feet away and out of any possible line of fire should it become necessary. Drew recognized the approach, knowing if he moved, he would be shot.

Drew felt the first policeman's hand snake into his coat pocket and pull his department ID from the case.

"Andrew Chapman. CID," the policemen confirmed. "What've you got, Chapman?"

The cover policeman moved in. Both uniformed men had their

weapons drawn and leveled at Willie Henderson. The first officer took the .357 magnum from Henderson.

Drew replaced his Glock. "This one tried to kill me. And he didn't care who else he killed in the process. If you guys can take care of him, I've got to get to the Bubble."

"We can take him off your hands, but you can forget the Bubble, or at least driving to it. There's a huge pileup just a few blocks away. Emergency teams are responding right now, but it will take a while to clear it out."

Drew's attention was drawn to the growing dissonance around him. He had assumed the chaos was localized, a result of the shooting and chase he and Henderson had just finished.

He was only partially correct, he realized. Emergency vehicle lights were flashing in a garish display of colors, the high-intensity lights bouncing off the building facades. There seemed to be no open area. Certainly none of the vehicles as far as he could see were moving. Drivers were already out of their cars shouting, waving, displaying their displeasure with the current circumstances and delay.

"How long to walk?" Drew asked the second policeman.

"In this mayhem? Half an hour. Faster than driving. That's for sure."

Drew took off at a jog. Half an hour. He checked his watch: 8:10 P.M. Where had the time gone? The convention was well underway. Drew felt his legs begin to tire. He had to get there. He had to stop Benson from doing whatever it was that would signal the beginning of Operation Resurrection.

Lights still glared and flashed as Drew neared the heart of the congestion. His legs burned; his breath came in short gasps. Traffic was a maze of insanity all about him. The Bubble loomed just ahead, seemingly closer than it actually was. It was the same distortion one felt in the desert when viewing far mountains. Huge objects always appeared closer than they actually were.

When Drew finally reached the Bubble, it was ablaze with the activity of a full-blown convention in progress. The construction of the facility was such that light from the interior illuminated the great mass of synthetic fabric that formed the roof, displaying for all the world to see the genius of man and his abilities.

To Drew, the thing looked like an oversized cantaloupe whose skin had suddenly turned luminescent from too much radioactive water. Despite the burning and cramping in his legs, Drew smiled at the image.

He was close now. It was difficult to distinguish the pedestrians, conventioneers, and the unfortunate souls stuck in the heart of the city because of the burgeoning traffic and numerous wrecks.

Drew was always amazed at the sheer size of the Bubble. The structure towered above him like a huge rounded mountain. Masses of people were everywhere—around the building as well as in the city streets. Drew sprinted around the Bubble, wondering as he did so if haste were really necessary. Nothing concrete had caused his anxiety, only generalized references in the Garrison report. But for some reason the report and the CAM convention seemed too coincidental to be comfortable.

This is it, Drew thought as he ran, knowing that whatever Operation Resurrection was, it was going to begin tonight in the Bubble with William Benson. And people were going to die.

■　■　■

Cecil Barlow skirted the huge trailers whose insulated metallic ducts snaked from massive couplings attached to the end of the trailer.

There were twelve such trailers, all exactly fifty-three feet long, bearing the exact same corporate logo of a well-known refrigeration company.

Barlow had checked each of the trailers in turn. Satisfied that they were functioning exactly as had been advertised, Barlow pulled out his cell phone, punched in a number, and waited. The number was routed to a multisequencing server. The server activated an additional eleven cell phones. Each of the phones was carried by a maintenance worker who was also a member of the Brotherhood of the Ring, and each knew exactly what his task for the night was to be. Each man moved to a preassigned location. Each man carried the necessary tools to complete his assigned task, and each was eager to prove his loyalty to the Brotherhood.

That such proof came in the form of mass murder was of absolutely no consequence to these men.

Cecil Barlow moved to his own position. The time had come. He would activate the operation by the push of the paging feature button on his cell phone. All twelve maintenance workers would begin together.

■ ■ ■

What is different? Drew asked himself as he moved around the huge structure before him. Something was wrong. *Something* was strange, out of place. Again the inconsistent, the incompatible. But what was it? What was extraneous to the normal operation of the Bubble?

Drew forced the question from his mind. He had to get to the front of the structure. He needed to be inside, to stop whatever it was that William Benson was about to do or say that would begin the nightmare of Operation Resurrection.

The front of the convention center was impressive. Colorful banners touting the Caucus of American Minorities flew in wild abandon from every exposed surface capable of such a display. Huge searchlights glared into the evening sky as smaller but equally intense versions lighted the flat surfaces of the Bubble.

Some conventioneers were milling around outside, not prepared as yet to yield to the confines of the convention center.

All seemed normal.

Normal. *Normal?*

What is it? Drew thought again. All seemed normal, but normal was not what he felt. Something strange was taking place, something far from normal.

Drew bounded up the concrete steps leading to the main entrance doors. People were everywhere. Too many people, Drew realized. Even for a convention of this magnitude, there were too many people left on the outside. Somehow they had been locked out. And then it struck him like a sledgehammer blow: the purpose was not to lock out the people on the outside. *The purpose was to lock in the people on the inside.*

It had begun! The nightmare was reality!

Operation Resurrection was underway!

Drew fought through a smaller crowd at one of the side doors leading to the Bubble's main concourse. The door was locked. The people on the outside asked questions, quizzical looks on their faces.

"What's going on?" Drew asked the closest conventioneer, an elegantly dressed woman in her early forties. Her solitaire diamond ring sparkled as the high intensity lights reflected off it.

"No one knows," she answered. "We were just out here talking, and when we started back in, the doors were locked. There doesn't seem to be any rhyme or reason. They're just locked," the lady said, bemused.

Drew pushed past the few people crowded around the door and tried it. The door did not budge. Drew tried the next door—locked. Drew moved down the line. Every door was shut tight and locked from the inside. Drew could see some confused conventioneers trapped between the locked exterior doors and the doors leading to the main convention floor. What was happening? The doors to the convention floor were locked too.

No! Not locked, *chained!*

Drew could see large links of chain dangling from the push bars of the doors leading into the convention hall. Someone—the Brotherhood—had chained the doors, locking the conventioneers inside!

The sound outside was overpowering. Drew had not paid much attention to the superfluous noise earlier other than to note its existence. Now the sound flooded over him like a warm tidal wave. It was the sound that was out of place!

The sound!

That was it. Drew leaped from the steps, leaving the crowd questioning the actions of the strange young man who had been trying to get through the locked doors of the convention center.

Drew sprinted around the building, ignoring the calls of angry men and women he knocked out of the way as he rushed headlong for the service sectors of the Bubble. All thought of exhaustion and pain in his legs was gone. Blood pounded in his ears; his heart beat to bursting. His vision narrowed as his body tried to regulate available energy to continue the forced rush toward the rear of the Bubble.

As Drew rounded the corner of the building, revealing the Bubble's general service and delivery section, the sound was horrendous. Connected to twelve trailers, umbilicals of insulated ductwork snaked into the building, feeding refrigerated air into the Bubble's heating and air-conditioning system.

But that made no sense. The Bubble was a state-of-the-art structure. All systems were self-contained, including the air-conditioning system. This system was extraneous.

The trailers' logo was of a prominent national company whose main business was major appliances, including commercial air-conditioning systems. But why here? Had the internal system broken down?

Drew caught a movement out of the corner of his eye. The service and delivery area was not as well lit as the other exterior portions of the building. The movement had been that of light against dark, a light blue shirt against the darker background of the building. The shirt of a maintenance worker.

Drew headed in the direction of the worker. His hand on the pistol in his shoulder holster.

The man, Drew could now see, was a maintenance worker, or was at least dressed as one. The man moved in and out of the maze created by the huge ducts and the massive trailers. The noise was overpowering. The trailers obviously contained not only the equipment necessary to produce refrigerated air but power generators so that the trailers formed self-contained units.

But *what* exactly was taking place was still a mystery.

Drew followed the worker around one of the trailers, catching up to the man as he drew near the middle of one of the center trailers.

"Stop," Drew shouted, his words almost swept away by the overpowering sound emitted by the powerful machinery contained in the trailers.

The maintenance man turned, a perplexed look on his face. "What are you doing here?" the man shouted back.

Drew held the pistol in his right hand, but kept it hanging loosely at his side. He did not want to frighten what might only be a maintenance worker going about his assigned duties.

"Why the trailers?" Drew shouted.

The man nodded knowingly. "Internal system on the blink. Just had time to get these hooked up before the convention began."

Drew felt a flush of foolishness sweep over him. He had acted on impulse when he'd left the front door, thinking what he was seeing in the trailers was part of Operation Resurrection, and he had been wrong. This man was simply going about his business, checking the equipment necessary to maintain a comfortable temperature within the Bubble.

"Sorry to bother you," Drew said, holding out his hand.

The maintenance worker took Drew's hand. A thin shaft of light, almost invisible until some object crossed its path, reflected off the silver ring the man wore.

Drew felt his blood chill within him. The ring the man wore was the same one Drew carried in his pocket. The same ring Bannerman County deputy Mike Reece had given him. The ring that designated the wearer as a member of the Brotherhood of the Ring.

CHAPTER THIRTY-NINE

The man moved swiftly, surprising Drew. The shadows formed by the high-intensity lights from the other venues around the Bubble and the lack of illumination around the maze of corridors formed by the dozen trailers parked at odd angles gave the man a slight edge, but only for a moment.

Drew had switched his Glock from his right hand to his left when he reached out to shake the maintenance man's hand by way of apology. When the Death's Head ring reflected the light, the maintenance worker realized immediately what had happened and reacted first. He threw his weight against Drew, knocked Drew to the ground, and fled.

Drew was up in a flash. He holstered his Glock and pursued the fleeing worker among the shadows of the trailers. It was all visual. The sound coming from the equipment more than covered the running steps of the fleeing man. Drew caught sight of the man as he rounded the end of one of the trailers.

Power cords and other industrial paraphernalia lay between the trailers, impeding his motion, slowing him down. Drew saw the man go down in a heap, the victim of unseen fingers of either high-voltage cable or ductwork. Drew charged ahead.

The man was up again, running—limping—toward a maintenance entrance located at the rear of the Bubble. The man had less than twenty yards to go.

Drew redoubled his efforts, closing the distance between himself and the fleeing man in a matter of seconds.

Drew slammed into the back of the worker just as the man's hand contacted the latch of the maintenance entrance. Both bodies flattened at impact, the worker crushed between Drew and the unyielding surface of the metal door.

Drew heard a satisfying expulsion of breath from the man just before he slumped to the ground at Drew's feet. Drew jerked the man back to his feet. The name on the front of the worker's shirt identified him only by his first name—Cecil.

"Talk to me, Cecil, if that's your real name," Drew ordered as he tightened his grip on the man's overalls.

"You go to—," the man began.

Drew tightened his grip, cutting off the man's air before he could finish the sentence. "I can hold this position long enough so no air ever gets back into your miserable body," Drew said, his face close to Cecil Barlow's face. The implication was simple: talk or die.

Drew released his grip. Barlow gasped as his lungs fought to fill themselves with fresh air. Drew allowed the man one breath, then twisted the fabric again, cutting off Barlow's air with an ever-tightening grip.

"When I let go of your collar, you have exactly thirty seconds to begin talking. Understood?" Drew said, drawing Barlow's face even closer.

Barlow nodded.

Drew released the pressure. Barlow gasped once again, then fell to his knees.

"Yo . . . you . . . you should be wi . . . with us," he gasped. "You're one of us."

"What are you talking about?" Drew demanded.

"White. You're white, ain't you? Whites got to stick together. All us got to be part of the Brotherhood."

"What's happening here?" Drew shouted over the distant noise of the trailers. "Do those trailers have anything to do with this?"

Barlow smiled. "Everything, brother."

Drew was repulsed by the man addressing him as *brother*. He jerked Barlow to his feet. "Don't ever call me your brother. I don't know what you think you believe or what you think I should believe, but we're from two different planets. Now talk to me about Operation Resurrection."

The mention of Operation Resurrection had the desired effect. Drew watched as the man he knew only as Cecil seemed to shrink inside the maintenance uniform.

"Tell me now. It's over," Drew commanded.

"Ho . . . how . . . ?"

"Never mind how. *Talk to me!*"

Cecil Barlow's eyes glazed over in defeat. "The trailers. They're refrigeration units."

"That much I know. What about them?"

"The doors are chained inside. All the conventioneer seating is at ground level."

Drew exploded. The man was talking in riddles. Words with no meaning.

"Tell me!"

"Refrigeration units are special," Barlow said in a low voice, just barely audible over the distant noise.

"Special how?" Drew demanded.

"They produce dry ice."

Drew tightened his grip on Barlow. What was the man saying? *The doors are chained inside. All the conventioneer seating is at ground level. They produce dry ice.*

Ground level.

Dry ice.

Dry ice was nothing more than frozen carbon dioxide. Hardly dangerous. Unless . . .

Drew again felt the blood pounding in his temples, battering inside his head. The vision of what was happening in the Bubble made him ill.

Dry ice. Frozen carbon dioxide. The trailers produced carbon dioxide. Carbon dioxide was heavier than oxygen. Heavier gases displaced lighter gases.

All the conventioneer seating is at ground level! Ground level meant the lowest occupied spaces in the Bubble. More than twenty thousand people were seated at ground level in an area where at this very minute the oxygen was being replaced by carbon dioxide! Under ideal circumstances, carbon dioxide could kill as effectively as chlorine, mustard, or cyanide gas.

And the ideal circumstances included a closed space at ground level. *Angels in heaven above.*

The Brotherhood was killing some twenty thousand people with carbon dioxide—just because they were different.

Drew felt a wrath well up in him he had not thought possible until this moment. He wanted to kill the man now cowering before him. He wanted to destroy the Brotherhood of the Ring as surely and as swiftly as squashing a cockroach.

And William Benson has put it all in motion.

Except . . .

Except that Lieutenant Governor Benson was locked inside with the rest of the members of CAM!

William Benson was dying too!

Benson was not responsible!

Who had done this?

Drew released his hold on Cecil Barlow. The maintenance man slumped into a heap at the base of the maintenance door, whimpering. Drew ran back toward the trailers, scanning the area for help. He had to cut the power supply to the massive machinery that was pumping death onto the convention floor.

■   ■   ■

Lieutenant Governor Benson was seven minutes into his welcoming speech when he began to feel short of breath. Was he catching a cold? The flu, perhaps? A summer variety of some Asian or East Asian flu that hadn't been seen in the state for more than twenty years was going around. That had to be it.

As he looked up from the podium, however, he saw others who appeared to be having difficulty as well. Eyes were closing as if sleep the night before had been elusive. Coughing, usually sporadic and expected with large crowds of people, had become a chorus of discomfort.

What was going on? Did this have anything to do with the Brotherhood of the Ring and their Operation Resurrection? He knew they were planning something, but determining the time and place had eluded his every effort. The men he'd assigned to root out the perpetrators had yet to report. He'd talked to one of his primary investigators earlier, but the conversation had shed no light on the situation.

Now, as his breathing became even more labored, Benson wondered if he had miscalculated. Had he terribly underestimated the Brotherhood? Was this the night Operation Resurrection was to begin? And if it was, had he now become one of its first victims?

■   ■   ■

What was he looking for? Drew sprinted between the trailers, weaving his way among the power cables, ductwork, and other industrial items that lay strewn about. He tried the double doors at the rear of one of the trailers. Locked. He tried another. Locked. All were locked.

Because each trailer had its own generator, none of the power cables powered the engines of death contained in the trailers. The Brotherhood had covered that base. No one could extinguish the gas generators without getting inside the locked trailers. The pumping of carbon dioxide into the Bubble continued unabated. How long had it been going on? How long before people would begin to notice? How long before panic erupted?

Panic.

Panic in such a crowd would be as deadly as the gas. More so. Drew could visualize the scenario. Hundreds of bodies piled against chained doors, all scrambling to escape but unable to do so, crushed to death by an ever-growing mass of bodies. The instinct for survival would override all other considerations, and that instinct would lead to certain death.

"They planned that too," Drew cried as he left the trailer area on the run. He had to get to the doors, to get them open so the gas could spill out.

And where were the police? The security guards? The other Bubble staff personnel normally found at such functions? Surely the Brotherhood did not control them all. Some, certainly. But all? Impossible.

Drew ran for the front doors. Police cars were screeching to a halt in front of the Bubble. They were soon joined by fire department rescue vehicles, engines, and ladder trucks.

Someone had raised the alarm!

Police and firemen were everywhere. Fire tools and axes smashed into the glass doors at the entrance. Drew immediately chastised himself for not shooting out the glass when he'd first encountered the locked doors.

Panic was rampant. Screaming exploded from the interior of the Bubble. High strident voices mixed with deeper, more demanding ones. All were seeking release from the convention floor. It had become a death zone.

Drew heard the high-pitched whine of gasoline engines being started. The jaws of life, chain saws, and metal cutting saws were being used to breach the chains, to open the doors.

The first door came open. Men and women who had rushed for the doors and found them barred spilled from behind the damlike enclosure. Some were unconscious, others bleeding, others coughing.

Rescue teams attacked the other closed doors. The same scene was replayed at all thirty-six exit doors around the main convention floor.

Some men and women came out choking, some vomiting, others running from the unseen, the unknown.

■   ■   ■

The final count was fifty-three dead. More than three hundred were treated and released from area emergency rooms.

Drew found Lieutenant Governor Benson outside at one of the EMT vehicles, his face obscured by the oxygen mask he was wearing.

"The Brotherhood," Benson said behind the mask as Drew approached.

Drew nodded. "And I thought you were the one responsible for all this."

Benson smiled despite the mask. "You were meant to think that. If you thought that, then others might well think the same thing, and that, at least, would throw them off guard."

"*Them* being the Brotherhood of the Ring."

"Exactly. Confusion was the prescription. Of course, I never figured on this."

"You haven't seen the Garrison report," Drew replied.

"No, I haven't. I know about it. I know Marty Akers commissioned it, and I know what the preliminary findings were. But, no, I've haven't read the completed report."

Drew waited as Benson sucked in some more oxygen. The man was pale. It had been a bad night, and Drew had the feeling it was about to get worse.

William Benson took a deep breath and continued. "I've already ordered additional police protection at the hospital for Marty Akers, Samuel Reardon, and William Garrison. It's not a coincidence that all of them ended up in the same place. That was planned too. Not the injuries, of course, but as contingencies. Easier to solve protection problems if you can put all your eggs in one basket."

Drew suddenly felt a flash of anger begin to surface. "What else don't I know?" he asked testily.

Benson smiled. "There's more, but the important thing is what you may have learned from Bill Garrison's report."

"You're talking about the involvement of Joshua McGrath and McGrath Oil."

"See," Benson said, his smile broadening, "that's why I wanted you on this case. You're smart. Smart goes a long way these days. What else are you thinking?"

"That Marty Akers knew about McGrath, or at least suspected him, and ordered the report to forestall any surprises in Governor O'Brien's campaign. What he discovered via Garrison's report was a whole lot more. McGrath is in the Brotherhood up to his neck. My guess is that he's responsible for tonight, for this thing these crazies are calling Operation Resurrection. I think he's also responsible for the attempt on Reardon's life, the attack on the deputy in Bannerman County, the three dead men on Hallis Road, the murder of the young girl at the university, and probably even O'Brien's accident. And if what I suspect is correct, he's also responsible for the disappearance of Bannerman County prosecuting attorney, Jordyn Phillips."

Benson inhaled a deep gulp of oxygen, then put the mask aside. All around the Bubble the same treatment was being administered to hundreds. A triage system had been set up and was functioning at lightning speed—diagnosing, prioritizing, and shipping the most serious cases via a long queue of ambulances to area hospitals.

"I admit I miscalculated that one. I didn't think McGrath would go so far as to kidnap Jordyn Phillips. But then, anyone who would try to kill more than twenty thousand people at one time, just because he doesn't like their color or the way they talk, would think nothing of kidnapping a public official for his own end."

"Now the question is: Where is she?"

"That one's easy to answer. You would have figured it out, but since you asked, my recommendation would be McGrath Oil headquarters. You know the place?" Benson asked Drew.

"North of here. Between Spring Valley and here. Southern part of

Bannerman County. I've been by it a few times when I was on cases up there. Never been there, though," Drew added.

"Go there. You'll find her. I'll send backup, but I have a feeling you're not going to wait on it to catch up with you. You take off, and I'll have your help there, possibly before you get there."

As Benson finished, the first of the media trucks pulled into place. Drew watched as the crew got out and began setting up the satellite links that would carry the news of tonight's happenings to the rest of the world.

"I need a favor," Drew said to Benson. "I need you to work some of that government magic where the media is concerned."

Benson met Drew's gaze as Drew explained.

"Consider it done," Benson said.

Drew looked down at the lieutenant governor. He'd been wrong about the man, mistakenly blaming a good man for a horrendous deed. But he was right about Joshua McGrath. His gut told him that much. Operation Resurrection had been halted in its tracks, and McGrath would be furious. How would the man's fury manifest itself? That was one question. Another overriding question still remained: Was Joshua McGrath—the oil baron of the state—the man known as the Shepherd?

As Drew headed toward the flashing lights of a police cruiser, he knew he would find the answer to that question before the night was over. Already, William Benson was talking with the media group that had assembled to cover what would be known in the morning news as "The Bubble Disaster."

CHAPTER FORTY

Drew pulled the borrowed police cruiser over to the side of the road. In the distance he saw the lighted complex that housed the headquarter offices of McGrath Oil Company. Benson had as much as verified that he knew Jordyn was being held here. Had he known that or had it been an educated guess? He'd also assured Drew that backup would be waiting. *Where are they?* Drew wondered as he scanned the grounds laid out before him.

The complex was impressive. Built of actual logs hewn from the forest surrounding the complex, the place was rumored to have cost Joshua McGrath almost half a billion dollars. McGrath Oil was still a privately held corporation, giving McGrath the ability to spend what he wanted, when he wanted, and on whatever he wanted with no oversight from a board of directors.

That fact that Joshua McGrath was the chief financier of the Brotherhood of the Ring seemed to Drew to be a terrible waste of resources.

"McGrath," Drew said in the quiet of the car, "you have spent a lot of money on hate. It's time you learned your lesson." Drew looked around once more. No cars were approaching from either direction. Drew had chosen a small knoll more than a mile from the McGrath complex. The vantage point was a good one because it provided a view of the highway from both directions.

Drew raised the binoculars he'd retrieved from the trunk of the cruiser and scanned the area once again. Lights blazed in every building, spilling out onto the courtyards and the half-filled parking lots of the complex. The parking areas had their own illumination, but at this time of night, despite the workers in the buildings, computer programs had shut down half the parking area lighting system. Even McGrath saved money if possible.

Drew dropped the binoculars on the seat beside him, turned up the radio, and listened to the news broadcast with growing interest. Reports about the CAM convention were flowing over the airwaves now. Drew noted the details being broadcast and grinned with satisfaction. William Benson had come through like a champ. *Now it's up to me,* Drew told himself.

He looked in both directions of the highway. Still no headlights. No blue flashing lights were converging on the McGrath Oil complex. That meant he would have to go in alone and find Jordyn.

The thought of something happening to Jordyn had filled his mind on the drive north. What if something did happen? What he if lost her again? He'd already admitted to himself that he loved her. He'd been alone essentially all his adult life, and such an admission had been difficult. That he could need someone else was a foreign feeling to him. But that first day at the Carter House in Spring Valley had been the beginning of the end. The shooting, where he'd found himself covering Jordyn's body with his own as shotgun blasts rained in on them, had been an abrupt awakening. He'd not confessed a word of his feelings to her yet. The struggle had been an internal one, and that part was over. Admitting his feelings to her would be a difficult but not overwhelming problem.

In fact, now that he'd surrendered to his feelings, Drew found himself eager to confess his love to Jordyn. How she would react, he had no idea, and *that* did offer a note of concern on his part.

Of course, before any of what he was thinking could take place, he had to find her. She was in the McGrath complex somewhere.

Drew stepped out of the car. He had already formed his plan of attack. He could not drive into the compound or anywhere near it. Such a complex undoubtedly had the most sophisticated alarm systems available—laser, infrared, motion, seismic, and any other sensor that had ever been invented. Walking into the compound seemed his only option. Perhaps no one would pay attention to a lone figure who seemed to belong. At least that's what he hoped. The promised backup had not materialized. This would be a solo operation.

Drew headed for the lighted compound. The weather was cooling off a little. He'd estimated the distance at a mile, calculating half an hour to cover the terrain. By the time he got there, he knew he'd be sweating despite the cooling temperatures. How he would begin his search for Jordyn he wasn't certain, but he felt an urgency that penetrated his very being. Part of that feeling came from the agreement he knew William Benson had made with the media.

He needed to find Jordyn Phillips within the next two hours.

■　　■　　■

Robert Chancellor couldn't believe what he was hearing—because what he was hearing was coming from his own mouth! For the last few hours, he'd listened to Nanny Collins's theory of prayer and miracles. He'd been carried away with the words and sincerity of the woman, but he was so grounded in secular beliefs that at first he doubted what he was hearing. His skepticism did not last long.

Nanny Collins had spoken about miracles she'd seen and experienced, prayers that had been answered in terms that left little doubt of God's sovereignty. Chancellor listened at first with a smile of condescension plastered on his face; however, it hadn't taken long for that smile to change to one of spiritual realization. Not only did the old woman believe, *she had proof.*

"What are you thinking, Mr. Chancellor?" Nanny asked.

Chancellor smiled. "About how wrong I've been when it comes to religion."

Nanny held up a single finger of reminder.

"Not religion," Chancellor corrected himself. "A personal relationship with Jesus Christ. I never knew there was really a difference. I guess that's why I'm smiling. I have to admit to not knowing the truth, and now that I do know it, I'm surprised at what I didn't know."

Nanny smiled. "I heard that in your prayer. Now we need to pray for our state and nation. I can feel something ain't right."

Robert Chancellor kneeled once again, and once again his voice rose to the heavens.

He had no idea his prayer was also saving his own life at that very moment.

■　■　■

Five men approached the small cottage where Robert Chancellor and Nanny Collins knelt in prayer.

"Both of 'em are on the list," the man in charge said in a whisper.

"Then let's get that prayin' black woman and that meddlesome newspaperman," a second man said.

"Nice of 'em to gather together," another chimed in. "Two for the price of one," the man smirked.

The men moved stealthily, the only noise coming from the scraping of worn boots on the hard-packed earth.

The first man reached the small fence surrounding Nanny Collins's cottage. He stopped short, his pulse racing.

"What's the problem, man?" one of the men said, stumbling into the first man.

"You tell me, jerk. Do you see what I see?" the man said, pointing into the shadows.

Four men turned their heads in unison, their combined gazes looking in the direction the first man pointed. What they saw caused their blood to freeze in their veins. Their breath caught in their throats, and each man's heart beat a tattoo against the inside of his chest.

None spoke. No words could describe the vision before them. Slowly, deliberately, the five men backed away from the small fence and the cottage where Nanny Collins and Robert Chancellor prayed.

Each man wore the ring of the Brotherhood of the Ring. Each would denounce their membership in the Brotherhood within the next five hours.

CHAPTER FORTY-ONE

Drew had been right. He was sweating now, beads of perspiration rolling down his face, back, and chest. His head ached, a shallow pounding that matched the heartbeat he felt in his ears. The closer he got to the McGrath complex, the more confused he became. There was no evidence of a fence or any other form of perimeter protection. That fact alone made him nervous. The other problem was that there were no armed guards patrolling the grounds. Drew couldn't help but feel he was walking into a trap. But not even the feeling of impending doom would stop him now. He would find Jordyn no matter the consequences. He was fully aware that his thinking was clouded by his feelings for the young woman, but for some reason, it didn't seem to matter.

Still, he wished he had the backup Benson had so confidently promised. But even that concern took a backseat to his desire to find and see Jordyn Phillips. Even if it was their last few hours together, it seemed worth it.

Lights still blazed from the log buildings. Drew had to admire the entire complex. He could see how McGrath could easily have spent a half-billion dollars on its construction. The complex was essentially a high-rise corporate complex built of logs. The construction alone would have had its own inherent problems. One just did not build high-rises out of rough-hewn logs.

But Drew didn't have time to admire the craftsmanship of the place. He needed some help, some direction, if he was going to find Jordyn in the monstrous complex.

Then, as if he'd prayed a silent prayer that had been instantaneously answered, a faint odor wafted through the air. What was it?

"Candles," Drew whispered. "Candles? In this place?" Drew looked around. Where had the smell come from? He began moving toward a building that, until now, he had not noticed as being set apart from the rest of the complex. As he moved, the odor became stronger, more pungent. He was headed in the right direction.

The building was of log construction like the rest of the complex. Unlike the rest of the complex, however, it showed no identifying plaque or number. The other buildings were all numbered, their numbers displayed on brass shields illuminated by high-intensity lights. This building, on the other hand, had only minimum lighting and no identification shield. Drew had almost subconsciously eliminated the building from his search pattern when he'd first penetrated the area.

Now he was certain he was headed in the right direction.

The building was short and squat, nondescript,when compared to the others. No more than two stories, if that. Drew's eyes, now that his back was toward the brightly lighted areas behind him, began to adapt to the lower-intensity lighting. He moved slowly, still worried by the fact that he'd not run into guards or other warning devices. He half expected alarms to begin blaring in the night with every step he took.

Nothing happened.

Drew tried the building's exterior doors one by one. All were locked. Still no alarms intruded on the night. No prewarnings. A fire escape ladder crawled up the side of the building. Even buildings designed to perpetuate the myth of days gone by had to comply with current building codes. The ladder loomed as a possible entry point.

Drew began climbing. The smell of burning candles grew more intense as he climbed. He was sweating again. His legs were cramping even more than they had back at the Bubble. He made a mental note to increase his exercise regimen in the coming weeks—provided, of course, he lived long enough to do so.

The roof of the building was flat. The smell of tallow was almost overpowering. Somewhere in the bowels of the building, candles were burning. No, he corrected himself, the smell was not so much of burning candles as it was the smell of candles that had been burnt in times past. But why candles?

Drew stepped onto the roof. He found the building's service entrance, a flat door covering a scuttle hole in the roof. He twisted the handle and pulled the heavy, horizontal door open. He could just make out a steel-rung ladder attached to the wall. He stepped in, his foot on the first rung. Drew moved downward slowly, one rung at a time. When he reached the fourth rung, he gently allowed the service trapdoor to shut. Darkness enveloped him. The odor of candle tallow filled the air around him, as if a thousand candles had been burnt in the room below. The odor permeated the walls next to him. The air he was breathing had an oily, musty feel to it.

Drew waited for his night vision to adjust to the new, lower level lighting. He could see the rungs below him, but just barely. He stepped onto the next, then the next, moving ever downward into the dark abyss below.

The floor met him unexpectedly. How far had he traveled downward? Two, maybe three stories? Something like that, Drew calculated.

Now where? He was inside, but inside what?

A gentle swishing sound reached him from the far reaches of the blackness. The sound itself was innocuous, but for some inexplicable reason, it conveyed a menace beyond measure.

Someone was moving in the room!

Drew stood his ground, trying in vain to see through the darkness and discover the origin of the sound.

Suddenly a match flared in the darkness, its light penetrated the inky blackness. The flash of the match revealed a figure standing in a hooded robe, the match held in his right hand. The figure touched the match to a candle, which flared and caught. Instantly another match flared; another figure lit a candle. The procession continued until twelve candles were lit.

The candles were arranged along a low ledge that encircled the room. Their light illuminated the room just enough for Drew to make out a huge oak table surrounded by thirteen chairs.

Thirteen. There were only twelve candles. Twelve for the disciples, Drew surmised. That left the Shepherd.

Drew's pulse pounded in his ears.

No sooner had Drew thought of the Shepherd than a thirteenth match flared. This time the match was larger, the flame more brilliant, almost white in its intensity. The figure who held the match touched it to a massive candle located on the same two-foot ledge where the other candles were positioned.

"Please, Mr. Chapman, take a seat," the thirteenth figure said, whipping the match out as he spoke.

"You're the Shepherd, then," Drew responded, not moving. "Where is Jordyn Phillips?"

The Shepherd laughed. Its harsh, overpowering echo sounded obscene in the enclosed chamber.

Drew knew the laugh, the voice, the man.

"You may find your one true love here, but you will also die with her in the next few minutes," the Shepherd of the Brotherhood said. "Both of you will follow all those unfortunate souls who died tonight. Unfortunate for them, but very fortunate for us."

"If you mean for the Brotherhood of the Ring," Drew said, moving toward the Shepherd, "you can forget it. The Brotherhood is exposed for what it really is. A band of hatemongers with little or no compunction where human life is concerned."

"*Human life!*" The Shepherd spit the words. "Subhuman life. Mud races. Lesser human beings, no more," the man raved. "You should know that. You were once a member of the Brotherhood. That, by the way, will be to your advantage. We will kill you quickly."

"You might want to think twice about that. I have a feeling you are about to be disappointed at what you actually accomplished tonight. Oh, you killed some people. But the number will surprise even you," Drew challenged.

"Not so, traitor. We have heard the truth. The news. Every method of media coverage has transmitted the successful beginning, the success of Operation Resurrection."

Drew laughed now. "Since when can you believe what the media says. You should know better."

"What are you talking about?" the Shepherd demanded, moving toward Drew as he spoke.

"I'm talking about you murdering fifty-three people, not thousands. About you and the rest of these cretins standing trial for those murders, and about you getting a personalized ticket to the same gas chamber you thought you were creating tonight."

"We have freed society this night," the Shepherd said, his voice rising, filling the chamber. "The Brotherhood has done what no one else had the guts to do. We have begun the extermination of the mud races here in this, our promised land. We will be the saviors of our kind, of our race, of our country. Operation Resurrection began in the Bubble, and it will sweep across this country in a wave that will purge this country of every undesirable. It has been ordained. It has begun."

Drew watched with a morbid fascination as the man called the Shepherd, the titular head of the Brotherhood of the Ring, moved closer and closer.

"Where's Jordyn?" Drew asked. This time his voice was quiet, but nonetheless demanding. The tone carried a promise of retribution.

"My boy," the Shepherd answered. "She is right behind you. She has heard every word. I would not have denied her that privilege. You both deserve to know what will happen to you. It will happen together, just as I have promised, and then we, the members of the Brotherhood Council, will get on with the advanced planning to follow Operation Resurrection."

Drew turned as Jordyn stumbled into his arms from the dark reaches of the chamber.

"Drew, he's mad," Jordyn choked the words out.

"He is that," Drew replied as he placed his right arm around Jordyn, gently moving her to his left side as he did so.

"If you think you are going to reach for that Glock in your shoulder holster, think again," the Shepherd chuckled.

Instantly a gun was jammed into the small of Drew's back. From the feel of it, the gun was a twelve-gauge shotgun. The weapon would blow him in half if he made a move to reach for his weapon.

"We observed you the whole time," the Shepherd said. "You probably thought this complex was rather poorly protected, but the truth is, McGrath Oil is only vulnerable if I want it to be. Now, what were you saying about fifty-three murders?"

"That was the count when I left the Bubble. It may be more by now, but not much. The fire and police departments were working wonders with your would-be victims. Most will recover completely. You killed fifty-three people tonight. Not many by your standards, but a tragedy nevertheless, and enough to get you the gas chamber." Drew stopped, letting the words sink in.

"The news," the Shepherd ordered. "Pipe it into the sepulcher."

Within seconds, electronic sound filled the chamber in the form of a CNN broadcast.

"The official death toll at this point in time," the commentator was saying, "is fifty-four. Several hundred have been treated on the scene and released, and still others are being transported to local area hospitals. Sources tell CNN that a malfunction in the air-conditioning system caused the problem, but that is all we have at the moment. There have been rumors of arrests, but again, those reports are unconfirmed to date. To recap, during the National Convention of the Caucus of American

Minorities, what officials are calling a malfunction in the air-conditioning system produced carbon dioxide that suffocated fifty-four people at the group's national convention. Lieutenant Governor William Benson, the keynote speaker for tonight's event, has apologized for any errors that were broadcast earlier. Apparently incorrect information was passed on to us at CNN as well as to other networks and affiliates. Those incorrect reports indicated that thousands had been killed in this tragic event. What should have been said was that thousands had been displaced, but fifty-four were killed. The keynote speaker for tonight was to have been Governor Patrick O'Brien. Since the governor's accident, there has been speculation about his health. In an ironic twist of fate, Lieutenant Governor Benson is once again occupying this state's highest office, under a contingency plan that cast doubt on Governor O'Brien's continued ability to govern. Pat, this is Malcolm Adams reporting for CNN from the Bubble."

A piercing cry penetrated the depths of the chamber. Drew felt Jordyn cringe next to him. He pulled her tighter. The man with the shotgun had relaxed as he listened to the broadcast. The gun was no longer firmly jammed into Drew's back.

The outcry had come from the man Drew knew now to be the Shepherd. The man whose warped mind had fabricated the unspeakable Operation Resurrection. The same man who at this very minute was howling in the voice of the dead.

"You do not know what you have done," the Shepherd cried. "No idea. *None!* You have done nothing more than succeed in perpetuating an inferior society whose substandard theologies and practices give rise to nothing more than mediocre human beings."

"Human beings are human beings. That's the part I think you've forgotten," Jordyn countered in her best courtroom diction.

"Do not speak to me in such a manner. You are both about to die. If nothing is accomplished this night, I will have that satisfaction," the Shepherd retorted.

"That will be all the satisfaction you get. William Benson is in the governor's seat now. You will never get that back." Drew waited for another cry of anguish from Patrick O'Brien.

Governor Patrick O'Brien was the Shepherd.

"I thought you might recognize my voice," O'Brien continued, his voice now controlled, his hood removed. "Jordyn recognized me immediately. That, of course, is too bad. You will both surely die now." Without warning, Patrick O'Brien ordered in an emotionless voice, "Kill them."

Gunshots rang out in the chamber, the sound deafening in the narrow sepulcher.

Drew rolled with the first sound. Had Jordyn been shot first? He was still functioning, moving, evading. He could feel Jordyn to his left. She was moving too. Where had the shot come from?

Drew was behind the oak table now, Jordyn by his side. The thirteen candles still burned, the yellow light casting an eerie hue over the high walls and oak furniture.

"You all right?" Drew asked Jordyn.

"Fine. What happened?"

From high above a voice drifted down. *"I happened,"* the voice called down.

"Sheriff Lawrence." Jordyn recognized the voice. "Dewayne? Is that you?"

There was a shuffling from above and more movement to the side. Electric lights flared, and the room was bathed in bright light. There were thirteen figures in red robes. Behind them stood half a dozen Bannerman County deputies backed by a dozen state police officers. The first to step forward was Deputy Mike Reece. His face was still black-and-blue from the beating, but he seemed OK otherwise.

"Good to see you, Drew," Reece said, grinning.

"Wha . . . ?"

"Save it," Lawrence ordered gruffly. A wide smile on the sheriff's face revealed his true feelings. "Good to see you guys could make it tonight."

"So Benson came through after all," Drew said.

"Yeah," Lawrence confirmed. "He called as soon as you left. He also arranged for the false media coverage. He told me that was your idea. And it worked. It's a good thing too. We've been out here for the last four hours. It took that long to disable the warning devices and surveillance cameras with a special laser device. That allowed us safe entry into Mr. McGrath's property. We just had time to position ourselves and our NVGs and attached cameras."

"NVGs?" Jordyn asked.

"Night Vision Goggles," Drew explained. "Unless I miss my guess, our good sheriff got everything that went on in this chamber tonight on videotape."

"Get these jokers out of here," Lawrence ordered. "Read them their rights, and be sure they understand them. That's more than they do for their victims."

Drew and Jordyn watched as the robed figures were escorted out of the chamber. Joy Hartford, Joshua McGrath, and Bannerman County deputy Danny Boggs were three that Drew recognized. Other faces were familiar, but he couldn't recall their names. Ex-governor Patrick O'Brien was the last to leave under armed guard, a mask of unconcealed hate plastered across his face.

"This organization doesn't seem to have the best taste in personnel," Drew commented.

"And your point is . . . ?" Jordyn responded, leaving the implied question unanswered.

"There's never a good reason for hate," Lawrence said as he walked up.

Drew disagreed. "I can think of about thirteen good reasons at this moment."

"You can hate them if you want to," Mike Reece said from behind the trio. His badly bruised face accentuated by the lighting. "But remember, that puts you in the same ballpark with them. Is that where you want to be?"

Drew, Jordyn, and Lawrence looked in amazement as Mike Reece turned on his heel and walked away.

"Nothing left to say after that," Drew said.

"Nothing at all," Lawrence agreed, a look of pure admiration on his face.

EPILOGUE

The only customers in Banners in Spring Valley sat at a booth toward the rear of the small restaurant. Jordyn Phillips sat next to the wall in the last booth. Drew Chapman was next to her. Across the table sat Robert Chancellor, publisher of the *Spring Valley Courier*. Next to Chancellor was Bannerman County sheriff, Dewayne Lawrence.

"Still doesn't make a lot of sense, does it?" Jordyn spoke first. The nightmare of Operation Resurrection, thrust upon an unsuspecting public by the Brotherhood of the Ring had been the singular news topic for the last two days, particularly the rumor that Governor Patrick O'Brien was the Shepherd—the head of the organization.

Drew sipped at the soda in front of him. Chancellor looked around to see who would respond first. No one did.

"Depends on how you look at it," Chancellor finally answered. "Hate doesn't make sense. It's a waste of good energy, but that doesn't stop people from hating."

"I thought I wanted to hate William Benson for a while," Drew said, staring into his soda. "I was sure Benson was the Shepherd. It all seemed to fit."

"It did fit," Lawrence said. "That was part of Benson's plan. Have himself set up to take the fall, or so it would seem, in an effort to smoke out O'Brien."

Drew shook his head. "And you were working with Benson all along. How did Benson know O'Brien was the Shepherd?"

"He didn't. He only suspected. But when you add some facts you don't know to what Benson knows, it's all logical," Lawrence explained.

"And the fact that O'Brien was in the wreck with Marty Akers was just a fluke. Irony has its own twist." Drew said.

"*That* was certainly unexpected," Lawrence agreed. "Akers talked O'Brien into going to the campaign rally at the last minute. Joshua McGrath had set up the hit on Akers, knowing Akers had spent the money on the Garrison report that McGrath suspected would implicate the Brotherhood. McGrath had no idea O'Brien was going to be in that car."

"I imagine that almost stopped Operation Resurrection dead in its tracks," Chancellor said.

"Probably not," the Bannerman County sheriff continued. "McGrath or someone else would have stepped in to fill the void. Doesn't take much to generate hate, and that appears to be the Shepherd's primary responsibility. Understandable in a warped, twisted way. The Brotherhood also went after Akers, Reardon, and Garrison in the hospital." Lawrence cleared his throat. "Benson had ordered additional security at the hospital, and that turned out to be a fortuitous move. Police picked up Jefferson Caine, one of McGrath's 'special assistants,' shall we call him. Caine was there to kill Akers, thinking that would put a final end to the trail leading to the Garrison report. Caine hasn't confessed yet, but we suspect, and it's only logical, that Caine would have killed Reardon and Garrison. The Brotherhood was going for all the marbles."

Jordyn chimed in, "Like the Community Services Agency computer system."

"Exactly. Benson was the titular head of that, working within state government to set up the system and see that it functioned to help those in need. But O'Brien actually initiated the first studies on the system, skillfully maneuvering Benson into setting up the system with one slight twist. But Benson was not as stupid or naive as O'Brien thought. Benson started researching the system's genesis, everything he could find in the state's archives. CSA was a valid concept, but with an additional feature."

"An additional database that kept track of minorities working in the state," Chancellor said.

"Every name on your list"—Jordyn turned to Chancellor—"was in the CSA computer system. That's what I discovered the night I was kidnapped. Joy and Kerry Hartford were the front people for the Brotherhood here in Bannerman County. Every county in the state had the same type organization. O'Brien and the Brotherhood had been systematically using the organization to locate and kill people."

"Not just any people. People they thought didn't meet their standards," the sheriff added.

"Hate's as deadly an enemy as it is a powerful ally," Chancellor concluded almost in a whisper.

The four fell silent for a few minutes, each deep in his or her own thoughts.

It had been only two days since the failure of Operation Resurrection. The media had pounced on the story, linking every murder of a minority group member in the last five years to the Brotherhood of the Ring. The Brotherhood had been revealed, its members rounded up and arrested, its financial assets—mostly McGrath Oil—frozen.

"Strange, isn't it," Chancellor said finally. "We're sitting in a restaurant that celebrates various cultures by serving foods from different countries, and all we can talk about is how those differences divide people."

Again no one spoke.

Drew reached over and covered Jordyn's left hand with his, feeling the engagement ring against his palm. Drew had wasted no time after getting out of the Brotherhood's detestable chamber. He had asked Jordyn to marry him the next morning on the porch of the Carter House. She accepted immediately.

"By the way, Robert. Nanny Collins told me you were with her the night Operation Resurrection went down." Drew was still holding onto Jordyn's hand, but he was looking Chancellor directly in the eye.

Chancellor flushed for a moment. "I was."

"Praying?" Drew prodded gently.

"Praying," Chancellor confirmed. "I guess you could say Nanny taught me what real miracles are all about," the publisher said sheepishly.

"Don't worry," Lawrence said in a low voice. "No one here is going to make fun of that. We know Nanny, and we all know miracles exist. For example," Lawrence continued, "you may or may not know about the five men my deputies arrested coming away from Nanny Collins's cottage the night of Operation Resurrection."

The others glanced up at the sheriff with perplexed looks.

"Five of the Brotherhood were sent to the cottage to kill Nanny Collins because they considered her a black activist, and they were going to kill you at the same time. Orders. They were going to kill two trouble-makers with one blow."

Drew, Jordyn, and especially Robert Chancellor were now gazing in amazement at Lawrence. "My men caught them. Each was wearing the Brotherhood ring, and each of them told the same story independently."

"What story?" Drew asked, inching forward in his seat, the hair on the back of his neck standing up as Lawrence spoke.

"About seeing the two biggest men they had ever seen in their lives guarding Nanny's cottage that night. To hear them tell it, those two guys were more than a match for the five of them, and for some reason, those guys knew it. They got out of there as fast as their legs would carry them. Ran right into my boys and started babbling like schoolboys. Said the two guys had eyes that burned like glowing coals in the night."

"Your men?" Jordyn asked. "Guarding Nanny's cottage, I mean."

Lawrence shook his head. "Nope. All my boys were accounted for. Needed them in the sweep at McGrath's. And besides, I was short at least one deputy. Danny Boggs was part of the Brotherhood. I couldn't have mustered an extra man, much less two. My men went back to Nanny's house, but those two men were gone, if they were ever there."

"State police, then?" Jordyn persisted, turning to Drew.

"Nope. The state's part was pretty hush-hush, obviously. I didn't even know what was going on. They wouldn't have risked rocking the boat by sending two men out to guard an old woman and some newspaper publisher."

"So, who were they?" Jordyn asked.

Robert Chancellor looked up. "Nanny knew about them. I thought I'd seen movement in the bushes when I first arrived at her house. I went there to talk to her about miracles and such. The kind of things people say really happened. I'd just been doing some research on the subject that night. Why I was so interested at that point is beyond me, but I was. Anyway, I saw the same two guys. Or at least I think I did. Nanny confirmed it." Chancellor lowered his voice, as if what he was about to say might be taken the wrong way, and he didn't really want anyone else to hear. "That's usually the way it happens. Just enough presence to let you know they're there, but not so much as to overwhelm you with the reality of it all."

"You're talking in riddles, Bob," Jordyn responded nervously. "What do you mean, *that's usually the way it happens*? That's usually the way *what* happens?"

"Angel sightings," Chancellor said even more quietly. "Those two men guarding Nanny's house that night were angels."

"I think you really believe that," Jordyn replied in an amazed voice that indicated she, too, believed what she'd just heard.

Drew squeezed her hand.

Lawrence smiled.

"I think I do too," Chancellor said. "In fact, I *know* I do."

■　■　■

If you enjoyed this book, contact the author via E-mail at
JohnFBayer@aol.com